By Kara Louise

© 2004
© 2006 by Kara Louise
Cover image by Kara Louise

ISBN 978-1-4303-1999-3

Published by Heartworks Publication

Printed in the United States of America

Library of Congress Cataloging-in-Publication Data

Kara Louise
Pemberley's Promise

Note from the author~

A few thanks are in order for those who helped me along the way.
First of all, to my Australian friend, Sharni, whom I trust implicitly for advice
and who gave the story a good look through.
Thanks to Roya and Mary Anne, who were a great help in
editing and cleaning up my sentences.
Thanks to Philippa from Derbyshire, England,
who gave me a beautiful description of that county
and what a small village like Lambton may have looked like.
Thanks also to all who read this story when it was first written
and encouraged me along the way.

Finally, I am deeply indebted to Jane Austen.
She shared with the world her wonderful story and characters
in *Pride and Prejudice,*
and touched hearts and captivated readers for two centuries.
I owe my inspiration to her and am first to admit that
her writing and story is far superior
than anything I could ever think or imagine.
Thank you, Miss Austen!

To my readers ~
I hope you enjoy reading *Pemberley's Promise!*

Prologue

Elizabeth stood patiently with her Aunt and Uncle Gardiner at the post station where they awaited the carriage that would take her from London to her home in Hertfordshire. Her journey would take about a full day, including having to transfer to another carriage that would convey her to Meryton, where Elizabeth's family's coach would be waiting.

It was the end of summer, an exceptionally warm day, and she had just finished spending a month with her aunt. Her uncle's trade had taken him to Bath for an extended time, so Elizabeth joined her aunt to help her care for their four young children. It had been a little more difficult than anticipated, as she had the misfortune to sprain her ankle just before leaving for London and was still favouring it because of the pain.

As the time for the departure drew near, Elizabeth kissed her aunt and uncle goodbye and slowly limped to the carriage. She took care to step on her sprained foot gingerly.

It appeared that there was only one other person leaving London at this particular time. Elizabeth had earlier deemed this gentleman, whom she had noticed while tarrying at the station, as fine and tall with dark, handsome features. By his dress, she concluded that he was a man of wealth, so his taking this carriage for hire seemed curious, indeed.

As she turned back to wave one last time to her dearest relatives, she felt a bump and was almost knocked to the ground by the gentleman who had likewise been waiting.

He had charged abruptly for the carriage and seemingly did not see her, colliding with her and sending her off balance.

Elizabeth let out a cry and made a mental note to add to her quick judgment of him - preoccupied and interested only in himself.

He quickly reached out and retrieved her, pulling her back up and steadying her. But her foot was now painfully sore and she most assuredly let him know with a frowning glance up at him.

She reached down for her foot and her aunt and uncle came running over.

"Dearest Elizabeth, are you all right?" Her aunt took her arm and looked into her face, noting her wince.

"I shall be fine, Aunt." She looked directly at the gentleman and stated, "I shall just have to be more careful to watch where I am going!"

The gentleman narrowed his eyes at her and shrugged off a quick and seemingly insincere, "I am sorry, miss." He took a deep breath and briskly ran his fingers through his hair. With what seemed to come from a source of guilt rather than civility, he offered, "Allow me to lend you a hand, please."

Elizabeth, keeping her eyes directed on him, replied curtly, "My uncle will assist me, thank you."

The gentleman turned abruptly and extended his arm toward the carriage to allow her to enter before him. Elizabeth's Uncle Gardiner took her arm, as she now limped to an even greater degree, and he helped her in.

"Are you sure that your foot is all right, Lizzy? You are limping a vast deal."

"I am well, Uncle. But thank you for your concern."

The driver loaded her luggage and the gentleman's in the back as Elizabeth pulled herself in, and she slid over as far as she could to the other side of the carriage. The gentleman followed her in. Immediately he turned his face away and stared out the window on his side. She was quite convinced that he was most unhappy with his travelling arrangements, as well as his companion. Upon making a sly glance back at him, she resolved further that he had uninviting manners, most likely due, she was sure, to his inclination to associate only with those of his own superior society.

Her overactive imagination, stimulated by his fashionable dress and stiff manner, credited him with an intolerance toward anything and anyone not his equal in consequence. He most likely was one who felt that his wealth and status in society secured him anything he wanted and he would definitely not give the time of day to someone he deemed beneath him or of little advantage to him.

There! She had him figured out. That was most easy. An easy subject, he was. As she finished up her scrutiny of him, he turned back and met her startled glance with a discerning perusal of his own. She was not expecting this and felt a sense of uneasiness as she realized he had caught her staring. She quickly turned to look out her window.

The carriage finally began to pull away from the post station and Elizabeth gave one last wave to her aunt and uncle. When she could no longer see them, she turned back and saw that the gentleman continued to gaze upon her. He seemed to be about to say something, so Elizabeth waited. When no words came forth from him, she turned her attention to the book she had brought along.

After a few minutes of silence, he finally spoke. "I am truly sorry, Miss, for my inattention back there." The words did not seem to flow out easily. "I was not watching where I was going as I was only intent on getting on this carriage. I needed to depart London early today and my own carriage was unfortunately in need of repair. It has been most inconvenient for me to have to take a post carriage. It is not something I normally have to do."

So that explained why he was travelling in this carriage. She simply smiled and arched one eyebrow as she considered his overwhelming plight. "I imagine not. It must be most disagreeably inconvenient for you."

Most disagreeably inconvenient! He shifted in his seat, as he realized how she had taken this. He turned to the window again, tapping the fingers of his left hand against the window well. He turned to her again, making an attempt at civility and asked, "What happened to your foot? How did you hurt it?"

"I sprained it. It only hurts when I… when I… step on it wrong… or take a spill." The look she gave him emphatically reminded him he was the cause of the pain she was again experiencing. The smile that then appeared on her face revealed to him she did not harbour resentment toward him.

With a long ride ahead of them, he continued attempts to be civil. "How did you sprain it?"

The question caused Elizabeth to sigh heavily and she averted her eyes from him. She wondered whether she should own the truth to him. He would laugh; of that she was certain. Or he would scoff at her for her impertinence and unladylike behaviour. But she never allowed anyone to intimidate her before and would not this time. She boldly looked at him and declared, "I was climbing a tree, Sir, and I fell!"

Elizabeth had a difficult time keeping the smile off her face as she saw his reaction. He arched one eyebrow and shook his head in the most infinitesimal manner; all the while he pursed his lips in a vain attempt to hide a smirk. Elizabeth, however, noticed the disapproving furrowing of his brow. It took him a moment to respond, and Elizabeth thought for a moment that he had been rendered speechless.

He finally said with a sly smile, "Certainly if you fell from the tree as a young girl, I doubt that you sprained your foot if you are still limping on it. You must have unknowingly broken it." He stared at her, waiting for her to respond.

Elizabeth took in a deep breath. His statement indicated an assumption on his part that a lady would not have climbed a tree, certainly not someone her age; therefore she must have done it years ago. He was mocking her, but she refused to give him the upper hand. "I beg your pardon, Sir, but I did not do it when I was a young girl. I did it just a little over a month ago."

This time he openly smirked and nodded his head, as if confirming to himself that indeed, this lady had engaged in a very unladylike manner.

"Delightful diversion for a young lady such as yourself."

She felt indignation rise up within her as she felt his mocking censure. Elizabeth suddenly blushed and ignored his comment. *Delightful diversion!* She echoed his words to herself as she turned back to look out the window on her side. She had prodded herself to try to astonish him with the truth; now why did she suddenly regret that she had?

The gentleman made a concerted effort to reconcile the image of this young lady sharing the carriage with him. He estimated that she was close to twenty and apparently was an accomplished tree climber. She seemed refined enough, well mannered, and nicely -- but moderately -- dressed. She was commonly attractive, her figure light and pleasing, but not altogether striking. Her hair was attractively styled, but not overstated.

He continued. "Do you often climb trees, then?"

Elizabeth blushed and dropped her eyes to her lap, but resolved to not back down. She cast her eyes toward him. "Only when they afford me a better view or…" She paused and then added, "Or they give me a better chance to hide than the ground does!"

"And what, pray tell, was the occasion this time? Was it a better view or a better hiding place that prompted you to climb this tree?"

Elizabeth winced. She seriously wished that she could bring this conversation to an end, but again, she was not one to become easily embarrassed. She finally decided to tell all, knowing it would most likely shock him further. She reasoned that it really did not matter, as she would never see him again. Besides, she had already assessed his character; she was quite certain he had already done the same in respect to her.

"This particular time, I climbed the tree to hide from someone who was coming up the road." She said this without taking her eyes off him, with a forced sort of audacity. She would not look away. She would not let him think she was discomfited.

"Pray tell then, from *whom* were you hiding?" Elizabeth noted the apparent amusement he was receiving from this line of conversation.

Elizabeth took a deep breath and continued. "From an unsolicited suitor, Sir, whose attentions I was in no mood to receive! I could not endure one more meeting with him, so when I saw him coming -- and I knew he was looking for me -- I scurried up the tree!"

The gentleman smiled, as if conjuring up this image in his mind. "And did it do the trick? I mean, were you able to stay out of his sight?"

Elizabeth laughed unexpectedly. "Most definitely! The tree spared me at least one unwelcomed walk with that man." Thinking back to the incident made her laugh even more and he eyed her more acutely as the smile brought a sparkle to her eyes and illuminated her face. The gentleman was caught off guard by the magnetizing effect this had on him. He had to make a conscious effort to pull his eyes away. She seemed oblivious to his plight and continued to laugh.

He looked back at her again, this time more cautiously. "What is it that is so humorous? I cannot imagine your fall causing you so much mirth."

"It is merely that… he knew I had been ahead of him and he looked all around for me, calling out my name. He had no idea I was above him watching. I had to keep my hand over my mouth to keep myself from laughing aloud so he would not hear me. I cannot imagine what he would have done if he had looked up and seen me."

"Perhaps if he had seen you up that tree, it would have discouraged him from pursuing you any further." He paused. "Or perhaps he would have climbed up to join you." A small smile tugged at the corners of his mouth and his eyes crinkled, causing Elizabeth much consternation within. For a moment, his severe countenance eased and was almost inviting. His next words sent her reeling even more. "I think perhaps *I* might have been tempted to climb up there with you."

Elizabeth blushed as she imagined this gentleman discovering her up a tree and wondered whether he truly would climb up to join her. "No, never!" she struggled to continue. *"He* would never have done that!" she replied, completely ignoring the statement that this gentleman seated across from her might have.

"And then how did you fall?"

Elizabeth shook herself out of her reverie to answer his question. "After he had passed by a considerable distance, I started down the tree. My foot stepped on a small branch which broke and I fell to the ground."

"How did you get back home?"

"I hobbled back on my own."

"I see. It was not far, then, that you had to walk on your sprained ankle?"

"On the contrary. It was close to a mile."

"What were you doing walking that far from home? No, wait. Do not tell me. You were trying to put as much distance between you and this gentleman."

"Why a mile is not far at all. I actually enjoy walking. I do it all the time. I prefer it exceedingly to riding when I have the chance."

He tilted his head at her comment, wondering at the dichotomy of this young lady. She was pretty, indeed, but obviously of a country breeding and most likely had little to offer a man in terms of wealth or connections. He did give her the benefit of the doubt and in his estimation proclaimed her to be a gentleman's daughter. For some incomprehensible reason, however, he was strangely drawn to her. "You prefer walking to riding then." He repeated it as if he was making a mental note of it. "Would that be on horse or in a carriage?"

"Both, actually. I definitely prefer it to riding horses, but I also prefer it to riding in a carriage when it is an easy distance to walk."

She was now uncertain whether the conversation on his part had been patronizing, critical, or simply courteous. They rode in silence for a while, but Elizabeth noticed him occasionally glance up at her.

She set her attention back to the book she was reading when she noticed the gentleman straining to see its title.

"It is 'Richard III' in case you were wondering."

"*Now is the winter of our discontent; made glorious summer by this sun of York*," he quoted. "I have read it. It is very good. You enjoy reading, then?"

"When I am not climbing trees, I do."

He could not stifle his smile. "Have you read other works by Shakespeare?"

"Several of his sonnets. A few of his plays. My father loves reading as well and he has a small library. He is fond of Shakespeare and this is one of his own that he allowed me to take with me on my visit to London."

The two of them began a discourse on literature. His knowledge far exceeded hers in the extent of what he had read, but her discussion on what she had read equalled his. He enjoyed the fact that she was willing to question his views, even disagree with his opinion. They settled into an easy parlay of words and before they knew it, the carriage was slowing down and pulling into a livery station.

She watched as the gentleman began to gather his things. She smiled inwardly, convincing herself that he was probably used to fashionable women from polished society who would never walk across a street on their own accord, let alone climb a tree. His heart was not likely to be touched by a poor country girl such as herself. He was most likely eager to get off this carriage for hire that he had just shared with a decidedly inferior woman who had the impertinence to challenge his every thought.

The gentleman looked out the window and then back to her. "This is where I get off. I see the carriage from my country home is already here." The door was opened and he looked out and then back at Elizabeth. "I enjoyed travelling with you. I confess I was not looking forward to this ride when I first boarded the carriage. But you have, somehow, made it pass most pleasantly and I thank you." He stepped down and looked back at Elizabeth as if he was about to say something else, then turned away as if he had changed his mind.

Elizabeth blushed at his words of praise and smiled. "It was my pleasure," she said softly to herself.

As the carriage pulled away, the gentleman thought to himself how odd it was for him to be drawn to a woman like her. Perhaps it was because she was so unlike most of the women he had met over the years. He turned to watch as the carriage continued down the road, then walked slowly toward his own. He realized he had not even asked her name.

"Good day, Barstow. It is good to see you."

"Good day, Mr. Darcy. Sorry to hear about the other carriage. Hope it was not too much of an inconvenience taking the one for hire. I shall get you home in no time."

Elizabeth sat still in the carriage, her heart beating wildly as she furtively turned back to watch him easily step up into his own carriage. Why was she feeling this way? She had to admit he was one of the most handsome men she could remember meeting. Something inside of her ached at the thought of never seeing him again. She was not sure why, when he was obviously a man who would never lower himself to the likes of someone such as her. Why someone of his wealth and station even bothered to talk with her she was not sure. For one short carriage ride, she enjoyed his presence and he acknowledged her, yet she did not even know his name.

Chapter 1

Two years later

Elizabeth Bennet walked into the parlour at her Aunt Madlyn and Uncle Edward Gardiner's empty home in London. She and her father had spent the day travelling from their home in Hertfordshire and were now spending the night at the Gardiners' home in Cheapside, where they would both depart early the next morning for the harbour on the River Thames. Elizabeth would board a sailing ship, which would take her from her England homeland to America. Her aunt and uncle were already in America, where they had been these past three months, so this evening they had the house to themselves.

Mr. Gardiner's business had taken on additional work that spanned the two countries separated by the Atlantic Ocean. Elizabeth understood only that it involved some importing and exporting details that needed to be worked out on the American side. The Gardiners had expected to remain there between six to nine months. Elizabeth planned to visit them for the remainder of their stay. The Gardiners and their four children had all made the crossing together, taking advantage of this opportunity to see some of the sights in the new world.

With her uncle's work taking him to New York, Elizabeth understood that she and her aunt would have sufficient time to tour the area together. When her uncle's work was completed, they would all travel back together to England.

Elizabeth's only regret was that her sister, Jane, was not able to join her. She had also been invited, but due to Jane's tendency for severe motion sickness, she declined. She knew from past experience that she would have a very difficult crossing. From her experience on a boat for a short time in the English Channel and suffering greatly from it, she knew that four to five weeks on a ship out on the ocean would be exceedingly difficult for her. Consequently, Elizabeth was setting off by herself, much to her father's consternation.

When the letter from her aunt had arrived, the discussion between herself, her mother, and father had been very typical of the conversations that took place in the Bennet home. Elizabeth tried to remain calm as she gave her reasons for desiring to go. Her father was adamant against it and her mother wavered back and forth, giving her nerves full reign as one moment she saw no reason why her daughter could not go, and the next, change her mind.

It was Elizabeth's steady, calm, and rational argument that finally persuaded her mother. She knew it would take more to convince her father to allow her to travel unaccompanied, but she knew she could appeal to his love of history, geography, and books, as well as her own love of those things. To pass up an opportunity such as this to see America would be something she would always regret if she did not do it now. She appealed to his trust in her character, her wisdom, and maturity, and in due course, he gave in.

Elizabeth sat down on one of the chairs that occupied the Gardiners' sitting room. Her thoughts went nostalgically back to all of the times she had come here to visit her aunt and uncle over the years. She was extremely fond of them and practically considered them a second mother and father. She closely identified with her aunt, and as a young girl would scrutinize her closely and try to imitate her ways. She had never understood her own mother's ways and knew at a very young age that she did not wish to grow up to be like her.

The Gardiners' home in London, although neither exceptionally fashionable nor elegant, was very warm. Elizabeth always found it to be a respite away from her own home. The Bennet home in the village Longbourn, was by society's standards, neither modest nor extravagant. Situated in the country on a good parcel of land, it did give Elizabeth a chance to enjoy her favourite pastime, which was to walk. Their own home was a good distance from their nearest neighbour, while her aunt and uncle's home was located on a busy street in Cheapside. Yet she felt the Gardiners' home was more tranquil because of their easy nature and that of their children. It was far too often that the Bennet household resonated with the nervous ranting of her mother and the uncontrolled outbursts from her youngest sisters. She enjoyed every visit she ever made here. Now, she was looking forward to seeing them again, this time in America.

She pulled out the letter that her aunt had written to her and her sister. From the moment she read the letter, she knew she had to go. She looked down at the letter and began to reread it.

My dearest Jane and Elizabeth,

How we miss you all! It is such a different world here, but we are enjoying it immensely! So often we will see something and say, 'Oh how Elizabeth would love doing that' or 'Jane would love seeing that!' You are often in our thoughts and conversation.

Edward's work is proceeding along well, although slowly. We knew it would be very challenging, as he must acquaint himself with the diverse import and export laws in America. Some are very unlike ours in England, but he enjoys it.

One reason for my letter, dearest nieces, is to extend an invitation to you both to come over if your parents agree to it. We anticipate being here quite a few more months, possibly another three or four. How we would love to have you both make the crossing over and visit us. While Edward is occupied with work, how I would treasure your companionship. When his work is complete, we will then all sail back to England together.

I know that this might seem like an unreasonable request, but we would be most delighted if you could endeavour to come. Our children would love to see you, and we, of course, would hold dear your company. If this is acceptable to both your parents, please check into getting tickets as soon as possible. We will, of course, be willing to help out with the cost of passage. The trip for us took about four weeks. It was not always easy, but we made it without too much difficulty.

Please write back as soon as you have made some sort of decision. We look forward to hearing from you.
All our love,
Your Aunt and Uncle Gardiner

Elizabeth folded up the letter just as her father came in. "Well, my Lizzy, are you still determined to do this?"

"Yes, Papa. I am so looking forward to it." She stood up and walked over to him, taking his hand in hers. "Do not worry. All shall be well with me."

~~*

The next morning, Elizabeth pulled her wrap tightly around her as the carriage carrying her and her father drew them closer to the harbour in London. She shivered, not so much because of the cool, foggy mist enveloping them, but because of her realization that the day had finally come. She could admit to herself, but not to her father, that she was indeed nervous about all that was in store for her.

The only way Mr. Bennet had agreed to allow Elizabeth to travel alone was for him to take her onto the ship himself and put her under the protection of the ship's captain until she reached the foreign shore. But even then, he felt very troubled. The journey would take anywhere from four to five weeks, depending on the weather, the winds, and a multitude of conditions. He had heard too many tales of ships that never made it across, sickness spreading throughout the passengers and crew, and other adversities that could befall them. But he also feared for his daughter arriving in this new world and the type of people who made up this melting pot country. He absently shook his head.

"What is it, Papa?" asked Elizabeth.

He turned to her with a sad look in his eyes. "You know what it is, my dearest Lizzy. I would give anything to talk you out of this right now and turn this carriage back around to the safety and security of Longbourn."

"But Papa, this is an opportunity that I may never get again! Think of it! All of those places I have only read about. Aunt and Uncle Gardiner certainly would not have asked for us to come if they did not think it was safe. Do not worry about me. I shall be well." Elizabeth smiled to reassure him. The only betrayal to her words and her smiling face was her rapidly beating heart. It continued to remind her how nervous she actually felt.

They soon saw the tall masts of the ships that were docked along the harbour on the River Thames. One of these very ships would transport the crew and passengers out to the eastern coast of England and down around the English Channel. From there they would sail out into the open seas of the Atlantic Ocean, farther from any source of land than either dared comprehend.

"Elizabeth, if anything were to happen to you…"

Elizabeth quickly put her hand over her father's. "Nothing will happen to me, Papa. Please try not to worry."

The smile he returned to her was weak. Elizabeth noticed, but did not comment on, the tears that welled up in his eyes. He quickly turned his head to look out the window of the carriage. She knew this was difficult for him and she wanted to do all she could to set his mind at rest. She could think of nothing else to say. She knew he would not rest easy until she was back here in his sight, in a few months.

A very soft, sad voice suddenly said, "We are almost to the port." He brought his hand up and apprehensively pointed toward the harbour and then turned to her. "Are you sure, Lizzy, that I cannot talk you out of this?"

"This is something I *have* to do." Elizabeth strained her head to look out the window. She saw the masts of the ships, some with sails completely unfurled and already sailing, and others with the sails still furled tightly about their masts. Elizabeth's heart skipped a beat as she suddenly felt a wave of excitement pour through her. *Yes, this would be a life changing adventure. I will not be the same when I come back!*

~~*

As the carriage pulled up as close as they could to the dock, Elizabeth and her father kept their eyes on the ships they passed for the one on which they had booked her passage. It was one of the first of the packet ships that were being used to travel at regular intervals between London and New York. Her father had done much investigating into the ships that were offering passage to America and was most pleased with this particular one. Even though they could not afford a private room for Elizabeth, they understood that the steerage accommodations in this ship were one of the best.

Despite Elizabeth having to sleep with many other women and children far below the deck for the next month, he was sure she would be in good hands. But that was only the least of his worries concerning her. His only consolation was in believing that his second eldest daughter was not one to shrink from discomfort, draw back in fear, or yield to adversity. She would face anything head on, speak her mind if she felt any injustice, and would stand up to anyone who provoked her. Of all of his five daughters, he had to admit that Elizabeth was the only one he felt confident enough to make this kind of trip without some kind of mischance occurring. She was also his favourite, however, and knew that if anything happened to her, he would never be able to forgive himself.

James, the driver of the Bennets' carriage, slowly pulled along the dock, keeping his eyes vigilantly searching for berth number 44, until he finally spotted it and the ship which would take his favourite of the Bennet ladies away. James had been their carriage driver for many years and had enjoyed many lively conversations with Elizabeth during his employ. She always took an interest in how he was doing, how his family was, and treated him as much an equal as anyone. She was sensible, intelligent, and very much a lady, but not afraid of getting her hands dirty or doing a little work. He often told her how much he regretted that she preferred to walk instead of ride, as she would walk to Meryton rather than require his services in the carriage.

His eyes took in the tall ship. There was a flurry of activity as the crew climbed up the masts and readied it for an imminent voyage. In an area just off the gangway, he saw carriages pulling up and unloading passengers and freight. He pulled up behind the last carriage and brought it to a halt.

Elizabeth had brought along one large trunk, which would be stowed down below in the ship. She had packed enough other items in a large, heavy duffel which she would keep with her in her accommodations.

When they stepped down from the carriage, some workers checked her ticket and then took her trunk. She was given her bed number and instructions on how to get down to the steerage deck.

Mr. Bennet tightly gripped Elizabeth's arm and escorted her toward the ship as James went ahead of them with her duffel. It appeared that there were many people making this trip and that was comforting to Elizabeth. Surely they felt everything would be all right.

As they approached the ship, Mr. Bennet inquired of one of the crew where the ship's captain might be.

"He is inside greeting everyone. Just step right on in and you will not miss him."

"Thank you." Mr. Bennet looked down at Elizabeth. "Seems like a nice, young man."

"Yes," Elizabeth laughed. She knew her father must have been scrutinizing everything and everyone on this ship. She felt that the captain would get the fiercest scrutiny. She only hoped he would live up to her father's expectations, or she was certain he would haul her off this ship without one further thought.

When they stepped inside, there were several crewmen helping the passengers find their quarters. In the centre was an older gentleman, obviously the ship's captain because of the uniform he was wearing. Elizabeth thought to herself, *Older is preferable; that means much experience and maturity.*

A crewman, standing by the captain, asked Mr. Bennet if he required assistance. Mr. Bennet politely declined, stating that he preferred speaking with the captain. He and Elizabeth waited until the captain was free and they stepped up to him.

"Good day, Sir. I am Captain Willoughby. How may I be of assistance to you?"

Mr. Bennet introduced himself and Elizabeth. "My daughter is making this journey without anyone to accompany her, as much as I dislike the idea. I had been informed that, under these conditions, I might put her under your protection for the trip. Would you be willing, Sir, to accept that responsibility?"

"I have done it many times before, Mr. Bennet, and you can be confident I will do it again, especially for this young lady. I would be most happy to. We frequently have ladies who have to make the trip alone for one reason or another."

Mr. Bennet looked somewhat relieved, but a lingering touch of nervousness spurred him to vigorously rub his hands together.

The captain turned to Elizabeth. "Miss Bennet, I will do everything in my power to assure a safe trip for you." He glanced at her ticket. "You may proceed down to the steerage compartment for the ladies and children and get settled in there. Mr. Bennet, you need not worry. Once we are safely out at sea, I will be going down to give all of the ladies some common sense guidelines."

Elizabeth and her father walked down the steps that took them first to the deck that accommodated people in private cabins. They followed the signs and proceeded down another two sets of stairs that took them to steerage. The steerage section had been divided; one side was for men and the other for women and children. They walked in and glanced around. It appeared clean enough, but very dark, with no natural light coming in save for the hatchway, which was now opened. Elizabeth was sharp enough to realize that in bad weather it would be tightly closed. The room was filled with bunk style beds, many of which already had a person or parcels upon them. They walked down the rows, looking for bed number twenty. That would be Elizabeth's bed for the next month.

They found her bed and she was grateful it was a lower bunk. There was a small wooden chest next to each bed, where Elizabeth determined she would stow most of her possessions. Her large duffel would be stowed under the bed. They greeted a few people and Elizabeth was amazed at how many children were sailing. As they left to return up to the main deck, Elizabeth made a mental note of where the bath chambers were.

She knew, as she walked up the steps with her father, that each step was taking them closer to their inevitable moment of parting. Her arm was wrapped tightly around his as they came up and once again stepped into the sunlight. Word was being sent out among the passengers that all non-passengers would be required to disembark shortly.

Mr. Bennet turned to Elizabeth and cupped her face in his hands. "I will be praying for you each and every day, Lizzy. You can count on it."

"Thank you, Papa. I appreciate that."

"And it would not hurt for you to say a prayer each day, too. When you see the sun rise, thank God for taking you through the night. And every night, when you see the sun set…" He stopped, choking on his words. "When you see the sun set, thank God that he took you through another day."

"Yes, Papa, I promise." Elizabeth hugged her father and kissed his cheek. It seemed an eternity before he let go. Finally as they were giving the last call for visitors to leave, he turned slowly and walked away. She noticed his shoulders raise and lower in huge sigh. With one last look back at her, he exited the ship.

As the ship slowly pulled away from the dock, tears welled up in her eyes as she continued to wave at her father. She looked at the name of the ship on a hanging sign that was carved out in wood. It gave her hope that this crossing would be most exceptional. The name of the ship was *Pemberley's Promise*.

Chapter 2

Fitzwilliam Darcy walked behind his valet, Durnham, down the stairway to his cabin. "Watch your head, Sir. This is a particularly low ceiling."

It was too late. Darcy had already bumped his head. "Drat!" He wondered with great consternation how he would ever survive a month in the confines of this ship. He *had* lowered his head at Durnham's words; however it was not enough due to his tall stature. He would have to remember to duck his head a vast deal more than usual in walking down to the first deck of the sleeping berths, where his was located.

They walked to the fore of the ship, to the premier of rooms, and entered. He gave a quick glance around his room, the finest on *Pemberley's Promise*. But despite its elegant furnishings and expert craftsmanship, he was not looking forward to this journey, particularly if he had to spend an excessive amount of time in this exceedingly small vestibule.

"Sir, I hope you know what to expect. A month on a ship can be quite daunting, even on one of the finest ships around." Durnham looked at him sternly. "Are you quite certain you do not wish me to accompany you?"

"Your father is ill and needs you. There is no need to concern yourself with me, Durnham. I shall manage quite well."

"Still, it will not be easy. Even the most exceptionally constructed ship, such as this one, can be tossed and ravaged like a piece of driftwood in a storm. And storms come up frequently and quite suddenly out at sea."

Darcy took in a deep breath, acknowledging the truth in Durnham's words. He looked around his room and mumbled an agreement. Even though this ship, *his* ship, was one of the finest built, and this particular cabin was the premium on the ship, he knew he could be facing a physically demanding month at sea going, and then another month, returning.

He had purchased the ship from his friend, Edward Stearnes, as an investment. Stearnes had been a fellow student at university who had gone into the ship building business. Stearnes was known for building only the finest and expertly crafted ships, and Darcy looked upon it as an excellent prospect. He handpicked the captain for the ship, Captain Martin Willoughby, a long time friend of the family. He knew this man had an excellent reputation as both a captain and gentleman, and paid a high sum to lure him from his previous ship.

He had never actually intended to embark on one of the ship's crossings to America once he purchased it. He found himself today on board, nevertheless, facing a voyage that would most likely tax his patience and unsettle his nerves. He was not looking forward to it, but it had to be done.

He had been guardian of his sister, Georgiana, for the past five years since their father had died. She had recently been put under the companionship and care of Mrs. Annesley, who was a long time friend of the Darcy family. Her husband had passed away and she eagerly welcomed taking on this responsibility for the young girl. She had taken Georgiana under her wing after a most distressing and embarrassing incident. Distressing to Darcy and embarrassing to his sister. Georgiana had come very close to eloping and marrying a most deceptive and conniving childhood friend, under the complete approval and encouragement of her companion at that time, a Mrs. Younge.

Mrs. Annesley had always been well liked and trusted by Darcy. When he approached her to take the position as Miss Darcy's companion, she heartily agreed. But subsequently, a few months after consenting to do this, she received word from her son and his wife from America that they were expecting their first child and invited her to come for a visit when the child was due to arrive. As she greatly desired to be there when her grandchild was born, as well as continue in her responsibility to Miss Darcy, whom she had known since she was an infant, she approached Darcy with a plan.

Her solution, which she proposed to him, was to take Georgiana with her to America. Initially Darcy was adamantly against even considering it. Although he trusted Mrs. Annesley to the fullest and he certainly could not deny trusting his ship and its seaworthiness, he was not quite certain if he was willing to entrust Georgiana to it. Mrs. Annesley, armed with the arguments that Georgiana might never have this opportunity again and they could have many historical and varied lessons in seeing the new world firsthand, presented her case to him. But her greater argument in favour of it was that she felt that the young girl needed to be as far away from the presence and power of George Wickham, the deceptive suitor, at least for awhile.

Georgiana was also in favour of this. She had been hurt, deceived, and embarrassed by what happened. She had believed herself in love with Wickham and had foolishly agreed to elope with him. Looking back, she realized he had wormed his way into her heart with nothing more than a lust for her fortune. She felt that she had let her brother down in allowing herself to be deceived by him, by displaying a wanton lack of wisdom and maturity, and now she wanted an opportunity to get away and grow into the woman he expected her to be.

With the two of them pressuring and encouraging him, Darcy wrote to his cousin, Colonel Richard Fitzwilliam, who was Georgiana's co-guardian.

On the surface, Fitzwilliam tended to not take things as seriously as his cousin. He had a lively personality that Darcy lacked and often envied. Darcy therefore enjoyed their special familial relationship, close friendship, and joint decision-making responsibility regarding Georgiana. Fitzwilliam had strongly encouraged Darcy that this would be good for her, an experience which could bring about much growth and maturity, and he gave his hearty approval. Darcy knew the only thing hindering her from going was his own fear and concern for her safety. Finally, and most reluctantly, he gave in.

He waited anxiously for that first word back that they had arrived safely. He was grateful at length to learn they had a good, uneventful crossing. But he received word, soon after, that Mrs. Annesley had taken ill and it was unlikely that she would be able to make the trip back for some time. Darcy adamantly refused to allow Georgiana to make the return voyage unescorted, so he was now sailing on his own ship to America, to bring her back with him.

Darcy sat down on one of the two benches that sat astride a very small table in his cabin. Two beds were situated on opposite walls in the narrow berth and a small closet, a chest of drawers, and a dressing table and mirror would be the extent of his world for the next month.

Durnham finished putting away Darcy's belongings and gave him some well needed advice. "I have heard, Sir, that the ways on board a ship differ greatly from what we have come to expect in good society. You may likely have people boldly approaching you without first seeking an introduction." He looked over at Darcy and raised his eyebrows as he fixed his eyes on his master. "The ladies, Sir, when they find out who you are, will not, I fear, leave you alone."

"Then they will not find out who I am. I am quite certain that there is no one on this ship who frequents the same circles I do. And I shall have a little talk with the captain so that he does not let anyone know anything about me, especially the fact that I own this ship."

"That is wise, Sir, but I fear it will not stop the ladies… or their mothers." He smiled a knowing smile when he said this.

Darcy shifted uncomfortably on the bench upon which he was seated. The last thing he wanted was to be pursued on this trip. A month in the confines of a ship, where anyone would be bold enough to come up and strike up a conversation with him, would disconcert him to no end. He could certainly be polite when the situation demanded it, but there most likely would be times when he would prefer solitude. He knew he would not be able to stay in his cabin for extended lengths of time. For his own sanity he would require to be out in the open, getting some fresh air, and taking ample opportunities to walk up on deck.

"Then what do you suggest I do?" Darcy asked, not really expecting an answer.

"I suggest you find yourself a *wife* for the duration of the voyage." Durnham laughed and Darcy grimaced.

Darcy had always respected his wise, faithful valet. But Durnham had a tendency to occasionally tease him and it had taken Darcy years to accept it as part of his personality. Darcy had never nurtured the ability to tease others himself and sometimes wished he could. Whenever he *did* make an attempt, it usually was not taken in the way he intended. He *had* learned over the years to read his valet's face to determine whether or not what he was saying was in jest.

Durnham continued. "Oh, and sea sickness, Sir. Until you get your sea legs, it is probably likely that the movement of the ship will cause you to be sick. Eat just enough during your first few days to keep food in your stomach, but do not overdo it. If you begin to feel sick, breathe slowly and deeply. Keep out in the fresh air as much as you can. It will help."

"Thank you, Durnham. I shall heed your advice. Er… the sea sickness part, not the *wife* part."

"Yes, Sir." Durnham tried to hide a small smirk as he thought of all the years he had been with this man and how, slowly but surely, Darcy had come to recognize his teasing as an indication of his appreciation and respect for the man. But Durnham strongly felt that his master still took himself too seriously and it was only in very rare and exceptional moments that he let his guard down and really enjoyed life. He felt that was truly his only fault of character.

With his task completed, Durnham asked if there was anything else he could do before he disembarked the ship.

"No, Durnham, but I thank you for everything. Let me accompany you back aloft. I want to be up on deck when the ship pulls away from the dock and the sails are unfurled." He was anxious to watch the crew as they climbed the rigging and manoeuvred the sails when she set out.

As they readily walked up to the top deck, Darcy resorted to the stern, taciturn mannerism he had come to perfect over the years. He avoided eye contact with the multitude of people about him, hoping to disappear in their midst. They had not yet called for non-passengers to depart the ship, so the deck was replete with tearful farewell hugs and kisses as loved ones prepared to depart.

Durnham solemnly turned to his master, whom he had been with for five years, having moved into that role when Darcy's father died. He had kept the position of head valet, merely changing masters. He had not been out of his presence save a few days here and there for all those years.

"Sir, I must now take my leave. I pray you have an excellent crossing now and again when you return with Miss Darcy. I hope that your sister is well and I look forward to your return."

"Thank you, Durnham. I hope all goes well with your father. I shall see you, hopefully, inside three months."

The two men shook hands and Darcy sadly watched him leave. He was an exceptional valet, and even though Darcy was capable of taking care of himself, he would miss the respectful friendship they both shared. Durnham was without equal in his ability to know when Darcy needed solitude or companionship, silence or a tactfully placed word, and when he would tolerate teasing and when he best refrain from banter of any sort.

Darcy found a place to stand out of the way of passengers, but one that gave him an excellent prospect to watch them. He was anxious for the voyage to begin and passed the time by watching the other passengers as, one by one, the family members or loved ones of the travellers departed the ship. He similarly tried to conjecture why those passengers sailing on his ship were going to America. It touched him to think that families were possibly being separated for the rest of their lives. It had been hard enough to know that Georgiana was such a distance from him for only a few months. He could not imagine her going off indefinitely. But he had heard of many doing that very thing.

He stood with his back to the side of the ship, leaning against it and his elbows bent back, resting upon the rails. He was grateful that at this point, everyone was more concerned with their goodbyes than with noticing him. He could watch without drawing any unwanted attention to himself.

He noticed a young, dark-haired woman he estimated to be about twenty, on the arm of an older gentleman. He initially thought she looked familiar, but given the clothes she was wearing, he judged she most likely did not frequent the same social circles as he. As he watched them, he was surprised when the elder gentleman gave her a fervent hug and, with tears in his eyes, he left the ship.

Could she be travelling unescorted? He found that impossible to comprehend and would never have allowed Georgiana to do such a thing. He wondered what her circumstances could be that would have induced her to do this. Perhaps she had secured a position as a governess in America. Perhaps she was a mail order bride. No, he absently shook his head. He did not like that idea.

He looked over at an older couple. He pondered whether they might be travelling to see a son or a daughter who had set off for the new world to find a better life. Perhaps they had finally sent for the parents, having secured work that raised them to a higher position than they had been in England.

There was the young man who, Darcy conjectured, was off to America solely for the adventure. Perhaps he loved to travel and for him, this was just another exciting place to visit.

He saw many ladies, fashionable and not so fashionable, and began to feel their eyes and the eyes of their plotting mothers and sometimes even their fathers, upon him as they noticed the absence of any lady on his arm. He knew his patience would be tried and his composure stretched to the limit as he would have few places on this ship to seek the solitude he needed and desired, except for his room. And that was too small for him to remain secluded in for the length of the trip!

It was announced that the people who were not sailing had to depart the ship. Loved ones bid their final farewells and the passengers lined the railing for one final glimpse. He looked over at the dark-haired young lady who now waving at the man he supposed to be her father. The gangway was removed and shortly after, a few sails were unfurled. Darcy looked up at the beautiful white sheets that billowed like clouds against the deep blue sky. Only a few were set free, to give the ship just enough wind to slowly pull away from the dock.

He brought his eyes down and noticed that the young lady, whom he had seen earlier, was watching the sails, as well, and she was smiling with apparent joy. He kept his eyes on her as she turned back to her father on the shore. The ship slowly began to sail away from the dock and she continued waving. As people on the shore grew smaller to the eye, many left the railing. But this lady remained as long as she could see the dock where the gentleman stood. He wondered whether she was ever going to see her family again.

He walked with long strides toward the front of the ship. He knew he would enjoy being out on the deck, and hoped that at least two things would be in his favour on this crossing. The first was that the weather would be accommodating so that he could come up often and take undisturbed walks. He knew in bad weather one would need to remain below. The other favourable condition would be that he not be assaulted by single ladies or their matchmaking mothers, fathers, brothers, sisters, or friends, looking at him as some sort of prize in the pursuit of a husband. He was in no mood to contend with such intrusions as his thoughts were singularly focused on reuniting with Georgiana and returning her to England.

Darcy noticed a few people had begun greeting one another and were making new acquaintances with the other passengers who would live within the same sphere for the next month. Most everyone extended amiable courtesies toward one another; impervious to one another's standing in society.

As the ship slowly made its way down the River Thames and out of London toward the open seas of the English Channel, Darcy continued to quietly conjecture about his fellow passengers instead of converse with them, and stood off by himself, content in his preference for solitude.

At length he was grateful to find his good friend, the captain, up on deck, and walked over to him. "Good day, Captain Willoughby."

"Darcy! How do you find your room?"

"Excellent, Sir."

"Good. It is one of our finest; only the best for the owner of the ship."

"Yes, well, I would prefer that you not make that fact known to anyone. I would not want people coming to me with their problems and concerns."

The captain laughed. "And neither would I want them to do that. Take no offence, Darcy, but I fear your knowledge of sailing and this ship would be most inadequate to help them with their concerns."

"That is true." Darcy looked at him wryly. "May I inquire something of you, Willoughby?"

"Certainly!"

"If we are now on our way, and as you are Captain, who is sailing the ship?"

"Ah, how often I am asked that question! I do have others perfectly capable of taking the helm. Be not dismayed, Darcy, you are in good hands."

"I did not doubt that, Sir."

"Good."

Darcy noticed the young lady that he observed earlier coming toward them and pass by them. She nodded to the captain, cast a slight glance in Darcy's direction, and continued on.

"Captain, another question, if you do not mind."

"Yes?"

"Do women often make this voyage unescorted?"

"Yes, frequently. On each voyage I normally have a handful. They do it for various reasons, usually financial. But do not fear, Darcy, I issue them some commonsense guidelines and try to ensure that there is no impropriety aboard this vessel. You can be confident of that."

"Thank you, Captain. I am reassured to hear that."

"Good. I would not want to have to use my upper hand in keeping *you* in line with the ladies on board."

"Do not worry yourself, Captain. I have only seen meagrely tolerable women on this ship; certainly none handsome enough to tempt me in the least."

The captain laughed. "Darcy you have not changed one bit in the years I have known you. You and your impeccable, fastidious nature. I have seen several that I would regard as quite pretty."

"I have no intention on this voyage to give consequence to ladies who have been unable to secure a husband for themselves in England and who are determined to find one aboard this sailing vessel even before arriving in America. It is apparent to me that the ladies on this ship, for the most part, have very little beauty and no breeding at all. Most are decidedly beneath my station." At this the captain raised his eyebrows. Darcy continued, "As it is, my main goal is to retrieve Georgiana and return her to England, not to seek out a female diversion; let alone secure for myself a wife."

"You are still the interminable critic. Always determined to be displeased with everything and everyone you meet. Well, Darcy, I shall leave you to your scrupulous musings. If you will excuse me, Sir, I need to see to the passengers on my ship." The captain smiled and walked away, wondering just what it would take to penetrate the Darcy armour with which he had shielded himself for as long as he could remember.

"Of course," Darcy nodded as the captain turned and walked away.

Elizabeth's eyes opened wide and her jaw dropped in derision as she heard the gentleman's disagreeable assessment of his fellow passengers. She turned and eyed the man who had been standing with his back to her, talking with the captain. She had not intended to eavesdrop, but as she walked past them, there was a vague sense of familiarity with the gentleman, but not such that she could put her finger on. When she saw a bench situated directly behind where they were standing, she decided to take a seat there, hoping to hear something that would help her determine if she had met him before. However, after overhearing his caustic words, she was quite certain she had never made his acquaintance and was even more certain she did not wish to.

At that moment, Darcy turned to walk on and saw Elizabeth sitting directly behind him; her eyes mocking, one brow raised. Inwardly Darcy tensed, feeling at the moment the object of this young lady's scorn, believing she had heard his every word. He turned away from her and briskly walked to the other side of the ship.

He certainly seems to think himself above everyone, she mused. *Not one lady handsome enough to tempt him, and most everyone decidedly beneath his station.* She stood up and brushed her hands lightly over her dress, walking over to the ship's rail. Elizabeth developed no cordial feelings for the gentleman due to his manner. If Jane were here or perhaps her good friend, Charlotte, she would heartily laugh at his blatantly proud and arrogant manner.

Darcy proceeded to the other side of the ship and leaned against the hull, holding himself stiffly. He watched people coming and going, trying to appear as indifferent and as invisible as he could, so he would be left alone. At present he had no desire for company. When he caught the eye of a young lady or her mother walking towards him, he averted his gaze, giving them no doubt that he did not wish to make their acquaintance and enter into conversation with them.

As the ship sailed toward the English Channel, the winds picked up a little and the sails billowed out even more. Darcy was anxious to see the Dover cliffs and watch the coast of England as they sailed past. He turned to walk over to the other side of the ship and took in a deep breath, recognizing that first scent of salty air. He contentedly let it out slowly when suddenly a great sound from above caught his attention and prompted him to look up.

Elizabeth had been drawn out of her reverie, watching the land pass by, when the remaining sails were unfurled, and in catching the wind, abruptly propelled the ship faster.

"Oh, my!" exclaimed Elizabeth in awe as she glanced up at the magnificent ship in full sail. She brought her hand up to secure the bonnet on her head as she stepped back a few steps to get a better view.

Darcy continued to gaze upward at the magnificent sight as he strolled across the deck of the ship. Being more captivated with the sails than where he was going, he was suddenly dismayed when he inelegantly collided with someone. He looked down and found himself face to face with the young lady he had seen earlier.

Elizabeth's eyes continued to sparkle in delight from the sight of the sails as she turned her gaze to the man into whom she had just collided. Unwittingly, Darcy found himself captivated by those eyes, but when Elizabeth saw who it was, the sparkle quickly departed.

"Excuse me. Please forgive me!" As he said these words and reached out his hands to steady her, a very fleeting memory teased his thoughts. He looked at her, wondering if she would return a look of recognition, but instead she gave him one that reflected an air of indifference, laced with a touch of agitation, as she coolly replied to him that no harm was done.

After Elizabeth collected herself and walked past the gentleman, she wondered, as well, what it was that swept through her mind when they collided. He was of a higher class than she and not someone she would have an occasion to know. So what was that tenuous recollection that touched her mind and then evaporated? She shook her head absently as any sort of remembrance eluded her. She doubted that he would have ever heard of the little village of Meryton, let alone visited it. And when she was in Town visiting her aunt and uncle, it was highly unlikely that he would frequent the Cheapside area in which the Gardiners lived. It was just as well, as she construed from his manner that he obviously was proud and arrogant and his comments to the captain, although not intended for her to hear, assured her of his character.

Her determined departure from his presence, however, did not remove thoughts of her from his mind. He concluded she was definitely not a woman of society, most likely had very little fortune and connections, and would, by all means, be most ill suited for him. He turned back to the cliffs, which were now growing smaller in the distance and for some strange reason found himself sighing.

Chapter 3

Elizabeth walked briskly away from the gentleman whose character she had determined as being proud and disagreeable, but lingered up on deck as long as she was able to see the coast of England. She leaned against the rail of the ship, letting the breeze lightly play against her face as she kept her eyes set upon the shore. At length it slowly grew smaller and smaller and soon the last vestiges of it disappeared from the horizon. At that moment her stomach quickened and she wondered with a fleeting sense of apprehension whether she had made a sensible decision in making this voyage. Tears pooled in her eyes as the realization hit her that she would be at the mercy of the unpredictable seas, changing weather conditions, and this large piece of floating wood for at least the duration of a month, and then have to endure it on the return voyage. Would she ever see her family and England again? She would not allow herself to even ponder the possibility.

With land no longer visible, the ship was completely surrounded by a vast array of blues from both the sky above and the sea below. Each was dotted with splays of white, in the puffy clouds and the tips of the waves as the ship glided through the water. The weather was comfortably warm, but the constant breeze demanded that she wear a shawl she had brought along. She hugged it closer to herself as a chill swept through her. Whether it was from the breeze or a disquieting feeling, she could not settle on.

At length, she decided to make her way back down the steps to the steerage quarters to unpack her belongings. With each step that took her further down into the dark bowels of the ship, her heart tightened. When she had come down here earlier with her father, she had assured him that the accommodations were adequate enough and she would manage comfortably in them. But in reality, she hoped she would not have to be confined to this place very often, as it was dark, dank, and very musty smelling.

It was not that the ship's accommodations were inferior or unclean, but it soon became apparent that it was considerably crowded with people in a tightly confined space. There was very little room to move. They had been assured that the steerage accommodations on *Pemberley's Promise* were among the finest. Now, however, with the quarters being filled with people, luggage hauled in, and the first indications of sea sickness taking hold, the conditions rapidly deteriorated. In an environment such as this, even the finest accommodations would become daunting. Elizabeth found herself wondering how she would fare down here for any considerable amount of time.

When her aunt and uncle invited her and Jane to join them in America, the

Gardiners offered to pay for the return voyage if the Bennets could pay for the voyage over. As it turned out, Jane decided she would not be able to make the long voyage over. Elizabeth, anxious to make the journey, but knowing her family had not the means to spend a vast deal on a trip such as this, insisted they purchase the least expensive ticket for her. That meant she would have to travel in steerage.

As she walked down into steerage and returned to her simple bed, she naturally and easily greeted those around her. This confined compartment that was to be her home for at least the next month housed ladies and children. Elizabeth soon discovered, much to her consternation, that many of the children were doubled up in the beds.

She sat down upon her bunk, absently smoothing it with a wipe of her hand as her thoughts drifted to her bed back home. For the next month a simple pillow, sheet and two coverlets upon a thin mattress were to be extent of the bedding. This was a far cry from the soft, comfortable bed, overflowing with warm coverlets and a colourful quilt, in which she normally slept. She was grateful she had brought along an extra light coverlet in case it was needed.

As Elizabeth unpacked her duffel and stowed her belongings in the drawers beneath her bed, she struck up a conversation with a woman who was in the bed next to hers. Mrs. Rawlings was travelling to America with her husband and two daughters; Pauline, who was five, and Penelope, who was seven. She was four months with child, and her husband was in the other half of steerage with the men. The two girls were sharing a bed and Pauline had begun complaining of feeling ill. When Elizabeth finished packing away all her things, she offered to entertain Penelope while Mrs. Rawlings looked after Pauline.

Little Penelope boldly handed Elizabeth a book she had brought along with her and eagerly climbed up onto her lap, squirming around to get comfortable for a reading of the story. Elizabeth obliged this little girl who was very close in age to her Aunt and Uncle Gardiner's daughter, Amanda. When Elizabeth made extended stays with the Gardiners in London, she enjoyed entertaining her little cousins and, sensing that Mrs. Rawlings had her hands full with Pauline, was grateful that little Penelope was warming up to her very nicely.

Elizabeth read the story to Penelope with much animation, securing the young girl's affections and approval. Upon finishing the story, Elizabeth inquired of Mrs. Rawlings whether she would consent to both of them going up on deck to get some fresh air. Mrs. Rawlings heartily agreed, which allowed her to concentrate fully on trying to help her other daughter feel more comfortable.

Elizabeth held on to the little girl's hand tightly as they ascended the three flights of stairs and came up to the top deck of the ship. Elizabeth savoured the fresh air as she took in a deep breath, taking delight in the sights about her. There was a gentle wind propelling them forward, and to Elizabeth's novice eyes, it appeared as though every sail was unfurled. The sailors seemed to have an excellent knowledge of what was required of them, and she watched in delight as they climbed up and down the rigging. It reminded her of the acrobats at the circus she had seen once in town, who climbed the ropes with ease and with seemingly no sense of fear that they might fall.

Penelope, confined so long in steerage, was anxious to get out and run. Elizabeth was afraid to let go of the young child's hand, so she walked briskly while Penelope ran alongside of her, occasionally breaking into a slight run herself. She enjoyed being up on deck again, and relished the opportunity to expend some of her own energy and pent up emotions she had been feeling since leaving the coast of England.

Elizabeth knew the only way she would be able to enjoy herself for the duration of the month on this ship was if she could be up on the deck and walk. It was something she enjoyed immensely at home, and hoped the weather would oblige them and be favourable enough for a brisk walk frequently upon the deck.

Suddenly Penelope squealed and called out, "Daddy!"

Elizabeth looked up and saw a young man rush over to Penelope, sweeping her up in his arms. "Hey, there is my little girl!" He swung her around. "Where are Pauline and Mother?" He glanced questioningly at Elizabeth.

Penelope answered. "Polly is not feeling well, and Mother is taking care of her. Miss Bennet is taking me for a walk on the boat."

"Excuse me, Sir, but I am Miss Elizabeth Bennet. Your wife is tending Pauline who is feeling a bit unsettled, so I offered to bring Penelope up to allow her to get some fresh air and exercise."

"That is very kind of you, Miss Bennet. I am Jack Rawlings."

"It is a pleasure, Mr. Rawlings."

Penelope held on to her father's hand and twirled around him as they talked. Elizabeth laughed at the playfulness and endless energy of this young girl.

Her father looked down at her as she continued to dance around him. "Now, Penny, remember what we told you, you must engage in calm and quiet activities while on the ship."

"I am afraid, Sir, that, if she is anything like me, she will need to engage in some brisk activity occasionally to make up for the confinement down below."

"She is a lively young girl."

"I have noticed."

He proceeded to ask Elizabeth about how his wife and daughter were faring. She was drawn to his easy manner and evident care and concern for his family.

Oblivious to Elizabeth's notice, Darcy had wandered into the eating area, a large room filled with tables and benches, where the meals would be served and people could congregate and visit. He had walked in hoping to find something light to eat or drink, and discovered, much to his consternation, that it was filled with noisy travellers who, for the most part, and upon his initial assessment, appeared unpolished and hailed from exceedingly low connections. Most were engaged in conversation, either with friends or family with whom they were travelling or with new acquaintances they had made since coming aboard.

He looked around for some obscure place to sit down where he could be by himself, but none was to be found. People were spread out everywhere and it was irritatingly loud. He scanned the crowd, and not observing anyone whose manners or company looked inviting, at once began to feel uncomfortable. He was able to secure some tea for himself and walked toward the outer wall, one which was dotted with small windows looking out to the deck.

He gazed out the small window as he drank the tea, leaning against the wall with one shoulder, tilting his head as he looked out at the people walking by on the deck. Over the years he had become proficient at putting on this façade of aloofness which, as a rule, allowed him the privacy and solitude that afforded him personal comfort. He suddenly realized he was watching the movements of the lady he had encountered earlier, walking by with a child.

His eyes narrowed as he witnessed this, straining his neck to watch them proceed toward the front of the ship. She was holding on to the young girl's hand, walking along with her and occasionally allowing herself to slip into a skip or a run. He found himself unexpectedly drawn to her vivacious and unreserved nature. She seemed not at all concerned what others might think of her actions.

With his mind engaged on the scene playing out before him, he gradually became aware of someone standing next to him, disturbing his preoccupation and speculations.

He turned to see a woman standing by his side. She was definitely striking, more so in a fashionable than handsome way. She had been gazing off across the room, but when he turned his eyes upon her, she met his gaze and knowingly mistook it as a sign of the gentleman's interest.

"Good afternoon, Sir." He was taken aback by her forwardness. "What a relief it is to finally find someone on board this ship who obviously frequents the same circles in society as I! I can certainly guess your thoughts at the moment. You are thinking how insupportable it will be to spend a month in such tedious company as found on this ship."

Darcy's jaw tightened as he pondered his response. "Your assessment is more correct than you would imagine."

She smiled, pleased with his apparent agreement. "My name is Eleanor Brewster." She held out her hand, extended with her palm down, in hopes that he might take it and bestow a kiss upon the top of her hand.

She was more than disappointed when he merely answered, "I am Fitzwilliam Darcy," and gave a quick, short bow.

Despite her disappointment, she asked, "Are you travelling with family?" She looked around him and quickly added, "Are your wife and children with you?" She put on a smile that was intended to evoke a response.

Darcy eyed her suspiciously and felt the all too familiar sense of discomfiture come over him as she continued her ploy of persuasion. The very fact that she claimed to frequent the same circles of society as himself, yet was completely disregarding the dictates of that society by approaching him and beginning a conversation with him, appalled him. She obviously thought herself above the dictates of polite society, having the unrivalled audacity to approach him so boldly.

He forced a civil smile upon his face and offered a simple, "I am travelling alone."

Pleased with this response, her every movement was meant to entice and ensnare, and Darcy was more annoyed by this than allured. Desiring nothing more than to continue the conversation, she asked, "May I inquire, Sir, as to why you are heading to the colonies?"

Darcy, *lacking* all desire to continue this conversation or encourage this woman, replied with a paramount lack of enthusiasm, "Strictly to retrieve my sister and then return to England as soon as possible."

"Oh, Sir, what a kind brother you are! To have such concern for your sister, to give up at least two months of your life to travel to and fro…" Her hand went up to her neck and she fingered a rather large brooch that hung there as she calculated her next comment. "But perhaps, Mr. Darcy, while you are there, you might find the need for a companion to show you around. I would be…"

"I think not," Darcy interrupted.

The response it elicited was not the one she wished for. Darcy felt a surge of agitation infuse throughout his body and he impatiently excused himself, bowed, and turned away. He quickly finished the tea, and set his cup down, anxious to put as much distance as he could between this woman and himself.

As he quickly headed for the door, an older man and his wife entered, followed by a young lady in her late teens. The older man greeted him and immediately introduced himself.

"Good day, Sir. My name is Gerald Summers." He extended his hand and Darcy reluctantly, but civilly, extended his.

"Fitzwilliam Darcy," was his only response.

Summers jovially expressed his pleasure at making the acquaintance. "And may I introduce my wife, Henrietta Summers, and my lovely daughter, Miss Angela Summers."

Darcy bowed to both, sensing that the father and mother were eyeing him and going through a checklist of sorts of eligible suitors for their young daughter. He sensed uneasiness rather than eagerness, however, in the young girl's demeanour.

"May I assume that you are travelling alone, Sir?" Mr. Summers inquired.

Darcy nodded reluctantly. "You assume correctly."

"Good, good! You can complete our table tonight at whist. Can we count on you?"

Darcy took in a deep breath. His natural tendency would lead him to brusquely brush him aside and not give a second thought about putting him in his place. But he knew spending a month with the same people in the confines of this ship required him to make more of an effort at civility, so replied, "Thank you, Summers, but I rarely play. If you will excuse me…"

Darcy removed himself again from a most discomfiting situation for the second time in just a few minutes. As he walked past them, he sighed. *How am I ever going to endure a month on this ship without keeping myself sequestered in my cabin?*

Darcy walked out, eager for some fresh air before he finally succumbed to temptation to return to the solitary confines of his small, private room.

It has begun, he groaned to himself, and it was only the first day.

He absently found himself turning in the direction in which he had seen the young lady and the child earlier, but apparently she was no longer up on deck.

~~*

Later that afternoon, the captain made his way to the steerage compartment holding the women and children. It was announced that he was arrived to make an announcement to them. When he came in, he welcomed them to his ship and informed them that he had come to give some general guidelines for travelling aboard *Pemberley's Promise.*

"Ladies, I know that some of you have husbands in the men's steerage compartment, but I do not want you thinking that this announcement is not intended for you. I have some things to say to all the women as commonsense guidelines, and you would be wise to listen. I am especially directing this to those women who are travelling unescorted, however. I strive to make this ship and the journey we are on a safe and pleasant one. But I cannot guarantee the character of everyone on board this ship. Of my crew, I will say without doubt that they will behave as gentlemen around the ladies. If I hear word otherwise, they will suffer severe penalties. But as for the other passengers on this ship, I cannot vouch for them all. Therefore I say this to every woman. Do not walk around this ship after dark unescorted. I can only guarantee your safety to a degree. There is no reason to be walking alone around this ship after dark. Again, if there is any impropriety that you become aware of, please inform me. If there is anything you need, please let me know."

The captain ended by giving instructions for various things they would need to know for this voyage, ending with meals. The meals were served in a large dining area that would also be available to lounge in during the day and into the evening. He gave them the hours meals would be served, along with some other essential information, answered some questions, and then left.

Later that afternoon Elizabeth found her way to the large dining room. She seated herself at a table with some women she had met in steerage who were now joined by their husbands. She enjoyed making their acquaintance and conversing with them.

The meal that night, as it would be for only a few days, consisted of some fresh meat and vegetables, a little fruit and a light bread. They had been told, however, that due to the length of time at sea, they would eventually have to subsist on a dried, salted meat, hardtack biscuits, and some hardy vegetable such as potatoes. Most other vegetables and fruits, unless dried, would spoil.

Elizabeth glanced out of the corner of her eye at the tall man in the far corner of the room who had so earnestly expressed his views to the captain earlier about the lower class citizenry of the passengers. He was unquestionably holding to a position of superiority as he seemed loath to assemble with the others and make new acquaintances. But there was something else about him that puzzled her. She could not place it at the moment, but his look and posture suggested something else, as well. It intrigued her and she was determined she would figure it out by the time they reached the American shore.

She settled into an easy conversation with a young lady just about her age who was travelling with her husband. Her name was Jenna Michelson and Elizabeth discovered that when they arrive in America they would make their way to the Dakotas, where her husband's brother owned some land. Elizabeth listened in awe as Jenna read a letter from her brother-in-law describing the winters there; how they would be housebound for days, even weeks on end, when severe snowstorms came upon them.

"And this is your dream, to live in such a place as this?" asked Elizabeth incredulously.

Jenna smiled and nodded softly. "It is the only way. We had no hope for a better life in England. At least here we shall have some land and our own home."

Elizabeth smiled sympathetically. She was grateful for Longbourn, their modest home, yet knew that unless a marriage by one of her sisters was made with someone of fortune, they had little hope for much more. With their home entailed to a distant cousin, whom they had never even met because of a family dispute between her father and his father, they could hardly hope that Longbourn would always be there for them.

Jenna interrupted Elizabeth's thoughts. "We saved for years, giving up many things so we could make this trip. For us this trip means everything." The young friend looked over at the gentleman sitting off by himself. *"We* sacrificed quite a lot to make this voyage. For *that* gentleman," she discreetly motioned towards him, "it was probably no sacrifice at all for him to take this trip."

Elizabeth, with her eyes turning back to the gentleman, whose impeccable dress and manners more than hinted at his wealth, asked, "Do you know anything about him? His name or where he is from?"

Another woman at the table, a Mrs. Nichols answered for her. "His name is Darcy, so I hear. Has a home in London and in Derbyshire somewhere."

Another one answered, "I heard he owns a great estate."

From across the table, someone added, "No, I think I heard he owns his own castle that he doesn't let anyone come close to."

Elizabeth was amused at the rumours that were already circulating about this man of wealth.

"Perhaps he even owns his own island, or even his own country somewhere," said another.

Everyone laughed.

"Not a very sociable person," added Mr. Michelson, "but from the looks of him and his dress he is definitely a man of wealth and therefore has no need for any of us. Almost certainly the only sacrifice *he* is making in taking this voyage is being in the same room with people he deems beneath him."

"You are not far from the mark there, Mr. Michelson," Elizabeth smiled. "I overheard him say to the captain that the women on this ship were not handsome enough to tempt him, and most everyone decidedly beneath his station."

Michelson added, "I am glad to hear that for the sake of the ladies on this ship. He may have the looks and the wealth to attract any number of ladies, but I would wager that he would consider it a punishment to even *speak* to any lady on this ship." He nodded towards a table where a young lady was seated with some other passengers. "Now *she* has had her eye on him all evening. I would wager that she deems him as someone most suitable for herself."

"Well she looks like she deserves him. But you do not have to worry about me." Elizabeth stated emphatically. "I believe I can safely promise you *never* to cast an interested eye in his direction."

At this, her eyes gave a teasing glance at Darcy just as he looked up to see three sets of eyes upon him. Somehow he suspected that they were talking about him and he shifted uncomfortably on the bench. At times he wished he was more like his outgoing friends… Bingley, for instance, who could speak so easily amongst strangers and would, in very little time, be acquainted with the whole room.

Yet in reality, when Bingley was with him in situations where he had few or no acquaintances, he would watch Bingley circulate about the room while he remained anchored at some window or mantel, unable to keep up with him; unwilling to make the effort. No, having Bingley around did not always help.

Darcy had brought with him a book in to read, but no longer had a desire to remain in here. He knew that in time he would get to know a select few of the passengers, most likely as he found opportunity to speak to them alone. When in the company of one or two, he more often than not could summon up all effort at civility and get through the very basics.

He looked over to the woman who had boldly come up to him earlier, noticing that she was still eyeing him most overtly. If he really wanted to, he could put on a charming façade and a civil demeanour, endure her company, and charm her and her companions. But at the moment, his thoughts were not inclined toward viewing this voyage as something that would offer him any modicum of pleasure or refined enjoyment. He was solely focused on the task at hand; to secure his sister and return home with her. Finally, deciding he needed the solitude of his room, he slid himself out from the bench.

Elizabeth had turned back to her friends and she excused herself, wanting to get back down to steerage before darkness settled across the ship. As she turned toward the door, she again inadvertently collided with Darcy, who was also walking hurriedly in the same direction.

Elizabeth gave a wry smile as she saw who she had bumped into again. "Perhaps we ought to stop meeting like this, Sir. One of us is bound to get hurt!" Her eyes flashed a lively, almost mischievous look his way that caught him off guard and seemed to pull him in and, at the same time, back to some fleeting memory again.

"I would hope not. Again, I apologize."

He walked on ahead of Elizabeth and she thought, *Just as I would expect. He wants to distance himself from the likes of someone like me. He cannot endure being in the presence of one so decidedly beneath him!*

But instead of continuing on, when he reached the door he opened it, stood off to the side, and allowed her to pass through ahead of him. His unexpected action pleasantly surprised her and at once she regretted her previous thought about him. *At least he can choose to display good manners when he wants*, she thought. "Thank you," she replied and made her way to the stairs that took her down below, wondering at the difficulty she was having in attempting to sketch his character.

Darcy stood still and watched as she left, noticing that she was headed down another flight of stairs. He found himself captivated by her eyes and found it difficult to pull *his* away. As he finally turned to proceed to his cabin, he had to abruptly divert his direction to avoid encountering yet another woman he determined had planted herself in his path to make certain to attract his attention. His decision to walk completely around the other way to his cabin brought him to it in a most exasperated state.

Chapter 4

As darkness encased the ship, the environment within steerage became markedly bleak. Elizabeth made her way toward her bed and found Mrs. Rawlings still tending to her daughter, Pauline, who still felt exceedingly ill. Penelope had fallen asleep in her mother's bed, and Mrs. Rawlings decided she would sleep on the floor, as she did not want to disturb her sleeping daughter. Moreover, she would not fit upon the narrow mattress with the little girl in the state she was in.

Elizabeth would not have it and offered her bed to the woman. "Please, I insist that you take my bed. Allow me to sleep on the floor!"

"Thank you, Miss Bennet, but no. I cannot do that."

"Mrs. Rawlings, I am younger, and you need a good night's sleep to keep yourself and the baby healthy."

"I appreciate your generosity, but we chose to save money by having our girls sleep together. It is my dilemma."

Elizabeth shook her head firmly. "Mrs. Rawlings, I have oft slept on the floor in my sister's room. I would sneak into her room at night and we would lie on the floor whispering and giggling, falling asleep before we knew it."

Elizabeth extended her hand toward her bed while gathering her coverlet and a coat to use as a pillow, placing them on the floor. "Please."

Mrs. Rawlings was more than grateful to Elizabeth, but remorseful for causing Elizabeth such discomfort. They sat and talked for awhile; Elizabeth continually reassuring her that she would be more than happy to do this. Elizabeth eventually changed into her nightdress and robe, and then crawled between the folded warmth of her coverlet.

She and Jane often ended up asleep on the floor in either one of their rooms, although it had been many years. As Elizabeth lay there in those first few moments of darkness, she thought it was not so much the hard floor that might keep her awake, but the rocking of the ship and the noises from this crowded room of women and children. At home, she had her own room and she knew, much to her consternation, that she was a very light sleeper.

As she lowered her head upon the pillow, she remembered the words of her father and offered up a silent prayer thanking God for taking them through this first day. She was grateful she did not seem affected by the swaying of the ship and prayed for those who were, especially little Pauline. As she closed her eyes, she added to her prayer a request that she would be able to sleep well on this ship for the duration of the voyage. But the noises from children crying out and other odd sounds of so many people sleeping together did little to help this part of the prayer being answered that night.

~~*~

Being blessed with pleasant weather, the hatch to steerage had been left open all night, which allowed for a meagre amount of light to seep down into its depths as soon as the sun began announcing the new day. At the earliest signs of dawn, Elizabeth awoke, silently cursing her propensity to awaken with the morning sun. At some point in the night she had fallen asleep, but now she was stiff and sore, and believed herself to have only had a few hours of sound sleep.

She sat up slowly, working out the sore muscles and stiff limbs that were painfully letting her know they were not happy with the sleeping arrangements last night. Most of her steerage companions were still asleep and she sat quietly, leaning her head against the wall, contemplating what this new day would bring.

She looked up toward the hatch, and watched the thread of sunlight sneaking through. She stifled a deep breath because of the variety of odours that were building throughout. As she sat motionless, she thought of her father's words again, and thanked the Lord for her first night on the ship and then beseeched Him that He would continue to carry them safely across these waters.

Her attention was drawn to Pauline, who had awakened and began to whimper. Elizabeth stood up as Mrs. Rawlings awoke and they both went to the little girl. Elizabeth felt the little girl's forehead and found it to be feverish. "She does seem to have a fever, Mrs. Rawlings. Perhaps her illness is something other than seasickness."

Mrs. Rawlings pulled the blanket off the bed and brought it up to Pauline, covering the little girl who had begun to shiver.

Elizabeth gently reassured the woman, who was quite concerned for her daughter. "Let me go freshen up, and then I will go up on deck and see if I can secure another blanket for her."

"Thank you."

Elizabeth changed into a simple muslin dress and quickly brushed out her hair, easily pulling it up and securing it. She put on a bonnet and tied it securely under her chin, then set out for one of the small necessary rooms they had for the women. When she had readied herself, she wrapped a shawl around her, climbed the stairs, and instantly felt strengthened by the gradual increase of sunlight that poured down on her. Upon reaching the floor just below the top deck, she obliged herself and took in a well needed deep breath. She filled her lungs with the fresh air and immediately felt strengthened and more alert.

She decided to walk down the hall, looking for some sort of linens storage room. To her delight, she found a door marked "linens."

She did not see anyone around, so she turned the door lever and was pleased to find it unlocked. She walked into a very pleasant, clean room that had shelves of blankets, pillows, towels, and assorted other items. A small window let in some light and a fleeting thought passed through Elizabeth's mind that she could curl up in here and sleep for the night so soundly and no one need to know. It would be much more endurable than steerage. As she was musing over this very foolish, yet appealing idea, the slight listing of the ship closed the door behind her, bringing her back to her purpose in being there, and she set out to collect a few things she needed. She decided to pick up an extra pillow for herself, as well as two more blankets in case they were needed.

Her arms were full as she managed to open the door. As she backed out, she slowly closed the door behind her. She turned and found herself staring into the face of Mr. Darcy, who was walking down the hall.

A look of surprise crossed his face as he saw her arms laden with linens, closing the door behind her. He smiled slightly, tilting his head as he spoke, "I did not know when I collided with you yesterday that you were a stowaway."

"I am not a stowaway, Sir," Elizabeth declared as she shook her head in irritation and for emphasis. She looked down at the blankets and pillow. "I am bringing these down to steerage for a little girl who has a fever and the chills, and where, I might add, I am a *paid* passenger."

"I see," he said. "I am sorry to hear that a child is unwell." He had never seriously considered that she was a stowaway, but he should have known that his attempts at teasing usually were not taken as such. This was unfortunately one of those occasions. "Were you not given enough blankets and pillows, then?"

Elizabeth was eager to let this gentleman know what she thought about this very poor policy on the ship. "We would have had enough if only one person was assigned to each bed."

"There are people doubled up down there?" asked Darcy incredulously.

Elizabeth started at his question. She tilted her head and looked at him askance, pondering yet another example of his unpredictability. "Many of the children are. Unfortunately one of them is the sick little girl. The child's mother, who is four months with child, gave up her bed to her other daughter." Elizabeth pondered whether to go on to tell him that she gave her own bed to the mother, but decided against it.

Darcy looked at her with not much more feelings of disbelief than displeasure at what he learned his ship's policy was and what had happened as a result. "So this woman, who is four months with child, is left to sleep on the floor?"

Elizabeth now looked at this man whose character was becoming increasingly difficult to sketch. That he seemed concerned did not harmonize with the image she had of him.

"No, I could not allow her to do that." Elizabeth paused, "I gave her my bed." Darcy nodded. "So you slept in the linens room instead?"

"Not quite, Sir," Elizabeth let out a sparkling laugh. "I went in just a few moments ago to secure these items." She paused, and when Darcy said no more but seemed highly disconcerted about this whole thing, she added with a touch of mischievousness and a sly smile, "Although while I was in there, the thought *did* cross my mind that it might be just a bit more comfortable sleeping in there than on the floor in steerage. Do you think that anyone will mind?"

She did not wait for an answer, but pressed the need to get the blankets down below. "If you will excuse me, these are required downstairs."

Elizabeth walked away, surprised by this man's character. Her first impression of him had been that he entertained feelings of superiority and disdain for the common passengers on this ship, and that out of his own mouth. Now she had just seen evidence that he might possess a little compassion for others. And then there was something about the way he reacted to her comment about the sleeping conditions. *What was it? Why would he even be concerned about how people in steerage were faring?* She walked away from him exceedingly puzzled.

~~*

Darcy sought out the captain immediately upon leaving Elizabeth. He was not aloft, so Darcy made his way to the captain's cabin, which was at the front of the ship, just down the hall from his own room. He knocked firmly and impatiently at the door.

Captain Willoughby opened the door, holding a cup of coffee in one hand and a piece of bread in the other. "Come in, Darcy. I am just having a small breakfast. Would you care to join me?"

'No, thank you, Sir. That is not why I am here. I was disturbed by some news I heard and wanted to inquire about it."

The captain looked up at him questioningly. "What is it, Darcy?"

"I understand that in steerage some of the passengers, the children to be specific, are doubled up in the beds."

The captain turned and returned to his chair, sitting down and motioning for Darcy to sit down. "That is true. Several ships allow this policy to enable more passengers to afford the crossing. Usually the children do fine sharing their bed with a brother or sister."

Darcy walked over to the table and sat down opposite Willoughby, regarding him intently. "There is a young lady down there who has been forced to sleep on the floor after giving up her bed to a sick child's mother. She did not ask me to inquire about this, but Captain, might there be another bed available for her? I would gladly make up the difference in her fare."

The Captain eyed him suspiciously, wondering of his sudden generosity. "I am sorry, Darcy. The ship is full to capacity. There are no extra beds at all on this ship… except the one in your cabin, and I most certainly will not allow her to take *that* one."

"There is not another available anywhere?"

The captain shook his head, wondering whether his concern over this matter was directed toward the young lady or how people would feel if they were to find out he was the owner of the ship and go to him with complaints.

"I am sorry, Darcy. This particular young lady friend of yours should claim her bed back. I am sure the child down there will improve in time. It is most likely the motion of the ship, and that should pass soon enough once she is used to it. If I were you, I would not worry about it. There is nothing you can do, and unfortunately, it happens all the time."

Darcy turned in exasperation. *She is not my particular lady friend!* he thought to himself. Yet for some odd reason he was repeatedly being thrown in her presence, and he continually found his mind agreeably engaged on this lively, perplexing, and slightly familiar looking woman with very fine eyes!

"Is that all, Darcy?" the captain asked.

"Yes." He turned towards the door.

"Darcy?"

"Yes, Willoughby?"

"I do not fully understand why you are taking such an interest in this lady's situation, but I would not go about entertaining thoughts about her."

Darcy tried to interrupt and deny that he had any intention of doing such a thing, but the captain raised his hand to stop him. "Darcy, just remember. I will not allow any impropriety on my ship."

Darcy took in a deep breath. "Yes, Sir. As I said earlier, I am grateful for that."

He left, closing the door behind him, and set out for the top deck to take a determinedly brisk walk before the majority of the passengers came up.

~~*

Elizabeth returned below and placed the folded blankets and extra pillow on her bed to use that night. People were beginning to stir, and Elizabeth was grateful she was already up and dressed, although if she could, she would curl up in her bed and fall asleep. It was now vacated and had been straightened out by Mrs. Rawlings. And despite the narrow, thin mattress, it looked extremely inviting.

She inquired how Pauline was faring, and Mrs. Rawlings answered that she was sleeping, but still had a high fever. She was now, however, concerned for Penelope, who was complaining of feeling unwell, herself.

Elizabeth recognized the drawn look of fatigue on Mrs. Rawlings face, as well, and wondered if she was beginning to come down with what was ailing her daughters.

"May I inquire how you are faring, Mrs. Rawlings?"

"Thank you for your concern, Miss Bennet. I am just a little tired."

By the way she avoided looking at her, Elizabeth concluded that she did not own up to the complete truth. Elizabeth believed her to be concealing her ailment so she could continue to care for her daughters.

"Mrs. Rawlings, if there is anything I can do to help you, please do not hesitate to ask. If you need some rest, or if you need to get up and get some fresh air, I would be more than willing to watch over your girls for you."

A swathe of relief passed over Mrs. Rawlings. "Miss Bennet, you are too kind. Have you had anything to eat, yet?"

"Actually, no. I might go up now and secure a bite, and then I shall return immediately to keep an eye on your daughters so you may go up. If I see your husband, I shall let him know you will be up shortly."

"Thank you, Miss Bennet."

"Please, call me Elizabeth."

"And you must call me Lenore."

"I shall return momentarily, Lenore."

Elizabeth walked up the two levels of stairs to the deck where the eating area was located. She glanced around the room and recognized some women from steerage who were eating with their families. She walked over to join them; greeting those she had already met and introducing herself to those she had not, and settled into an easy conversation with them.

Elizabeth had a natural gift for meeting and conversing easily with people, and her sharp wit and lively personality endeared her to many. But the prominent thing that people noticed about her was how she reached out in concern to others. They saw a prime example of this in her aiding the Rawlings.

When Elizabeth returned to steerage after eating that morning, she found Mrs. Rawlings fatigued and feeling quite ill. She knew it would benefit her greatly to get some rest, so Elizabeth offered to run back up, get some food for her and her daughters, and bring it back down to them.

Elizabeth returned with some hardtack bread, a few pieces of fruit, water, and tea, but Mrs. Rawlings took only a little liquid nourishment. Neither of the girls appeared to be hungry; they seemed not at all interested in what she had brought them. Elizabeth did all she could to get them to at least take some liquid, and when it was quite apparent that they would not eat, she simply made an effort to keep them comfortable and still.

She later returned up to the top deck when the girls and Mrs. Rawlings had fallen asleep. She was anxious for a walk, although it was quite difficult with so many people aloft. The ship itself also had obstacles that made it difficult to take a leisurely, pleasant walk without having to walk around things. Elizabeth decided if she wanted to get a walk in each day, something she definitely desired, she would have to do it early in the morning when few people would be up.

While up on deck, Elizabeth noticed Mr. Rawlings and informed him that his wife and daughters were unwell. She told him she had brought them something to eat, but they would likely be resting for the remainder of the day.

By late afternoon, Elizabeth was weary, having spent much of her day sitting with either Mrs. Rawlings or her daughters, and occasionally going aloft for a break and a respite of fresh air. She ate as soon as the meal was ready, but instead of staying up to visit with others as she would have liked, she returned to steerage and readied herself for bed, hoping to fall asleep early and get a good night's sleep. She curled herself up on the floor and while a trace of light was still making its way down the hatch, she pulled out a sampler she had brought along and began stitching. As the sun eventually diminished sending its light, and with her eyelids growing heavy, she lay down, but the sounds of coughing, sickness, and children crying continued to assault her, preventing any real success at falling asleep again for the second night in a row.

Earlier in the evening, but after Elizabeth had returned to steerage, Darcy entered the dining area, book in hand, and searched for a place to sit. As his eyes quickly scanned the room, he looked for a suitable place to sit, but in reality he was seeking out a particular young lady. Being unable to locate her, he settled for a table off to the side that had some room on the end of one of the benches. There were other people sitting there, a family, but since none of the women he had been trying to avoid were anywhere near, he decided to settle himself there. From where he was sitting he was also able to keep an eye towards the door, enabling him to see who walked in.

Seated with him were a middle aged gentleman, his wife, and their two sons. Mr. Jennings made the introductions to his wife and sons. Darcy did not need to worry about making any kind of effort in conversing with his dining partners, as Mr. Jennings seemed content to carry on quite admirably himself, with Darcy only making an occasional sound of agreement or nod of his head. Mrs. Jennings occasionally looked at him with a somewhat embarrassed look as her husband carried on, but she contributed very little to the discourse. Darcy was content to sit and tune out the endless chattering of this man while his mind was solely preoccupied with one particular lady whom he was hoping to see tonight.

If he had only to put up with Mr. Jennings' droning monologue, he would have been able to endure the evening. As the evening grew later, however, his frustration increased as he was not allowed to be content just sitting -- had not even been able to pick up his book -- but was approached by several others requesting him to join them in their table games, or conversation, or a smoke or drink. He was easily suspicious of their reasons for singling him out for company. He politely declined, knowing he would not be able to concentrate on anything but where *she* might be tonight.

She, the vivacious woman with the fine eyes, did not come up at all that he could see. Instead of being able to even dwell on her, he was continually assaulted with the presence of several, whose sole objective was to make sure this man took notice of them.

After enduring only what enabled him to remain civil, he finally excused himself from those around him, grasping book in hand and retreated to his room for the remainder of the evening.

~~*

The next morning, as soon as sunlight poured down through the hatch, Elizabeth awakened. She was not sure how much she had slept, but by the way she felt, she knew it had again been insufficient. There were only a few others in steerage that had awakened. She slowly pulled herself up and began readying herself for another day, remembering to offer up a prayer for the Lord to continue to watch over them.

Once she came up on deck, she breathed in the fresh air. How invigorating just a breath of fresh air made her feel. The staleness of the air down below seemed intent on taking away any morsel of energy she had, but up here she felt alive and revitalized, despite her lack of sleep.

She began walking, up one side of the ship and back on the other. She walked briskly, watching the sailors man the sails and attend to their morning chores and looking out to the vast sea, hoping to catch the sight of dolphins that she had heard often could be seen soaring alongside the ship. She quickly plotted out the best course for her along the deck that would best avoid obstacles scattered throughout.

After having walked up and back a couple of times, she became aware of someone walking behind her. Thinking it was a crewman, she stepped over toward the right so she would be out of his way and he could pass. At length that person's strides brought him to her side. But instead of passing her, he slowed his pace and began walking alongside of her. She glanced over; surprised to see that it was Mr. Darcy.

She was not sure whether he seemed surprised to see her when she turned her head, but he did appear uncertain about what to say.

Never to be at a loss for words or intimidated by wealth or rank, Elizabeth greeted him. "Good morning, Mr. Darcy! Pleasant morning for a walk."

"Yes it is." They both continued in their stride and he looked at her oddly. "It is apparent you know my name, but I am at a loss to know yours."

For some inexplicable reason her heart made a tiny erratic leap as he inquired about her name. It went undetected by Darcy, however, and she answered, "Please forgive me. I overheard someone mention your name the other day, Mr. Darcy. I am Miss Elizabeth Bennet."

Darcy glanced down at her. "I am pleased to make your acquaintance, Miss Bennet."

They turned their attention to their walk, and after a brief silence, Darcy asked, "They mentioned me? And what precisely did they say?"

Elizabeth cast a glance up at him, a single eyebrow briefly arching. A smile crept across her face, recalling the rumours that people were spreading about him.

"I believe, Sir, that one person claimed you owned your own castle."

"Is that so?"

Elizabeth nodded. "I am afraid it is, Mr. Darcy. It was settled that you almost certainly own a large estate, a castle, an island, or I might add, possibly your own country. I am surprised no one thought of the likelihood that you might also own this ship!"

Darcy tensed as she made this last remark, but realized by the smile on her face that she was saying it in jest. "What do *you* think?" he asked.

She pondered whether to tell him what her opinion of him was, which was based on what she overheard him say that first day. "What I think is of no importance. And it is no one's business but your own, at any rate."

He turned his eyes forward, feeling fairly secure that word had not leaked out of his ownership of *Pemberley's Promise*. The two walked practically in step. Elizabeth felt awkward that he most likely felt obligated to remain with her as they continued, given that they were the only two passengers up on the deck. They had walked nearly the full length of the ship before he was to speak again.

"May I inquire, Miss Bennet, have you worked out the sleeping arrangements in a satisfactory manner?"

She turned to look up at him, almost as surprised that he remembered as that he was asking about it.

"Unfortunately no. The woman to whom I gave my bed is now ill, and I could not, in good conscience, ask for it back. So I find myself sleeping on the floor again. It is of no consequence. I have done it often enough at home."

She detected a deep, aggravated sigh from him, but he said nothing. His only response was to bring up his hand and brusquely rub his chin.

He did not make further effort to converse with her, and seemed lost in thought as they walked. She cast a furtive glance up at him to see if she could detect whether he was irritated by her presence, oblivious to it, or took any sort of pleasure in it. She was certain it was not the latter, but was hard pressed to discern which of the other two it was.

They walked another two lengths of the ship in silence; Elizabeth pondering why he felt he must remain with her if he had no intention of talking with her, other than about the sleeping conditions in steerage.

But if she was surprised by his earlier question, she was astonished by his next comment.

"I did not see you up in the dining area last night."

Elizabeth stammered for some sense to come forth. Certainly he was simply stating a fact. He could not mean anything by it and she would be a fool to interpret it any other way.

"I went in early for supper and then went back down to steerage directly."

Darcy nodded but wondered if her sleeping on the floor was as tolerable as she claimed it to be.

During the course of their walk, more passengers began making their way up, and Elizabeth felt the necessity for her to return to steerage and check on the Rawlings.

"Mr. Darcy, if you will excuse me, I need to return down below."

"Thank you, Miss Bennet. I enjoyed our walk this morning."

As Elizabeth walked away, there was a moment when a memory teased her thoughts like an image from a dream that you try to recall but evaporates before it can be fully recollected. She had an odd sensation of having been at the receiving end of his approving deference before. A long time ago.

~~*

Darcy returned to his room. He did not have to remind himself that he enjoyed the company of Miss Bennet a great deal more than he should. She had neither the breeding, nor was she of the sphere of society into which he was expected to marry. Everything about her position resonated against his better judgment. Viewed in a rational light, he knew he should take his walks at some other time in the course of the day and thus avoid any more of Miss Bennet's delightful company.

He shook his head. He did not want to give up his early morning walks, but for his own peace of mind, he determined it would be best that he keep his distance from her at all other times while on this voyage.

Chapter 5

The following day, Elizabeth rose at the first signs of dawn and quickly made her way aloft, beckoned by the promise of sunshine and fresh air. As she opened the door that brought her out on to the deck, she took in a long deep breath that invigorated and roused her from any last remnants of sleep.

She politely nodded to the crew she passed as they hurriedly set out to ready the ship for another full day of sailing and she determinedly set out to walk. She stepped briskly, holding her shawl tightly around her shoulders as the morning air was cool, and the breeze from the sea, coupled with the movement from the ship, made it cooler than it really was.

At length, just as she began her second time around the deck, she noticed Mr. Darcy step out. He looked her way and she was surprised to see that he refrained from walking until she reached him.

"Good morning, Miss Bennet."

She nodded and replied, "Good morning Mr. Darcy."

He joined her in her stride, walking with his hands clasped behind him, looking either straight ahead or out across the sea. Elizabeth sensed that he was far away and was perfectly satisfied with the silence between them. She felt an awkwardness that stemmed from her uncertainty concerning whether, if he had his preference, he would wish to walk unaccompanied.

She occasionally slowed or quickened her gait to see if he would pass on ahead of her, but each time he adjusted his steps accordingly. She finally settled in her mind that he was content to walk in this markedly silent manner, which was broken only occasionally by one or the other in a comment about the weather, the sea, or how other passengers were faring.

Elizabeth stole some glances at him and marvelled that his stern demeanour, while walking, seemed to soften somewhat. He seemed at peace, almost at home, in this activity. They continued to walk briskly and talk little, but when they did, he offered very little information about himself and she did not pry.

As more and more passengers came up, it became increasingly difficult to walk in a leisurely, unobstructed fashion. Elizabeth commented that she should get back down to steerage to see how the others were faring.

Darcy seemed inclined to say something as he took in a deep breath. Fully expecting him to speak, Elizabeth waited, but when he did not, she turned to leave.

In an action that surprised her because she did not expect it from him nor did she expect the stirring feelings it provoked in her, he reached out and stopped her by slipping his hand through her arm.

"Miss Bennet, will you be walking again tomorrow morning?"

Elizabeth pondered whether his question was to ascertain if he would finally have the pleasure of a walk in solitude, or, however unlikely in her opinion, he looked forward to a walk together again. Her rapidly beating heart made it terribly difficult to think, let alone be rational and reasonable.

"I love to walk in the early morning hours, Mr. Darcy. It is one of my favourite pastimes at home, and as the exercise and fresh air are all I need to keep up my strength and endurance on the ship, then I imagine I will."

He merely nodded, letting go of her arm, almost reluctantly. She did not believe that he could truly enjoy having her as a walking companion. They had not engaged in any kind of lively discussion or divulged any personal information. But, when she left and as she made her way down to steerage, she wondered whether his question reflected a desirable anticipation.

Elizabeth laughed and shook her head. *No! How absurd!* She was one of those very women who were *intolerably beneath him*, as he had so adamantly informed the captain!

Elizabeth spent that day helping Mrs. Rawlings and her daughters, as well as a few others who had taken ill. She was grateful that she felt well enough to come up for a break for some intermittent fresh air and sunshine. She found herself in a routine acquiring food and drink, applying cool cloths to fevered foreheads, and simply sitting with, talking with, and encouraging those who were not doing well.

~~*

It continued in this manner for several days. If Elizabeth came up first for her walk, Darcy joined her when he made his way aloft. If he was up first, when he noticed her he either quickened or slowed his pace until she was by his side.

He never said a great deal, nor did she give herself the trouble of talking or questioning much, but she was struck with the fact that he did ask some questions occasionally that bordered between civility and genuine interest. In addition, he continued to be peculiarly concerned with not only the sleeping arrangements, but the living conditions down below.

In the course of those few days, they shared very little about themselves save that Elizabeth was heading to America to visit her aunt and uncle who were there on business. She hoped to remain over there for a couple of months before returning to England with them.

Darcy, in turn, talked to her of his sister and how he was making the voyage simply to secure her return to England. He told Elizabeth how her governess, who had taken Georgiana to the States with her, had become too ill to accompany her home.

Elizabeth did find, on about the fourth day of their walks, that Darcy was an avid conversationalist when it came to discussing books. She had noticed him reading in the dining area the night before, still keeping to himself, and a simple inquiry about what he was reading seemed to capture his interest.

That began a very diverse, animated, and enjoyable conversation between the two. Elizabeth loved to read, and although she enjoyed indulging in some of the current romance novels of her day, she also eagerly read meatier novels, plays and prose by Shakespeare, interesting biographies, and had even ploughed through some historical books with great enjoyment.

Elizabeth looked at each successive day after that as a challenge; to discover a subject that interested him and get him involved in a healthy discourse. She loved to question his opinions and disagree with him. She thought it odd that he seemed to enjoy it when she expressed an opposing view.

When they first began discussing books, Darcy assumed Elizabeth's knowledge would be limited. He was pleasantly surprised to discover otherwise, but what intrigued him most was the fact that she did not pander to his opinions. She expressed her views without hesitation, albeit politely, and did not try to align them with his solely because he was a man of wealth and connections.

On the morning of their sixth day out, Elizabeth began to feel the effects of not sleeping well for several successive nights, but anxiously looked forward to her walk. As she readied herself to go aloft, she determined that on this day they would discuss poetry. She wondered at all whether he enjoyed that literary genre. She imagined he would not.

Later, after they had walked the perimeter of the ship a couple of times, she finally inquired, "What do you think of poetry, Mr. Darcy? Is it the food or foolishness of love?"

"I believe it is said that poetry is the food of love," answered Darcy, fairly suspicious that she was ready to challenge his statement.

"So they say. But how often has poetry actually driven away love. If it is a good, strong, healthy love, then anything will nurture it and cause it to grow. But a weak love… I am afraid that one good sonnet will starve it entirely away."

"But would it not also have to do with the sonnet itself? A good, strong, healthy sonnet should have a positive effect on even the weakest love, whereas a weak sonnet, in even the most fervent and ardent love, might it not even be injurious to it?"

Elizabeth smiled. "But would not the recipient's knowledge and appreciation of sonnets be essential? What is pleasing to one person may not be to another."

A fleeting thought crossed his mind that she was much like a young lady he had met years before. The memory was merely a faded blur, having spent only a couple of hours with her in a carriage, but she stirred him in the same way. He could not remember her name or where she had been travelling to.

They continued to banter back and forth, but this morning Elizabeth had to excuse herself early. She had grown more weary and even the fresh air was not obliging her as it normally did in reviving her spirits.

Elizabeth retreated back down to steerage and did a little to help out Mrs. Rawlings and her daughters, as she normally did, in addition to a few others who were struggling with illness. She soon found herself growing more and more weary, and finally was compelled to curl up and take a short nap, even though she felt she needed to help out those who were suffering from more severe illnesses. She ended up sleeping for most of the day; something that she rarely did.

~~*

With the rising of the sun the following day, Elizabeth struggled to open her eyes. Her head ached, as well as her body, and she was only vaguely aware of the sun sending its light and warmth down into the depths of the ship in a futile attempt to awaken her. She shifted her position on the floor, but could not get comfortable. The voices she began to hear were only murmurs, and she could not make out any particular words. Her one thought was that perhaps she was becoming ill as well, as she dug herself deeper into the coverlet, covering her eyes from the light that was beginning to filter through the room.

Darcy had eagerly pulled himself out of bed, looking with anticipation toward his morning walk. That he found himself looking forward to being with Miss Bennet altogether surprised him. He rarely had, in all his adult years, been so captivated by a woman. Although he knew it was an injudicious partiality on his part, as she was not at all suitable for him, he was helpless to put her out of his mind.

She had become the one thing on this ship he found tolerable; a refreshing, lively distraction from both the unpleasant obligation this journey had become and the intolerable array of women seeking his attention. She enjoyed doing things he enjoyed doing. He tried to convince himself that there was nothing more to it than the simple fact that they enjoyed their morning walks together talking about books they had both read.

She does not seem to particularly seek out my attention as so many women do. What a pleasant change! That last thought surprised him. He shook his head, contemplating the oddity that he considered a woman not interested in him a pleasant change.

He vigorously splashed himself with the water from the pitcher and managed a frugal attempt at bathing using the hand basin in his room that was the only provision for bathing on this ship. He looked at himself in the small mirror, frustrated with his unruly, curly hair that was becoming more unmanageable with each passing day. He wished he had his valet along, who could work wonders with very little. He wished he could don a hat and cover what he considered his least favourable attribute, but the wind up on deck would only whip it away, so he resigned himself to just walk up and face her with his hair looking the way it was. And it was certain to only get worse.

He readily walked up and out on deck, pleased to find another fine day, and he began his walk. Each time around, when he approached the door that led to the stairway, he paused, hoping to see her appear. Several times during his walk he glanced behind him, thinking that possibly he would find her there, but each time he was disappointed.

He inwardly scolded himself, arguing that he had no business dwelling on this lady whom he would most likely never see again and one that he would probably never have given a second glance to in Town. She was simply a young lady from a small, inconsequential country village somewhere in England.

His strides became more determined as he contended with himself regarding the disparity between the two of them. Resolving to cease his musings of her, however, and the actual realization of it are two different things. He continued on with the hope of seeing her. After a disappointing walk, he finally returned to his room and wondered of her absence.

Later that morning, he went to the eating area for the prepared meal that was becoming less and less desirable as there was nothing remaining that was fresh. He overheard passengers talking about the sickness taking hold in steerage.

"With all those people confined together, what do you expect?" one man asked in frustration.

Another spoke up. "I have heard o' ship's fever that takes hold and runs rampant. Sometimes it can be fatal. I heard o' ships coming to port having lost a whole one fourth of their passengers."

"Excuse me," Darcy spoke and a look of silent surprise passed each face as they looked toward this man who usually extended only the minimal courtesy of conversation that civility required. "What was that you were saying about disease spreading through the ship?"

"Not the whole ship, Sir. Just down in steerage."

"Do you know what it is?" he asked.

"No. It's mainly in the women's and children's area and a fever seems to be part of it." After a pause the man added, "I just hope it's not the typhoid."

Darcy tensed and his jaw firmly tightened as he thought of Miss Bennet. He knew she had been caring for the Rawlings, as well as a few others, and wondered if she had grown ill herself. His mind went back to his walks with her and he recalled that she appeared increasingly tired and worn each morning. "Has anyone inquired of the captain for some medical assistance for them?"

"I believe so, but he can do nothing. At this point he does not think it is anything serious and it will run its course. Till then we must wait and hope."

"And pray!" added another.

Darcy stood there silent, as all the eyes in the group were upon this man who, for most of the past week, had been distant, aloof, and exhibited a very austere persona. That he was suddenly conversing with them was surprise enough, but that he appeared concerned, astonished them even more.

Darcy felt a presence behind him and he turned to see Miss Brewster standing behind him.

"Mr. Darcy, what a pleasure to encounter you this morning."

The last thing Darcy wanted was to endure this woman's wearisome presence. Each day it seemed she had sought him out at exactly the time he least wanted it. There were two or three other women that seemed to take pleasure in finding him unattached and wanting for company. Yet now she was displaying the audacity to approach him while in the midst of a conversation with a group of men. Would it never cease?

He turned politely to her, yet inwardly felt very much otherwise, and nodded. "Miss Brewster."

"It is such a lovely day and I particularly recall you enjoy a pleasant walk on deck. Would you mind accompanying me?"

"Thank you, no, Miss Brewster. I have already had an early morning walk, and it is imperative that I speak to the captain directly."

He excused himself from Miss Brewster and the others, intent on finding Captain Willoughby, and leaving Miss Brewster to wonder what she could do to get this man to notice her.

Darcy was pleased to find the captain on deck and free from any imminent responsibilities.

"Good morning, Darcy," the captain greeted him when he saw him approach.

"Good morning, Captain."

Willoughby eyed him with a suspicion that Darcy was again approaching him with some concern about the ship.

"What is it, Darcy?"

"I understand that there is sickness, a fever spreading through steerage."

"It is a normal part of the voyage that a few of the weaker passengers come down with something. Unfortunately it does spread more readily in steerage because of the closeness of quarters, the lack of fresh air, and the number of people down there. There is nothing that can be done about it, other than to let it run its course."

Darcy let out a frustrated sigh, guarding his motivation for asking and seeking a way to bring up Miss Bennet without raising the captain's suspicions.

"Do you suspect it to be typhoid?"

"At this point we cannot tell. There is one young lady who has taken ill quite unexpectedly and suddenly. It may be a simple case of influenza, but she has been weakened quite dramatically by it, more so than the others."

Darcy could not hide the alarm on his face. "Who is this woman, Captain?"

"Her name is Mrs. Trimble. She is travelling to America to join her husband who is already there."

The captain saw a wave of relief pass across his old friend's face, which was replaced immediately with a voiced concern.

"Captain, is there anything that can be done to alleviate the potential for an epidemic breaking out down there among the passengers?"

"Apart from moving everyone out of steerage? No, I am afraid not."

The Captain watched as Darcy nervously rubbed his hands together and wondered whether it was truly a concern for all the steerage passengers or one in particular, having noticed his walks each morning with Miss Bennet.

Darcy was frustrated that he still did not know anything about Miss Bennet and decided to be frank with the Captain.

"What do you know of Miss Bennet? I have not seen her yet today and I know she has been aiding several down there who are unwell. Do you know if she has taken ill herself?"

Captain Willoughby looked intently at Darcy, seeing something in his countenance he had never witnessed before. "I understand she has taken ill, as well. Whether it is as severe as Mrs. Trimble's case I do not know."

"Is there any doctor on board?"

"Not as such. The head cook serves as our doctor. He has training in preparing medicinal remedies. He is aware of the illness and has been doing all he can for those passengers. If I hear anything more I will let you know."

"Thank you, Captain."

"Darcy…"

Darcy looked up at the captain. "Yes?"

The captain slowly shook his head. "Never mind," he sighed and he turned to leave. He wondered with grave concern whether he would have to come down hard on the man who owned this ship and who had ultimate authority. Darcy had been spending a vast amount of time with a woman who had been put under his very own protection. He wondered how he would do it. He wondered if he would be able to do it.

Chapter 6

Darcy stood still for a few moments feeling frustrated and helpless. If diseases like typhoid did come upon this ship, those who were in steerage were the most susceptible because of the living conditions. Elizabeth, who was helping those very people, was at an even greater risk, in view of the fact that she was getting very little sleep. He knew disease was a possibility on every ship, but he felt acutely responsible himself, being the owner of *Pemberley's Promise*.

Darcy was pondering the situation when he looked up to see another of his adoring women, Miss Evans, strolling toward him. At the moment, he was feeling anything but civil, giving her only an infinitesimal nod of his head, then turned and quickly returned to his room before she was able to utter a word.

He remained there for some time, trying to read a book but making little progress. They had been just over one week at sea, and had about three more to go. He suddenly slammed his book closed and set it down abruptly on the table.

He felt a restlessness suffuse through his body. He did not know what he wanted to do, but he felt he needed to be out of the confines of this room. He refused to be a prisoner on his own ship.

Perhaps if he went to the dining area he would find out something more. He battled with the thought that it would likely throw him again into the presence of one of those annoying, persistent ladies, and he was in no humour for it. But he did not wish to remain in his room. *Hang those blasted women!*

After contemplating his options, he finally stood up, opened the door to his room, and walked down the hall; his concern for Elizabeth stronger than his concern to shield himself from unwanted advances.

As he passed by the stairs, he was suddenly put off balance by an unexpected swell that rocked the ship, but he steadied himself easily. Hearing a soft cry for help and the sound of tumbling, he hurried to the stairway and looked down. He was stunned to see that a young lady had lost her footing and crumbled upon the steps. Darcy immediately rushed down the few steps to reach her and bent down. When she looked up his direction, he saw that it was a very tired and pale looking Elizabeth.

"Miss Bennet, are you hurt?"

She let out a meagre smile. "I had to come up and get some fresh air. Perhaps I should not have."

She reached down and grabbed her ankle. "I believe my ankle just went out on me when the boat listed."

"Let me help you. You may have broken it or sprained it."

"No, I will be all right, truly."

Before she could protest, Darcy reached down and agilely picked her up. "My room is right here. Let me take you there and see what can be done."

"Please, Mr. Darcy, you do not have to do this." Her words did not come effortlessly, as being unexpectedly lifted by his strong arms added confusion to her already feverish and foggy mind; more than she wished to acknowledge.

"No, I insist."

He carried her with ease to his room, calling out to a woman who was passing by. "Could you help us? Please come with me and see to Miss Bennet. She seems to have injured her ankle."

"I would be glad to," the woman replied.

They walked into Darcy's room as Elizabeth struggled to keep her head upright, although the pleasant scent that seemed to emanate from him strongly tempted her to lean her head against him and turn her face into him. He gently placed her on the small bench next to the table. He stood up while the woman, a Mrs. Mullins, as she introduced herself, stooped down to look at the ankle.

"Not to worry, Miss Bennet. I have raised five children, and I have seen many sprains and broken bones in my life."

Elizabeth reached down to rub her ankle and felt quite foolish that all this attention was being paid to her when it was her fault and she was quite certain there was nothing seriously wrong. She was fighting against the effects of lack of sleep and illness, but was able to glance around the room and notice the splendour of Mr. Darcy's accommodations.

Mrs. Mullins stooped down and addressed Elizabeth as she gently began unlacing her boot, "Where does it hurt, Miss Bennet?"

"The inside of my ankle, Mrs. Mullins. I twisted it two years ago and it goes out on me occasionally. It shall be back to normal in no time." Elizabeth took some deep breaths as this was all extremely arduous for her in her ailing state.

Darcy, trying to avert his eyes from the most desirable sight of her now bootless slender ankle casually asked, "You said you sprained it?"

Elizabeth lifted her head slowly, looking up at him, and Darcy immediately noticed her pale and worn appearance. "Yes. Two years ago I fell out..." she abruptly stopped then, as if she changed her mind simply said, "I fell."

Her fevered mind seemed to make an attempt to recall something, but it evaporated as quickly as it had appeared. Whatever it had been was gone, but she had a clear enough mind to know that she did not want Mr. Darcy aware that only two years ago she made it a practice to climb trees.

Elizabeth turned her attention back to Mrs. Mullins and therefore did not see the startled look upon Darcy's face. From out of the past, a voice finished her sentence... *out of a tree.* He looked upon her and realized that it *had* to be her! Elizabeth had to be the one he shared the carriage ride with two years ago! His mind raced. What did he remember about her and that ride? *She told me how she had fallen out of a tree and sprained her ankle. We had a lively discussion about books. She challenged my every thought. I was not able to get her out of my thoughts for months after. I chided myself for never asking her name!*

Mrs. Mullins advised that they wrap it tightly and that she avoid walking on it. Darcy stepped out and called a member of the ship's crew who was passing by to obtain something with which to wrap her foot. Darcy was grateful for the chance to step out of the room. His mind now reeled with the almost complete conviction that Miss Bennet was the very woman who ended up haunting him two years earlier.

He tried desperately to remember any details about that day. *Where was she going on to after he departed the carriage?* He did not recall. He recollected a man and a woman waiting with her and who gave her assistance as she stepped into the carriage, when he carelessly ploughed into her. *Her aunt and uncle.* She was on her way *now* to visit her aunt and uncle in America. *All right, but most everyone has an aunt and uncle.* He turned to look at her and thought he could simply ask her if she sprained it by falling out of a tree, but that would most likely embarrass her. He was quite sure she did not finish her sentence because she did not want to let on that she had climbed a tree and fallen from it. He did not believe it would do any good to ask her if she remembered him and the carriage ride, as she most likely would not.

The crewman returned with some rolled up cloths and Mrs. Mullins began the slow, delicate process of wrapping her foot. Darcy stood back with his hand firmly planted against his jaw, rubbing it briskly as his mind searched the deepest recesses of his brain to try to recall anything more about her. Elizabeth glanced up and noticed a very disconcerted look on his face and she felt he was most irritated and impatient with this interruption.

"I am so sorry. So sorry," was all she could say. She was convinced he was put out having to assist her, when he must have others things he wanted, or needed, to tend to.

Darcy watched as Mrs. Mullins gingerly wrapped Elizabeth's ankle with the cloth. It was very evident to him how weak she was. His anger had increased now and he directed it at the ship's policy, of which he had been unaware, allowing children to be doubled up in beds. He was angry at the conditions in steerage, even though, on the whole, they were better than most other ships. He was angry that he could do nothing about Elizabeth's situation.

She was very ill and she would not improve unless she was out of steerage. But how to get her out was the question. Where else could she go? There was not one available bed on the ship.

Once her ankle was wrapped, Darcy came over and helped Elizabeth stand up, asking her to try to put some pressure on it. As she stepped down upon it, she winced in pain.

"Miss Bennet, I am afraid you are not going anywhere with your ankle like that for a while."

"Well I certainly cannot stay here!"

Her liveliness, even when she was feeling as poorly as she was now, humoured him.

"You need not worry about that, Miss Bennet. I shall carry you to the dining area so you can get something to eat. Right now you need to eat for strength."

Elizabeth tried to protest, but he was correct; she did not have the strength. This time when he picked her up, she was too tired to do anything but relax against him, and as her head fell against his chest, not only could she smell a pleasant scent that came from him, but she could feel his beating heart, which in itself, soothed and comforted her.

As he carried her toward the door, Darcy looked down at her and spoke. "You are not well. I can see that you are not getting enough sleep. Miss Bennet, this can turn quite serious if you do not take care of yourself. You must claim your bed back."

Elizabeth let out a frail sigh. "Perhaps in a few days. The Rawlings girls are improving," she took a few shallow breaths before she continued. "But I fear it is not so much for want of a bed, but that I am a light sleeper, and am kept awake more by the sounds of the crowded room than the discomfort of sleeping on the floor."

"Miss Bennet, certainly there is something you can do."

"Mr. Darcy, I am unfortunately ill, as are several people in steerage. I just need some fresh air and something to eat." Her words were almost whispered, and fatigue prompted her to close her eyes.

Darcy looked back into his room and rested his eyes upon the second bed in his room, the only vacant bed in the ship. If ever he had come up with a crazy notion, he had one now. The words of his valet in this very room came back to him. *Get a wife for the trip.* He looked back at Elizabeth as he closed the door behind them and carried her to the dining area.

There were not many people inside, for which he was grateful. He placed Elizabeth on a bench off by herself and secured for her some hot tea and some hardtack biscuits.

"Thank you, Mr. Darcy."

Darcy watched her as she slowly sipped the tea but he did not leave. She looked at him curiously. He seemed intent on saying something, but no words were coming.

"Was there something else, Mr. Darcy?"

"Miss Bennet, I… I have a proposition that I would like you to seriously consider."

Elizabeth raised one eyebrow at him, wondering what it was he was proposing. "What would that be, Mr. Darcy?"

"I… uh… I am concerned about your sleeping conditions…"

"I have told you there is no need for your concern."

"Since you do not seem to be inclined to ask for your bed back…" He did not seem able to go on.

"Yes?" She lifted her eyes to his face, but seemed unable to lift her head.

Darcy sat down on the bench opposite her. "I would like to offer you the spare bed in my room."

He saw the flash in Elizabeth's eyes just a moment before he felt the sting across his face.

She would have indignantly stormed off, but was prevented by her sore ankle and the weak state in which she found herself. Darcy reached up to the place on his now stinging cheek she had just slapped. "Perhaps you are not as weak as I believed."

Elizabeth turned her angry eyes back down to the meagre nourishment in front of her. "Please leave me alone, Mr. Darcy. I beg you, please."

Darcy took in a deep breath. "Miss Bennet, I ask that you just hear me out. I am not suggesting anything unseemly." He continued to rub the area on his cheek that had just been the recipient of a very brisk slap.

Incredulous, but with extreme fatigue consuming her, Elizabeth turned to him. "And just what are you suggesting then, Mr. Darcy?"

"You need a bed, and I… I have the only spare one on the ship. Obviously it would not do for you to share my room with me as we are not married."

Elizabeth almost laughed that he seemed to be struggling to articulate something, and she was more curious about hearing him than serious about considering it, whatever it was. She did not say anything, but patiently waited.

"I suggest we have the Captain marry us and then there would be no problem with you sleeping in my room… on that bed. It would be strictly a marriage on paper, not a… I would not… it would, of course, be strictly platonic."

Now Elizabeth did laugh, however weakly. "Mr. Darcy, you are certainly a man of unexpected surprises. If you will excuse me now, Sir, I would like to be left alone."

"Miss Bennet, walking up and down these stairs will be even more dangerous for you now that your ankle has gone out. You are ill and are not sleeping well, which makes you more prone to getting seriously ill down there. Heavens! You are not even sleeping in a bed!"

"Mr. Darcy," Elizabeth's head felt light and she wondered whether she could even express her arguments in an intelligible way. "I appreciate your concern, but what would induce you to make such an offer? What is in it for you, if I dare ask?"

Darcy leaned toward her. "I am tired of being harassed and pursued by the women on this ship. There are times I prefer solitude, and while, granted, most people leave me alone, there is a desperate group of women on this ship who will not. My getting married will bring an end to their disturbing me."

Elizabeth shook her head, trying desperately to clear the thoughts that were now so foggy. "You want to marry me, so that these ladies, who are solely interested in securing a husband, securing *you* as a husband, will stop bothering you?"

"That is a correct assessment." Elizabeth was stunned at how matter-of-factly he spoke.

"Mr. Darcy, I find this a highly foolish idea. What is to become of our marriage after the voyage? A marriage ceremony performed by a sea captain is as valid as one done by a clergyman."

"I will have it annulled once I return to England."

At this, Elizabeth was speechless. At her look of shock, Darcy continued. "There will be no problem in annulling it, as the marriage will never be consummated."

Elizabeth looked down, blushing, as Darcy added, "I am sorry to have to speak frankly, but I want you to be assured, in advance, of what my intentions are… and what they are not."

"Mr. Darcy, you may think you have an admirable idea that will solve your problems as well as mine, but there is one obstacle you have not considered."

"What is that?"

"Captain Willoughby! My father directly asked him if I could be put under his protection! He will never allow it!"

Darcy leaned in toward Elizabeth and tightly gripped his hands together, asking, "And if he does agree?"

Elizabeth was tiring more and more by the minute, and it was a strain for her to have to argue her point. "He will not, Mr. Darcy. I think we should leave it at that."

"Miss Bennet, if he agrees to perform the ceremony, will you agree to it?"

Elizabeth strained to look up at him. She could not make any rhyme or reason of Mr. Darcy's proposal, nor come up with any argument against it. Finally, in great fatigue and weariness of mind she answered, "Mr. Darcy, if the captain is willing to do such a thing as this, then yes, I will agree." She turned her attention back to the cup of tea and bread in front of her. "But I assure you, he will not!"

Darcy did not respond, but simply stood up. "Miss Bennet, if you would be so kind as to wait for me here until I return. I am going to speak with the captain immediately!"

Chapter 7

Darcy hurriedly departed to seek out the captain, whilst Elizabeth sat quietly with her hands wrapped around the small tin cup that was holding her hot tea and providing warmth and steadiness to her hands. She felt weaker by the moment and knew she required nourishment to aid in her recuperation from the fever, and needed to stay off her foot to aid in her ankle's improvement. At the moment, eating was cast aside as her hazy mind struggled to ponder Darcy's proposal.

She could not entertain any serious notions about it, as she was convinced the captain would refuse. As she pondered the extent of Darcy's wealth, however, she wondered if the captain would be prone to taking a bribe. Elizabeth shook her head. Darcy would have no reason to bribe the captain to perform a wedding ceremony to a common lady as herself.

If the captain said no -- *when* he said no -- Darcy would have to accept it. She would express her appreciation for his concern for her welfare, but would assure him she would manage as well as she could with the rest of the passengers in steerage.

She slowly sipped the tea and began taking small bites of the hardened bread that she softened by dipping in the steaming liquid. Although it was not truly palatable, it was sustenance. She forced herself to partake of it, thinking that if she had a clearer mind at the moment, she would be able to make better sense of what Darcy had just put forward. But try as she might, she could not!

She was torn whether to remain up here savouring the fresh air or to ask for some assistance getting back down to steerage. She knew Darcy would soon be returning from seeing the captain. For some reason she felt anxious about what news he would bring. In the state she was in, she had difficulty discerning whether she was troubled more that the captain might agree to marry them than she was that he might refuse. But neither did she look forward to returning to steerage as yet, so she determined to remain where she was and deal with Mr. Darcy when he came back.

If truth be told, at the moment and under the present circumstances, Darcy's proposal actually began to sound quite appealing to her. She was surprised to find herself now rationally and practically viewing it as having some merit and see the benefit in it. He reassured her it would be strictly platonic, and she would no longer have to sleep on the floor or breathe in the stale and stifling air in steerage anymore. She would be in a better state to help those who were faring worse than she. She would actually be in a nice, clean, quiet cabin. Most importantly, he would later have the marriage annulled and no one ever need know. *No one.*

The alternative was not very appealing. Elizabeth had found each successive day and night in steerage more difficult. Now that she had taken ill herself, she knew it would likely be a lengthy illness without fresh air or sleep.

Elizabeth shook her head. No, she *must* be feeling the effects of the fever. All the other steerage passengers had to endure the same thing as she! She was not a weak, spoiled little girl who could not endure a little discomfort. *No, it was not a good idea*, she tried to tell herself, *not at all*!

~~*

When Darcy went in search of the captain, his determined strides surprised even him. That he was pursuing such an uncommonly foolish path was highly out of character for him and his normally rational behaviour. For every action he took there was usually a methodical line of reasoning behind it. This time was a rare exception.

Each step he took away from Elizabeth was a constant reminder to him of the vast difference in their standing in society. If his family, *particularly* his aunt, were ever to discover that he had done such a foolish thing, that he had even *considered* such a thing as to marry a woman like her, his aunt would not hesitate to renounce him and cast him out of the family.

Is this really something I should be even considering? A man of my means and status... He was distracted by his line of argument, reasoning, and questioning when he found himself face to face with another *Miss whatever*. He could not recall her name and had no desire to.

"Mr. Darcy, such a pleasant day it is. Would you not agree?"

This is why I am doing it! The women assaulting him day in and day out when all he wanted was to be left alone. They would never learn that he was in no humour on this voyage to entertain thoughts of reciprocating their interest.

"It is a very nice day, and as such, I unfortunately must take my leave and discuss something with the captain!"

He quickly strode off, leaving *Miss whatever* very disappointed and at a loss for words.

He thought of Elizabeth. She seemed to have a gift for knowing when to speak and when to be silent around him. He felt as comfortable in their silence as deeply as he felt invigorated by their intelligent dialogue. For these other women, any pause in the conversation prompted them to fill it up with nonsense and idle chat, none of which was satisfying to him in the least.

Darcy made his way to the captain's cabin and paused. He thought back to the woman he met two years ago in the carriage -- the woman he was fairly certain was Elizabeth. Could it be that the real reason he asked Miss Bennet to marry him was because he did not want her to get away again? Darcy closed his eyes and rolled his head back. *I cannot think like that! This is solely for her benefit now and I cannot allow myself to dwell on any future possibilities, because there can never be any!*

Darcy knocked sharply on the captain's door, hoping he would find him there. A wave of nervousness began to roil up inside of him.

"Come," a voice from inside called out.

Darcy slowly opened the door and peered in, finding the captain entering some notations in his log book. When he saw that it was Darcy, he pursed his lips together as if fighting off the urge to make some comment.

"Good day, Captain. Do you have a moment?"

"For you, Darcy, of course. Come in."

Darcy walked in and the captain waved for him to sit down. Darcy obliged, but never really settled into the chair, constantly adjusting himself in it and nervously tapping his fingers on the armrest.

It was apparent to the captain that Darcy was obviously distressed or nervous about something. "What is it now?" Willoughby asked, folding his hands firmly in front of him on the desk.

"I have a small favour to ask of you, Willoughby."

"Is the food not to your liking? Are you beginning to tire of the hardtack bread and dried meat? Are they not up to your expectations? Or perhaps you would prefer a more varied array of entertainments on board?"

Darcy looked down at his hands that he now gripped together and held firmly in his lap. "No, Sir. It is a rather odd, personal request."

"Pray, continue."

Darcy took in a deep breath, held it for a few seconds and then slowly let it out. "I would like you to perform a marriage ceremony."

The captain's eyes widened, then immediately narrowed. "Between who?"

Darcy leaned forward and spoke with forced decisiveness. "Miss Elizabeth Bennet and myself, Sir."

The captain remained gravely silent, gathering his thoughts and wondering what had prompted this man to make such a preposterous request. Finally he stood; his towering presence over the seated Darcy intended to make an impression.

"Darcy, I have only been approached with this particular request but a few times. I have presided over a couple of weddings in my years as Captain. But being as how Miss Bennet was especially put under my protection by her father, it is very unlikely that I will agree to it."

"Captain Willoughby, are you refusing me?"

"Are you asking me as a passenger or as the owner of this ship?"

Darcy placed his hands on the armrest and pushed himself up, now looking directly in the captain's eyes. "I am asking you to trust me, to vouch for my character, have confidence in my reasons behind this, and agree to marry us."

The captain's brow furrowed. "I have known you for many years, Darcy. I have always thought highly of your character. This is foolish; your family would disown you for marrying a woman from her class, and besides, I can hardly believe that she would agree. She barely knows you, and from what I have seen of her, she is not the type to latch onto a man solely based on his wealth."

The captain watched Darcy's face as he asked, "What exactly has prompted you to such an inclination as to marry Miss Bennet? Do you find yourself suddenly longing for a woman's company?"

"On the contrary, Captain. This marriage is strictly to allow her the opportunity to get out of steerage and the propriety to sleep in the extra bed in my room so she may regain her health back. You must have heard yourself how she has been helping out passengers down in steerage who have taken ill themselves… to the point of endangering her own health. She gave up her bed, has now become ill herself, and just now she turned her ankle. Taking those stairs up and down will only cause to aggravate it. She cannot remain down there and this is the only solution! You, yourself, said there was no other bed available."

The captain firmly placed his hands behind his back, tilted his head down and began pacing around the room. "And Darcy, what is in this for you?" His question sounded grave.

"Captain, I swear upon my dead father's grave that I have no ulterior motive. I give you my word that I will not lay a hand on her. You know, Sir, that I do not give you my word unless I am willing to keep it. She gets the chance to improve her situation while on board this ship, and I…"

The captain looked up. "And you?"

Darcy felt somewhat sheepish now, but confided to the captain, "Being married will bring a stop to all the ladies on this ship who have been plaguing me with their unwanted attention!"

The captain forced a laugh, feeling very little humour in the situation. "Your dilemma is heavy indeed. And what is to happen after the voyage, Darcy? Are you determined to go through life married to a woman you do not love, who you have vowed you will never touch?"

"My plan is to have it annulled once I return to England."

The captain stopped pacing and turned to look at Darcy. "Are you now?" He rubbed his chin vigorously as he wondered whether this was truly an act of compassion on his part. "And what do you really know of Miss Bennet? How do you know she will not come after you for your money once she is legally married to you, even attempt to stop the annulment?"

Darcy looked at the captain. "I do not believe she would."

"Neither do I," admitted the captain. "But I still do not like this. I assume you have spoken to her on this subject?"

"Yes I have."

"And she is willing to marry you solely for propriety's sake so that she can avail herself of the empty bed in your cabin only to have this holy union later annulled?"

"Yes, she is willing if you agree to perform the ceremony." His hand clenched in reaction to this minor stretching of the truth a bit, something he disliked doing immensely.

"Again, Darcy, I ask, is this request of yours being made as a passenger or as the owner of this ship? As the man whose ultimate authority I am under?"

"Whichever it takes to get you to agree."

The captain went back to his desk and sat down. "When do you wish to have this *ceremony* performed?"

Darcy let out a breath as he realized the captain was leaning toward agreeing, however sceptical of it he was. "As soon as possible. What do I need to do?"

The captain opened his desk drawer and pulled out some forms that had been filed toward the back. "Fill these out, you both need to sign them, and bring them to me when you return with Miss Bennet. We can begin as soon as you like."

Darcy grabbed the forms. "Thank you, Captain. She is waiting in the dining area. I shall return with her promptly."

The captain only nodded as he could scarcely believe what had just transpired in his cabin; let alone understand it. He wondered what had ever prompted him to agree to perform such a ceremony, and what had ever gotten into the Master of Pemberley to even conceive of such a course of action!

~~*

When Darcy returned to the dining area, he found Elizabeth making a concerted effort to talk with some passengers who had gathered around her, inquiring about her ankle and her illness. She still looked tired, and he hoped the other passengers were not causing her too much exertion. As she turned her head and saw Darcy walk in, her heart made a barely noticeable leap, especially when she saw papers being carried in his hand.

Darcy walked toward her and apologized to those she was conversing with, asking that they forgive him, but he needed to speak with Miss Bennet alone. They gave Elizabeth some reassurances about her health before leaving, turned a curious eye to Darcy, and then departed.

Darcy took a seat across from her. "The captain has said all that is required is for us to fill out these forms."

Elizabeth took in a slight gasp of air and felt her body shudder as he spoke the words she had assumed she would not hear. Obviously the captain was willing to perform the wedding! She could not look at him, but looked down, eyeing the very formal looking papers that he had spread out in front of her. Words refused to come and she could not formulate one thought to press her argument against doing this.

Darcy had secured a pen and some ink, and pushed them toward Elizabeth. "The Captain is willing to do this, Miss Bennet."

She looked up at him with weariness flooding her surprised eyes. "As are you?"

He nodded. "It will benefit us both, but primarily yourself."

"And you will have it annulled once you return to England?"

"Your family and friends need never know. And you will certainly never see any of the other passengers on this ship again, as they will be staying in America. As far as they know, we fell in love on the ship and decided to marry."

"We hardly have looked like a couple in love, Mr. Darcy."

Darcy cocked his head. "Who is to say what love looks like, Miss Bennet?"

Elizabeth looked up and met his gaze. She felt as though she was simply entering a business transaction with someone and yet there was something in his eyes now that had not been there before. She also felt there was a stronger beating of her own heart that she could not ascribe to anything. She took another deep breath as she pondered this man. She wondered if he had ever been in love. Had there ever been a woman who lived up to his impeccable standards?

Darcy's attention was directed toward the papers. "It looks like all you need to do is sign here, and I sign here." He gently nudged the pen into her hand while she studied the paper. She looked up at him one last time before signing 'Elizabeth Julianne Bennet' and 'Hertfordshire' for residence. She slowly pushed the papers toward Darcy.

"Now what?"

Darcy filled in a few more entries. "Now we go to the captain."

"You mean we are to do this at once?" A sense of panic began to rise up within her.

Darcy nodded. "Tonight, Miss Bennet, for the first time on this ship, you will get a good night's sleep."

He stood up, came around, and picked her up again. "Shall we go to our wedding?" A reassuring smile swept across his face, but quickly disappeared as he looked at the concern etched on Elizabeth's face.

As he picked her up, he was even more aware of how weak she was, and suddenly wondered if she would look back on this with regret when her mind was free from the effects of the fever. Would she harbour resentment against him for pressing her for a decision when she was feeling so poorly?

When he picked her up and began to carry her, her heart pounded even more fiercely. She was not sure whether the warmth she felt was a result of fever or being held so securely by him. But she knew it was *not* the fever, but the feel of his arms around her that prevented any rational thought or objection to this course of action to penetrate her mind.

~~*

The captain was still in his room when Darcy arrived carrying Elizabeth. He was surprised, yet not, to see him return so promptly. He had always known Darcy to be a man to quickly accomplish what he set his mind to do. Usually it was based on sound reason and judgment. He believed his reasoning on this particular occasion was based on something other than rational thinking. Perhaps it was emotion, but that was something which he rarely saw in Darcy, who prided himself on always remaining in control. Although Darcy was trying to appear level-headed, there was something else that was prompting this decision, and Willoughby could not quite place what it was.

Could it be love? He could not determine it one way or another, but for some reason, he chose not to fight Darcy about his determination to pursue this course of action. Perhaps it was his own fondness for Miss Bennet and the fact that he saw something between the two of them that neither of them had yet realized was there.

"Darcy, come in. Good day, Miss Bennet. I understand you have not been feeling well and that you turned your ankle today."

"Yes, Captain, but it is nothing. It shall be back to normal in no time," she replied weakly.

The captain motioned for them to sit down. Darcy placed Elizabeth in the chair and he stood behind her.

"Miss Bennet, I understand that Darcy has made a rather peculiar request in this offer of marriage to you."

"Yes, Sir. I realize it must appear odd, but I think we are both of like minds that it will benefit us to pursue this course of action."

Darcy raised his eyebrows as he heard Elizabeth's words, which now sounded very much in favour of proceeding with the marriage. Elizabeth, herself, was surprised at how easily they flowed out of her mouth.

"Hmmm," murmured the captain. "I would wish you to take under advisement to consider all the ramifications of such a marriage before I proceed."

"I have, Sir," Elizabeth said softly.

"As have I, Captain," added Darcy quickly.

"Well, then. Let us proceed." The captain rang a bell and his first mate entered. "Webber, here, shall be witness. Normally I have the bride and groom stand, but in your case, Miss Bennet, seeing as how you are quite unwell, I shall allow you to remain seated."

The captain looked up at Darcy and raised his eyebrows, as if giving him one last chance to change his mind.

"You may proceed, Captain."

"Do you have any kind of a ring?"

Darcy suddenly frowned, having not thought of it.

Elizabeth lifted up her hand. "I have this ring I usually wear on my other hand. We can use it."

She took it off her one finger and handed it to Darcy, who looked down and saw a small ruby stone set in a gold band. He held it in his hand until it was time to place it on her wedding ring finger.

The ceremony was simple. The vows were spoken with little attempt to disguise the fact that they were going to be null and void once Darcy returned to England. When they were pronounced husband and wife, Darcy simply reached for Elizabeth's hand and placed a kiss on the back of it.

"Congratulations. You are now married." The lack of enthusiasm in the captain's voice was recognized by all in the room and Elizabeth swallowed hard as she contemplated what this would now mean.

The captain excused the first mate and the three were left with feelings of awkwardness. "What do we do now?" asked Elizabeth.

The captain looked at the two of them. "If this were a *real* marriage, you would not have to ask me that question. As it is, we must get word out before rumours begin circulating, especially if you return to his room now. I suggest we make an announcement to those in the dining area later this afternoon."

"Thank you, Captain." Darcy shook his hand, but felt a twinge of guilt that he had pressured the captain into doing something that had gone against his conscience by reason of his owning this ship. He was not proud of the fact and hoped Elizabeth would not find out.

"What about my things?" asked Elizabeth weakly.

"I could send someone to collect them," Darcy offered.

"I should like to retrieve them myself, if you do not mind. I should like to tell Mrs. Rawlings and her daughters myself... about our... our... marriage."

"I shall take you down after you have had some rest and a good meal."

"Very good. I have done all that I needed to do," the captain said austerely. "I shall see you both later."

Darcy picked Elizabeth up and walked out the door. Elizabeth hoped that no one would see her being carried to his room and she was grateful when they were able to make it there and inside without encountering anyone. It helped that Darcy's room and the captain's were up towards the front of the ship away from most of the other rooms. She felt awkward this time, being carried into his room and hearing the reverberating sound as the door closed behind them.

He set her down on the bench again, inquiring how she was feeling.

"Tired. I think I should like to sleep, if I may."

Darcy nodded. "I have done some thinking about the arrangements in here. I will hang up a sheet across your bed so you can have some privacy and separation from my side of the room at night. Of course we will remove it during the day so if anyone notices it, they will not become suspicious as to why it is there."

"That is very considerate of you, Sir."

"It is nothing, Miss Benn…"

Darcy stopped and looked at Elizabeth. "I cannot call you Miss Bennet, now, can I?"

Elizabeth looked down; neither of them had contemplated this.

"What would you have me call you; Mrs. Darcy or Elizabeth?"

Elizabeth flinched slightly as she pondered what each would mean. Mrs. Darcy sounded so official, so legal, and so wifely. Yet Elizabeth sounded so intimate, so familiar. Her hand was nervously drawn to the small necklace she wore around her neck as she pondered an answer. She fingered it momentarily and finally answered, "Elizabeth, please."

"Very well, Elizabeth." He walked over and easily picked her up, carrying her over to her bed and placing her upon it. Exhausted from fatigue and illness, Elizabeth practically fell across the bed, laying her head upon the pillow and bringing her legs up on the thick, soft bed.

For a few moments Darcy let his eyes rest upon her pleasant, reclining figure before sternly admonishing himself about what that kind of indulgence might lead to. Without allowing his eyes to linger any longer, he reached for the coverlet and pulled it up over her. He suddenly realized how difficult this arrangement might end up being for him.

"I shall leave you to rest now." His words were spoken most reluctantly.

As she heard him walk slowly toward the door and open it, she opened her eyes and quietly asked, "And what shall you have me call you?"

Darcy stopped in his movement and turned back to her. "My given name is Fitzwilliam, but I should prefer that you call me William."

Elizabeth nodded as he turned to leave.

"Thank you, Mr. Darcy." He looked back at her, shook his head, and walked out. She closed her eyes, plumping up the pillow underneath her head, and fell into a deep sleep that she had not had the pleasure of having for almost a week now.

Chapter 8

When Darcy returned somewhat later, he was not surprised to find Elizabeth in a sound sleep. Not wanting to disturb her, fully aware that she needed as much rest as she could get, he quietly laid out the tea and an assorted array of foods that he had secured from the captain's private supply. At times like this, there was an advantage to being the ship's owner and he did not have to twist the captain's arm too severely to get what he desired.

He turned towards her and stood silently observing her, intrigued by the calm demeanour that had spread over her face in sleep, captivated by the few long, dark tresses that had escaped from her pinned up hair, but greatly disturbed about the pallor that was taking hold of her features. He fought the temptation to reach over and gently run his fingers through her hair or stroke her cheek, compelling himself to turn away instead. He could not allow himself the liberty to dwell on things that could not be.

Sitting down on the bench at the table in his room, he absently picked up the book he had been reading. He opened it to the page he was on, but found his attention reverting back to the sleeping form in the bed on the other side of the room. He had always found time to read, enjoyed reading, and looked for any excuse to read, but at the moment he was easily finding a justification *not* to read.

He finally gave up and closed the book, setting his mind to trying to recall more about the carriage ride two years ago and the young lady who shared it with him. While he was fairly certain it was her, he tried to think of other things he remembered about her from that day.

Vigorously rubbing his chin, as though that would help facilitate his memory, he did vividly recall that he had been impressed with her knowledge of the books she had read and they had shared a lively discussion about many of them. He remembered afterwards crediting her as being an accomplished woman who sought the improvement of her mind by extensive reading. She had been willing to express a difference of opinion and even argue with him about some aspects of literature and his opinion of them. That was certainly descriptive of the lady asleep in his room.

He furrowed his brow as he tried to recall any part of the conversation they shared. What else could there have been that would enlighten him as to whether or not it was her? He recollected that she had dark, sparkling, fine eyes, as did Elizabeth. She had sprained her ankle falling from a tree that she had climbed...

she had to walk home injured... she loved walking! Yes, that would be true of Elizabeth.

Suddenly he remembered a vague discussion they had about horses. She had told him that she preferred walking to riding a horse and sometimes even to riding in a carriage. Darcy smiled. That should be easy enough to discover without raising suspicion. He would wait for the right opportunity and then work it into his conversation. If he found that to be true of Elizabeth, he would be certain it was her!

Darcy stood up and walked over to the small port window. He looked out at the vast sea that surrounded them and realized that it had been days since his thoughts had turned to Georgiana and the sole reason for his coming on this voyage. He had boarded this ship with her retrieval being first and foremost on his mind, and having to cross the ocean to fetch her was something that had originally caused him great consternation.

He had come aboard with a very poor disposition, to the point of being irritated with his fellow passengers even before becoming acquainted with them. He felt anger towards Mrs. Annesley and his cousin Fitzwilliam for their persistent and persuasive arguments to allow Georgiana to go to America in the first place. He had not looked forward one bit to the crossing and had it settled in his mind from the first that he would not enjoy the voyage at all.

Added to all this was that upon boarding the ship, he still reeled from the recent blow of Georgiana's close call with that deceitful, scheming George Wickham. These past few months had been taxing on his ability to handle the things life dropped in his lap, had affected his decision-making ability, and altered the way he had begun to look at life.

Certainly he had boarded the ship angry at the very people he was having to journey with. He cringed with shame as he recalled the comment he made to the captain that first day and he still wondered whether Elizabeth had overheard him.

He turned to look at her. Somehow she had made him forget all his anger, frustrations, and even some of his resentment.

He left the window and looked around the small room that they now shared. He took in a deep breath as he contemplated the close quarters of this room. Once her health improved and she could think more clearly, would she feel comfortable spending the rest of the trip in the confines of this cabin with him? Would she continue to trust him or would she harbour suspicions that he had ulterior motives in proposing this arrangement? Would she think he forced her to make a decision she had been in no condition to make? Would she have second thoughts and regret her decision?

Darcy let out the breath he had been holding. It would be too late for second thoughts. The captain had married them and they were now husband and wife -- at least until he had the marriage annulled back in England. It may have been something he had done with very little rational thought behind it, but he believed he had done it with her best interest in mind.

Knowing he would be unable to simply sit still and wait for her to awaken, he began to nervously pace around the room, going to the window and looking out, walking the short distance over to Elizabeth, and then back to the window.

Darcy's movements eventually awakened Elizabeth. She opened her eyes, aroused from the deepest sleep she had enjoyed in close to a week, and took a moment to get her bearings. Darcy was standing with his back towards her, as he stood at the window, and she was able to watch him for a few moments before he turned and saw that she had wakened.

"Good afternoon, Elizabeth. Did you sleep well?"

Feeling a little self-conscious lying in the bed, she struggled against her weakness to pull herself up. "Yes, Mr. Darcy, thank you."

Darcy ignored her persistence to acknowledge him formally.

"I brought you some tea and something to eat, as well. I think it would be best for you to eat something first before we go to the dining room. It would be wise not to spend too much time with anyone until we know that you are improved. Try to eat and drink a little, and then we will go up and join the captain for the announcement."

The announcement. He spoke those words devoid of any emotion. She could certainly comprehend his feeling, or *lack* of feeling about this whole arrangement. But at the moment, although she greatly enjoyed the welcomed sleep, she was hard pressed to know exactly what *her* feelings were regarding this marriage. She still felt the assault against her body from illness and lack of sleep, and she could barely conjure up a reasonable sentence, let alone discern her thoughts at the moment.

Elizabeth brought her feet around to the floor, quite convinced that she looked as poorly as she felt. But she had slept soundly, and for that she was grateful.

Darcy walked over to her. "Here, let me help you over to the table."

As he reached out his hand to her, her initial response was that she could do it herself, but due to her ankle's continued tenderness and her unsteadiness upon sitting up, she accepted his offer. He pulled her up and slipped his arm underneath hers, supporting her body as she used one foot to propel herself along. Surprisingly, she felt a strength from him that seemed to boost her energy even more.

He set her down at the table and she looked down at the plate of food in front of her. Instead of the normal fare of dried, hard, unpalatable food, she found a very pleasing array of some fresh fruit and chicken.

"This looks delicious." Her appreciation was apparent, but subdued. "Is this what everyone is having this evening?" She dabbed a little at the food, unwilling to pass it up, but suffering from an untimely lack of appetite.

"Not exactly. This is something special from the captain's cupboard. He had some fruit that was still good, however very little, and there is a pen of chickens on board that he gets eggs and an occasional chicken meal from."

Elizabeth looked up at him curiously, wondering what he had to pay the captain for him to turn over some of this delectable fare.

"Thank you." As Elizabeth took some small bites, she wondered how often he himself had been privy to these kinds of meals all along.

"If you would like, I shall leave you to finish eating and then you can tidy yourself up before going to the dining area. Is there anything I can get for you before I leave?"

"No. Unfortunately all my things are still in steerage."

"Help yourself to anything of mine that you require." He pointed to a dresser full of items. "The captain will join us to make the announcement in the dining area. We shall linger but a short time to allow you to speak briefly with your acquaintances. We shall then retrieve your things from steerage. You must not exert yourself."

Elizabeth merely nodded in weak acquiescence. She had a difficult time fully comprehending all that Darcy had just said, but knew that he was resolutely laying things out the way he expected them to be. She realized if she had a morsel more of strength and even a remote ability to think more attentively, she would have been inclined to challenge these dictates he was giving.

Darcy left the room and the first thing Elizabeth did was to take her unused napkin and hide the remaining morsels of food into it, slipping the napkin into the pocket of her dress. She would take it down to her friends in steerage.

She hobbled over to the dresser, propelling herself along with her arms braced on the tabletop and dresser top, putting as little pressure on her injured foot as she was able. She sat down in front of the mirror and for a few moments silently looked at her reflection. Elizabeth weakly picked up a brush and combed out her hair, pulling the dark, thick locks back on top of her head. She reflected back on how uncomplicated and unemotional their conversation had been. He talked as if he were discussing with her the details of a business arrangement. She sighed as she looked at her weakened, pale reflection in the mirror. Perhaps he was.

When she had finished, she called out and Darcy returned into the room. He looked over at the empty plate on the table, wondering how she could have eaten it all so quickly, but said nothing. "Are you ready to go to the dining room?"

"We might as well get it over with." Elizabeth replied, suddenly feeling very uneasy. She wondered what the reaction would be from those with whom she had formed acquaintances.

Darcy's jaw tightened at her response, speculating whether now, after having had a good sleep, she regretted what they had done.

He walked over to her and his arms easily scooped her up. She made every attempt to view being held in his arms as strictly a necessity born out of her clumsy stumble earlier in the day. She had begun to feel an unanticipated warmth and appreciation towards him, however, that in her condition, she could not dwell on.

They proceeded to the dining room which was already crowded with people. As Darcy walked in carrying Elizabeth, a sudden quietness fell over the room as people noticed the couple walk in, followed immediately by some whispering and rising speculations about the pair.

The captain quickly walked up to join them and raised his arms to silence everyone. "Ladies and gentlemen, I have an announcement I wish to make. Today, as Captain of this ship, it was my privilege and honour to unite Mr. Fitzwilliam Darcy and Miss Elizabeth Bennet in holy matrimony. I am honoured to present Mr. and Mrs. Darcy."

A very audible buzzing was heard as people came around to bestow upon them surprised, but sincere best wishes. Darcy accepted their words of congratulations with a simple nod of the head and "thank you." He watched as Elizabeth received their attentions warmly and she graciously offered back words of encouragement herself, despite her weak and fragile state.

Not everyone was inclined to approach; some from simply a lack of introduction to either of them. A certain handful of ladies sat rather stupefied that the one man they deemed most eligible and desirable among all the available men on board, had somehow been underhandedly snatched by this singularly common woman. They thought it was most unreasonable!

Darcy carried Elizabeth to a table and set her down, whispering to her as firmly as he could that they would only remain for a few minutes because of her health. They accepted continued words of congratulations from their well wishers and soon were joined by Mr. and Mrs. Jennings, who had made Darcy's acquaintance earlier, but not Elizabeth's.

The Jennings expressed their congratulations to the newly married couple.

Mrs. Jennings looked at the two and asked, "What a surprise this is! How long have the two of you known each other?"

Darcy replied, "We met only upon coming on board the ship."

"So the two of you just met? You did not know each other before?" Mr. Jennings asked incredulously.

"That is correct," Darcy replied.

He could tell by Jennings' look that this did not sit well with him. Knowing his tendency to speak his mind without giving thought to what he said or how he said it, Darcy was quite surprised when he simply raised an eyebrow in a manner indicative of inner speculation and silently nodded.

The Jennings soon left, and after spending what Darcy considered a reasonable amount of time allowing Elizabeth the chance to visit, but not too much time that she would become too wearied, he offered up an apology that they must leave and reached down to lift her up again.

"Come, Elizabeth. Let us go down and get your things."

He carried Elizabeth quickly down to steerage, very much aware that she was becoming weaker and weaker. He took the three flights of stairs easily and agilely. Bringing her in, and per her direction, he brought her over to where Mrs. Rawlings and her girls were. He set her down and she sat toward the foot of the woman's bed. She was glad to see that Pauline and Penelope had improved and Mrs. Rawlings seemed a little bit more on her way to recovery. Darcy had agreed to step out until she had broken the news to her.

"I have something I need to tell you, Lenore."

"Oh, Elizabeth, I understand you hurt your ankle today. You must want your bed back," Mrs. Rawlings contritely said. "I have been expecting that. You have been unwell yourself. It would be very wrong of me to insist on keeping it." She began to pull the blankets off of herself, but Elizabeth stopped her.

"No, no, Lenore. You stay right where you are." Elizabeth found herself at a loss to explain what had transpired that day. "Lenore…" Elizabeth looked down at her hands that she was rubbing nervously together. "Today I was…" She paused, almost afraid to say the words. "Today I was… married, and I shall no longer be travelling in steerage but in the room with my… with my… husband." Her heart tightened when she softly uttered those words, as suddenly a more acute awareness of what she had done, the vows she had taken, swept over her.

She looked into Mrs. Rawlings face and knew she needed to explain. "Lenore, today Mr. Darcy and I were married. I wanted to come down and tell you myself when I came to get my things."

Mrs. Rawlings face showed a great deal of surprise. "Mr. Darcy? When did you meet him? How did this happen?"

"I actually met him the first day on the ship." She had not quite met him then, but rather bumped into him. There was no need to go further into that.

Mrs. Rawlings reached out for Elizabeth's hand. "Please forgive me, Elizabeth, but can you really know a man in such a short time?"

Elizabeth nodded. "Do not worry, Lenore, he is a fine man." She felt awkward discussing this and greatly desired to change the subject. She reached into her large pocket and withdrew the napkin. "Here, I brought you something from my dinner."

Mrs. Rawlings looked with amazement as Elizabeth slowly opened the napkin. Her eyes widened as she recognized the delectable array before her not just by sight but by the pleasant aroma.

"Elizabeth! How did you come upon such fare?"

"That does not matter. I just want you and your daughters to enjoy something that might make you feel a little better and help you get your strength back."

"You are too kind, Elizabeth. That husband of yours got for himself a mighty fine lady!"

"That was him who brought me in. He is outside the door, waiting to retrieve my things. May I ask him in and introduce you?"

"Yes, please, I should like to meet him."

Elizabeth called for Darcy. That he was feeling the uncomfortable effects of steerage was very noticeable. Its stifling air and putrid odours began to take a toll on him.

He walked back in and Elizabeth introduced him to Mrs. Rawlings and the girls. "It is a pleasure, Mrs. Rawlings. Elizabeth speaks highly of you."

"Thank you, Sir. You have chosen well, Mr. Darcy. There is none finer than Elizabeth."

Elizabeth blushed, grateful for the darkness of the room. She quickly pointed out to Darcy where her things were, and he picked them up, helping her put them in her duffel. "I shall take these to our room and return for you shortly."

He turned to leave and Elizabeth turned her attentions back to Mrs. Rawlings. "Oh, Elizabeth, he is indeed a fine looking man. When did all this happen?"

Elizabeth knew she could not lie to her friend, but she did not have to tell her the whole truth. "We became acquainted on early morning walks together. He and I both arose at sunrise and found we enjoyed many similar things." Elizabeth marvelled at how easily those words came.

Mrs. Rawlings nodded, still at a loss to understand this, but very happy for her friend.

Elizabeth played with Pauline and Penelope, who were well enough to have some energy, but still not well enough to venture up. They eagerly partook of the delicious offering that Elizabeth had brought down.

Before Darcy returned, Elizabeth carefully hobbled over to Mrs. Trimble, finding she could put a little more pressure on her ankle without too much discomfort. Mrs. Trimble was very pale and weak, but it was apparent that she was more than grateful for Elizabeth's visit.

Elizabeth sat down with her, giving her a portion of the food she had set aside for her. As she watched the woman take small bites and eat appreciatively, she wished she could pass on some other morsel of strength to her. She did not like the way she appeared, almost as if she was giving up the fight to get well. If she was not eating the supply of food Elizabeth brought her, she was certainly not eating the food the rest of the passengers were getting.

Elizabeth remained with her for just a short while, and then returned to Mrs. Rawlings until Darcy came back down.

"I shall visit you tomorrow, Lenore."

Mrs. Rawlings put up her hand. "Now Elizabeth, you are just married. You need to be with your husband and not worry about us! Besides, I can see that you are still not well. We are doing just fine!"

Elizabeth shook her head and smiled. "If I can, I shall see you tomorrow!"

Elizabeth stood up as Darcy came over to her. He assisted her in walking to the door and out. He began to reach down to lift her up, but she stopped him. "I can walk on my own now, thank you."

Darcy paused, taken aback by Elizabeth's stubbornness, but only for a brief moment. "Not when there are three flights of stairs and I am around to carry you!" He spoke his words and lifted her up with such authority that she tensed with anger.

"Put me down, please! I can walk on my own!"

"Elizabeth, do not be a fool! It has been only a few hours since your ankle went out and you are still unwell! Just relax and let me carry you."

Elizabeth had not the strength to fight him. This evening had taken its toll on her, but deep down inside she knew he was right. Being carried in his arms was affecting her in quite a different way, and she was disconcerted to find there was something stirring within her as he carried her through the now darkened ship to his room -- their room.

Darcy sensed Elizabeth's fighting spirit doing battle with her diminishing energy. "Just relax, Elizabeth. You are tired. Rest your head against my shoulder."

Elizabeth felt she could not relax and that was the last thing she could allow herself to do. She feared what might happen if she relaxed in his arms. She kept herself rigid and tense, purposely avoiding that which she knew she needed and wanted -- to lose herself in the arms of the man who was now her husband, because she knew he would only be her husband for a very short time.

When they reached their room and entered it, Darcy set her down on the bench at the table, still silently angry at her for her stubbornness. Elizabeth noticed that he had put the sheet up across her bed. He must have done that when he brought her things back to the room earlier.

"Elizabeth, in the morning, I shall rise first, get myself ready and then leave. That will give you the opportunity to come out from behind the sheet, and do what you need to do in privacy. As long as you are still unwell, I expect you to get as much sleep as you can. When you are feeling improved, then you can join me up on deck for our morning walk. Only when you are completely well, *only* then, will I allow you to go back down to steerage to help out those that are ill. Not one moment sooner!"

Her eyes widened as she listened to his orders, spoken in a severely authoritative tone, of how things would be! How things must be! Her mouth opened to respond with a vehemence of words unleashed, but was halted by her lack of strength and his continued commands.

"You must now get yourself ready for bed, so I shall leave you to it. You have had an exerting afternoon. I shall return later and expect to find you asleep."

"Yes, Captain!" Elizabeth gave him a mock salute.

Darcy looked at her, his eyes darkening. "Elizabeth, this is for your own good."

He stood silently watching her, very aware that if she had the strength she would have had much more to say to him on the subject. Instead she simply replied, "Yes, Mr. Darcy, I am sure it is."

She lifted her eyes to watch him walk out the door as it slammed behind him. He did not enjoy being so forceful with her, but he needed to set up boundaries for her sake as well as his own. The sheet was a safeguard against what could be the greatest temptation he had ever faced. The sheet itself would not be enough to hold him back, but it would be a reminder to him of his resolution and his assurances to Elizabeth.

He was impatient to get out on deck, to breathe in the fresh night air after having been down in steerage. He wondered how anyone could endure that for a month. He came up and filled his lungs to capacity with the cool air and let it out slowly.

He was also anxious to get outside where he could better clear his thoughts about the woman in his cabin. Two years ago he had looked back at the carriage conveying her away, annoyed at himself for not thinking to ask her name, while at the same time berating himself for becoming so captivated by a woman so decidedly beneath him. It had not been easy to remove her from his thoughts. Several months following that carriage ride he still found himself thinking of her.

Whenever he made a trip to Town, he looked for her, hoping he might encounter her there. He held her up as a standard to every woman he met, and found that they all lacked something he had found so appealing in her. But the memory of her gradually faded... he had almost completely forgotten about her... until meeting her on his ship!

He walked over to the ship's railing and rested his elbows upon it, clasping his hands together. He looked out at the vast sea of blue surrounding him and took in a deep breath. Elizabeth was truly a remarkable and attractive woman in all aspects of her person, and he was honestly concerned for her health. He just had to remember that this marriage was solely to get her out of steerage to allow her a better chance to improve her well-being. He could never seriously consider a real marriage to a woman who was not of at least equal birth and connections as himself; to a woman whose family was not in the first circles of society and had little or no fortune.

He shook his head. Apart from that, however, she was the type of woman who stimulated him; who entertained and challenged him at the same time. She brought out something in him that very few other women did. She had a vivacious personality, something that he lacked, being more often than not quiet and reserved. She had an engaging nature that actually drew him out of his fastidious shell without her even making a decided effort to do so. This was very unlike so many other women who, in making the same exerted effort, actually drove him deeper inside himself and further away.

But then she can certainly be obstinate! It was very apparent to him that she disliked the fact that he was taking charge. *Perhaps we have gotten off to a bad start; no doubt due to her feeling unwell and the awkwardness of the situation. Things will improve. I certainly hope they do.*

~~*

Back in the room, Elizabeth looked at the duffel containing all her things. She would have preferred to put everything away before retiring, but she was fatigued from the exertion of the evening. She felt completely unable to attempt anything of that sort now, and although she had enjoyed a good rest earlier, she felt sleep strongly beckoning her again.

She quickly put on her nightdress, modestly covering it with her robe, ever conscious that Darcy could, at any moment, walk in through the door. Although he said he would return later, she was fully aware that this was his room and he had every right to return to it whenever he desired.

She let down her hair, grateful for the weight of it now set free, and brushed through it a few times. Just the exertion of the few strokes of the brush tired her even more, and she resigned herself to the fact that all she cared to do right now was crawl into the bed and lose herself to a night of deep slumber.

She pulled aside the sheet that Darcy had hung and climbed into her bed, taking off her robe once the sheet fell back down into place. She eagerly crawled under the blankets. This time, as she lay her head down, she did not succumb to sleep right away, as she had done before. She was able to truly appreciate the comfort of a real bed, its soft mattress beneath her. She breathed in the fresh air, very unlike that which had been in steerage. As she looked over at the sheet that would act as a barrier between her and the man who was now her husband, she actually felt a sense of gratefulness for the thought he had put into this. That was the last thought that passed through her mind as sleep stole upon her and took her quickly into its depths.

Darcy later returned, quietly moving about the room readying himself for sleep.

He crawled into his bed and lay down; his eyes wide open at the knowledge that Elizabeth was asleep in the other bed. He lay awake, listening to the sound of her deep, steady breathing, savouring a very faint scent of lavender that must have been the lingering essence of perfumed toilet water. Even though the room was bathed in complete darkness once he extinguished the oil lamp, he found himself glancing over to where she slept. He did not have to see her with his eyes, for he had a very detailed image of her in his mind that would not go away.

Elizabeth slept soundly, barely moving a muscle as her body tried to make up for her lack of sleep and discomfort the past week on the ship. For the first time since coming on board his ship, Fitzwilliam Darcy slept very poorly.

Chapter 9

Instead of improving in the comfort of Darcy's cabin, Elizabeth seemed to grow steadily worse those first few days. She was barely able to get herself out of bed; her fever climbing dangerously high. Darcy secured whatever remedies he could acquire to aid in her recovery from the ship's cook, who was the only expert on board pertaining to these illnesses.

He also enlisted the help of Mrs. Jennings to give assistance to Elizabeth where he believed it would be more prudent for a woman to aid her than himself. She came to the room several times a day, helping Elizabeth out of bed, taking her to the necessary room, encouraging her to eat and drink, and securing her back into bed. Darcy needed only to remember to remove the sheet first thing in the morning so she would not have any questioning suspicions as to the nature of their marital arrangement.

Mrs. Rawlings, for the first time since boarding the ship, was eventually well enough to come up out of steerage and repaid Elizabeth's compassion with some of her own. The two women eagerly and graciously helped Darcy out with his wife's care. Elizabeth slept a lot, said very little, was growing increasingly pale, and Darcy was concerned.

Between Mrs. Jennings and Mrs. Rawlings, they took good care of her, but saw little improvement. Mrs. Rawlings was compelled to repay Elizabeth for all she had done and stopped by at every available opportunity. As Elizabeth's fever spiralled higher, Mrs. Rawlings took damp cloths and applied them to her face and encouraged her to drink plenty of fluids, advising Darcy to do the same with her, as well. When Elizabeth was too weak to do anything but sleep, she brushed out her hair for her and tidied her up.

Darcy was at a loss to know what more to do. He found himself gravely concerned for her health; wondering whether he had been too late in bringing her up out of steerage. He received varied accounts of Mrs. Trimble, and it was apparent that she was not making any sort of recovery. He wondered whether Elizabeth had contracted the same thing she had.

The evening of the third day that they had been married, Elizabeth was at her worst. Darcy awoke in the night to find Elizabeth moaning and thrashing about in her bed. He quickly pulled himself out of bed, lit the oil lamp and walked over to her, removing the sheet that separated them. He sat down beside her and felt her forehead. Even to his inexperienced touch, he had the unsettling feeling that her fever was higher than it ever had been or should be. He did as Mrs. Rawlings had advised, putting moist cloths across her forehead and trying to get her to drink some fluids.

In the light of the oil lamp, Elizabeth's face appeared flushed. He gingerly let his hand trail down her cheek, delighted by its softness, disquieted by its scorching heat. As she began again to thrash and cry out, Darcy tried to waken her by gently shaking her and calling out to her. "Elizabeth, do you hear me? Elizabeth wake up, you are having a bad dream!"

He seriously doubted that it was merely a bad dream, however. He was quite certain she was delirious from the effects of the high fever. She did not respond to his voice or touch, would calm down for a short spell, and then frantically cry out again. He steadfastly stayed by her side as he continued to apply the cloths to her face, hoping the fever would break.

As he sat there, he silently pondered whether her ailment could be the judgment from God on the two of them taking solemn vows so lightly. Could this be a punishment for entering into a marriage covenant without due consideration? He closed his eyes and uttered what he considered a meagre prayer. He was not a man who normally found himself relying on God, but having no other options available to him, he appealed to God's mercy for the plight he may have brought upon them and beseeched Him for her healing.

Elizabeth began murmuring again, and then frantically cried out, "No! No!"

Firmly grasping her shoulders, Darcy drew his face close to hers and called out to her, "Elizabeth, wake up! I know you can hear me!"

She mumbled something unintelligible, tossing her head even more and then suddenly stopped. Her eyes unexpectedly opened and he found himself staring into her beautiful, wide eyes, unsure whether or not she was really awake and seeing him. She then cried out, "Mr. Wright, Mr. Wright!"

Darcy took in a quick, sharp breath, fully convinced now that she was not awake, although she seemed to be looking right at him. He briefly wondered who this Mr. Wright could be when she cried out again.

"I did not know... I did not know..."

Elizabeth continued to thrash about while Darcy diligently applied wet cloths to her face, feeling more and more at a loss to know what to do. He wondered what it was that she did not know, and again, who this Mr. Wright might be.

Darcy lingered with her the remainder of the night keeping watch over her, alternating between attending her and pacing the floor. She cried out a few more times, but in the early hours of the morning, her fever finally broke. She fell into a deep, restful sleep, and relief flooded Darcy, knowing that she was on her way to recovery. He sat with his elbows resting on his knees, and his head buried in his palms. He could do nothing until he offered up another short prayer of thanks to God for bringing her through this. Exhausted, and ever so reluctantly, he walked the short distance over to his bed and crawled in, just as the sign of first light broke through the window. He did not bother to put the sheet back up.

~~*

After a few days of little more than bed rest, Elizabeth steadily began feeling improved. For those first few days after her fever subsided, she resisted the urge to rise with the sun; prompted principally by Darcy's strong admonition that she remain in bed to allow her the rest she needed to fully recover. Her more than satisfactory meals from the captain's private cupboard, although provided only occasionally now due to diminishing supply, strengthened her. She regretted that she was not feeling well enough to go visit the friends she had made, but greatly appreciated the visits from the now healed Mrs. Rawlings. On more than one occasion, she enthusiastically relayed to Elizabeth how Mr. Darcy showed such compassion and concern for her while she was ill. It was apparent to Elizabeth that he had secured Mrs. Rawlings' approval.

On those mornings while she had been ill, she had been only vaguely aware of Darcy rising and readying himself for the day. She had barely been able to open her eyes, and before she knew it, he would quietly remove the sheet and be gone, followed by either Mrs. Jennings or Mrs. Rawlings who would come in to help her up.

It was dark one morning and Elizabeth could hear rain pelting the ship. The overcast skies did little to give light to their room. When Darcy arose, he lit the oil lamp and began readying himself. Being the most alert she had been since their marriage, she found herself entranced by the shadows his movements projected upon the sheet.

It was by no means a distinct silhouette of the man, but she continued to watch it in silence. It was when he began walking closer toward her that the shape took on a more definite form, and she was surprised to find her heart had begun to beat a trifle more erratically. When he unexpectedly spoke to her from the other side of the sheet, she practically jumped, reeling from the irrational thought that he must have known she had been watching his shadow through the sheet.

"Elizabeth? Are you awake?"

It took a few moments for Elizabeth to compose herself, and she manufactured a loud, long yawn. "I… I am now," she answered softly.

"I am sorry to have awakened you. I wondered if you needed me to fetch Mrs. Jennings or Mrs. Rawlings this morning."

"No, no, I believe I am feeling well enough to take care of myself this morning."

Darcy smiled. "Good. Unfortunately it looks as though it is raining. I will go to the dining room for a while to allow you to get ready and then bring you back some food if you like."

"Thank you, no. I should like to partake of my food in the dining room itself. It has been too long since I have seen everyone."

"I shall return for you shortly, then."

Later that morning, when she went to the dining room with Darcy, Elizabeth was grateful to renew those acquaintances that she had not seen since she took ill almost a week ago. Sitting with her, Darcy was more intent on keeping an eye on her to insure that she did not overdo it rather than be inclined to join much in any conversation. But he did occasionally contribute, and for that Elizabeth was glad. She remained there until early afternoon, but fatigue gradually demanded she return to the room and rest, and she complied.

A couple of days later, she finally felt well enough to join Darcy on deck for their first walk since becoming husband and wife. The rain storm had passed without too much of an inconvenience. As the sun gradually rose above the horizon, she felt more compelled that morning to engage in the activity that she enjoyed best and had sorely missed. Elizabeth waited until after Darcy left their room that morning; then she promptly arose, readied herself, and proceeded to join him up on deck.

She peered out when she came aloft, feeling almost completely back to her old self. She took in a deep breath, anxious for a walk. She looked up one side of the deck and down the other, when she saw Darcy coming toward her.

"Good morning, Elizabeth."

"Good morning, Mr. Darcy."

By now Darcy was resigned that this woman would continually insist on being formal with him when they were not in the company of others.

The sun poured its warmth down upon the deck, but the breeze seemed to compete for attention. Elizabeth had inadvertently come up without her shawl and Darcy insisted he go back down for it.

"You cannot walk without your shawl. I shall run down after it."

"I am fine, truly," Elizabeth attempted to assure him.

"I do not want you coming down with a chill immediately after recovering from your fever! I shall return shortly."

He left without giving Elizabeth the chance to utter another word.

When he returned, he spread out the shawl in his hands and brought it around her. As he draped it around her shoulders, his hands came up and straightened the shawl around her neck, brushing against it lightly with his fingertips. If she had felt nothing this past week other than the effects of the fever, suddenly a fever of another kind swept through her at his touch.

She had been unaware of the extent of his care for her, too ill to be attentive to much of anything, and now was greatly discomfited that this simple touch, although most likely unnoticed by him, greatly stirred her. And there was something else. When she had been ill, she had dreams of him, and yet it had not been him. They were too hazy for her to clearly recall, and she was left again with a sense of something she was trying to recollect, but could not.

Elizabeth was incorrect in her assumption that Darcy most likely had not been affected by the touch. He had, in fact, been just as affected by the simple act of placing her shawl around her as she had been. He had cared for her these past few days, and there was something in caring for her that seemed to strengthen his regard for her. As he felt his irrational feelings toward her doing battle with his rational mind, he reprimanded himself for being so adolescently affected by something as simple as a fleeting touch.

They both turned to walk; Darcy politely extending his arm to Elizabeth. She gingerly placed her hand inside his arm and they began to stroll leisurely up on deck; their first time since becoming man and wife.

It was different now. They both sensed it. It had been over a week since they had taken their last walk together, and so much had happened since that day. A sense of awkwardness hung over their walk, as they both recognized that since Elizabeth was now well, their marriage would be more open for scrutiny by others. They would have to play the part convincingly and well.

Their conversation that day seemed stifled and forced. She could not think of any subject to introduce that might interest him. He appeared miles away in thought, apparently content in his silence, and so, apart from some general comments and observations, they said little.

In reality, though, both of their minds were full of thoughts that they wanted to pour out, but held themselves back.

As they were greeted by other passengers and some of the crew, Elizabeth found it disconcerting to be called Mrs. Darcy. She wished to be able to have everyone call her Elizabeth, instead of that name that was only a pretence, but that could not be. As they walked, she considered that Mr. Darcy had been spending almost this whole week posing as her husband while she had been ill in bed. Now she was faced with doing the same thing, and she wondered if she would be able to. In the fogginess of her mind when she agreed to his proposal, she could not have foreseen the awkwardness it would cause her.

She stole a look up at the man walking next to her, who seemed content to walk in silence and seemed oblivious to the moral or ethical dilemma she was facing. He was obviously one who did not struggle with lies and disguises. Did she really know him at all?

Darcy kept their walk that day short due to Elizabeth's only recent recovery and she was grateful when he suggested they had walked enough for the day. Feeling invigorated by the walk, but suddenly unnerved by the whole idea of living a deception in front of others, Elizabeth was grateful to return to the room.

When they stepped back inside the room, Darcy strongly suggested to her that she should not overexert herself, and that she should occupy her time resting in the dining area with a book or visiting with some of her acquaintances in there.

"I believe, Mr. Darcy, that I should prefer to pay a visit in steerage. I know there are some ladies who are still not well, and I would like to see Mrs. Trimble."

"Not yet, Elizabeth. You are not yet fully well. There is no reason for you to exert yourself and put yourself in harm's way."

He spoke to her in a way that, in his mind, it was a settled fact.

"On the contrary, Mr. Darcy, I believe there are several reasons for me to go down, and whether I exert myself or put myself in harm's way is left to be seen."

Darcy's eyes narrowed as he recognized the look of challenge permeate Elizabeth's features. He readied himself with an answer and girded himself for an expected retort. "I beg to differ, Elizabeth. You are not the only one capable of taking care of these people! You must think of yourself!"

Elizabeth's ire, coupled by the awkwardness she had felt earlier with him, rose. "Upon my word, Mr. Darcy! I believe I know myself well enough to know that I am perfectly well enough now to go down! You may think what you like. I will be paying a visit to steerage!"

She turned and walked toward the door. Darcy reacted by reaching out and grabbing her wrist, yanking her to a stop. She angrily turned back to him.

He stood facing her, unable to speak for the mesmerizing sight of her fiercely dark, challenging eyes. They arrested any thought he might try to conjure up and an uncomfortable silence ensued. How could he tell her that he was only concerned for her? How could he convey to her that he only had her well-being in mind? At length he realized she would most likely do as she pleased anyway and he released her hand.

"You may go, Elizabeth, if you are so strongly inclined. But I beg you, do not spend too great a length of time down there, and when you come back up, wash your hands thoroughly!"

She paused before turning to leave, debating whether she desired more to speak out again and have the last word, sarcastically inform him she did not need his permission, or whether she should apologize to him for her obstinacy and unreasonableness. At length, she opened the door and walked out, saying nothing further.

Darcy stood still for a few moments, contemplating this woman who was so independent, strong-willed, stubborn, compassionate, intelligent, lively, and beautiful! He had no idea how any man would be able to handle her as his wife. But a thought quickly materialized that he would surely love to give it a try and find out how!

Elizabeth sullenly made her way down the three flights of stairs to steerage, being ever so careful to step gingerly so as not to injure her ankle again. She was not happy with herself and wondered about her outburst. Whereas she told herself that Darcy was only looking out for her, she found it difficult to hold her tongue at his inclination to oblige her to do things the way he wanted without question.

She sighed as she approached the door that would take her into the steerage accommodations. She could already feel the stifling effects of being down within the bowels of the ship and the lack of fresh air. How grateful she was to be out of here. With that thought, she had to admit she was grateful for the man who was her husband, however temporary it might be.

When she walked into the large room, she was happy to see that many had completely recovered. Their were only a few left who were still ailing, including Mrs. Trimble who did not seem to be able to rise above her illness. Elizabeth did whatever she could to aid in their recovery and comfort.

When she met Darcy again later that day, Elizabeth was a bit more subdued than normal. Darcy could not determine if it was due to their argument earlier, that she had done too much that day, or both. As they sat together at dinner that night, he noticed she was exceedingly quiet, and he was pretty much left to his own devices to converse with those around him.

He was grateful to discover the next day that Elizabeth was one who rebounded quickly and completely, both in her health and in forgetting the conflicts of a previous day. By the next day she was pretty much back to her former self, and Darcy made every attempt to avoid appearing overbearing and controlling, for he knew exactly what her response to that would be.

The length of their walks each day grew longer and longer. As long as they kept the conversation from becoming too personal, they both began to enjoy the time and feel comfortable again. At length she even resorted to a little teasing.

One morning when she joined him for a walk, she commented on his attire, which she had found to be much too formal and elegant for an ocean crossing. She often contemplated how she must pale next to him in her simple muslin dresses.

"Tell me, Mr. Darcy, are these the only clothes you have?"

Darcy's eyes narrowed, looking down at his clothes in bewilderment. "May I inquire what you find wrong with these clothes?" he asked as he waved a hand over them.

Elizabeth smiled. "Nothing, if you are planning to go to a ball!"

Darcy looked at her incredulously. "A ball? These are not clothes one would wear to a ball!"

"Perhaps not yourself." Laughing lightly, she asked him, "Did you not bring any travelling clothes with you on this voyage?"

Darcy turned his head away from her, took a deep breath, and then brought his eyes back to see a most sparkling pair of dark eyes taunting him. He smiled at her and said, "Elizabeth, these *are* my travelling clothes!"

Now she let out a lively laugh. "Then perhaps you ought to bring out your work clothes for a change! I dare say you might be more comfortable!"

Suddenly Darcy turned serious. "I have no work clothes."

"You have no…?" Elizabeth paused, perceiving that he felt rather discomfited at the moment and checked her laugh. But she wondered whether he meant that he did not have any work clothes on this ship or not at all. She turned her attention away from him as they continued to walk, pondering whether this was the kind of man who never lowered himself to a menial task. She cringed as she thought what his life must really be like.

Elizabeth became increasingly concerned about Mrs. Trimble, who was growing weaker and eating and drinking less. Others in steerage recognized the look of impending death spreading across her features. Elizabeth continued to do all she could to make her comfortable while others tended to stay as far away as possible from her, fearful that what she had may spread to them.

Darcy and Elizabeth continued their daily walks, keeping the conversation to general things. When in the dining room, Elizabeth encouraged Darcy to meet others and prompted the conversations to veer towards those subjects he enjoyed talking about. He did not appear as withdrawn as he had, and Elizabeth found that he seemed to relish conversation on politics, religion, and current thought, but she also found he rarely offered any real insight into his personal life.

She was surprised with the effort at civility in which Darcy had begun to speak to those seated around him. He certainly did not seem to be at a loss in communication skills when in the company of a few. Why he would deliberately choose to sit off by himself in a crowd of people, as he had those first days out at sea, she had assumed was because he thought himself above everyone. But now she was of the opinion that it might be due to the fact that it took him some time to open up to people he did not know.

Darcy was convinced that Elizabeth was completely back to her former, spirited self a few days later when the dolphins made their appearance. They took their walk earlier that morning, and then went their separate ways, much like they had done each day since Elizabeth's recovery. In the early afternoon

Elizabeth went back on deck looking for the Rawlings when she saw a group of people congregated at the rail.

When she walked over, she was amazed at the sight she saw. Several dolphins were swimming alongside the ship, their bodies gracefully coming up out of the water and then going back down. She watched for several minutes quite engaged in the sight before her, believing she would never see anything else like it again. They seemed intent on staying alongside the ship, and Elizabeth, although finding it difficult to pull herself away, went in search of Darcy.

She found him in the dining room reading, and excitedly exclaimed, "William! You must come up and see this!"

Curiosity, as well as satisfaction propelled him to get up and follow her, for in her excitement, she had completely forgotten to use his formal name. She practically pulled him up onto the deck, lightly holding his hand in hers, and when they came up and looked out, Darcy was quite impressed.

But it was not so much the dolphins with which he was impressed, although they were definitely quite a sight. It was the fact the Elizabeth had thought to come down and find him to bring him up so he could share in this sight with her. As he continued watching the dolphins, he experienced an even greater pleasure in watching Elizabeth as she took infinite delight in observing the dolphins almost as if they were at play.

"Are they not the most beautiful things you have ever seen?" she turned to him and asked.

He had never seen her eyes more sparkling and lively than at this moment. "They most certainly are." At the moment, he felt a leaning in his heart that he wished he did not have to push away.

~~*

It had been almost two weeks since their marriage; the ship had been making good progress and they heard that they had but a week to go. The captain came to their room early one morning. The sun was just up over the horizon and there was a knock on their door. Darcy pulled himself out of his bed and opened it. The captain, holding an oil lamp to light his way in the early morning, asked to speak with Elizabeth.

Elizabeth looked out from behind the sheet. "Yes, Captain?"

"Excuse me, Mrs. Darcy, but Mrs. Trimble is fading. You may want to go down to her. I shall wait outside your door and take you down if you like."

"I shall be there directly, Captain."

Darcy thanked the captain and closed the door as Elizabeth scrambled out of bed. He turned, and in the palest light coming from the window caught a glimpse of her quickly donning her robe. He swallowed hard as Elizabeth looked up to see a look of discomfiture cross his face.

"Shall I go with you?" he forced himself to say. He really did not want to go for himself, or for Mrs. Trimble, but he would go solely for Elizabeth if she wished it.

"No, I shall go alone."

Elizabeth went down with the captain and found a few of the passengers gathered around Mrs. Trimble. Her breathing had grown shallow and her eyes were open but did not appear to see.

"Mrs. Trimble, it is me, Elizabeth." She watched as the woman's eyes fluttered, but there was no other response. Elizabeth took her hand and held it firmly as each breath seemed to be a struggle. Elizabeth lightly touched the woman's forehead and tears came to her eyes as she contemplated how sad it was that this woman had no one on the ship to grieve for her. Her husband, who was already in America, would not find out about his wife until the ship reached the shore.

Elizabeth sat for what seemed an eternity of intermittent breaths until finally, one last breath was sucked in and then slowly let out, her lungs never to fill with air again. Elizabeth watched as a peace overtook the woman's face; a peace that she had not seen in this woman at all since meeting her. Perhaps she had had a rough life, and now, she was finally in a much more desirable place.

But that comfort still did not prevent Elizabeth from collapsing in a heap crying. Others around her sniffled, some merely walked away, offering simple words of prayer or comfort, but Elizabeth could not tear herself from this woman. Perhaps she could have done more. Perhaps she should have spent more time with her instead of Mrs. Rawlings or remaining down here instead of going back to her comfortable room with Mr. Darcy. She thought with regret that if Mrs. Trimble had been given the opportunity to come up out of steerage as she had, perhaps she would be in good health and still alive today.

At length she felt a strong arm reach down and pull her up, and she looked up to see that it was Darcy. "Come, Elizabeth. She is in better hands, now."

He picked Elizabeth up, and as he carried her up the stairs, she turned towards him, burying her head against him, letting the tears fall. His arms tightened around her as she sought to find some sort of solace in them. He carried her upstairs back into their room and sat down with her on her bed, still holding her in his arms. He began to slowly rock, as he often had to do with Georgiana when she was downcast, and waited for her tears to cease.

"I am sorry," Elizabeth struggled to say between sobs, feeling completely foolish and unable to stop her crying. "I cannot help but think there might have been something more I could have done for her."

Darcy reached up and stroked her long hair that she had not had time to put up when she left so abruptly earlier. "I assure you, Elizabeth; you did all you could have done for her. The captain said she was in a gravely weakened state when she came on board, but no one was aware of it soon enough."

He did not say any more, being content to simply hold her and stroke her great length of dark hair, occasionally letting his fingers dig deeply into her thick tresses. He kept his face averted from hers, for her close presence was greatly unnerving him and he felt that if he looked down and she were to look up and meet his eyes, he would be hard pressed not to lean down and kiss her. They continued to sit in silence until her sobs ceased.

He could have held her in his arms indefinitely. Hesitantly, he turned and placed her beside him on the bed. "I shall leave you now so you can get dressed.

The captain has said he will have a service for her at ten o'clock."

"That soon?"

"Yes, it must be so." His voice oddly sounded firm and resolute. 'I shall be up on deck if you wish to have a morning walk."

Darcy stood up, and Elizabeth suddenly felt an emptiness replace his presence. He had been there to comfort her, and it had been an indescribable strength to her, however momentary. She wished he did not always have to leave. She found herself suddenly wishing that this marriage was real; that she could find solace in his arms, and he did not have to pull away.

When Darcy left the room, Elizabeth forced herself to walk over to the mirror and reluctantly looked at her reflection. Her red eyes and splotchy face were certainly not the looks of a woman who would attract the eye of a man such as Darcy. She splashed some water on her face trying to rid her eyes of the redness.

After doing all she could to freshen herself up, she looked through her meagre selection of dresses, each one becoming more and more wrinkled and worn. She thought how much she must pale next to Mr. Darcy's fastidious wardrobe. She finished by putting up her hair and soon left to join her husband up on deck.

When she stepped out, she found Darcy with his arms resting on the side of the ship; his gaze looking out across the water. He had come here to think; to sort out the thoughts that had continued to swarm in his head about Elizabeth. His thoughts went back to the image of her that morning as she climbed out from behind the sheet; to the feel of her in his arms as he consoled her and how it felt so right. As much as he wanted to concede that she was everything he had ever wanted in a woman, a deeper, more practical voice argued that she was not.

What he had done in arranging this façade of a marriage had certainly been a great help to her. But in the long run, could he really seriously consider her as Mrs. Fitzwilliam Darcy, Mistress of Pemberley? *What would others think?* he repeatedly asked himself. *What obligations do I have to my name? To my family?* The rationale that he could take her back as his wife to his circle of society gnawed away at him in a way that he could not reconcile.

Darcy closed his eyes to that thought. As much as he hated to admit it, he had to think about what others, especially his family, would think. He had to consider his elevated position, her much lower position, and the expectations to marry someone in his sphere. His mind was miles away when Elizabeth came up to him.

They walked in silence that morning. Darcy could not summon up any words and Elizabeth was too filled with grief to talk.

Chapter 10

As Darcy and Elizabeth made their way up on deck for Mrs. Trimble's service, she willingly slipped her hand into Darcy's extended arm, knowing she would need his strength to get through. People stood or sat on the few available benches, and Elizabeth was grateful they had come up a little early so she could stand close to the captain and hear what he had to say.

The captain began the service reading a passage from the Bible and then opening in prayer. Standing off to the Captain's side, Elizabeth bowed her head deeply. Darcy lowered his head, but kept his gaze upon Elizabeth, enjoying her closeness. He then chided himself for being so distracted by her presence when he should be focused on the captain's words. At length he closed his eyes as he heard the captain close with an "Amen."

Elizabeth saw that Mrs. Trimble's body had been put in a white canvas bag of sorts. About halfway through the service, when a brief eulogy was spoken with what little information had been gathered about her life, Elizabeth realized what was going to happen. Darcy knew the moment she realized that Mrs. Trimble's body would be let out into the sea, as she tightened up, tears filled up her eyes again, and she gripped Darcy's arm for even more needed support.

Even the prior realization of what was to transpire was not enough to prepare Elizabeth for it. When the sailors lifted the bag and sent it over the edge to sink into the depths of the sea as the captain prayed a prayer, Elizabeth turned to Darcy, trying to stifle her sobs. His arms reached around her and drew her more deeply into his chest. They did not move for the longest time, even as everyone slowly began to disperse, and Elizabeth wished that he would never let her go.

Elizabeth seemed to have no inclination or capacity to leave. They were two of only a few people up on deck. As Darcy continued to hold Elizabeth close to him, he noticed the captain eyeing him. Silent looks exchanged between the two men conveyed what each was thinking. From the captain, a cautionary lifting of the eye was sent Darcy's way, and from Darcy, a shrugging of his shoulders, tilt of his head, and the raising of both eyebrows signalled that there was little he could do. To be a little more truthful, there was little else he wanted to do.

After the service, Elizabeth desired some time by herself in their room. Darcy obliged her request and spent most of the day in the dining area where people had gathered and much of the conversation was about Mrs. Trimble. There was also much praise for Elizabeth, which he received graciously.

Feeling a little better but not yet ready to venture out and visit, Elizabeth pulled out the needlework sampler she had begun earlier in the voyage. She felt the healing effects of each embroidery stitch as a few flowers and words appeared by her own doing. She was working on it when Darcy returned.

He sat down, wishing there was something he could do to engage her spirits. He never knew what to do when Georgiana was feeling down, and he felt the same awkwardness of not knowing what to do for Elizabeth. He nervously tapped his fingers on the table bringing a smile to Elizabeth.

"Mr. Darcy, you do not need to stay here with me. I am feeling improved."

Feeling a sense of disappointment that she still chose to address him with such formality he responded, "I do not mind being here with you, as long as you do not mind." He sat down across the table from her.

Elizabeth looked at him and saw a tenderness she had never before seen. "Thank you." She wondered of his behaviour at times. She had to continually remind herself that their marriage was a pretence, but there were times when her husband played the caring, concerned, even loving husband all too well. It was those times when his behaviour had her most confused.

"Do you want to talk about it?" he asked.

Elizabeth shrugged. "It just seemed so sudden, so definite." She put her needlework down and looked up at him. "It is not that Mrs. Trimble was really that close to me, but that I had been seeing her almost every day for some time now. I have never had anyone close to me die before. At least that I can remember."

"You are fortunate. I have lost both my mother and my father."

Elizabeth's eyes widened at this personal disclosure. "I am so sorry." She was surprised that he had not mentioned that fact before and she impulsively reached out her hand to place it on his in a comforting gesture. When he looked down upon it resting on his hand, she hesitantly pulled it back.

"So it is just you and your sister?" she managed to ask, nervously tightening her withdrawing hand into a fist.

"And a few odd relatives." He looked back at her hand, almost willing it to return atop of his.

Elizabeth laughed. "I have a few odd relatives myself."

Darcy smiled, grateful that she was not so despondent that she could not laugh. Elizabeth was suddenly struck by how attractive he was when he smiled. She mused to herself that she would like to see him smile more often.

Then Darcy said something quite unusual. "I have one cousin, a younger cousin, who actually prefers walking to riding. Can you imagine?" He seemed intent to watch her, waiting for her response.

"I most certainly can! I prefer that myself!"

Darcy's heart leaped as Elizabeth continued. "I actually have never felt safe around horses. I merely try to keep my distance if I can."

She laughed as she wondered why he would consider this an odd trait, and continued, "And Mr. Darcy, if this is the extreme of your odd relatives, I would gladly trade any of my odd relatives for yours!"

He was drawn to her fine eyes when she laughed and felt himself becoming more and more lost in the depths of them. It was especially difficult now, being fairly confident that Elizabeth was the one in the carriage who so briefly captured his heart two years prior.

With this confirming revelation and the amount of time he had spent with Elizabeth, he found it difficult to hold firmly to his resolve to keep his distance emotionally from her. He began to wonder whether it was prudent to remain in the room with her.

Elizabeth expected Darcy to make a retort about her fear of horses, but he remained silent, an odd expression on his face. An eyebrow was briefly lifted on Elizabeth's face in speculation of what he was all about right now.

She wondered whether he regretted sharing personal things about his family. She decided to keep things light-hearted. "Although my father is most definitely a gentleman in every sense of the word, his humour can sometimes be sarcastic and teasing. My mother has her sole objective in life to marry off all her daughters and my younger sisters are all very silly, indeed."

Darcy smiled, not being able to take his eyes off her. She returned his gaze curiously. She could not entertain any serious notion that it was out of admiration, and could only construe that it was because he was experiencing uneasiness due to the personal nature of their conversation. They remained in silence for a time as Elizabeth turned her attention back to her needlework.

"What is that you are employing your time with there?" He struggled to ask.

"A needlework sampler." She turned it around for him to see. "It is not much. It will be surrounded with flowers and script."

He looked at it and began reading the words that she had begun to form with a steady line of stitches. "Think only of the past…"

"Think only of the past as its remembrance gives you pleasure."

"Is this your philosophy in life?"

Elizabeth nodded. "It is one. I actually have several."

Darcy began to wonder how she would look upon her time on this ship; how she would look upon *him* when this was all in the past. Would she be able to consider him with any pleasure?

"You are fortunate if you can truly live by it." He looked down in reflection. "I have a very unyielding temper. I cannot forget the follies and vices of others so soon as I ought, nor their offences against myself. My temper would perhaps be called resentful. My good opinion once lost is lost forever."

"That is unfortunate, indeed. I pity anyone who may have wronged you."

Darcy looked at her with an odd expression on his face, as if he were recalling some particular person who had hurt him in the past.

He stood up and walked over to her, lifting the sampler from her. She grew somewhat unsettled as his tall, close presence and attention stirred those feelings again in her that she knew not how to counter. The satisfaction it gave her, however, left her feeling that she did not want to counter it.

An unspoken mutual admiration and respect drew them closer that day. As the last days of the ship's journey were upon them, Darcy knew he was faced with making a decision regarding Elizabeth that, if dependent solely upon his feelings and, even now, his intellect, would be easy to make.

His feelings he had no control over. They had grown increasingly stronger just by being in her presence, enjoying her company. He believed she enjoyed his as well, although he had to admit that she seemed to enjoy the company of most people on this ship. His intellect was stimulated by conversations he had with her that gave evidence of her own intellect and liveliness.

But the deeper recesses of his being still demanded he think beyond his personal partiality and consider how she would, or would not, be accepted by his whole circle of family and acquaintances. Surely there would be those who would graciously accept any woman he deemed worthy of his hand. But there would be others, who, because of unreasonable expectation, would go out of their way to openly take umbrage at his choice, disregard her, and make life unbearable for him and her alike.

He lay awake those last few nights on the ship, listening to the sound of her breathing, and he tossed and turned as the battle waged even more fiercely. He struggled for that which was so close to him, yet so far.

He knew himself too well to know that once he had it settled in his mind, he would adamantly set forth to attain that which he so greatly desired. He knew it would put him in an awkward position with Elizabeth if she did not return similar leanings of her heart toward him. If he approached her with his strong feelings of regard and she did not return them, she would most likely no longer feel comfortable sharing the room with him, but that would be comparatively minor compared to the anguish he would suffer. At length he determined he would have to wait until they were just upon American soil. He knew, however, where the inclinations of his heart lay.

Elizabeth, unaware of his struggle, tried not to look ahead at what lay before her. She put aside all thoughts about their inevitable parting, and daily strove to simply enjoy their time together. They got along exceedingly well, apart from her stubborn nature that tended to clash fiercely with the authoritative streak he possessed. Although she was not a woman who easily retreated from obstacles she faced in life, she would never consider pressuring Mr. Darcy to go against his original intent to annul the marriage and retain her as his wife. She was all too aware, although she did not agree with, the irrational obligations those in the first circles of society placed on the position of the person they married.

With these thoughts and feelings surrounding Darcy and Elizabeth, the last few days of the voyage passed with a camaraderie between the two, and before they knew it, they found themselves facing the fact that it was their last day upon the ship. They would be reaching America sometime the following day.

On the final day of sailing before arriving in America, the winds picked up and clouds began to form. They had previously passed through several storms along the course of this voyage, but none had been anything too severe. The captain could tell this storm was different, and he began taking precautions well before the storm hit.

The first thing that became noticeable to everyone was the increase in the size of the swells, causing the ship to be severely tossed to and fro. As passengers gathered in the dining room anticipating their final evening of revelry, they had to keep a firmer grip on their cups of tea and coffee, their plates of food, and utensils. Revelry soon turned to a struggle to maintain order.

The captain knew they were heading straight into the storm, as the storms came off the east coast of America. He had heard many tales of vicious ones that spun ships around and easily ripped them to pieces.

Although the sun had not yet set, an eerie darkness settled over the ship. Lightning flashed around them and the winds picked up fiercely. The crew scrambled to furl the sails to prevent the ship from being blown over by the forceful gale of the winds.

At sunset, the storm hit with a fury very few had ever seen. The festivities were abruptly cancelled and everyone was ordered to their rooms as rain began to pour down in torrents. What was earlier thought to be a savage tossing of the ship proved to be nothing compared to what they now experienced.

When Darcy helped Elizabeth return to the room, as it was exceedingly difficult to even walk, she watched in utter frustration as Darcy pulled out a coat and began to put it on.

"What are you planning on doing?"

"I am going out there to see if there is anything I can do!"

"Are you a fool? You could get yourself killed up there!"

"Elizabeth, I cannot just sit here, knowing that the ship could break apart at any minute! You stay here!"

He opened the door and slammed it behind him as the boat encountered a swell that tipped it precariously on its side.

"William, please, no!"

Elizabeth grasped for something to hold on to as she cried out for him to stay. Her voice was lost in the crashing of the waves against the boat. She was left alone to ponder in anger why this man insisted on doing such a thing as to venture out into the storm when the captain and crew were most capable of handling things. Who did he think he was?

As her mind unwillingly became engaged with the worse scenarios of what might befall them due to the intensity of the storm, she was gripped with fear.

The ship made a sudden, violent lurch to the side and Elizabeth was harshly flailed against the wall. She frantically tried to grasp hold of the table to keep from falling. She then leaned against the table to secure her own balance as the ship swayed in the opposite direction. It returned to its upright position only for the briefest moment, and then continued its tremulous tilting. The ship tossed as if it was in the hands of a mighty, relentless force, and its pitching was increasing in intensity by the minute.

She stubbornly refused to let her fear get the best of her and consequently decided to do something. She determined her first course of action must be to stow away and secure everything that was susceptible to falling down, toppling over, or scooting precariously across the floor.

She worked quickly, fighting against her fear and the savage tossing of the ship, quickly and adeptly stowing everything that was not secured. The ship swayed one moment from one side to the other, and then would rise up from the front as it encountered a swell head-on and then proceeded to come crashing down again. Her heart pounded as realization swept through her what a storm like this could do to a ship.

When she had secured all she could, she made the decision that it would be best for her to stay low to the floor. She felt that even trying to secure herself in the narrow bed for the night would be fruitless due to the extent of the ship's unremitting tossing. She knew she could easily be thrown from the bed onto the floor. She took her pillow and propped herself against a wall, bringing her knees up and grasping hold tightly with her arms. She whispered a silent prayer that the ship would remain intact and all on board would remain safe.

Her thoughts and prayers dwelt particularly of Darcy and his safety, as he had gone aloft so see what, if anything, he could do to help.

What a fool he is! her thoughts repeatedly echoed. Why must he always insist in being in control of a situation, when it is not even his place to worry? She let out a frustrated sigh and a cry heavenward for his safety.

Chapter 11

Elizabeth sat still, keeping her eyes on the door, hoping and praying that Darcy would return. After what seemed an eternity of waiting and imagining every horrible thing, it finally opened and a very wet Darcy stomped in.

"The captain says it looks to be quite a severe storm!" He had to compete with the thunderous resonance to be heard. Pulling off his coat as it left puddles of water on the floor, he informed Elizabeth, "He has all hands on deck and they have furled all the sails. There is as much water coming from the swells over the sides of the ship as there is rain coming down from the heavens! It is going to be a long night."

A tremendous sense of relief had washed over her when he walked in, causing her to close her eyes in a quick, prayerful "thank you." But it was tempered with residual anger toward his foolish stubbornness. She knew there would be no benefit in expressing her anger now. "Does the captain appear concerned?" she asked.

"The captain says not to worry, but we need to stow everything that is not secured or it will come crashing down." Taking a quick glance around the room he said, "Oh, I see you have done that already."

"Yes."

"Good." He began to take off his coat and water cascaded from it onto the floor. He hung it up on a rack, and raked his hand through his hair, only slightly removing some of the water with it. His coat had kept out some of the water, but his shirt was soaked in some places.

Elizabeth made her way over to the dresser and secured a towel, handing it to him. "You should get out of your wet clothes."

Darcy looked at her and nodded. "That is something I plan to do." He took the towel and briskly rubbed down his hair, removing the excess water. "It would have been better for me up there if I had had an oilskin coat. That is what the crew all wear in a storm such as this and it really helps them keep somewhat dry." He walked over to the small closet, and as he did, the ship made a sudden lurch to the left, propelling him off balance and sending him against the table, his shoulder going right into its edge. With a moan, he grabbed his shoulder with his other hand, and promptly slid himself down to the floor.

"The other thing that captain said is to stay as low to the floor as possible." He grimaced painfully. "I now see that is a wise idea."

"Are you hurt?" Elizabeth asked as the ship rose and fell mercilessly.

He vigorously rubbed his shoulder and replied, "I do not think it is fatal."

Elizabeth smiled as she realized he was trying to be light-hearted with his last remark, possibly to help ease her fears. He continued, "I shall most likely be sore for a few days, that is all." He sat on the floor continuing to rub his injured shoulder and soon made another attempt to retrieve a dry shirt. When he reached out the arm with the injured shoulder, he withdrew it back in pain. "Ohhh!" His hand immediately went up to rub it again.

"You are not all right." Elizabeth said as she reached him. "Let me help you." She easily took hold of the dry shirt he had been attempting to reach and then turned to look at him. "Can you unfasten your shirt?" she asked.

He tried to untie his neck cloth with his unhurt hand, using his injured arm as little as possible. Elizabeth watched with the expectation that she would help if he needed her assistance, although in this area she wondered whether her fingers would be a help or a hindrance to him as they had begun to nervously shake. As he began to undo the buttons to his shirt, she forced herself to look away.

As much as she would have liked to approach this circumstance in a very practical, unemotional way, her heart's pounding and her rising tide of feelings began to overpower her. That he was hurt almost made him more vulnerable, more desirable. She suddenly felt that she would be very happy taking care of this man until they were old and grey. But she halted that thought immediately, knowing it would not do any good to think about things that were not to be.

As her thoughts were engaged in this direction, Darcy attempted to remove his shirt, and Elizabeth was stirred from her reverie by another groan of pain from him. The pain in his arm was such that he could not manoeuvre the shirt down off his arms, and he looked helplessly at Elizabeth.

"I am sorry, but I do not seem able to accomplish this. My arm is causing me a great deal of pain."

Elizabeth positioned herself behind him and calmly responded, "Drop both of your arms down by your side." When he did so, she gently took the shirt by the collar, her fingers lightly brushing his neck, and brought it down along his long arms and slid it off. She was glad she was situated behind him, as this simple action and the sight of him shirtless from the back caused some unexplainable stirrings within her and a very noticeable blush across her face.

She quickly fumbled for the dry shirt and lowered the sleeve so he could easily move his hurt arm into it, and then she brought it around and he was able to slide his other arm into it as well without any problem.

Darcy felt her breath on the back of him, and the very slight touch of her fingers upon his neck produced an involuntary shiver. When she slid his shirt off, he thought how different it was to have a woman do the same task that Durnham had done throughout the years. He enjoyed this much more than he should have allowed himself to.

Once the dry shirt was on, he quickly reached up with his good arm and nimbly began buttoning the buttons one handed. An awkward silence had enveloped them, and his jaw tightened as he considered that Elizabeth must feel exceedingly uncomfortable.

"Thank you for your help, Elizabeth. I would not have wished to cause you any uneasiness."

He spoke softly and with much gratitude.

Elizabeth drew herself around from behind. "I only did what I knew I must."

She sat aside him, marvelling at the goodwill that had come to exist between them in just the last week. The ship suddenly tipped again violently, and she fell against him, causing him to reach out for her with his good arm and he planted his sore arm against the floor for stability.

Another groan escaped him, and Elizabeth apologized profusely. "Mr. Darcy, I am so sorry."

He looked down at her, not wanting to let her go. "Elizabeth, do you not think we have been through enough together, that even when we are alone you can call me by my given name?"

Elizabeth closed her eyes and blushed. When she found herself unexpectedly wanting to draw nearer to him, she became more intent on reverting to formalities in addressing him.

"Mr. Darcy, we are almost at the end of our voyage. I think it best we keep things between us as we agreed." He was still holding her when she met his eyes. "Our marriage is on paper only."

Darcy sighed softly and released her. His idea to marry her solely for the duration of the voyage had indeed caused him greater consternation than if he had allowed himself to be tormented this past month by all the single women, their mothers, and their fathers, and all the other matchmakers and fortune hunters on board this ship. He had fallen in love with Elizabeth, and it was clear that she did not love him in return. *On paper only*. That was certainly not how he felt toward her now.

Mustering all the strength he had to keep from succumbing to the storm of emotions that were erupting within, he calmly and deliberately spoke. "The captain said it would be wise to sleep on the floor, as a storm such as this will even throw one out of bed. We need to bring the bedding down to the floor for the night." He looked around the room, much as Elizabeth had done earlier.

"There is not much room…" He looked over to the space between the two beds. "This is probably the best place for us to sleep tonight. There really is not any other room on the floor." He tried to control his voice to sound calm, rational, and not at all ruffled, which was not at all what he was feeling. "With the dresser drawers underneath the bed, that will give us some stability from the rocking and keep us from sliding all over the floor."

Elizabeth looked over to the small area. It was certainly long enough for them to stretch out in, but suddenly it seemed very narrow. "Yes, it seems to be the wisest," she reluctantly agreed.

Darcy looked at her and recognized the look of discomfort written across her face. "Perhaps it would be best if I sleep over there. I could easily sit against the wall behind the table… if you prefer."

"No, no," she stammered. "I could not allow you to do that. We are both adults." How she wished she did not sound so nervous. Then, in almost a whisper she added, "We are, after all, married."

Darcy's chest suddenly constricted and his jaw tightened as he heard her speak those words so dispassionately. He looked into her eyes and saw the pain. *Does she really regret this marriage that much?* he asked himself. "There is not much more we can do. We might as well try to make ourselves as comfortable as we can."

As the ship continued its relentless rocking, they both began to pull the blankets off their beds. There was room for only one mattress on the floor and Darcy pulled it off of his bed. Elizabeth pulled two blankets off her bed, one to go underneath her and one to cover her. She scooted as closely as she could to the dresser on her side, and lay her head down on her pillow. The room was dark now, except for the frequent flashes of lightning that ripped across the sky, lighting up the room through the tiny window. There seemed little likelihood of them falling asleep any time soon, with the clamouring of the forces of nature outside as well as in. The rumble of the thunder, the howling wind, and the crashing of the waves against and over the boat seemed to take their toll on the ship in addition to their nerves, as did the rising tide of their feelings.

Earlier, Elizabeth's fear had propelled her to do something. She had tried to secure everything that was not bolted down so it would not fall over or come crashing down. Then she had set her mind on helping Darcy after he hurt himself. But now as there was nothing to do but listen to the tumultuous sounds and feel the assault on the ship as it laboured and strained, her fear began to spiral, as the storm seemed to be intensely overpowering and growing in severity by the minute. With each pitch of the ship, Elizabeth grabbed either the mattress, the dresser, or the floor itself, hoping it would keep her in her place.

But as the ship rocked and swayed, as it creaked and groaned, there was little either could do to keep themselves settled in one place. More often than not, Elizabeth either slid into Darcy as the boat tipped his way, or he slid into her when it tipped the other way. The worse of it occurred when the boat encountered a wave head-on. The fore of the ship would rise up, and then come crashing down violently.

There was little chance that they could grow accustomed to the constant swaying, dipping, and crashing down, but they lay there together, each one consumed by their own thoughts and feelings. At one sudden, very strong jolt of the ship, Elizabeth cried out as she was pelted against Darcy. He immediately wrapped his arm around her, driven by a protective instinct, but he let it remain there out of a selfish desire to feel her in his arms.

She lay there still, suddenly feeling very safe in his arms. The thunderous beating of her heart competed with the sounds of the storm outside. Whether it was simply fear or the fact that she was now being held tightly in his arms, she was not sure. But she had this very strong assurance that while in his arms, no harm would befall her.

Despite her overwhelming sense of fear, she became aware of some other feelings that were awakening within her. It was more than just a sense of being protected by this man. There was a yearning inside her to draw closer to him. A stirring within that she had never experienced. She wished to be able to turn toward him and bury her head in his chest. She closed her eyes tightly, wishing away these thoughts and feelings. He was not really hers to think about. Her regard towards him that had been growing these last few days could never be reciprocated. She took in a deep breath to steady the overwhelming feeling of despair that began to overtake her. But it was not enough to prevent a tear from escaping her eye and travelling down her face.

She had two pictures in her mind, and neither of them was at all pleasant or desirable. The first was that the ship would not make it through the storm this night and they would all perish, being lost at sea. The second was that they would make it through the storm, and once the ship pulled into the harbour in America and they left the ship, she would never see him again. As the ship violently rose and fell, the thought came to her that perhaps she wished for the former. For in that case, they would at least be in each other's arms for eternity.

All the while, Darcy closed his eyes as he considered how right it felt to have his arm wrapped around Elizabeth. If it were not for the extremely dangerous and trying conditions they were in, and the violent rocking and swaying of the ship, he knew he was in danger of another kind; that is, overstepping his bounds with her and breaking the agreement they made for the conditions of this marriage. He was not sure how he would survive an entire night with Elizabeth by his side, without struggling with the temptation she presented.

After lying awkwardly in silence, stirred both by heightened feelings in the midst of the storm waging outside and in, Darcy attempted to engage Elizabeth in conversation, if nothing more than to take his mind off her discomfiting proximity, since neither of them would be able to sleep anyway.

"Did you ever finish your sampler, Elizabeth?"

"Why, yes, I did." She lifted her head and looked around as if she suddenly realized that she did not know where it was, even though in the darkness she would not have seen it.

"I should like to see it now that it is finished."

Elizabeth smiled, knowing this was a very meagre, but appreciated, attempt to keep her mind off the storm.

Attempting to keep their minds engaged on other things he asked, "And may I inquire what other accomplishments you employ while you are not sailing across the oceans of the world?"

Another round of violent swells delayed her answer, as she gripped tightly to him, but smiled. "You know I enjoy reading, I do a little sewing, enjoy singing, and play the pianoforte, but very ill indeed."

"Those are delightful diversions." He spoke the words softly, but the reaction Elizabeth had was almost as if he had screamed them.

Her eyes opened widely in an acute sense of stark realization.

Delightful Diversions! The very same words the gentleman in the carriage two years ago had said!

She stared into the darkness, the room flashing with light from the bolts of lightning outside, and she suddenly recalled the image of the man who, for several months after their encounter, never left her thoughts! Her heart tightened and she suddenly felt as if she could not catch her breath, tightly closing her eyes as she deliberated this disclosure.

Suddenly it all became very clear! She knew why he had seemed so familiar! Those fleeting memories that she could not pull to the surface since she first saw him on the ship were from that carriage ride, the gentleman sharing the ride with her, and the following months that held her captive to his memory.

He had uttered those exact words when, as a young, impetuous eighteen year-old, she told him how she had recently climbed a tree and fallen from it, spraining her ankle. She had thought he was mocking her behaviour, but in the course of their time in the carriage, she found him to be quite engaging, very attentive, and effortlessly charming.

For weeks and months following the carriage ride, she found herself repeating those words at every opportunity as a reminder of her short time with him. 'Mary is reading Fordyce's Sermons!' Delightful diversion for her! 'Jane! Guess what! We are going to visit Aunt and Uncle Gardiner!' What a delightful diversion that shall be!

And when she and Jane would talk about life and love into the wee hours of the morning, Elizabeth could only talk of him. For months, she talked of her 'Mr. Wright,' the man whose name was unknown to her, but seemed so right for her.

At length the memory of that day had faded. As months passed into years, she no longer was able to draw up an image of what the gentleman looked like, or what his voice sounded like that had been so pleasing to her ears.

Her thoughts assaulted her. *Could he really be the same man?* It was as if she suddenly remembered everything very clearly! It *was* him! *The man who visited her in her dreams in the past week was both Mr. Wright and Fitzwilliam Darcy! The same man!* She simply had no idea.

She hoped that he would not sense her discomposure. At least in the darkness of the room she could hide her face of shock and make a futile attempt to still her shaking fingers. At once, all those little episodes trying to recall a vague memory made sense – her colliding with Mr. Darcy that first day, feeling that she had been on the receiving end of this proud man's praise once long ago. She took a deep breath as she tried to gather her thoughts.

She knew that now she would have an even greater struggle getting off this ship without him. If she could not forget the man with whom she only spent a couple of hours, how could she ever forget the man who had posed as her very own husband over the course of several weeks?

Elizabeth was rendered silent by this realization and Darcy, receiving no further response from her, assumed she was in no mood to talk. Their conversation for the night ceased.

For several hours the storm continued mercilessly with wind, rain, and occasionally hail battering the ship. In the early morning hours, the storm gradually weakened, and Darcy and Elizabeth fell into a sound sleep. Darcy awoke a few hours later and discovered his arm still protectively wrapped around her. She had turned in the night and her head was snuggled deeply against his chest and her arm wrapped securely around his waist. He could only see her when the occasional flash of distant lightning lit the room. She was beautiful and he found it exceedingly difficult to remove his eyes from her.

Her hair was splayed around his arm and he found himself anxiously waiting for each successive bolt of lightning off in the distance to light up the small cabin so he could better see her. How he wanted to comb his fingers through her hair, caress her face with his hand, kiss her lips.

Darcy lay very still, but his heart pounded mercilessly. When Elizabeth moved in her sleep and drew herself up against his chest, Darcy gave in to the temptation, leaned his head over, and gently kissed the top of her head, letting his lips linger there. He wanted to draw her into a fervent embrace, but that kiss would have to suffice for the time being. He lay there for some time, listening to every breath she took, sensitive to every slight movement she made, and breathing in the flowery scent of her hair from the toilet water she most likely sprinkled in it.

At length, the only way Darcy felt he could endure the prospect of spending the remainder of the night with Elizabeth in his arms and remain the gentleman he promised he would be, was to think of her as his best friend's sister. He forced a mental image to appear of the woman who grated his every nerve, tested his patience, and pushed the boundary of his civility. The only way he found to deal with this temptation was to imagine that she was Caroline Bingley! Never before had he thought so much about that annoying woman in his whole life! At length he fell asleep.

As the sun began to peek up over the horizon through the scattered clouds that were remaining from the storm, Elizabeth awoke. She had been in the middle of a dream. In the dream she had been up on the top deck of the ship and a fierce storm was raging, much like the one that night. One of the masts had broken and crashed down over her, the sails from the mast and yardarm falling atop her. She was sure that no one knew she was trapped under them, and felt frantic, unable to move... unable to scream.

When at last she awoke, it took her moment to realize where she was and that it had only been a dream. Her mind gradually cleared and she recalled how she and Mr. Darcy had come to sleep on the floor that night. Darcy was asleep next to her. She could tell by his heavy, steady breathing that he was sound asleep. She also came to realize that the masts that were lying across her in her dream were actually his leg that was draped across her leg and his arm that was slung over her. The sails that had entrapped her in that dream were the blankets that she was wrapped in.

Her head was buried deep within his chest and she not only recognized the constant rhythm of his breathing, but could also hear and feel the steady pulse of his heartbeat. She lay there quietly, unwilling to move so as not to awaken him.

As more light began to seep into the room, she pulled herself away slowly and looked at his sleeping face. Something about watching him sleep halted her. While asleep, he appeared very vulnerable and unassuming. He had a very pleasing countenance that she only wished could permeate his features more often while awake. Here was a man who was so fastidious about his looks, and yet now he lay with his curly hair dishevelled and askew. She thought how much more unpretentious he appeared. Here was a man with a large fortune, and yet as she looked at him, she felt that at this moment, he was purely flesh and bones as she, and his fortune meant no more to him than her lack of fortune meant to her. Finally, here was a man who normally put on a mask of pride, and yet now that mask had fallen away, and he was as innocent as a baby.

She thought how attractive he looked in this state. No airs, no pride, nothing to recommend him. She could easily fall in love with someone like that. In fact she did, two years ago!

She steadily watched his face, and without even thinking, her hand went up and pushed aside an unruly strand of curly hair that had fallen across it. As soon as she let it go, it fell back down. In doing this, another thought came to her. Darcy was a man who took meticulous care in his appearance. She was aware of how tediously he worked to get his hair in place, often with fruitless results once he went up on deck and the wind whipped through it. His dress was always immaculate, and he was of exceptional height and build. All these things inevitably drew attention to him.

That was it! That was what she could not figure out that first night she saw him in the dining area. His fashionable dress, exceedingly handsome looks, and tall stature all commanded attention; yet that was the very thing he loathed!

Elizabeth had to keep herself from chuckling aloud. Here was a man who considered his good looks a curse because they drew attention to him. Attention that he did not want. When he planted himself against a wall or a window, he hoped to disappear. If he was just anybody, he would have succeeded without too much notice or idle speculation. But due to the very nature of the man, it simply drew more attention to himself; attention that misinterpreted his actions as prideful.

Elizabeth closed her eyes with this thought, as she savoured the novelty of lying in his arms. She did not want this to end and for the very first time, began to fear what it would mean to them when the ship docked. As she dwelled on these thoughts, she noticed him begin to slightly stir.

She closed her eyes so he would not see her watching him if he awoke. She was surprised when his arm closed around her more tightly, securing her against him. She could barely breathe, and suddenly felt ill at ease that if he should awaken, he should not find them tangled as they were. She tried to carefully pull away so as not to awaken him, when suddenly he spoke. "Lay still, Caroline, you are safe in my arms."

Elizabeth gasped in a sharp breath as he spoke these words. She lifted her eyes to his face. He did not appear to be awake, but his words pierced through her and she felt a real sharpness of pain. She had never once considered that he might have a woman back in England waiting for him. How foolish she had been to entertain thoughts about this man, when from the start, he made it clear that their marriage would be annulled and forgotten once he returned.

She grabbed her pillow and blanket, pulling herself away with little attempt to be careful in her movement so as not to awaken him further. Once that was accomplished, she climbed into her own bed.

She closed her eyes, her body trembling slightly. She was not sure whether it was due to her strenuous effort to pull herself away from him or if it was due to her feelings for him that were now so overpowering that she was not sure how she would endure one more day. As she turned her head to the wall and closed her eyes, she felt them swell with tears and one slowly escaped down her cheek.

Darcy slowly opened his eyes, awakening when he became aware of Elizabeth leaving his side. He looked over to her as she returned to her own bed.

He was grateful to see it was Elizabeth, as he had just been suffering in a dream where his wife for the journey had been Caroline Bingley and he had the arduous task of comforting her in a storm! He was, needless to say, grateful it had only been a dream.

Looking back at Elizabeth, he was disappointed that she left his side, but if she had remained, it would have been exceedingly difficult to maintain even a modicum of restraint. The storm outside had ceased, but another storm had taken hold in his heart.

Chapter 12

Darcy lay quietly absorbed in thought for almost an hour after Elizabeth left his side, unable to keep from thinking about this captivating lady. The sun was now up, fighting for dominance in the sky with the remnant of clouds left behind by the storm. The storm for the most part was over and Elizabeth was asleep in her own bed, but a storm of emotions continued to rage in Darcy's heart.

A soft, hopeless moan escaped him. How did this happen? How did she do this? Was it with some sort of feminine allurement that she had set out from the beginning to entrap him?

He thought back to those months after the carriage ride when he had first met her. He had not been able to get her out of his mind. Now, he had just spent a month with her, posing as her husband, living within the close confines of their small cabin, and he was supposed to forget her when they got off this ship? He knew there was very little chance of it. She expected him to return to England and annul this marriage when he, in all truthfulness, wished to keep it intact! In a frustrated sigh that deepened into a yawn, he stretched out his arms and began to sit up.

He grimaced in pain as he had forgotten about his sore shoulder and brought up his other hand to briskly rub it. He looked over at Elizabeth, who was still sleeping soundly in her bed. She was facing the wall, so he could only see her hair flowing down her back. He sat up and leaned against his bed, keeping a watchful eye on the sleeping maiden. Due to the storm, last night they had never put up the sheet separating their two beds, and he enjoyed the sight of Elizabeth as he gazed upon her sleeping form.

As he worked out his stiff muscles, he thought of those first few nights on the ship when she had to sleep on the floor in steerage. How did she do it? He did not think he would have been able to, due to the fact that he had been pampered and spoiled all his life. She was not afraid to step out of the comfort of her world; something that he personally found exceedingly difficult!

Now he was faced with stepping into a discomfort of another kind. He knew that today would demand that he address his feelings. Today, before they reached shore, he would somehow manage to convey to her his love and admiration. He felt his chest constricting and his pulse racing just at the prospect of it.

His thoughts went back to last night and how Elizabeth had so graciously and selflessly tended to him. From there his thoughts carried him to their laying together during the storm, and then awaking to find her nuzzled close against him.

These mindful recollections he had of her were most pleasant intrusions indeed, and as such, he was seriously displeased with himself. Why did he have such fierce reactions to the thought of speaking those words to her that would clearly express his sentiment and intent? *Why is the mere thought of that so difficult for me?* He could be articulate about a great number of subjects. He and Elizabeth shared deep, meaningful conversations. So why did the prospect of exposing his feelings leave him feeling so inadequate and vulnerable?

He longed to sit here watching her endlessly, but he knew he must get up and leave the room as she would want to arise in privacy. With a few quick adjustments to the clothing in which he slept, he prepared to go aloft. He knew how *he* had weathered the storm, now he was curious how the ship fared.

He quietly opened the door, turning back to look one last time at Elizabeth. Then he closed it behind him.

His first stop was down the long hall to the dining area. When he came upon it, he was stunned to find some windows had broken out and water had mercilessly flooded the room. As he looked in further, he noticed some tables and benches had broken loose and were no longer secured to the floor, but were now in a chaotic heap. One of the crewmen advised him that the dining area would be inaccessible until they got things cleaned up and repaired.

Slowly he walked to the deck, and as he came up, he deeply breathed in the fresh air that was laced with the scent of a recent rain.

He could immediately tell that the storm had waged a war with the ship last night, but in his novice opinion, it appeared as though the ship won. He noticed several of the crew mending sails. Apparently they had ripped in the storm before they had been furled. He saw a few yardarms broken, and some of the crew worked on repairing those. For the most part, the ship had endured satisfactorily. Several men were vigorously mopping down the deck, ridding it of the excessive water. He was grateful the ship had a good crew who all seemed to know exactly what needed to be done. It was good to see that firsthand. His ship was in excellent hands.

He inquired of the whereabouts of the captain and was told that he had retreated to his cabin as soon as morning broke and he was able to assess the damage. He remained on deck throughout the night and was likely getting some rest now. By the looks of the deck, it would not be a good morning to walk, as rigging, sails, and various pieces of equipment were strewn about and sailors were attempting to make amends. The topsail, gallant sail, and a few smaller sails had been unfurled and the ship was moving along nicely. Darcy inquired as to their bearings.

"We won't be arriving in the new world today as we hoped. We got pushed too far off course last night," answered one of the sailors. "We are currently further south and east than where we need to be. Prob'ly be making land early in the morning if we are lucky."

Darcy sighed. Another night aboard the ship. That gave him a little more time to formulate the words he wanted to say to Elizabeth, along with the decision whether to acknowledge his feelings today or wait until tomorrow. Darcy took in a deep breath as he contemplated what to do.

Since he could not walk easily on deck nor go into the dining area, all he could do now was return to their room. He knocked lightly and heard a soft, "Come in."

Walking in, he found Elizabeth sitting at the dresser in front of the mirror brushing out her hair. She had changed from the dress she had slept in, and looked surprised to see him.

Darcy felt awkward returning before she was ready, and offered an apology. "It is quite a mess up there, Elizabeth. It would be too difficult for us to attempt to walk this morning, and even the dining room is unfit for passengers until they get some work done in there." He walked over to the small bench and sat down.

From where he sat, he could watch Elizabeth brush out her hair, but she could not see him. He watched as she slowly and repeatedly brought the brush down through her thick, dark length of hair. Having only seen it down a couple of times, but never having had the pleasure of watching her brush it, he could not take his eyes off of her. As she deftly lifted its length up and easily pinned it into a very becoming style, Darcy was mesmerized by the sight, and noticed particularly how graceful her neckline was when she lifted her hair. The urge to walk over and gently kiss it was overpowering.

As she sat there brushing out her hair, she had been doing a great deal of contemplation about this man whom she discovered last night was her 'Mr. Wright.' Those two years had probably changed him in some degree, but it was most likely in her mind that he had changed. She reasoned that the greatest factor in not recognizing him was that after she had carried about the thought of this man for months and months, even giving him a name by which to refer to him, she eventually knew she must put aside this girlish infatuation and forget about him. It was a struggle that she had a difficult time conquering, but at length, after considerable willpower and effort, she let her 'Mr. Wright' go, determined to grow up and set her mind on more attainable aspirations in the area of prospective suitors.

That did not make the realization any easier. Her thoughts since awakening were mixed with the staggering recollection of his whispering the name 'Caroline' as he held her in the night and Elizabeth felt that any conversation with him today would be a struggle for her. A struggle because her heart was aching to love him and be loved by him, and because they would be arriving shortly in America and go their separate ways.

The silence between them was deafening to her ears. She struggled for anything to say. "Are we to see land shortly, do you think?" Her stomach tightened in a knot as she asked this.

"Not today, at least. The crew tells me that the storm pushed us off course. Hopefully we will reach land early tomorrow morning."

"Oh." Elizabeth turned back to the mirror. The tightening and tenseness grew worse as she heard his word 'hopefully.' He looked forward to moving on.

Perhaps that was what she needed. Once they had gone their separate ways it might be easier. In one way she wanted it over with. Perhaps when he was out of her sight and out of her presence, she would be able to put him out of her heart and mind. But if her former association with him was any indication, she would likely not forget him any time soon.

As Elizabeth turned her attention back to making some final adjustments with her hair, Darcy pondered again, for perhaps what was close to the hundredth time, what he should say to her, how he should say it, and when. Each time he even considered it, each time he would feel the impulse to begin his discourse, his heart would beat rapidly and he would feel a shortness of breath. He did not enjoy this feeling at all, as it was something he seldom experienced. He finally resorted to picking up his book to read, deciding he would attempt this later. He simply did not have the capacity at the moment.

As things up on deck were mopped down, cleaned up, and cleared away, people began congregating in the dining room again. Everyone needed to share their experiences from the night before, and Elizabeth found that many in steerage had been terribly frightened and exceedingly seasick. The conditions down there had been dreadfully terrifying. The savage tossing of the ship, coupled with the complete darkness and crowded conditions, produced a night most would not soon forget. She went down to see if she could help, and for her own peace of mind ended up spending most of the day down there away from Darcy.

Having a good amount of time to himself that day, Darcy put that time to use reflecting on what had been the greatest struggle of his personal life in deciding to preserve his marriage to Elizabeth. As he again began applying himself to further thought about what he would say to her, the formulation of any coherent, sensible, moving sentiment was proving to become his second greatest struggle.

There was also the underlying fear of what she would say. He would be going expressly against the conditions he had set forth and that she had agreed to. *And what of this Mr. Wright? Was he someone she had an understanding with back home?* The thought had gnawed at him intermittently since that night she spoke the name.

All these thoughts converged upon him. Did he even have the right to do this?

He did not think he would be able to live with himself if he did not. He would tell her tonight. The fact that the decision was made gave him a great peace. The prospect of doing it did not.

~~*

That evening, as anticipation again mounted that they would be drawing close to the American shore some time soon, most everyone gathered in the dining area for a final night together of conversation, reminiscing about the voyage, and a gathering of cards and games. Mr. and Mrs. Jennings pleaded with the Darcys to join them as a foursome at cards for this last night. Elizabeth looked at Darcy, who surprised her in every respect by saying he would be happy to.

The four settled into a spirited, and very competitive -- at least between the two men -- game of cards. Elizabeth was surprised to notice a more relaxed demeanour and openness in Darcy's behaviour. A few times he made some humorous comments, and even once he laughed without restraint. Her heart ached in believing him to be feeling a bit more relief in that he was bound to her but one more day. In her heart she realized that she would sorely miss him once they went their separate ways.

The activities in the room were lively, most everyone feeling a great sense of anticipation that the morning would bring a new life for them; a better life. An occasional strong wave that lifted the boat and sent hands scrambling to hold things down reminded them also that they had all weathered the storm together last night with little lasting damage.

When they were in the heat of their final round, Jennings leaned back in his chair, commented to Darcy on how well he was playing, and seemed to get a mischievous glimmer in his eyes.

At length he said, "Darcy, I do believe marriage agrees with you."

Darcy's eyes had been glued intently on his cards and he tensed before lifting them slowly to Jennings. He could do nothing to prevent his gaze from subsequently travelling over to Elizabeth, who was looking down at her cards with a blush that had overtaken her features.

Darcy did not respond except for a somewhat forced smile. Elizabeth made every attempt to disguise the discomfort she felt and hoped that would be the end of the conversation. It was not to be.

"But then, you have certainly found yourself a lovely wife."

Darcy saw Elizabeth's eyes slightly close as she took in a deep breath. When she opened her eyes, she still did not bring them up.

"Yes, that she is." He said it softly all the while keeping his eyes on Elizabeth. Darcy played a card, hoping to keep the game on track and the hand went around.

When it came to Jennings' turn, he began to pull up a card and then paused. "You know, Darcy, when I heard that the two of you were getting married after knowing each other for such a short amount of time, I had my doubts. I was very sceptical of whether such a marriage was prudent." He pulled out a card from his hand and laid it on the table. "But I must confess you have proven me wrong. The two of you certainly seem well suited for each other!"

That Elizabeth could barely concentrate on the game was expected, but when she saw that Darcy had played a completely worthless card and had uncharacteristically given the trick to Jennings, she realized he was just as troubled by this line of conversation as she was. Her emotions relentlessly roiled within her. She finally mustered the courage to look up at Darcy's face, which had discomfort written all across it as well. He had been rendered silent by this man, so she decided she must speak up.

"Mr. Jennings, I believe what makes a marriage successful is when the two partners completely agree on the direction they expect the marriage to go, know what each one wants out of it, and what each one is willing to give. William and I are in complete agreement about this marriage in all those aspects. Is that not correct, William?"

Darcy met the look of challenge in Elizabeth's eyes with a look of resignation in his. He had determined to enjoy Elizabeth's presence tonight and approach her later about keeping their marriage intact. With these words, she was essentially reaffirming the arrangement they made almost a month ago.

"Yes, Elizabeth is right. We do agree totally on all those things."

Jennings laughed. "Is it not amazing how Providence sometimes leads two people together, who are so right for each other, in the most unexpected way?" Darcy refrained from looking up, believing that if he looked at Elizabeth at this moment she would see in him all the depth of the feeling he had for her, laced with the despair at what he understood her to say.

Elizabeth was anxious to leave the table and any further conversation. With the ship reaching American soil sometime tonight and being in the dock by sunrise tomorrow, she did not feel it within her to maintain her composure with Jennings speaking as he was.

The game finally ended and this time Jennings took the win triumphantly. Elizabeth stood up. "If you will excuse me, I think it time to pay my respects to my friends in the room and then take my leave. Mr. and Mrs. Jennings, it has been a pleasure travelling with you and I wish you all the best."

Darcy saw the strained look on her face and stood up with her. He turned to the others, "If you will excuse me, I will accompany my wife. Good night."

"I certainly understand!" Jennings laughed. "I was a newlywed once myself," he looked at his wife who suddenly was the one who blushed, "and I remember how often we would be the first to leave a social gathering." His wink to Darcy was not missed by Elizabeth and she quickly turned and began walking from the table without waiting for Darcy.

Walking briskly to distance herself from the present conversation, Elizabeth suddenly felt Darcy's hand tighten around her arm. She walked over to Mr. and Mrs. Rawlings, expressed her gratitude for her friendship, gave the girls each a hug, and before she was even able to say the words, "Good bye," Mrs. Rawlings stood up and embraced her. The two could not hold back the tears.

"If I do not see you in the morning, Lenore, may I wish you God's blessing."

"And I hope and pray that you and Mr. Darcy will have a wonderful life together."

Elizabeth smiled nervously, Darcy bowed politely, and they made their way around the room, wishing everyone they had come to know the best in the new world.

As they turned back toward the door to finally leave, Darcy again took her arm. Naturally assuming she desired to go back to their room, he began to lead her that direction. She stopped him. "I need some fresh air, if you do not mind."

"Of course not. I could use some as well." There were a few other things Darcy believed himself to need, namely some courage, perhaps some courage-producing brandy, but fresh air would suffice.

They walked up to the deck just in time to see the sun had recently set and the endless horizon was a palette of reds, oranges, and purples that met the deep blue of the darkening sky. Without speaking, they both walked to the side of the ship that looked out to the colourfully vibrant sky.

"I am sorry if Mr. Jennings' comments made you uncomfortable back there," Darcy said to Elizabeth. "I would not have wished for you to have been put in that position."

"Deceptions are not always easy to live with, Mr. Darcy. I am as much a part of this deception as you are. It is not solely your fault and you have no need to apologize."

His hand still possessively held her arm and he closed his eyes at hearing her revert to his formal address. The two, standing side by side, turned their attention back to watch the colourful sky. Elizabeth's heart ached at the certainty that this would be the last time they looked upon a sunset together as man and wife.

As she looked out at the sunset, her thoughts suddenly went to her father when she saw him last. His parting words to her were a reminder to thank God for each day that He had given her. How odd, she thought, that my father's words were not first and foremost on my mind tonight in seeing the sunset. She was surprised that her thoughts went first to Darcy, and her father's words and parting request were almost an afterthought.

The two settled into their customary silence as their thoughts took a more similar path than each would have conjectured. As they enjoyed watching the sky give over its light to the coming night, they were suddenly caught off guard by a random, forceful wave that rocked the boat. Elizabeth was flung against Darcy's chest, and he reacted to the unexpected jolt by reaching out his good arm to steady Elizabeth while his injured arm grabbed the ship's railing. He winced as his shoulder wrenched with in pain, and Elizabeth pulled away.

"Is your shoulder still in pain?" she asked with candid concern.

Darcy reached over and rubbed his sore shoulder. "It is nothing serious. This is not the first time today I have been reminded about last night."

He may not have been able to see it written on her face, but if he listened attentively, he would have been able to hear her beating heart. At the moment, it betrayed her true feelings and seemed louder than the storm that passed through last night. He may have been referring to his injury, but when he mentioned last night, her only thought went to sleeping in his arms.

They stood in silence, facing each other in the darkness, when another wave propelled Elizabeth forward. This time the force of it was just enough for Darcy to reach out with both arms and secure Elizabeth safely against him as he was pressed against the side of the boat. After the wave passed and the ship settled, he told himself that he should release her, but he found it difficult to obey what he knew was gentlemanly and proper.

With the feel of his arms now wrapped securely around her, she suddenly did not care whether it was prudent, whether she might later regret it, nor whether there was some 'Caroline' waiting for him back home. She wound her arms around his back and pulled herself closer to him, all the while slowly lifting her gaze to him.

She knew she was in danger, but was without any facility to resist. His hands came up and took hold of the shawl that rested on her shoulders, adjusting it slightly and then pulling it -- and Elizabeth -- even closer towards him. Elizabeth felt as though time was moving exceedingly slow.

As Elizabeth was drawn up against Darcy, he slid one hand behind her neck and brought his fingers from his other hand up to her chin and lifted it up just enough to allow his lips to gently meet with hers. He was momentarily surprised that she offered no resistance. That thought, along with any other, was soon erased into oblivion as he lowered his lips to meet hers and savoured their softness against his.

As he more boldly deepened his kiss, he relished the response this woman, his wife, was displaying. Elizabeth, rendered breathless and feeling slightly askew in her equilibrium, brought her arms up to the upper part of his back, clinging to him more fervently as if for her very life.

Neither was aware how long the kiss lasted, nor were they aware of passengers that strolled past them smiling at their ardent display. Nor were they aware when the captain came up from below, quite stunned by what he saw.

Elizabeth unexpectedly sensed a change in Darcy. He tensed and purposefully brought his hands to her shoulders, drawing her away from him. She met his eyes warily; unsure of what she would see in them. In merely the light of the moon, she could make out that his eyes had narrowed, and he took in a sharp breath, letting it out slowly.

He spoke, his voice uneven and low. "Elizabeth," he paused, steeling himself for what he knew he wanted to say, but rendered incapable of any lucid thought by his fiercely beating heart. "What I have to say… I hope you understand. Elizabeth, I do not think…"

As Darcy struggled to put into words what he so greatly desired to tell her, the sound of someone standing nearby caught Elizabeth's attention and as she looked over, she saw the captain watching them. Without thinking, she pushed away from Darcy's embrace. Nervously acknowledging the captain, she expressed a rather shaky, "Good evening," to the one man who was aware of the extenuating circumstances surrounding their marriage. Feeling a great deal of mortification to have been found in such a state by him, and even greater distress at what she was sure Darcy was about to say, she promptly excused herself and left Darcy's side to return to their room.

Darcy turned to follow, but the captain gave him a friendly nod, and joined him at the side of the ship. As the two stood silently in the darkness, the captain finally spoke.

"It is amazing, is it not, Darcy, how a violent storm can rise up out of calm, idle waters so unexpectedly? I am always surprised, but never caught off guard. We can be travelling through what we think are tranquil waters, believing everything is going exactly as planned, heading in the exact direction we want, when in the blink of an eye, everything around us is jostled, tossed around, and completely shaken up. When it has passed, we are not at all where we thought we would be when we first set out."

"May I ask if you are referring to the storm we had last night or might it be something else?"

The captain did not answer, but was silent for a moment.

At last he said, "I believe there may have been another unforeseen storm that came upon this voyage." He turned and steeled his eyes at Darcy. "You know I was never in favour of this marriage between you and Miss Bennet. But I knew you well, trusted you, and I hoped that some good might come out of it."

Darcy looked at him quizzically. "Good?"

"That perhaps you would see what a treasure Miss Bennet was and would fall in love with her."

Darcy rested his elbows on the rail of the ship, looking out across the water.

"When *did* you fall in love with her, Darcy?"

Darcy closed his eyes. "I really cannot say. I was in the middle before I knew I had begun."

"But you do love her?"

"Yes, I do."

The captain smiled, knowing that Darcy could not see him. "So what do you intend to do about it?"

The captain heard Darcy's sigh. "I had planned to talk to her tonight. But with some things Elizabeth has recently said, I believe that she expects the marriage to be annulled when I return to England."

"From that kiss I witnessed, I would tend to disagree."

Darcy looked over in the direction Elizabeth had walked. "Do you really believe there is a chance she cares?"

"Darcy, all I know is that I have watched the two of you over the course of these few weeks. I believe I have not seen a couple more suited for each other, yet who are both completely oblivious to the fact."

The captain turned to Darcy and firmly planted a hand on his shoulder. "I would do some major thinking about what you need to say to her before you go back down to your room." He paused and inhaled wearily. "And Darcy, I beg you, do not do anything foolish!"

"Of course, Captain."

Willoughby walked away and Darcy turned back to look at the darkened sea. He had grown very accustomed to the sound of the waves splashing against the boat and the wind billowing in the sails. It was very comforting, but his heart still pounded from the kiss. As he contemplated going to their room and exposing the leanings of his heart to her, his heart resonated throughout his whole being.

Looking out across the sea, all he could see was blackness save the crescent moon and the stars which dotted the sky. He knew the course of the ship was determined by these stars and he wished at that moment that he could chart his own course so easily and with the confidence and the assurance that she would return his regard.

Being wrought with anxiety, he paced back and forth up on the deck for some time, compelled to rush into his room and declare his love, and yet held back by the apprehension of how she would receive it. Those little voices with whom he had argued earlier surfaced again, but this time more meekly, and he was able to rid his mind of them. He knew he could not live without her, and it was worth it to take the risk; the risk of what his family would say, what his friends would say, and most importantly, what she would say.

He lingered a while longer up on deck, rehearsing over in his mind his declaration; using every bit of concentrated effort to calm his nerves, and to recover from the effects of the kiss.

Later, when he returned to their room, he entered and found it dark. He was grateful; she would not be able to see the nervousness that relentlessly plagued him. He doubted that she was asleep, as she had only come to the room within the last half hour. He found his way to the bench in the room and sat down, but instantly stood up again, spurred to keep moving by his nerves.

He rubbed his hands together, reciting in his mind the words he wanted to say, the words that had not come to him when they were up on deck; the words he felt that as a gentleman he should have said before he ever kissed her. But even though he knew what he wanted to say, when he opened his mouth to begin his declaration of love, the words still did not come. Finally he came over and stood at the edge of her bed. With one last, concerted effort, words poured forth from his mouth, but his mind barely registered what he was saying.

"Elizabeth, in vain have I struggled. It will not do. My feelings will not be repressed. You must allow me to tell you how ardently I admire and love you." There he had said it! The rest came easier. "In declaring myself thus, I am fully aware that I will be going expressly against the agreement we made three weeks ago concerning this marriage, but it cannot be helped. Almost from the earliest moments of our acquaintance I have come to feel for you a passionate admiration and regard. I am asking, Elizabeth, for your agreement to keep our marriage intact. I am asking that you relieve my suffering and consent to remain my wife, a wife not veiled in deception and lies, but in truth and love."

Darcy was silent, waiting for Elizabeth's response. He waited patiently, but there was no answer. He began to dread that his words upset her, that she could not answer for her anger. "Elizabeth?" He nervously called out her name. Now he was anxious for another reason. "Elizabeth?" He reached out toward her bed, found that the sheet had not been put up, and when he gently reached down, discovered she was not in her bed.

He rushed out to get a light for the oil lamps and came back in, swaying a candle around the room to make an initial inspection of it. His heart felt like a lump rising in his throat as his eyes took a quick survey throughout the room, realizing with a start that not only was she not in the room, all her things had been removed!

Darcy dug his fingers through his hair as he stared at the empty room. She must have regretted the fact that he had kissed her. Perhaps he had frightened her with this bold, impulsive action, and she felt she could no longer trust him to spend this last night in the room with him. He shook his head as his breathing deepened with distress. He began to pace about the room again, trying to decide what his course of action ought to be.

He reasoned that when she returned to the room, she must have quickly packed her things. She most likely returned to steerage to spend the last night there. He closed his eyes as his fist slammed down against the wall. *Why did I overstep my bounds? What have I done? Why did I give in to my impulses before I declared my intentions?*

He could not go down to steerage now. It was too late. He would have to wait until morning. They had been told that the ship would reach the coast sometime in the early morning and remain off shore until the first light, when it would enter the harbour. He would get up early and find her. He would tell her then that he loved her and wanted to keep their marriage intact.

As he looked around the room, despairing at the thought that she was gone, his eyes lit on something on the floor off in the corner. He walked over toward it and picked it up. It was the sampler Elizabeth had been working on and had finished over the course of the voyage.

He fingered the stitches and his heart ached as he read the verse on it. "Think only of the past as its remembrance gives you pleasure." Would he be able to look upon this voyage with pleasurable memories or would they eternally plague him with pain and regret? Tomorrow morning would be crucial in answering that.

Filled with remorse and distress that spread throughout the depths of him, Darcy disconsolately walked over to the dresser and pulled out a small case, opened it, and removed a decanter of brandy. He pulled out a goblet from the same case and filled it with the golden liquid. He twirled the goblet and watched it as the liquid swirled around inside. He needed something to calm his unsteady nerves, ease his pain and anxiety, and give him a sense of boldness so that tomorrow he would be able to stand before her and declare his love.

He would speak those words again tomorrow morning before they left the ship. He took a sip and savoured the burning as it went down his throat. With each sip, his heart became a little less erratic, a little less sensitive to the pain and anxiety he was feeling, and he became a little bolder in anticipating his declaration to her when the new day had come.

After downing the contents in the goblet, he poured another glass, wishing to drown those aching and exposed feelings that continued to torment him. At length he put his head down onto the table, feeling the soothing, numbing, and emboldening effects and fell into a sound, alcohol-induced sleep.

Chapter 13

Elizabeth slowly opened her eyes and it took a few moments to grasp where she was. Her eyes were sore and most likely bloodshot from the tears she shed throughout the night. Her body ached from having slept on the floor all night. She had forgotten what it had been like that first week in steerage sleeping on the floor. But she had not gone down to steerage. She did not think she could bear unwanted questions and speculations.

Instead, she had quickly and secretively slipped into the linens room after rushing from their room. She stretched out her limbs, rubbed her eyes, and then threw off the blanket which was covering her. With much anguish and regret threatening to overwhelm her, she thought back to the events of the previous evening.

~~*

She had been quite disconcerted that the captain observed her and Darcy kissing, and reproaching herself that she had shamelessly encouraged it, abruptly left Darcy to return to their room. Hastening down the stairs, her heart refused to give up its incessant pounding. To keep her hands from shaking, she grasped them tightly together, rubbing her fingers raw. But every so often she would gently reach up and touch her lips with her fingers. She could still feel the gentle touch of his lips on hers; a kiss that she then unabashedly and foolishly encouraged to build into a fervently deep and passionate kiss.

She closed her eyes in contrition, tossing -- as did the ship last night -- between remorse for allowing the kiss, and pleasure at having experienced it. He must have seen her look of longing when she was thrown against him and looked up into his face. Her hands went up and felt the shameful blush of her face, as she wondered what had prompted her to draw her arms up and around his back and cling to him as if in immeasurable desperation.

As she entered their room, she sat down on her bed, wondering how she would face him and what she would say to him when he returned.

She dropped her head into her hands. *What must he think of me?*

She wondered whether he thought she was now expecting something from him beyond what he had stipulated in his proposal. Did he think she had been attempting to entice him to fulfil his duty as her husband on this final night solely to hold him to their vows? Did he think she was hoping to actually benefit from a marriage to a man of his means even though it began as a charade?

She violently shook her head as these thoughts and more continued to plague and torment her, causing a burden of doubt to weigh upon her.

She thought of his words last night when he pulled away. He did not finish what he was trying to say, but he did not have to. Elizabeth could see the look of discomfort written across his face. He was attempting to tell her that they should not have kissed, that he did not think it was prudent for them to continue. Although it should have been Elizabeth's duty, Darcy was the one who had to stop the kiss. Elizabeth would have allowed it indefinitely, and now she felt all the shame of having done so.

She sat still, fervently keeping an eye to the door, wondering when he would return. She absently fingered the coverlet that lay on her bed, sketching in her mind what she would say to him; wondering what she *should* say to him. She sat, rather impatiently, as her heart continued to remind her by its unremitting pounding that she still reeled from their earlier encounter. As each minute ticked away, she could not decide if she more greatly feared his prompt return or desired it.

When he did not return directly, Elizabeth began to feel a sense of disappointment as well as a rising sense of dread. She surmised that he had reservations about coming back to their room. Did he have similar regrets that he kissed her? Could it be that he thought she had behaved too recklessly? Too wantonly? Or was he now aware of those feelings and regard that she had striven so hard to conceal and was he now reluctant to face her? Did he regret the fact that he had married her, despite the conditions he had set forth?

As her thoughts and doubts gathered momentum, Elizabeth began to feel a stronger and stronger inclination to remove herself from the room before he returned. With a sudden surge of determination, she set her mind to the task of quickly packing her duffel, not taking the time to carefully fold her things as she normally would have done.

She grabbed a handful of dresses, all suddenly looking very plain and worn, and packed them away. Her personal items she put in a drawstring bag, placing that in as well. She picked up her shawl and held it tightly to her chest, then laid it beside everything else. When everything was packed, she looked toward the door again, as if to give him one more chance to return.

With her duffel filled with all of her things, and Darcy still not yet returned, she picked it up and half-carried half-dragged it to the door, glancing one more time around the room which was dimly lit by the oil lamp. She looked at her bed, then his, the table and benches, the smaller dresser and mirror. It was a small room, but it had been her salvation on this trip. His completely unexpected proposal to her had allowed her comforts she would not have known.

But she could not look upon it solely as a room that imparted her comforts this past month. There was so much more that happened to her. When did she actually begin to feel as though she was his wife? When did that foggy, confused, and selfish decision to go along with his scheme transform itself into a deep love?

She thought of him holding her as she cried, following Mrs. Trimble's death; how he sat with her upon her bed and rocked her while her tears flowed. She looked over to the corner of the room where she had helped him remove his shirt last night; then over to the floor where they had eventually fallen asleep in each other's arms. She then thought of this woman, *Caroline*, whose name he called out last night. It would be unfair to force herself between them.

No, she could not remain here. She dared not. He would see through any disguise she tried to put on and know her heart's leaning. He may have come to know it already. She did not want to put him in that awkward position. She would leave tonight so she would not have to face him again. And he would be free to follow through with the course he initially set forth.

Just before leaving, she looked back into the room. Whispering softly, she said, "Goodbye, William." She extinguished the lamp and closed the door behind her. With its closing, she felt as though a chapter in her life was closing as well, and wondered if she would ever be able to move beyond it.

She stepped out of the room, wondering how she would explain her presence in steerage. They would wonder what she was doing there. She suddenly thought of the linens room, and how, that morning she discovered it, she thought it would be pleasant enough to sleep in there. It was just down the hall, an easy enough distance to carry her duffel, and hopefully not encounter anyone.

When she came upon the room and entered it, it was dark save for a thread of light coming through the window from the light of the moon. She was grateful that no one had seen her, and she set about securing a pillow and a blanket, and spread them out on the floor. She practically collapsed upon them, grateful for the solitude that would allow her to unleash her tears that had been clamouring to flow.

She curled up and covered herself with the blanket, but knew that sleep would most likely evade her. She lay for some time with her eyes wide open, fighting back the tears, wondering if he had yet returned to the room and discovered she was gone. Would he consider looking for her? Rational reasoning pushed away any hopeful wishes she entertained and reminded her that he most likely would not. At length she let her tears fall unrestrained and buried her head into the pillow so no one would hear. She gradually fell into a fitful sleep, her dreams becoming surreal and haunting.

In the first dream, she seemed to be trapped on a ship that was sinking. Lifeboats were picking up passengers, but no one seemed to notice her. She could not move; she was alone and afraid. She could see William and knew his strong arms could easily pull her to safety. But he was looking the other way. She tried to scream, but could not. She watched in agony as he turned and walked away from her.

In another dream, she reached the shores of America and eagerly met her aunt and uncle. They greeted her with the startling news that they had arranged for her to marry someone the very next day and hurried her away to get ready. She was terribly confused and disturbed because she did not know how to tell them that she was already married. In a fragment of that dream, she was in a church dressed beautifully as a bride. standing up in the front next to a strange man. In great desperation she frantically tried to stop the wedding, but no one listened to her. As she looked toward the back of the church, she saw William standing there looking up the aisle at her; again he turned and walked away.

Her dreams finally ceased, at least that she could remember, and she fell into a more restful sleep for the remaining few hours of the night.

~~*

Now a new day was upon her, and as she saw the sunlight beginning to peer through the window, a strange noise drew her attention away from her thoughts. It was unlike any sound she had heard in the course of the voyage.

As she struggled to determine just what it was, she realized the movement of the ship was different as well. As the comprehension dawned on her, she opened her eyes widely. They were docked! They had reached land and the ship was being unloaded!

She thought it peculiar that her heart could pound so fiercely, yet at the same time feel so completely broken. How could it continue to beat like this when she was about to walk off this ship, away from the man she was married to? Away from the man she had spoken marital vows to? Away from the man she had come to love?

She sat up, knowing that the sooner she made the break, the better off she would be. Perhaps once she was in the loving presence of her aunt and uncle, she could leave this part of her life behind her. She would have to go on as if this month, this voyage, this marriage had never happened.

She quickly rose and peered out the small window, amazed at what she saw. She had not seen land for over a month, and now they had at long last arrived! She quickly readied herself for going ashore, dragging her duffel to the door and pulling it out into the hall undetected. She then found a sailor willing to assist her and carry her duffel up for her. As she followed him through the hall toward the stairs, she cast a glance in the direction of William's room. She wondered if he was already up on deck. What would she say to him if she saw him now?

When she came up on to the deck, she was not prepared for the sight. She looked out and saw land, trees, birds, people scurrying about, and carriages awaiting disembarking passengers. A flutter in her heart again reminded her just what it would mean for her to step off this ship. She slowly followed the sailor toward the gangway that would take her ashore and he pointed out where the stowed luggage was being brought out and where she could pick up a waiting carriage.

With each step toward the beckoning land, her heart grew heavier and heavier. She found herself looking back, hoping to see Darcy come off the ship in search of her. She knew he had to be up by now. It was much later in the morning than when they had normally taken their daily walks. Each time she looked back, however, she was disappointed.

With each step she took, she felt herself grow increasingly unsteady. It became more and more of an effort to walk away from the ship. Her eyes seemed glued to the last step of the ramp that would take her from the ship and on to land. She could not look beyond it. Just as she was about to place her foot down onto that first parcel of land, she paused. Was it really within her to leave like this, without any thank you; without any wishes for his health and happiness; without any goodbye?

Looking back one last time, she gave the slightest consideration to turning back. She swept her eyes back and forth over the length of the ship, as if giving him a chance to appear, willing him to appear. Faced with the bleak realization that he was purposely keeping himself sequestered in his room, she took in a deep breath and decided she must keep going.

She took that final step off the ship which brought her upon this new land, and as she did, she felt an unexpected and unexplainable pain grip her in the depths of her stomach. She wrapped her arms tightly about her, stooping down to help bear the pain.

It was a fleeting pain, but very real. As she pulled herself back up, she took some deep breaths, closed her eyes, and slowly took a few more steps onto American soil, feeling as though something had just been wrenched out of her.

She inquired of the carriages waiting, finding the one that had been dispatched to take her to the Gardiners' home. The driver quickly helped her aboard, securing her duffel, and going in search of the trunk she had stowed. She sat alone in the carriage, grateful to be hidden from inquiring eyes, but unable to keep her gaze from drifting back to the area where passengers were gathering as they walked off the ship. It became difficult to take each breath as she began to give in to the despair that he was not to come.

She prayed that the driver would delay in finding her trunk; that perhaps he would be required to wait for some other passengers he was hired to convey. He returned directly, however, stowing the trunk most efficiently.

He then addressed her. "The ride should take no more than a half an hour, miss. Just make yourself comfortable. And welcome to America!"

Elizabeth barely forced a smile in return as she turned her attention once again to the passengers coming off the ship. She scanned the crowd, knowing she would recognize his tall form easily, the way he walked, his unruly curly hair. As the driver gave the signal for the horses to begin drawing the carriage, she tensed up, her breathing becoming increasingly difficult. She knew that with this last look back, it was his last chance to appear, her last chance to ever see him again.

As she looked up, her eyes filled with tears, and she was no longer able to distinguish anyone in the crowd. The carriage slowly began to pull away and as it did, Elizabeth caught one last glance at the front of the ship where the name was inscribed - *Pemberley's Promise.*

Although it was blurred because of her tears, the name of the ship hit her with a greater realization than ever before. It was a name full of promise for those who were headed for the new world. But for her, it was a ship of broken promises. Upon this very ship she had made vows and promises, not three weeks ago, that neither she, nor the man she had married, intended to keep.

She leaned forward as the carriage pulled away, allowing her to have one final glimpse of the ship, and when she could see it no longer, she leaned back into the seat of the carriage and let her tears fall and her sobs pour forth from her, whispering a soft, "I shall never see him again."

~~*

Inside the ship, finally stirring within his room, Darcy lifted his head groggily from the table. He opened his eyes and strained to focus them as he glanced around the room struggling to form at least one coherent thought. His head throbbed with pain, and he succumbed to lowering it again onto the table in front of him.

He sat still for a moment, struggling to recall what had happened. Why was he in the state he was in? When he opened his eyes again, they fell upon Elizabeth's empty bed, and suddenly his heart lurched. He reacted with a sudden lifting of his head off the table, wincing in pain as he did so.

He fought back a wave of nausea as he struggled to stand, balancing his involuntary swaying by placing both hands firmly on the table. Only one thought came to his mind. *I must find Elizabeth before she departs!*

The will to put into action what his thoughts impelled him to do, however, was hindered by the state he was in. He glanced at the floor to find the empty decanter that must have rolled off the table sometime in the night and spilled.

Mercy! How much did I drink last night? With each faltering step he took, he fought a rising tide of dread and nausea combating with each other to bring him down into a state of despair.

He reached the door, opened it, and leaned against the doorframe, bringing his hand up to his head and taking in some deep breaths. He tried to rub out the pain that seared inside his head, but the pain would not relent. He decided he would have to take one step at a time, but he must get out. As he walked toward the stairway, he hugged the wall, using it as a source of support.

Pulling himself up the stairs to the top deck, he used his hands on the railing to the same extent that he pushed himself up with his feet. When he finally came up, he squinted in the brightness of the sun, which was too intense for his eyes and seemed to delve straight to the pain in his head. It was also a very strong indicator that it was much later in the morning than he really wanted it to be. He was fairly certain she would have risen by now and would most likely be close to leaving, if she had not already.

There were many people on the deck, scurrying about, carrying their belongings, saying goodbye to one another, and cheerfully getting off, heading in sundry different directions in search of a new life. His eyebrows pinched together as he frantically searched the crowd for Elizabeth. Throngs of people passed him but he did not even make an attempt to see if he recognized anyone. He made his way to the ship's railing and collapsed against it, closing his eyes for just a moment as he tried to regain some strength and clear his head.

He saw that carriages were already being loaded up, and noticed one was already departing. He dropped his head down, closed his eyes, and in a plea of desperation appealed to One mightier than himself. "God, please let her still be on the ship. Please let me see her before she departs!"

It hurt to open his eyes and look out among the crowd, but the pain of not seeing her was greater. With each passing moment, he became more and more convinced in the depths of him that she had already departed.

He remained where he was, more from an inner struggle not knowing what to do, than from the condition he was in. He had no idea where she had gone. She had told him that her uncle had arranged for an errand boy to watch for the ship's arrival, and this boy, in turn, would summon a carriage nearby the harbour to pick her up and take her to her uncle's designated address. He doubted that he would easily be able to find the single carriage that conveyed her away.

As despair began to take hold of him, the captain came by his side.

"Darcy you do not look well this morning."

Darcy slowly lifted his head. "You have the gift of discernment, Willoughby."

"I assume things did not go well with Mrs. Darcy last night."

Darcy turned to look at him. "She had already left when I returned to the room. I was hoping to come upon her this morning, but it appears I overslept and missed her."

"I understand she was one of the first off the ship."

Darcy winced as the words confirmed the finality of the situation. He hung his head at the captain's pronouncement.

"You are not usually one to sleep in, Darcy."

Darcy let out a frustrated sigh. "I… uh… had a little too much to drink last night."

The captain silently nodded. "Come back to my room and get yourself some strong, hot coffee. You will feel much better afterwards."

"I doubt that, Sir."

The two walked silently to the captain's room. He poured some strong coffee into a cup and gave it to Darcy.

"Drink this. You may not feel better, but you should be able to think better and decide what you must do."

Darcy gave in to the captain's suggestion and began drinking the coffee, as he gave in to his body's demands and closed his eyes. His head still pounded, but now there was a rising sense of despair as he knew he may have missed his final opportunity to tell Elizabeth how he felt; to tell her that he had come to love her.

The captain silently watched Darcy as he drank the coffee, and offered him some freshly baked bread and fresh fruit that had been brought aboard. Darcy declined.

Willoughby knew he should be up bidding his passengers farewell and making sure things were going smoothly. But at the moment he felt Darcy required some attention. He had never seen the man in this state, and now regretted having agreed to perform the wedding ceremony under the conditions Darcy set forth.

Out of the blue, Darcy said, "I do not even know how I am going to find her again."

"Darcy, you do not have to try to find her while she is here. Wait until you return to England."

Darcy looked up at him with bloodshot eyes. "We talked very little about our personal lives. I have no idea where she even lives, other than some small village in Hertfordshire."

The captain looked across the desk at his long-time acquaintance and felt moved by his sense of loss. Here was a man of great wealth, superior position in society, excellent connections, and one who most likely never had to think twice about getting what he wanted. It was amazing to consider how the one thing Darcy discovered he wanted had been completely in his grasp, only to slip away.

The captain opened a drawer and pulled out a booklet. "Let us look in here, shall we?"

Darcy looked up. "What is that?"

"The ship's manifest." He opened the large book and thumbed through a couple of pages. "We do keep a record of every passenger that boards this ship to America."

Suddenly Darcy's eyes widened, his heartbeat quickened in hope, and he reached his head over, trying to decipher the writings that were entered. Being unable to read upside down, in addition to his inability to focus clearly, Darcy walked around to the other side of the desk and began looking for the name, Elizabeth Bennet.

They scanned down the names on the first page but hers was not there. Darcy felt a sense of anxiety course through him as he looked upon the names. In no way could he call the manner in which they were written 'handwriting.' It was more like they were scribbled, and he wondered if they would recognize her name at all. He only hoped the captain would be able to decipher the entries better than he could in the state he was in.

After going through the first two pages, they were halfway down the third when the captain found her name. "Here it is! Elizabeth Bennet!" He took his finger and followed the line across the page. "Hertfordshire."

"Yes, I know that."

He followed it farther. "Hmmm." The captain and Darcy both had the identical thought. "This may be difficult to make out."

The first letter was definitely an '*L*' but what followed could only be described as a tumble of unreadable marks. The captain sighed. "Well, Darcy, it begins with an '*L*', and it looks as though there is a '*g*' or a '*p*' or maybe a '*y*' here."

Darcy rolled his eyes, eager to blame anyone for anything this morning. "Who wrote this anyway?"

"One of our clerks in the office." The captain stood up. "I'll leave you to sober up a little and try to decipher this while I go back to my duties. Drink as much coffee as you need, and please help yourself to something to eat. It is the best food we have had in weeks!"

As the door shut behind the captain, Darcy began to feel a sense of despair coming over him again. *Will I ever find her? Will I ever see Elizabeth again?*

After making a vain attempt to make sense of the writing, Darcy returned to his room. He was beginning to feel the sobering effects of the coffee, and began the emotionally arduous task of packing his things. He lifted the sampler Elizabeth had inadvertently left behind, taking prodigious care of it. He held it between his fingers, looking at it more carefully this time, and noticed how she had worked her initials, "*EB*" into the tendrils of a vine. He let out a soft "humph" as he contemplated that she had, unfortunately, used the letter "*B*" of her unmarried name.

As he emptied the drawers of clothes and placed them in his duffel, he unexpectedly came across their marriage certificate. As he looked upon it, he drew in a quick breath, having almost forgotten that he had secured it in one of the drawers.

His eyes narrowed at the sight of Elizabeth's signature, and he found himself drawing a finger over her name. Elizabeth Julianne Bennet. Hertfordshire.

He looked back up at the top, seeing his name and hers, united together in matrimony. He dropped the hand that was holding the certificate to his side. How long ago that seemed. So much had happened; none of which was what he had intended. Or had he?

He thought back to that day he asked for her hand in a marriage that, he told her, would be annulled once he returned to England. No one need ever know. But just moments before that impulsive proposal, he had discovered she was the same young lady who had captured his heart in a short carriage ride two years earlier. He wondered whether in truth he wanted to fall in love with her, wanted her to fall in love with him, and for her to be his cherished wife always. Could it be that deep down he felt this was the only way to secure her as his wife? That it was the only way to do it and not address their difference in station?

Darcy shook his head. *Then why did I struggle so with my feelings? Why did I wait so long to decide I could not live without her? Why did I have to wait so long that now I have lost her?*

Filled with remorse, Darcy attempted to finish the task of packing his things. His head was clearer now, but his heart was still reeling. *Why did I not ask her where she would be staying while here? Or where specifically she lived in England? Is there any chance I will see her again?*

These questions and more plagued him as he readied himself to leave. At length he picked up his duffel, took one last glance about the room, and departed.

Upon leaving, he took notice of the captain, and walked over to him to pay his respects. "Thank you for all you did, Captain. I know I was not the ideal passenger."

"Will you be returning with us to England in two weeks?"

"I think not. I think it best not to return on the *Pemberley*, as I would not want any of the crew to inadvertently speak to Georgiana of my marriage -- or my *pretence* of a marriage."

"One word to them, Darcy, and their lips are sealed."

Darcy shook his head. "No. I think it best that we return on another ship."

"I shall look into whether any of Stearnes' other ships are in port that will be leaving in the near future to return to England. You should have no difficulty securing passage on one if it is in port. Most people are sailing to America and not the other way around."

"Thank you."

"And Darcy..."

"Yes, Captain?"

"I shall look further into where your wife calls home. If I find out anything more, I will assuredly let you know."

Darcy extended his hand. "Thank you, and God bless, Captain."

Willoughby nodded as he watched his friend turn sullenly and disembark, wondering whether there would be anything he could do to help out his friend. He would certainly make the effort.

Chapter 14

For the greater duration of the carriage ride, Elizabeth was unmindful of the passing city of New York as it conveyed her to her aunt and uncle's boarding house. It had been their temporary home since arriving and would be the same for her for the next few months. The city swept past her in a blur as she looked out with eyes she believed to be red and swollen.

As much as she looked forward to seeing them again, the tumult of her emotions made her feel how unequal she would be to receive their affable and gracious attentions if she remained in this state. She knew not where they lived in relation to where she was, but at that moment she deemed it prudent to make every effort to put aside these heartbroken feelings and make herself presentable for her arrival.

She took in an unsteady deep breath, closed her eyes, and resolutely decided she would think no more of the man who offered himself as her husband solely to aid in her comfort and to ease his discomfort. She certainly benefited from his most unusual and unexpected proposal, but she looked back and wondered if her short term comfort had come at the expense of her long time comfort. Her body may have been restored to good health, but her heart felt as though it had been ripped in two.

Pulling out a handkerchief, she dabbed at her eyes, steeling herself to shake herself out of this and rise above it. She finally turned to look out the window at the city that was passing by her.

It was a new, sprawling city; similar to London but without the buildings that had been erected hundreds of years ago. They lived in an area called Manhattan, an island, the Gardiners had said, that extended for several miles out between the Hudson and East Rivers, that both then reached out to the Atlantic Ocean.

She straightened herself up, secured a few loose strands of hair that had escaped, and nodded, affirming that she was going to enjoy her stay here, take in as much as she could, and hopefully put the last four weeks behind her.

Elizabeth's attention was soon turned to the neighbourhood through which they were driving as the carriage began to slow down. It drew up in front of a large, two-story brownstone building that had flowers blooming in flower boxes that hung from the windows, a beautiful green lawn, and a small white picket fence bordering the front. A small sign hung from the front porch which read, 'New Amsterdam Boarding House.' Elizabeth warmed to a smile. This would be her home for the next few months and it could not be more delightful.

The carriage driver promptly opened the door for Elizabeth and offered his hand to bring her down. She felt a tinge of nervousness as she looked around her.

It was not just being in a new place, but a completely different country! She had never even travelled outside the borders of England before.

"Let me take you in and make sure your kinfolk are here, and then I'll come back for your things."

"Thank you," Elizabeth said and smiled. She had heard many things about the Americans, but this young man was most polite and helpful. She thought her first impression, through him, had been most positive.

Walking alongside Elizabeth up the long walk to the front door, he opened it and held it for Elizabeth to pass through. They walked into a large reception room and a friendly woman, who was busily dusting some large pieces of wood furniture, greeted them.

"Hello," Elizabeth returned the greeting. "I am Elizabeth Bennet, the niece of Mr. and Mrs. Gardiner. Are they by any chance here?"

"Why I believe they are! I know they have been most anxious for your arrival!" She waved for Elizabeth to follow her, and mentioned to the carriage driver, "You may bring her things upstairs to room 4."

"Yes, ma'am."

Elizabeth followed the woman, and in speaking with her, found out her name was Mrs. VanderHorn and that she and her family had come over from the Netherlands about ten years ago. Elizabeth enjoyed hearing the English spoken by this woman who had a slightly different accent.

When they came to the room, Mrs. VanderHorn knocked at the door. In just a few moments the door opened very slightly and a pair of eyes, about half the height of Elizabeth, peered out.

The door suddenly flew open and she was announced with a wail, "It is Wizzy! Wizzy is here!"

Little four -year old Caleb threw himself at Elizabeth, and as she kneeled down, she drew him into a big hug. How good it felt, and Elizabeth felt the first glimmer of joy flow through her since last night. They were soon joined by the rest of the family, the children jumping up and down, and Edmund and Madlyn Gardiner waiting patiently for their chance to greet their niece.

When the children finally finished with their greeting, her aunt and uncle together drew Elizabeth into an embrace. Mrs. Gardiner patted her lightly on the back, repeating over and over, "It is so good you have come! It is so good to have you here!"

Tears spilt from Elizabeth's eyes, but this time they were tears of joy.

Her aunt pulled away a little asking, "Was it a difficult crossing, Lizzy?"

"Oh, no," Elizabeth said through her sniffles. "It is just so good to be with family again!"

"Well, come in, dear girl." Her uncle offered. "It has been too long!"

Elizabeth walked in and savoured the modest, yet comfortable room that she just entered. Sitting down in a large, overstuffed chair, she soon had the two smaller children on her lap, and the two older ones standing at her side, anxious to hear about how things were back home, but competing with each other to tell her about the adventures they all had been having here in America.

The driver returned with her things, and her uncle showed him to the room that would be hers, which she would share with cousins Lauren and Amanda. He thanked the driver, paid him his due, and sent him on his way.

Elizabeth spent the whole day catching up on all they had been doing the past few months. With great detail and excitement her uncle told her of how his business back in London would be able to really expand with his ability to export a good deal of product to America. He had discovered while here that London would not be the most profitable place to export from, but instead he would be shipping mainly from Liverpool. And with that news, he informed them that they would probably be able to leave New York a little sooner than anticipated; travelling to Liverpool instead of London when they returned. He needed to finalize his business arrangements there before returning home.

Madlyn filled her in on all the places of interest they had visited since arriving, and let her know which ones they desired to visit with her. She told her of the wide variety of people, from every country she could imagine, the little shops that sold Dutch, or Greek, or French, or Norwegian foods and products.

The children insisted on telling her about all their new friends, the new games they had learned to play, and some of the words they learned from children who had come from other countries.

Mr. Gardiner had to leave later in the day after a most delectable fare for midday meal. Elizabeth remarked that she had never tasted anything as delicious, while her aunt assured her that it was most likely due to the bland, dried food she had been eating the past few weeks on the ship.

Elizabeth and her aunt enjoyed their time together talking alone as the children went out in the afternoon to play with the VanderHorn children. Madlyn could see that Elizabeth was tired, but began to wonder if there was something else causing her distress. There seemed to be something just beneath the surface that Elizabeth seemed not inclined to share.

"Tell me, Elizabeth. Was it terribly bad in steerage? I so wished you could have had a regular cabin."

Elizabeth took in a deep breath, knowing she could never tell her aunt the truth about what happened on the ship. Yet she truly did not want to lie.

"It was difficult at first. Above all else, when I had spent a good deal of time down there, I found myself yearning for fresh air. Fortunately I found early morning walks most desirable after being in the confines of steerage all night."

"Oh, I know how much you enjoy walking!" Her aunt exclaimed happily. "I am so pleased that it was not excessively distressful. But I want to assure you that on our return trip, we shall be in a cabin."

"I am very glad to hear that."

Elizabeth smiled, but her aunt noticed that the smile did not reach up to her niece's eyes as it normally did.

"Come, Elizabeth, you must tell me how everyone was faring when you left home."

Elizabeth looked at her aunt most appreciatively. She always knew exactly what to say at the exact moment she needed it. At the moment, Elizabeth needed to focus on something other than the voyage and she eagerly told her of all that had been happening back home.

"Mama was, to the last minute, her usual self. She was constantly swayed by the whim of the moment debating whether it was prudent for me to come or not. I believe she was more concerned that I might run off with some American than anything else." Elizabeth chuckled. "But even in that, she could not decide whether that would be a bad thing or not. Papa was visibly concerned with my leaving, wishing up to the moment that I boarded the ship that I would change my mind."

"I knew it would be difficult for them to let you come." Her aunt reached over and took her hand. "But I am so glad they did. I selfishly wanted you here so much for my own enjoyment." She looked intently at her niece. "I hope it was not asking too much."

"Oh, no, Aunt Madlyn. I am very happy to be here and I am looking forward to our time together."

Elizabeth continued to tell her about her family, and how her two youngest sisters were particularly looking forward to the militia coming to Meryton. Word had been circulating that a branch would be stationed there for at least a few months, and the two girls were beside themselves. She had no idea how their presence would affect her sisters, and confided in her aunt that she worried whether they would be able to behave fittingly around the officers.

Elizabeth enjoyed the good conversation with her aunt, but fatigue drew her to bed early that night.

She was grateful to be with her aunt and uncle and her little cousins, to have good, bountiful meals again, and to sleep in a plush, soft bed. She only wished that her heart could fare emotionally as well as she was faring physically. She hoped that in these surroundings she would recover from her heartache without delay.

~~*

Darcy solemnly departed *Pemberley's Promise* and secured for himself a carriage that was awaiting passengers seeking a ride as they disembarked the ship. He gave the driver the address of Mrs. Annesley's son and daughter-in-law, and waited while the driver secured his duffel and went in search of the trunk that had been stowed. It was a short wait and soon they were off.

Darcy's motionless figure stared blankly out the window of the carriage, his hand cupped around his chin and mouth, as if attempting to keep down what was fighting to come up. His condition, the result of his actions the night before, did little to help either his emotional or physical state.

He knew he must pull himself together. He would be seeing Georgiana shortly, and would need to put aside all these feelings of regret and remorse, and concentrate on her well being and safely returning her to England.

Darcy closed his eyes, the numbness from the effects of alcohol definitely wearing off. He was thinking more clearly now, but that meant he was also suffering again the depths of emotional pain. He looked around him at the city through which they passed; throngs of people going about their daily routine in this land they called home. As he looked out at the sprawling city passing by, he realized that the chance of encountering Elizabeth while he was here was very slim.

The ride from the dock to the Annesleys' home took close to an hour. The house was situated in a hilly area with modest homes built on narrow streets. As he watched block after block of neat little houses pass by, he suddenly realized they had stopped. His eyes looked up and down the house that bore the number he knew would belong to Mrs. Annesley's son; the house where Georgiana had lived the past few months. Suddenly he ached even more, desirous to see his sister again and return to some sort of normalcy in his life. Seeing Georgiana would be the first step.

The driver hopped down, opening the door for Darcy, and he proceeded up to the front door while his things were procured. He came upon the door and before knocking, took in a deep breath, brushed a hand through his hair, and straightened his clothes. Then he knocked.

The last he had seen Mrs. Annesley's son was at their wedding, which had been several years ago. That was also the first and last time he had ever seen his wife. So when the young Mrs. Annesley opened the door, he did not at first recollect her.

"Excuse me, but I am Fitzwilliam Darcy, looking for Georgiana."

The woman smiled and opened the door wider for him to enter. "Yes, of course! We have been expecting you, Mr. Darcy! I am Christine Annesley, Martin's wife. Please come in!"

Darcy walked in and looked around the modest room. He had not known what to expect their living conditions to be, but knew that Martin Annesley was making only a moderate living.

Christine Annesley invited him to sit down and she excused herself to call his sister. Darcy, however, remained standing as she quickly ascended the staircase.

The sound of feet purposefully hitting the floor drew his attention upwards and he waited anxiously for his first glimpse of Georgiana. She appeared at the top of the stairs, clasping her hands together, and then took the stairs down in a very brisk, yet ladylike manner.

Darcy started toward her and met her a few steps up from the bottom. Being a step above him, Georgiana was able to easily throw her arms around his neck while he brought his arms around her in a firm hug. Normally the affection this brother and sister showed for each other was fervent, but displayed in a rather swift manner. Georgiana was quite surprised, then, when he held on to her for an unusually prolonged amount of time. She attributed it to her considerable absence and the distance that had separated them.

Darcy's things had been brought in and Christine suggested she show him to his room so his things could be taken to it. He offered to stay at an inn if need be, but neither she nor his sister would hear of it. Georgiana had determined that when he arrived, she would move in with Mrs. Annesley and he could have the room she had been staying in.

They went upstairs; Darcy carrying his duffel and the driver carrying his trunk, and walked into a very small, but practical room. He placed the duffel on the floor, as did the carriage driver with his trunk, who then took his leave after Darcy took care of the fare. Darcy looked around him, feeling very much out of place, very far away from home, and exceedingly torn as to whether he wanted to leave and return to England as soon as possible, or remain and take every opportunity to find Elizabeth.

Christine Annesley observed Darcy look about him at the room and was troubled that he might consider the accommodations inferior to his impeccable taste. She offered up a soft apology. "I know, Mr. Darcy, that the room is not what you are used to…"

Darcy put up a hand, and began shaking his head. "Mrs. Annesley, please do not worry yourself about it. It will do very well."

Georgiana walked up to him and, leaning up to him, gave him a kiss. "You must want to settle in. I shall be downstairs and look forward to hearing about your voyage."

Darcy tried to smile. "And I shall enjoy hearing about your adventures here!"

Georgiana and Christine left the room and Darcy began unpacking his things. He was anxious to get most of his things and himself washed, as there had been very little opportunity to do that on board. The clothes from his trunk had not been worn, and he eagerly pulled them out. He began putting things away, and was halted when he came upon Elizabeth's sampler and his marriage certificate. His heart pulsed as he considered how he must conceal them so they would not be found. He pulled out one of the books he had brought along and, carefully folding the license, placed it inside. He took the book and placed it in one of the drawers underneath his clothes.

The sampler he was not too worried about, although he would have an awkward time explaining it being in his presence if it was found. He glanced again at the meticulous stitches, her script that so easily flowed from one letter to the next, and her initials that had so cleverly become a part of the flowers. He simply slipped it underneath the book that was now holding the marriage certificate.

With his things put away, he collapsed into a medium sized chair that was situated in a corner of the room. Anchoring his elbows on his knees, he brought his hands up; making a cradle for his forehead that came crashing down. He dug his fingers through his hair as he stared down at the floor beneath him. He needed to pull himself together, for his sake and for Georgiana's sake.

He lifted his head and one hand came down to his jaw, rubbing his chin briskly. Realistically he could not expect to see Elizabeth while he was here. If he were to see her, it would be purely accidental. With that realization, he set his mind to seek her out when she returned to England.

He began to contemplate when he would be able to do that at the earliest. Elizabeth had said her aunt and uncle were to be in America six to nine months. They had been there three months when *Pemberley's Promise* had left England. When they arrived in America a month later, four months would remain. She might return anywhere from two to five months from now. He sighed. Five months seemed like an eternity! Then there would be the month long voyage home.

It would make it easier if Willoughby met with success in finding out where she lived. If need be, however, he would visit every village and town in the county of Hertfordshire that even began with the letter "*L*" until he found her. He stood up, looked in the mirror, and straightened his coat. Somehow he would get through this. Right now he had to think of Georgiana.

~~*

The next few days with the Gardiners had proven to be a safe, healing haven for Elizabeth. She was able to rest, take wonderful walks with her aunt and the children, visit the main town, and taste some exotic foods that she found delicious. The thing that intrigued her the most was the patchwork of people from numerous countries that made up this city.

New York had originally been called New Amsterdam, and Manhattan had been settled predominantly by Dutch immigrants. She saw the effects of that everywhere, as stores and businesses had a very distinct Dutch sound to them. But interspersed among them were little sections of the town boasting names from Germany, Italy, Spain, Norway, and places Elizabeth had never heard of.

Ethnic pockets seemed to form, with people from one country settling together, their language and culture being their bond. But they all made up this great place called New York.

When Mr. Gardiner was able to spare a few days away from his business appointments, they took small excursions around the area. They enjoyed taking small barges across the Hudson and the East Rivers, and visited other parts of New York, although Manhattan seemed to be the most sprawling and growing place they visited.

Elizabeth found herself looking forward to these little excursions, as they provided her with an appreciation for the area that she would have never known.

But as much as she tried, she could not disguise or hide her pain from her aunt and uncle. They were acutely aware something was not setting right with her, and only hoped in time Elizabeth would feel comfortable enough to talk with them about it. In the meantime, Mr. and Mrs. Gardiner tried to make her feel as much at home and loved as they could.

One evening, after everyone had gone off to bed, Elizabeth felt compelled to remain up and read. She sat alone in the sitting room, trying to concentrate on a book she was reading, but was making very little progress. She knew if she were to climb into bed now, her thoughts would overwhelm her. At least with a book in hand, she could attempt to divert her thoughts from the direction they were inclined to go by putting herself in the novel that was before her.

As she sat there, she heard a noise, and turned to see little four year-old Caleb quietly walking toward her.

"Why Caleb!" exclaimed Elizabeth. "Why are you not in bed?"

"I cuddunt sweep. My eyes aw wide awake!"

Elizabeth smiled. "Caleb, all you have to do is close your eyes and you will fall asleep."

Caleb adamantly shook his head. "When I cwose my eyewids, my eyes aw stiw wide open unduhneath!"

Now Elizabeth laughed. She had to admit that sometimes she felt like that. Even though her eyes would be closed, she felt very little inclination to sleep.

"Do you want to sit here with me awhile, then?"

Caleb nodded and climbed up into her lap. When he was comfortably situated, he asked, "Wizzy, aw you unhappy?"

Elizabeth gave a start and looked down at him. "Now why would you ask that, Caleb?"

Caleb shrugged his shoulders. "I heawd Mama and Papa saying how unhappy you seem."

Elizabeth closed her eyes and drew in a very slow breath.

Caleb continued. "Aw you not happy to be with us?"

"Oh, no Caleb! I love being with you! You must believe me. I am very happy to be here with you!"

Caleb smiled, content with his older cousin's words. He sat there quietly, while Elizabeth drew her fingers back and forth through his hair, and at length she recognized the telltale sound of his deep breathing. He had fallen asleep.

She carried him back into his room and gently placed him on his bed. Her heart ached that her aunt and uncle knew she was hurting, and even now, this little boy knew as well. She determined that beginning tomorrow she would make every attempt to return to her former, lively self.

And that she did. Even though Mrs. Gardiner saw occasional glimpses of pain beneath her lively exterior, Elizabeth put every effort into enjoying her stay in America. The places they saw and the people they met were beyond Elizabeth's expectations.

~~*

Darcy and Georgiana were able to take in some of the sights in the area, despite his original intent to bring his sister back with him directly. He willingly acquiesced to Georgiana's insistence that he visit some historical and scenic places in the area, thereby delaying their return a few weeks. But it was not so much out of a desire to see anything that he put off their immediate return; it was the lingering hope that he might have a fortuitous encounter with Elizabeth.

Willoughby had done some investigating about the ships in port, and found that another of Stearne's ships, the *English Maiden*, was scheduled to depart New York for London about two weeks later than *Pemberley's Promise*. Darcy booked passage for himself and Georgiana aboard that vessel, securing again one of the finer cabins, and they made plans to leave accordingly.

The month in America passed more quickly than he would have anticipated. He had begun to feel out of place and in the way staying with the Annesleys, and although they always extended him gracious hospitality, he was ready to leave when the time came.

The elder Mrs. Annesley, although burdened with an illness that made getting around difficult, was very grateful that Mr. Darcy understood her predicament and took it upon himself to retrieve Georgiana. She would have felt terribly distressed if she thought Georgiana would have to return to England unescorted.

After a tearful goodbye on Georgiana's part, knowing that she most likely would never see her companion again, they departed the modest Annesley home. Their belongings were stowed in trunks and duffels, and they looked ahead to another month-long voyage at sea heading home.

Driving through the streets of New York on the way to the harbour the day they were to depart, they passed through a rather crowded business district. Both Darcy and his sister sat quietly in contemplation. Georgiana was suddenly startled by Darcy violently jumping from his seat, pressing his face to the windowpane. She watched in complete amazement as something seemed to unnerve him immensely. At first he violently pounded on the front of the carriage for them to stop. When the carriage continued at its moderate pace, he lowered the window, putting his head out, and called out, "Elizabeth!"

Georgiana's eyes widened as he pounded again, and then yelled out the carriage window for the driver to stop. This time the driver heard him, and as the carriage slowed, Darcy quickly opened the door and jumped out. Georgiana strained her head to see what he was about, and watched him run toward a lady who had walked past. All she could see of this woman was her bonnet as she continued down the crowded street.

When he caught up with her, she saw him speak, and then he suddenly backed away, looking rather sheepish, and returned slowly to the waiting carriage.

Georgiana was in complete shock, never having seen her brother behave in such a reckless way and wondered who this Elizabeth was, and why she caused such a reaction in him. When he returned, she sat completely bewildered, as Darcy climbed back into the carriage feeling somewhat foolish.

With her eyebrows pinched together in confusion, she asked him, "Will, who was that?"

He nervously rubbed his hands together, and avoiding her gaze only answered, "It was someone I thought I recognized. I was mistaken."

She continued to watch his countenance and could not help but consider his brooding disposition lately and this most uncharacteristic outburst. She wondered if both had something to do with someone named Elizabeth.

Chapter 15

Pemberley - Eight Weeks Later

Georgiana walked over to the window up in her room at Pemberley, looking down at her brother. He was outside with one of the stable hands preparing to mount his horse, Thunder, and take him out for a ride. He had been going out on Thunder frequently since they had returned from America almost a month ago, with the excuse that he had missed riding for the duration of the time he had been away and he wanted to take advantage of the nice weather that was still holding off the approaching days of winter.

Georgiana knew there was something troubling him still. She had hoped that their return to Pemberley and the normalcy of life would have been the impetus to bring him back to his usual self, but it had not. He still appeared distracted, discouraged, and easily disturbed.

Inside she ached, blaming herself that this was all the result of her imprudent actions with George Wickham. It had been over six months now and she had hoped her brother would have forgotten, despite the fact that *she* had not. She fretted that he was more deeply wounded by her poor judgment and Wickham's callous deception than she had ever thought possible. Whereas time should be lessening the pain, his behaviour reflected the opposite. Thoughts of great remorse threatened to overwhelm her.

Now, watching him mount the great black horse, she knew he was still troubled. She was all too aware that he did his deepest thinking whilst out riding alone in the countryside. He worked out his frustrations as he glided easily on Thunder's back galloping through the woods. He disciplined himself into control as he endured the arduous jarring of a solid trot down a lane. He pondered alternative options in decisions he was facing as Thunder ran a fast canter through the hills. He let his mind wander away from the responsibilities of being Master of Pemberley as he took the horse leisurely through a meadow.

She watched him take the reins and lead Thunder down toward the road. How she wished he would talk to her. Was his anger now compounded against her because he was forced to endure a crossing over to America and back all because of her? She closed her eyes as she dealt with a burning uncertainty whether her brother still loved her, despite his assurances that he did. His inattentive actions recently had just not reflected it.

On this particular day he was gone for several hours. Georgiana knew that being gone that long would mean he most likely journeyed out to Dovedale; possibly taking Thunder up to its peak where the view of the surrounding gentle rolling hills was unsurpassable.

She knew her brother all too well, as he was, indeed, heading out to Thorpe Cloud, a little hill at the entrance to Dovedale. Darcy prodded his horse higher along the dirt path to the rocky summit, where he knew the view out across the rolling hills and woody copses made one feel at the top of the world. He hoped looking out from the top would boost his spirits and help him rise above his melancholy.

When he had taken Thunder as far up the hill as he could go, he dismounted and tethered him to a tree. Taking the easy climb to the summit, Darcy walked out to the edge. He looked out and his eyes surveyed the beautiful diversity below him; the hills, dales, some small meandering rivers, and the peaks in the distance. He saw the numerous little villages below, many of them hidden by a small hill or because they were nestled in a valley. He turned until he spotted the dense woods that cloaked his Pemberley estate from the view from atop. As he looked down, he pondered how small everything looked, and he realized how small he really was in the whole scheme of life.

Recently he had been feeling so small and powerless that he wondered whether God really cared about him. He had not seen any indication of it lately, yet he knew he rarely gave God much consideration in his life. When they had arrived back in London, they spent several days there as he attempted to find out the information he wanted about Elizabeth. The records on this end were as cryptic as the ship's records had been, and the clerk who had written down the name of the village she lived in was no longer working in the office and had moved away. Darcy felt an anguish that everything was going against him. He had begun to realize that there were some things that even his wealth and position in society could not secure.

As he looked out from Thorpe Cloud on all the splendour that was Derbyshire, his thoughts turned to Elizabeth again and how he wished she could be enjoying this with him. Looking up to the heavens in a manner brought on by desperation, he clumsily prayed a prayer offering to God that he would be more attentive and most grateful if he was allowed the chance to see Elizabeth again.

Wondering whether his prayers were heard, and reluctant to return just yet to Pemberley, he remained up at Thorpe's Cloud reflecting on the desperate straits his life had taken on since that last day on the ship. If he was waiting for any answers to come, they eluded him. Finally, after sitting sombrely for some time, he walked back down to Thunder and began the long ride back.

As Georgiana awaited her brother's return, she passed the time practicing on the pianoforte, which always soothed her. It was something she knew she could do well, and she put all of her effort into improving herself even more. There were few things she felt confident doing, and even though she did not have the fullest confidence to perform in front of many people, she knew that her ability was such that those she did play for enjoyed it immensely.

Just as her brother would go out riding to sort out his thoughts, so she did while playing. Of course she would not tackle new or difficult pieces whilst allowing her mind to wander, but she would play those pieces that she knew so well, that her fingers literally would dance around the keys with little concentrated thought or effort.

As she played, she thought about the difference in her brother's demeanour now from when he first found out about her and Wickham. Back then, he was angry at Wickham she was certain, but he displayed a more protective, forgiving, and nurturing attitude toward her. She had not doubted that he was disappointed in her, but it was tempered by his obvious display of love. She knew that in spite of her immaturity and foolishness, he had still loved her!

But now she was uncertain. Whereas he went through the motions displaying brotherly affection towards her, she felt he was not fervent in it at all. His mind was definitely elsewhere and she did not know what to do about it.

She began to seriously wonder, as she had occasionally in the past, that perhaps it was due to the fact that he held this responsibility to be her guardian when, it all reality, he wished to be free from it. Her fingers stopped playing as she hit a wrong key, which resonated with a most discordant sound.

She had a strong belief that he should be married by now. He should have found someone to bring alongside him and with whom he could share his life. Was it because of her that he had not? Was he waiting until she had grown and had married herself to allow himself that liberty?

Georgiana now dropped her hands in her lap as she let out a soft sigh. What a nuisance he must consider her! What a burden and a restriction she must be to him! Because of her, he was deeply hurt when she almost ran off with Wickham. Because of her, he had been required to be occupied for over three months just retrieving her from America! Because of her, over the past few years he had spent considerable time trying to secure an appropriate governess or companion for her, and now, because of Mrs. Annesley's need to remain in America, he was in the process of doing that again!

She knit her eyebrows together as she rubbed her hands in regret. She could not ask for a finer brother, and she felt deep regret for what she had put him through! A single tear slowly left a trace as it fell down her cheek, and she wondered if there was any way she could make it up to him.

She heard him return and began playing again. She knew he always enjoyed hearing her play, and wondered whether he would come in and sit. It was quite a few minutes that had passed when she heard footsteps come down the hall, but instead of coming to the music room, she heard him enter his study and close the door. The single tear that had fallen was suddenly joined by a multitude of others.

Later that evening, they sat together at the table. Georgiana wanted so much to persuade him to talk, but had no idea how. Fear that she was the cause of his dismal disposition tempted her to refrain from asking what was troubling him. But love and concern for him overtook her fear, and at length, she finally drew up the strength and courage to approach him about it.

They were both quietly eating as she stole a quick glance up at him. "William, do you mind if I ask you something?"

Darcy looked up at her and smiled; a smile that was more out of effort than joy. "Of course not, Georgiana. What is it?"

She winced slightly and her jaw tightened as she deliberated what she would say. "I… I am worried about you."

Darcy, who had been bringing a fork full of food to his mouth stopped and put it back down on his plate. "Why would you be worried about me?"

Georgiana took a deep breath, feeling the need to fill her lungs. "I... um...I have just noticed lately, that ever since you...ever since you arrived in America, and even now that we are back at Pemberley, you seem... you seem unhappy."

She looked down quickly, and therefore did not see him close his eyes and drop his head as she said those words. A look of sorrow swept across his face as he looked back up at her.

"Georgiana," Darcy reached out for his sister's hand and she looked back up. "I appreciate your concern. I have just been preoccupied lately. There is nothing to concern yourself with."

Georgiana's eyes pooled with tears as she began again. "But I have never seen you like this before. I feel terrible that it was because of me you had to journey all the way to America and back, and that I put you through so much anguish."

Darcy brought his other hand over and grasped her hand in both of his. "Georgiana, I do not want to hear any more of this blaming yourself for anything! It has nothing to do with you! You must know that I love you and nothing will ever change that!"

Georgiana pulled a handkerchief from her pocket and, bringing it up to her eyes, wiped them. "But then what does it have to do with?"

Darcy leaned his head back and closed his eyes. "I cannot discuss it with you now." He lifted the napkin from his lap and brought it up to his mouth, needing a distraction, needing to formulate what he should say to Georgiana to reassure her. "It just has something to do with the voyage over to America. That is all. Please do not worry yourself, Georgiana. I shall be fine in no time."

"Are you sure it is not because of me? I would do anything to make it up to you!"

"Georgiana, believe me, it has nothing to do with you."

Georgiana felt somewhat relieved but a deeper curiosity set in. When her brother was set against talking about something, there was very little she could do to draw it out of him. She would have to be content to wait until he was willing to talk about it, or hope that the hold it had on him would soon pass.

They finished their dinner in relative silence, again, although Darcy did make more of an effort to converse with her just to assure Georgiana his gloomy temperament lately was not directed at her. He was having a very difficult time rising above the feeling that he may never see Elizabeth again, but he had never thought that Georgiana would misconstrue his behaviour and blame herself for it. He would have to be more careful.

He had returned to Pemberley to find an excessive amount of work needing his immediate attention. Part of his struggle since returning from America stemmed from having little time to think about how he would or when he would begin to search for Elizabeth. Now he realized that it had so overtaken him that he had begun to neglect Georgiana. He made a decision then and there to make every effort to show Georgiana he loved her.

~~*

Back across the great Atlantic, Elizabeth had finally been able to push aside, though not completely eliminate, the emotional pain she felt when she had first arrived. As great a help as her aunt was to her, she realized how much her aunt looked to her for the same. With her uncle gone frequently during the day, Elizabeth did her share of helping with the children and around the home, and was always eager to sit down with Mrs. Gardiner with some tea and simply talk.

It was at those times that Elizabeth truly grasped what it was about her aunt that made her so special in her eyes. She could sit down and have an intelligent, meaningful conversation with her; something she simply could not do with her own mother. The thought of sitting down and conversing with her mother about something of import would never be in her consideration. This was why she had so desired to come to America. She had looked forward to spending a good amount of time with her aunt, and she was grateful for every moment she had with her.

She spent her days savouring every new sight, every new experience, and soaking in all she could learn. It was during the day that she was able to direct her thoughts to those things around her that made up this place called New York. Whether it was strolling through the very ethnic downtown area, spending a leisurely day in a park, or making a three-day journey out to an incredibly beautiful sight such as Niagara Falls, she found herself truly enjoying her visit.

But it was in the dark, quiet moments of the night that she found difficulty reining in her thoughts, and a powerful loneliness and sadness would overwhelm her. At times she felt that William was right there in the room with her, or that she had just seen him, the image of his face so clear. At other times she felt there was a vastness of distance between them that most likely did exist because of his return to England with his sister. She found herself thinking of him as William, as though their intimacy on board *Pemberley's Promise* allowed her that right.

It was also during those dark, lonely nights, she determined one more thing. She realized that the vows she had made were solemn, and even though William might be able to easily run off and annul the marriage, she did not think that, in her heart, she could go against those vows. She knew what that meant. She would never remarry. She would be an aunt to all her sisters' children, always loving and generous, but a lonely spinster.

In God's eyes, she would uphold those vows in her heart. But it was not merely an act of sacrifice to appease God that she would never remarry. She knew that the love she had for William was ardent and strong, and she was convinced that to marry anyone else would be a futile attempt to remove him from her memory and from her heart.

~~*

Darcy sat at the table with Georgiana, having almost all his work caught up, and could now begin to see that light at the end of what had been a very dark tunnel. He believed he finally would have some free time that would afford him the opportunity to do some exploring around the county of Hertfordshire.

He interviewed several genteel ladies about the position of companion for Georgiana, and hired a Mrs. Chatham, a widowed woman from a nearby village. He had been pleased with her manners, her accomplishments, and her references. She moved into Pemberley and began working immediately with Georgiana.

As he and Georgiana were just finishing the evening meal one evening, Mrs. Reynolds came in. "Mr. Darcy, two posts have come for you. From the looks of the blots on one of the envelopes, I believe it must be from your good friend, Mr. Bingley."

Darcy let out a slight laugh as he took it. "You are very astute, Mrs. Reynolds. Nothing gets past you, now, does it?"

As she handed him both letters, she informed him, "The other is posted from Captain Willoughby."

Darcy was curious why his good friend, Bingley, would write when he abhorred writing letters, but he had an even greater interest in Willoughby's letter. Could he have found something out about Elizabeth's whereabouts?

He looked up at Mrs. Reynolds. "Thank you."

He ripped open Willoughby's letter as Georgiana watched the fixed demeanour spread across his face. They often received letters from Willoughby, or someone from the ship's line, to update Darcy of the business details of *Pemberley's Promise*. He normally took those letters back with him to his study to open. She had never seen him open a piece of business mail so determinedly, and in addition to that, opening it before a letter from a close acquaintance.

Darcy quickly opened the folded missive, and saw before him simply one name, written boldly across the page from the lower left corner to the upper right corner, **LONGBOURN**.

He smiled. The good Captain had met with success! He sat looking at the name for some time, realizing he would need to get out a map to find the location of this little village.

Quickly recollecting his other letter, he carefully opened it up and wondered at the feasibility of reading this letter through all the blots of ink. In addition, the pounding of his heart and the direction of his thoughts were not conducive to comprehending what his friend would have to say.

His eyes scanned the letter and Georgiana witnessed another very slight change in his posture. She detected a very slight sense of surprised delight.

"What does he say?" she asked, curiously.

Darcy, suddenly finding himself *very* interested in Bingley's letter, read it aloud to Georgiana.

My Good Friend Darcy,

I understand you have returned now from your voyage to America. I hope it was enjoyable and that this letter finds you well.

I have gone and done something that I would like your approval of. I found a very nice manor about a month ago, and I liked it enough to decide to let it. It is not as grand as Pemberley, but I believe it is just right for me at the present. It is in Hertfordshire and is called Netherfield. I would love to have you come take a look at it and assure me that I made the right decision. Or at least pretend you like it and give me your blessing.

It is a few miles from the little village of Meryton. Anytime you can come, I would love to see you.

My sisters send their greetings.

Sincerely, Charles Bingley

Georgiana looked at him and asked, "Are you going to go, Brother?"

He inwardly rejoiced that this was a perfect opportunity to travel to Hertfordshire. Now he would not have to come up with some excuse to journey there. He could go visit his friend, and whilst he was there, he could make some inquiries. Hopefully it would be an easy distance to Longbourn! Two answers to prayer dropped completely in his lap at the same time!

"Yes, it has been too long since I have seen Bingley, and I do want to see what kind of a place this Netherfield is. I think I shall write to him directly and let him know that I accept his invitation." Darcy turned to Georgiana. "Would you care to join me?"

Georgiana shook her head. "No, I think I shall leave you to visit your good friend and his sisters on your own. I fear that if I go along with you, Miss Bingley should look upon it as my encouraging her attentions to pairing Mr. Bingley and me together. I shall enjoy remaining at Pemberley, getting to know Mrs. Chatham in the comfort of our home here, while you endure Miss Bingley's gracious attentions."

Darcy rolled his eyes at his sister, who knew all too well how much he detested Miss Bingley's anything but gracious attentions. With his hand firmly gripped on Bingley's letter, he stood, excused himself and informed Georgiana that he would set about making plans to visit his good friend within the coming week.

Georgiana watched him walk away from the table, sensing a complete change in him. She turned back to the table and saw the lone letter from Captain Willoughby that he inadvertently left behind. Curiously, she picked it up.

"How odd," she softly exclaimed, as her eyes looked at the single word, *Longbourn,* written across the page. She quickly returned the missive to its place upon the table just as the brisk footsteps of her brother announced he was returning and, without word, he picked up the letter with the mysterious message and again, left the room.

~~*

The voyage home for Elizabeth and the Gardiners was just as could be expected. They had two cabins on the ship. Elizabeth and her aunt shared one with her daughters, and her uncle took the other with his sons. Although the ship was not as grand as *Pemberley's Promise*, at least she did not have to spend any of her time in steerage. She did, however, make herself available down there and tended those that needed it. With a good tail wind most of the way across, it took a little under a month to finally arrive at the port in Liverpool and with little distress. When Elizabeth took her first step back on English soil, she was grateful that she had finally come home.

They planned to spend a week or two in Liverpool while her uncle took care of business. While Elizabeth was anxious to get home after being gone for five months, she continued to enjoy the time spent with her aunt and uncle. She was grateful that her time with them had begun to ease her aching heart.

Not that she had told them anything. But her aunt, having the gift of discernment especially where Elizabeth was concerned, knew something was amiss. She had a gentle way of reassuring her when she did not even know the circumstances that seemed to be closing in around her. Those reassurances had been a needed, daily salve to her.

They sat around the dining room table in the inn at Liverpool after being there close to a week. Mr. Gardiner was exceptionally jovial. As they prepared to eat, he made an announcement.

"I finished my work here today, much sooner than I expected. If you like, we can prepare to leave for home tomorrow and set out the day after."

Everyone cheered, the children clapped, and Mrs. Gardiner placed her hand upon her husband's. "You mean we are really going home?"

He smiled and nodded. "We can make it to Hertfordshire in two days, and then another one day to London." He paused and then looked at Mrs. Gardiner. "Or, we can take a little detour and spend some time in Lambton."

Mrs. Gardiner clasped her two hands together. "Oh, Edmund! Do you really think we have the time to do that? You know I would love to!"

He nodded as he continued. "I do not have to be back to the warehouse in London until next Monday. That gives us a few extra days. It is not directly on our way, but only a few miles detour." He looked at Elizabeth. "Do you think you could put off getting home a few more days?"

Elizabeth looked delighted. "To see the place where Aunt Madlyn grew up? Absolutely!"

The children all cheered again. The older two children had visited Lambton with their parents quite a few years ago, and enjoyed seeing the places where their mother grew up. The two younger ones were now equally excited.

The following day they all eagerly helped each other pack up their things in preparation for another day on the road. Elizabeth enjoyed hearing her aunt's tales of growing up in this small village, and of some of her friends who still lived there. Elizabeth was sure it was a most delightful place.

"How long do you suppose it will take us to get there?" asked Elizabeth as she put the final item in her duffel and closed it up.

"For most of the day. But it shall be a most pleasant journey. The county of Derbyshire is absolutely breathtaking!"

Elizabeth suddenly froze. The mention of Derbyshire brought about a wave of unsteadiness that coursed through her. *William's country manor is somewhere in Derbyshire!*

Her eyes were cast down and she felt that she could not meet her aunt's gaze, lest she suspect something. At length, she calmed herself and looked back up.

"I am looking forward to it very much, Aunt."

"Oh, Lizzy, I was hoping you would. I would so love for you to meet a few of my acquaintances with whom I have kept in touch!"

Elizabeth took in a deep breath. "I should like to meet them as well."

~~*

The next day was spent on the road travelling. Elizabeth had to admit that her aunt was correct in her assessment of the county of Derbyshire. It had a natural, striking beauty that Elizabeth truly appreciated. She looked out at the landscape they were passing through and wonder of Darcy's proximity and familiarity with it. Along the way, as they passed a handful of estates, she silently wondered if any of them could be his.

After a good day's travels, they pulled into the delightful village of Lambton. As the carriage slowly conveyed them down the main street, Mrs. Gardiner pointed out places she knew, mentioned who once lived or worked here and there, and what was new or what had been torn down or replaced.

Soon the carriage stopped, and they looked out to see the Inn at Lambton, a charming two story brick building that was set back from the road.

As their items were unloaded, Elizabeth and Mrs. Gardiner visited in the lobby. "When I was a young girl," began Mrs. Gardiner, "I used to earn a little extra money by working afternoons in the kitchen, here."

"Really?" exclaimed Elizabeth.

"It was not much, but it helped us out. The proprietors were good friends of my family."

"What all did you do?" Elizabeth asked.

"Oh, a little bit of everything. I mainly helped prepare some of the meals, but occasionally I would be allowed to serve."

Elizabeth smiled, having discovered something she never knew about her aunt and was quite sure she would discover more while they were here.

Mr. Gardiner arranged for their rooms and they all eagerly followed Mrs. Evans, a young woman who was pleased to hear that Mrs. Gardiner had grown up in Lambton, as she directed them upstairs.

They walked in and found their accommodations pleasant and inviting. Although most of the day had been spent sitting in the carriage, Mrs. Gardiner was most eager to take a seat in one of the plush chairs in the sitting room while the children explored their surrounding.

Once they had eaten a good meal and rested from the day's journey, they set out to pay some visits to Mrs. Gardiner's friends. The first house they came to was one of her closest acquaintances, Mrs. Irene Martin, who was most pleasantly surprised by the visit.

The Martins had children just about the same age as the Gardiner children, and when invited to come in and spend the evening together, they settled in for a very enjoyable time. Mrs. Martin and Mrs. Gardiner had much reminiscing to do, and Elizabeth listened contentedly as they each shared poignant facts about their families and caught each other up on other acquaintances that one or the other still had contact with.

Mr. Gardiner and Mr. Martin retired to his study and, although barely knowing each other, they enjoyed a friendship that came strictly from the closeness of their wives. The children had such a good time, that when it was time to leave, they did not want to.

As they were leaving, Mrs. Martin had a suggestion.

"Madlyn, surely you do not plan to leave Lambton tomorrow. You must take Miss Bennet around to visit some of the sights around the country here. The children all seem to enjoy one another's company, and I would certainly not mind watching them if you want to take a little driving tour of the area. It is such a beautiful time of the year."

Mrs. Gardiner did not want to impose, but Mrs. Martin would not hear of it. "Now I insist and beg you not to protest. Bring the children by in late morning, and then the three of you can have a leisurely drive around Derbyshire." She looked directly at Elizabeth. "What would you think of that, Miss Bennet? Your aunt has some favourite spots that I know she would love to show you."

Elizabeth could think of nothing more delightful. "If it is agreeable to my aunt, I would be most happy to have her show off the place of her youth and take us to some of her favourite places!"

Mrs. Martin clasped her hands together. "Good! It is settled! Tomorrow you shall see, first hand, some of the finest things Derbyshire has to offer!"

Chapter 16

The carriage conveying everyone to the Martins' home took a little side trip the other direction before dropping the children off there. They drove past a small, two story home that sat off from the road.

"This is the house where I grew up," Mrs. Gardiner said softly. She pointed to the large tree in the back recalling that it once held a swing; the window up in the upper right was her bedroom window; and the flower garden out front was always meticulously kept supplied with flowers by her mother.

"Shall we inquire about seeing the place?" asked her husband.

Mrs. Gardiner shook her head. "No, I think I should like to remember it the way it was when I lived there. I am sure it has been changed considerably over the years."

"Are you certain, dear?"

Mrs. Gardiner nodded. "Yes, I am quite certain."

From there, as they travelled down the cobblestone street on the way to the Martins', Mrs. Gardiner pointed out little points of interest in Lambton. There was the small church she faithfully attended every Sunday, and the fine chestnut tree on the green next to the smithy that always boasted of an abundant supply of chestnuts in season. A small pond was situated off to one side of the green and a gaggle of geese made the most of this very fine day.

Once the Gardiner children had been left in the care of the Martins, Elizabeth and her uncle set out on a tour of the surrounding county with Mrs. Gardiner as their excellent guide. Elizabeth looked forward with eager anticipation to the pleasures that this day would bring forth. She greatly anticipated being out in the open, walking through meadows, and looking out onto the vast countryside at the peaks she had long heard so much about from her aunt.

The early autumn day was mild and perfect for their outing. Mr. Gardiner and Elizabeth listened with enjoyment as Mrs. Gardiner related stories about her childhood, places she had visited, her favourite prospects at little turnouts in the road, and the perfect places to go see the finest set of peaks.

As the carriage made slow progress up a hill, Mrs. Gardiner commented on how a short walk to the top would give a wonderful view of the surrounding vista. Elizabeth asked Mr. and Mrs. Gardiner if they would mind waiting whilst she took the climb up to the top. She was told they would be happy to wait.

Upon reaching the small summit, she closed her eyes as she felt the breeze on her face and began to imagine that she was back on the ship; not returning to England as she had most recently been, but making the crossing to America. Her thoughts took her back to standing on the deck next to the man who was -- *who had been* -- her husband. She believed in all likelihood he had annulled the marriage by now.

With a slight stamp of her foot she reproached herself for letting her mind dwell upon these things. What she could not shake from her mind was that somewhere in this county of Derbyshire was his country home.

She turned and looked across at the view. She could see for miles, and as she looked at the peaks in the distance, and the hills and dales below, she also saw little villages. But what caught her attention were the woods that dotted the landscape below. She did not think she had ever seen a more delightful prospect!

As she climbed down to a very relieved aunt and uncle, she commented on how lovely it all was.

"The peaks in the distance are beautiful, and the woods off in that direction seem so dense and lush! Aunt, you did not exaggerate. It is the most beautiful spot in the world."

"I am so glad you like it, Lizzy. This is Thorpe Cloud, the entrance to Dovedale and its magnificent peaks."

As they walked over to the waiting carriage, Mrs. Gardiner made a suggestion. "We could go home through those woods if you like, Lizzy. It will be a little out of the way, but there is an estate hidden in their midst that is not five miles from Lambton and is well worth the drive to see."

"That sounds lovely, Aunt."

They settled themselves in the carriage, and Elizabeth watched in admiration as they descended the hill and eventually drew into the woods. With trees on all sides and some forming a canopy across the road, Elizabeth pulled her shawl more snugly around her. She took a deep breath and savoured the various aromas the trees and foliage gave off.

"So Aunt Madlyn, tell me about this estate we shall be seeing."

"It is a grand estate, Lizzy. Although the house and furnishings itself are well worth seeing, the woods and gardens around the house are just as splendid. It has been years, though, since I have had the privilege of viewing it."

Elizabeth clasped her hands. "It sounds beautiful."

"Oh, it is indeed, Lizzy. There is none as beautiful as Pemberley!"

Elizabeth looked to her aunt sharply. "Pemberley?"

"Yes, dear."

"Why, Pemberley was the name of the ship I went across to America on. *Pemberley's Promise.*"

"That is right!" added her uncle. "Do you think there is any connection, Madlyn?"

"There is a very good chance it is owned by the same family."

Elizabeth raised her eyebrows in a quick movement as she reflected on this happenstance. "The ship was indeed very grand; I can imagine what the house must be like."

"Who owns Pemberley, dearest?" asked Mr. Gardiner of his wife.

"The home belongs to Darcy family. The elder Mr. and Mrs. Darcy died since I moved away…"

Elizabeth had her head turned to watch the scenery pass and turned sharply at the mention of the name Darcy. Her eyes widened as if she had seen a ghost.

"Lizzy, is everything all right, dear?" her aunt inquired.

"*Who* did you say owns Pemberley?" she asked hesitantly.

"The Darcys. As I was saying, the elder Mr. and Mrs. Darcy died, and now their son, Fitzwilliam, I believe his name is, and his younger sister live there." Her aunt looked at her with concern. "Lizzy, is something wrong?"

The nervousness in Elizabeth's answer raised some concern on her aunt's part. "It is nothing; save that there was a Mr. Darcy on board the ship."

"He would be in his late twenties, I believe. I have not seen him since he was a young boy, so I could not tell you what he looks like now. But it is highly probable that it was him. He would be a man of ample means."

Elizabeth began wringing her hands together in a most disconcerted state. It was imperative that she talk her aunt and uncle out of visiting the home. She was in no way prepared to encounter him, and would feel the deepest sense of awkwardness if he discovered her in his home.

Her heart pounded in her chest and as she contemplated how she could discourage this visit, her uncle exclaimed, "Look!"

Everyone's eyes turned in the direction his eyes were cast as a grand edifice was suddenly before them. Elizabeth blinked several times, not believing the sight before her. Never had she seen a more beautiful home.

Her aunt looked at her. "Is it not beautiful, Lizzy?"

"Yes," Elizabeth answered softly, marvelling at the stately manor before them, and very cognizant of the fact that she had become, unknowingly, mistress of this place just a few months back. But she was drawn out of her reverie by the pressing concern that they could not stop here!

She put her hand upon her aunt's. "Aunt, I am truly tired, and I do not think we should stop and disturb the family. I would feel awkward encountering Mr. Darcy if he should be here."

"Oh, Lizzy. I am sure he would not even remember that you were on the ship." She, in turn, patted her niece's hand in reassurance. "A man in his position surely kept to those of his own society."

Her uncle then added, "Certainly if you were in steerage, you would have had very little contact with the man." As he looked back upon the house he commented, "I am sure he had one of the finest cabins on the ship."

Trying to appear calm, she applied herself to their conversation. "Yes, he did."

Her uncle's eyebrows raised and asked, "You saw his room, Niece? How did you happen to see it?"

Wishing away the blush that spread across her face, she was grateful she did not have to lie. "I turned my ankle while taking the steps up one afternoon, and he happened across me at that moment. I could not walk on it, so he carried me to his room which happened to be nearby." She quickly added, "But he did have another woman accompany us, and it was she who tended my ankle while Mr. Darcy secured some bandages to wrap it."

"That was very considerate of him," her aunt commented.

As the carriage drew closer to Pemberley, Elizabeth felt an increasing tightening of her heart and lungs and felt compelled to insist they turn back, but without any rational thought to offer up as an excuse.

"Please, Aunt. May we please just go home?"

Her uncle looked at her. "Lizzy, if you are that uncomfortable, I could go to the door and ascertain if the gentleman is at home. If he is, I shall tell them we do not want to disturb them. If he is not, then there can be no harm in viewing the house. What say you to that?"

The carriage pulled up to the front door and slowed down. Elizabeth thought how much she would love to see inside the home, but her fear of encountering William and her curiosity to see Pemberley battled within. She finally nodded. "But only if he is not at home."

When they pulled up, Mr. Gardiner got out of the carriage and walked up to the front door. Elizabeth felt as though hours passed as she sat there in the carriage, very cognizant of the fact that if he was at home, he could just as readily walk out and see them. Her heart raced as she waited.

At length her uncle returned with a smile on his face. "He is not at home. He is visiting a friend, and we have been invited in. Shall we go?"

Elizabeth felt both a sense of relief and disappointment. She was relieved that he was not here and that they would be able to tour the house and grounds without the chance of encountering him. At the same time, her heart felt a strong regret that she would *not* have the opportunity to see him.

They were let in by a Mrs. Reynolds and she graciously welcomed them, giving them a little background about the home and the family. Elizabeth listened in astonished awe as she looked around her at the elegant furnishings that decorated this home. The thought continually asserted itself that a month ago she was legally the mistress of this place, but at the same time felt as though she was trespassing.

As they walked in, Elizabeth heard music being played on a pianoforte. It was very beautiful and she wondered if it could be William's sister.

The first room they visited was a sitting room. It boasted a large fireplace with various pictures upon the mantel. Mrs. Reynolds pointed out that they were all the late Mr. Darcy's favourites, and were exactly as he had left them, in his memory and honour.

Elizabeth at once recognized William's likeness in a small portrait, one that was probably done quite a few years ago.

Mrs. Reynolds began going through each one. "This is my master here."

Mrs. Gardiner looked at Elizabeth. "Is that a similar likeness to the man who was on the ship, Lizzy?"

Nervously, Elizabeth answered, "Yes."

"Oh, my dear, do you know my master?" asked Mrs. Reynolds.

"We sailed on the same ship to America a few months back."

"Oh, you sailed on *Pemberley's Promise*, then! How was the crossing?"

"It was long, but I do not believe there could be a more superb ship."

"And what did you think of my master? Is he not the finest, most handsome man?" Mrs. Reynolds barely allowed any time for Elizabeth to answer as she continued with her praise of him. Elizabeth was rendered mute by clashing feelings of nervous distress and heightened elation.

"He is certainly the best master, kind to all his servants. How we missed him, and I must confess worried about him and his sister as they made that voyage back."

She turned to the other pictures on the mantel, but Elizabeth could no longer concentrate. She felt pale again, and her head was dizzy with all this news. She had finally found herself able to go through a day without feeling the pain and anguish of never seeing him again, and then suddenly, unexpectedly, she is thrown into his midst, his house, and into those things that were his very life.

They followed Mrs. Reynolds to a few other rooms. They were shown the library and Elizabeth commented to Mrs. Reynolds on the extent of the books he owned.

"Do you enjoy reading, Miss?"

"When I get the chance to, I do. I have never seen a personal library as extensive as this!" She walked from shelf to shelf eyeing the books and letting her hand brush softly over the spines of many.

"Oh, my master loves to read. He loves to stimulate and broaden his mind. If you like this, I could show you his study, as well, down the hall."

As they progressed on the tour, Mrs. Reynolds continued her discourse. "I normally do not show people into this room, but since he is not here, and I feel it is very reflective of my master's person, I think we can take a little peek. I believe you will enjoy how many more books he has in here."

She opened the door to a large study. The first thing Elizabeth noticed was more shelves of books that framed the fireplace. The desk in the centre of the room was of a strong, dark wood, and a leather chair was situated behind it.

"This is Mr. Darcy's study. He spends a vast deal of time in here, doing work, reading, and relaxing." She walked over to the large fireplace on the other side of the room. "And these pictures and various objects are some of *his* favourites."

Elizabeth glanced over at the fireplace, above it to the mantel, and then to the extent of the books on the shelves. Her love of books prompted her to walk toward them, but suddenly, her eyes went back to the mantel, seeing something that markedly drew her attention. She changed her direction and walked slowly over to it, feeling a tingling sensation course through her body. There, in the midst of all the pictures of his family, was the small sampler she had inadvertently left behind in his room, framed, and situated on a little stand.

Mrs. Reynolds walked over and joined her. "Most of these are likenesses of his family; his mother, his father, and here is his sister." She noticed Elizabeth's attention to the sampler. "This is something my master brought back after his trip. He must have purchased it from the person who made it, as it was not even framed. He had me frame it and set it up here. I believe he must have liked the verse upon it."

Mrs. Gardiner looked at the words on the verse, "Think only upon the past as it gives pleasure…"

How odd, she thought. *That is one of Lizzy's favourite sayings.*

Elizabeth was stunned and rendered speechless by its presence among his favourite mementos. But she did not know if she dared allow herself to think that his having her sampler framed and set here meant anything. But it did leave her with a rather blissful feeling. She turned to leave with the others, falling a little behind, and as she passed his leather chair, she could not keep her hand from sliding over the back of it. She could almost feel his warmth on it as if he had just been seated there. Before stepping out of his study, she gave one last glance back at her sampler and, without thought she drew her hand up to her heart, pressing firmly against it as if to attempt to calm it.

They walked down the long portrait gallery where a much larger portrait of Darcy was exhibited along with family members of long ago. She was grateful that Mrs. Reynolds stopped in front of it, as the sight of an even greater than life sized portrait of him abruptly halted her. It was a striking painting, one that captured him with a very peaceful and pleasant demeanour. As she gazed upon it, she realized how living here must afford him the peace and solitude he so thoroughly enjoyed.

As the party moved on, Elizabeth lingered a moment longer, regarding his likeness, finally having to will herself to continue. They continued through the house and Mrs. Gardiner noticed Elizabeth's reflective deportment. It was unlike her niece not to embrace an experience like this wholeheartedly and with an overt enthusiasm. She wondered whether it could possibly have something to do with this Mr. Darcy and his being with her on her voyage to America.

They came back down to the front of the house and Mrs. Reynolds expressed her regret that the rest of the house could not be seen today. "The young Miss Darcy is practicing in the music room, as I am sure you can hear. She is very shy and would feel most embarrassed if she knew she had an audience."

Elizabeth spoke, "She plays beautifully, Mrs. Reynolds. I hope some day she can overcome her shyness and perform easily before others."

"She does play beautifully. You are very kind."

Mr. Gardiner expressed his gratitude for showing them the house. "It is beautiful, and we are so grateful to have had this opportunity."

"It was my pleasure. Now, feel free to explore the grounds."

"Thank you, I think we shall," he added.

They bid their farewells and walked toward a small lake that was situated down from the front of the house. Elizabeth was grateful to get away from the house, feeling as though the farther she was from it, the safer she was from any chance encounter. Even though they had been told he was away, she knew there was always the probability that he could show up at any time. Yet accompanying that was an equally strong sense that she *wished* she would encounter him!

As they walked, Mr. and Mrs. Gardiner talked about, commented on, and praised the grounds. It did not escape Mrs. Gardiner's notice that Elizabeth was unusually quiet.

As they looked out upon the lake, and Mr. Gardiner was commenting on how much pleasure it would be to be able to fish in it, a voice called out, "Excuse me."

The three turned around in unison to see a young girl coming toward them. "I hope I am not disturbing you, but I understand one of you was on the ship with my brother when he travelled to America."

Elizabeth could see that it had taken a concerted effort on her part to say this, and immediately responded, "Yes, I was on the ship. My name is Elizabeth Bennet."

Georgiana tilted her head at her name. *Elizabeth. Could this be the woman my brother thought he saw that day in New York?* she wondered. "I am Georgiana Darcy. It is a pleasure to make your acquaintance."

Elizabeth introduced her to her aunt and uncle.

Elizabeth could see that she had been well trained in her manners and posture, but that it was something she was not quite comfortable with. Or at least she felt that the young girl worried too much whether she was performing adequately in her duties.

"Do you have a moment, Miss Bennet?"

"Certainly, Miss Darcy. What can I do for you?" Elizabeth noticed immediately the resemblance between Miss Darcy and her brother in their eyes, but in all other areas they were very different. He had dark brown curly hair, brown eyes, and a solid build. She had straight blond hair, blue eyes, and was rather thin in stature, although tall for her age.

Georgiana slowly, but articulately, laid forth her purpose in seeking them out. "I heard you leave the house just now, and when I inquired of Mrs. Reynolds who had been visiting, she told me it was some travellers who wanted to see the house. Then she told me that one of you had been on the ship with my brother when he sailed to America."

"And what can I do for you, Miss Darcy?" Elizabeth made every attempt to remain calm, quite unsure what Miss Darcy would say.

"I wondered if you could tell me whether something happened on the crossing over. When my brother arrived in America, he was changed... so dark and brooding. And he would not talk about it and he still refuses to talk about it."

Elizabeth involuntarily winced as she heard her concern, but her rationale forbade her from telling Miss Darcy anything about their marriage, however much she believed that could be the reason for his concern.

"I... I do not believe I know of anything that happened."

"Was it a rough crossing?"

"Not terribly. We had a couple of storms, and then the second to the last day we had a terrible storm that rocked the ship violently. But I do not think that would have affected him so."

Georgiana looked down. "I am sorry to have disturbed you. I was just hoping..."

Elizabeth took her hand, feeling an unexplainable sense of kinship and concern for the young girl. "Miss Darcy, your brother is very fortunate to have a sister who cares so much for him. I am sure that whatever it is that seems to be disturbing him will pass in no time."

"Oh, I do hope so."

Elizabeth smiled and gently squeezed the girl's hand and let it go. "Please try not to worry about him."

"I will try not to. Please excuse me." Georgiana turned to go, but then stopped. "Are you to be in the area very long?"

Elizabeth answered for the others. "We are staying at the Inn at Lambton. My aunt lived in Lambton as a child and we are visiting some of her friends. I believe we plan to leave tomorrow."

"Hmm." Georgiana nodded. It was not in her nature to pry into people's business, but she was curious about one more thing and felt compelled to ask. "And where do you all call home?"

Mrs. Gardiner replied, "My husband and I live in London, and Elizabeth lives at Longbourn."

Georgiana's eyes widened; another piece of the puzzle falling into place. "Longbourn?" she asked. "I do not believe I know where that is."

"Oh," laughed Elizabeth. "It is a small, inconsequential village in Hertfordshire. If you were to blink while passing through it, you would miss it completely."

Georgiana suddenly had an unquenchable inquisitiveness about Miss Bennet, and a determined inclination to get to know her much better.

"Would you mind terribly if I joined you out here as you walk the grounds? I should be more than happy to answer any questions you have, and then I should be remiss if I did not invite you back in for some refreshment."

"Miss Darcy, you are most welcome to join us," Elizabeth assured her, "but we really would not want to impose on your hospitality."

"Consider it a pleasure, Miss Bennet."

Georgiana remained by Elizabeth's side and the Gardiners followed behind as they continued their walk by the lake. Georgiana demurely, but diligently, informed Mr. Gardiner about the excellent fishing that abounded in the lake, and that if he felt so inclined, he would be more than welcome to come back anytime and try his hand at it.

He was profuse in his thanks and appreciation. They walked but a bit more, and as Mrs. Gardiner began to feel wearied from the walk, they turned back to the house.

Wanting to get to know her better, Elizabeth engaged Georgiana in conversation. "Miss Darcy, I hope you do not mind my saying so, but while touring your home we heard you playing, and I must say, I have not heard anyone play as well as you do."

"Oh, Miss Bennet, but I was merely practicing. I was not playing well at all!"

Elizabeth smiled and looked directly into the young girl's eyes. "You play very well, indeed, Miss Darcy."

Georgiana self-consciously accepted her praise. Drawing from all the lessons in conversation she had from various governesses and more recently Mrs. Annesley, and a determination to discover some answers, she applied herself to Elizabeth. "Miss Bennet, did you come to know my brother at all during your voyage?"

Elizabeth stammered, feeling another unwelcome blush come to her face. "I… um… he…" Elizabeth took in a deep breath. "We did get a chance to meet. He was very kind to me. I stumbled on the stairs one day and he was right there to help me out."

Georgiana smiled. "I am glad you think him kind. Many people consider him proud and aloof. But they really have not taken the time to get to know him." Georgiana was not sure why she felt compelled to defend him, but just in case Miss Bennet had formed a different opinion of him, as so many others quite often did, she wanted her to know what he was truly like.

They came back into the house, and Georgiana offered them some refreshment. She wanted to find out more, but had not the slightest idea how to go about it without unduly prying.

Miss Darcy and Mrs. Gardiner talked of growing up around Derbyshire. Elizabeth noticed the many times the shy, young girl mentioned her brother and that it was always in a positive light.

When they had finished, and the Gardiners announced they ought to take their leave, Elizabeth felt a pang of regret. She and Miss Darcy truly enjoyed each other's company. She would have loved having her as a sister.

"I am very pleased you came outside to join us, Miss Darcy. It was indeed a pleasure meeting you," Elizabeth told the young girl.

Quietly the girl answered her, "I do hope we meet again, Miss Bennet."

"I hope we do, as well." Elizabeth took the girl's hand and gave it a squeeze, taking a long look at her face, wondering if she would ever see her again.

During the drive home, Elizabeth was extremely quiet; her insides continued in turmoil. Her aunt occasionally glanced at her, concerned that she did not look well at all. It was not so much a look of physical ailment as much as an emotional one.

The quiet atmosphere of the five-mile ride to Lambton allowed Elizabeth to dwell on all that she had come to know in just the course of an hour. There was the fact the he owned the ship and had never bothered to tell her. There were implications to that fact that threatened to overwhelm her.

Her eyes widened as she realized the captain most likely had no choice but to perform the ceremony Darcy asked him to, as he would be subject to his every command. She had seen glimpses of his concern for passengers in steerage and during the storm; could they have been solely out of concern for the reputation and the seaworthiness of *his ship*?

Then there was the grandeur of seeing his home; the praise of his housekeeper and his precious sister. She could not escape the fact that this man was highly esteemed by those who knew him well. She also became all too aware that he had more wealth than she had ever considered, and in marrying her, he had married considerably beneath himself.

Her thoughts then turned to her little sampler which she had seen in his study. She took in a deep breath as she considered that he found it, kept it, and had it framed, setting it among his favourite things. Did she dare hope that it reflected something about how he felt about her?

She kept her gaze out the window, this time not soaking in the beauty of the woods, but swimming in the deluge of emotions that were building up within her as she thought of all that occurred today.

Her breathing was distressed and she had to force herself to act as naturally as she could whilst in the presence of her aunt and uncle. She knew very well how her aunt could easily detect when something was bothering her, and she knew the marriage between her and Mr. Darcy was something she would never be able to confide.

Feigning sleepiness, Elizabeth closed her eyes and leaned her head back. Not since stepping off the ship onto the American shore had she felt such an onslaught of emotions.

Her aunt and uncle, still in awe over the beauty of Pemberley, were not at all oblivious to Elizabeth's demeanour. Since arriving in America she had been subdued, and her aunt was now quite convinced there was more to her acquaintance with Mr. Darcy than she was willing to share. But she would not press her. She would have to wait for her to come to her in her own time.

Chapter 17

Hertfordshire

It was near evening when Darcy's carriage pulled up the long drive to Netherfield Manor. Sitting inside the carriage, Darcy still could not believe his good fortune that both Netherfield and Longbourn seemed to be in close proximity to each other. With the information Willoughby acquired, now he would not be required to search all over the countryside and visit every village that started with the letter '*L*' to find Elizabeth. As soon as he could, he would find the Bennet household and discreetly ascertain whether Elizabeth had yet returned from the States.

As he sat waiting patiently for the carriage to come to a stop, his spirits were high. He knew it was only a matter of time before Elizabeth would return. If he were to establish that she was not to return for some time, he could easily return to London or Pemberley as needed and then revisit when it was closer to the time of her arrival. A sense of hopeful impatience ran through him as he contemplated his stay here. The only thing he was *not* looking forward to was enduring the company of Miss Bingley!

As Durnham opened the door of the carriage and Darcy pulled himself out, he stretched his arms up over him and then pressed them into his back with the attempt to awaken the muscles that had remained idle over the course of the day. He looked up and gave Netherfield manor an appraising glance. It was very suitable for Charles; not too opulent and not too modest. He absently nodded to himself in conviction that it had been wise for Bingley to merely let it. He knew a word of encouragement to Bingley to remain at Netherfield or a prompting to move on would be taken to heart by him. But he would not broach that subject until he saw Elizabeth, was able to declare his intentions, and subsequently ascertain her sentiments. If she refused any consideration of keeping their marriage intact, he would not wish his best friend to live in such a close proximity to her and would, with a persuasive subtlety, advise him to find another, more suitable place to live, preferably in a more distant neighbourhood. But he would give all that was within him and without to win Elizabeth's heart.

Caroline Bingley and her sister, Louisa Hurst, were sitting in the drawing room when a servant stepped in announcing Mr. Darcy. Caroline jumped up with great joy at this very pleasant, unexpected interruption.

"Mr. Darcy! What a pleasant surprise! What brings you to Netherfield?"

"I have some business in Hertfordshire. I wrote Charles; did he not tell you?"

"Charles? Tell us anything? Never!"

"I apologize." Darcy looked at both sisters. "I do hope this is not an inconvenience."

Caroline edged up alongside him and slipped her hand around Darcy's arm, unaware that he tensed up as she did so. "Oh, Mr. Darcy, on the contrary! This is not inconvenient at all! You have come at just the opportune time!"

"It appears you are going out."

"Yes. There is a trifling party that Charles has insisted we attend at some lodge in Meryton and the worst part..." She paused to look at Louisa and nodded. "The worst part is that Charles has found himself enamoured by some decidedly inferior country girl with the most abhorrent family!"

"Where is he now?"

"You know Charles, always so anxious and optimistically cheerful. We are not looking forward to this evening as much as he. Needless to say, he has gone on ahead of us. Oh, Mr. Darcy you *must* come with us tonight and put some sense into Charles' head!"

Darcy shook his head. "I am sorry, Miss Bingley, but I am exceptionally tired. I really cannot go with you tonight."

"Oh, Mr. Darcy, please reconsider. We are certain that this infatuation of his is ill founded and foolish. You shall see for yourself!"

Darcy sighed. "I am sorry, but I really do not feel as though I can go." As much as he was aware that he might be able to find something out about the Bennets, and particularly Elizabeth, at such an affair, he felt too fatigued to make the effort required at such a gathering.

Suddenly, Caroline saw things in a new, more amiable light. "Why, Mr. Darcy, how insensitive I have been, selfishly looking at my own concern for Charles and not your own comfort. Of course you are tired. But I would be remiss and the poorest hostess if I were to allow you to remain here alone tonight. I shall stay back as well." She turned to her sister. "Louisa, tell Charles that Mr. Darcy has just arrived this evening, and I have remained back to make sure all is well with him."

A look of alarm spread across Darcy's features and he protested. "No, no! Perhaps it is best that I do go and meet this young lady of whom you speak!" The thought of spending an evening alone in Miss Bingley's presence quite easily convinced him to reconsider his state of weariness.

Caroline sighed, not really sure if that was the way she wanted it after all.

With Durnham's able assistance, Darcy bathed, changed, and came downstairs in a most reasonable amount of time. When he walked into the room, a very audible sigh was heard from Caroline, who was quite sure that she would be the belle of this affair on his arm as well as on the dance floor with him. She mused that perhaps it would not be so tedious after all.

Darcy endured the wearisome ride over with Miss Bingley, who gave him her unsolicited opinion of everything she disliked about living in the country, *this* country neighbourhood in particular, and how futile her attempts had been to try and talk some sense into her brother.

When they arrived, Darcy was eager to leave the smothering confines of the carriage, but hesitant to walk into this gathering of country folk. He immediately felt his usual reaction come upon him and he tensed as he walked in and surveyed the crowd. Even though they were dressed in their finest, they paled in comparison to the Hursts, Miss Bingley, and himself. Many turned and looked as he walked in, completely at a loss to know who this gentleman was, where he had come from, and why he was with Caroline Bingley. No one could conjecture with confidence, but many suppositions about his wealth began circulating.

Sir William Lucas, at whose lodge the party was being held, greeted them at the door. As he welcomed the Hursts and Miss Bingley, he graciously accepted the introduction of the man accompanying them. Trying to bring himself up in their estimation, he began to talk of his presentation at St. James and how he would have had a second home in Town, for he was so fond of superior society, but he was quite certain that the air of London would not agree with Lady Lucas.

Caroline Bingley, eager to move away from this insipid man, nudged Darcy away, rolling her eyes at her sister indicating her disapproval of their host. They walked through the crowd of people, working their way to an area where they could stand off to the side. Darcy eagerly watched for his friend while fighting off the barrage of unflattering thoughts that assaulted him about the nature of this gathering from a habit that had become deeply ingrained over the years.

It was a typical, small country assembly, and with the hint of whispers he heard between Charles' sisters, they were not impressed either. A sigh escaped Darcy, interpreted by Caroline that he was completely appalled at the company in which he found himself. But in truth, it was in the convicting realization that he was viewing with an overcritical eye the very people Elizabeth lived among.

The three of them stood off to the side as Mr. Hurst went in search of drink and a comfortable chair. Darcy was determined to counter his critical musings with the argument that he had been able to see the beauty within Elizabeth and certainly could give her neighbours the benefit of the doubt and look upon them, as well, without prejudice. But it was becoming more and more difficult as he observed more than one incident of unpolished and unacceptable behaviour.

At length, Caroline began pointing out to Darcy some young ladies and informed him that they were "her" sisters. They were the sisters of the woman Charles apparently was quite enamoured with.

The first sister he observed was at the pianoforte. Her playing was very heavy and with little interpretation. She seemed to have neither the inclination as to the preference of the crowd nor the desire to accommodate it. He compared her playing with Georgiana's, and believed this young lady had a lot to learn about the mastery of music. Her playing was sombre as was her countenance. If she was any indication of the woman Bingley had taken a liking to, she would hardly be an accomplished woman.

Darcy's critical musings of the one sister was suddenly made quite insignificant by the outrageous behaviour of another. In a voice that was not subdued at all, she demanded that her sister play something they could dance to. But in the ultimate degradation, Caroline gleefully pointed out her mother, and he witnessed a display of behaviour so want of propriety as she quite loudly and rudely made a demand of the daughter at the piano that he felt quite repulsed. He hated to admit it, but he had to agree with Miss Bingley on her appraisal of this lady's family.

"Did I not tell you, Sir?" asked Caroline, eyeing his disgust at what he was witnessing.

"Their behaviour is distasteful, indeed!" he answered. "It is hardly reasonable to consider how Bingley would be so taken by a woman whose family is so abhorrently ill mannered."

Caroline grinned smugly as a curiosity began to rise in Darcy to see this young lady and discover for himself just what it was that Bingley saw in her.

Caroline cast furtive glances up at Darcy, quite pleased that he was witnessing what had to be an excess of impropriety in the family. At length Charles was seen to walk in from another room with the young lady on his arm.

Darcy had to admit she was pretty. She was fair with gentle features. She had a soft smile, but as he watched them make their way through the crowd, he noticed that it was more of a surface smile; one that did not appear to reach to the depths of her. He began to wonder if she was even enjoying his company. Perhaps this was an attachment that was only one-sided. If indeed she was willing to make a match solely for his fortune, she might be willing to lead him to believe she loved him. For Bingley's sake he would keep an eye on this lady.

He knew Bingley's propensity for falling in love with any young lady who was sweet and pretty, but he did not always use the wisest judgment in discerning her true character and feelings. Being a young man with a reasonable fortune, Darcy had always taken it upon himself to watch out for him in this area. But as usually happened it the past, Bingley would grow tired of the association after a short time and Darcy would not be required to use any of his persuasive powers to talk him out of it.

After speaking to a few people as they came in from another room, Bingley's eyes looked up and he saw his good friend. His eyes widened with joy and surprise.

"Darcy!" Bingley exclaimed from across the room. He turned to the young lady next to him, "Come, I see a good friend of mine is here and I must introduce you to him!"

Bingley escorted the young lady over to Darcy and shook his hand fervently. "How are you, good friend? I completely forgot you had written to say you were coming!"

"I hope it is not an inconvenience."

"Not at all! This is splendid, indeed!" Bingley turned to the lady by his side. "Darcy, may I present this fine young lady to you? Mr. Fitzwilliam Darcy, may I introduce to you Miss Jane Bennet?"

Darcy's eyes widened and his jaw dropped as he heard the name, and could scarcely proceed with the barest civilities required of him. His heart pounded erratically as he contemplated whether this could truly be Elizabeth's sister.

Finally coming to his senses, Darcy bowed politely, but felt as though all colour had drained from his face. He knew Elizabeth had sisters, but he could not remember if she ever mentioned them by name. If she had, he could not bring himself to recall a single one. A sickening feeling in the pit of his stomach began to overtake him as he struggled to reconcile the fact that Miss Bennet could indeed be Elizabeth's sister and consequently, this *was* her family!

After exchanging the briefest of civilities, Bingley and Miss Bennet left him for the dance floor. As he watched them begin to dance the set, he felt even more distressed than when he had first arrived. He watched, as a man watches a play from his seat in a theatre, as events unfolded around him, trying to come to terms with what he was witnessing. Here was his good friend Bingley, beaming ever so acutely. He could tell he was falling hard for this young lady who shared the surname of his own Elizabeth, but the young lady exhibited nothing more than a sweet contentment upon her face.

Miss Jane Bennet had three sisters here, and none of them had anything to recommend them. The two youngest seemed to have been raised in a manner devoid of discipline, and behaved almost wantonly around the officers who were attending the party and in the very sight of their obviously approving mother. The father was not to be seen.

He had no desire to dance, as he rested against the mantel for physical support as well as emotional. He kept telling himself that this certainly could *not* be Elizabeth's family. He *hoped* it was not.

His disheartened demeanour did not go unnoticed by Caroline. Looking over to her sister Louisa, she whispered, "Poor Darcy! What agonies he must be suffering. How distressed he must be in having to endure this!"

With that she rose. "Louisa, I cannot sit here and watch him suffer so. I must go to his side." She eagerly walked over to him and placed herself beside him, hoping to ease his discomfort. She was all anticipation that he might be inclined to dance at least one set with her.

When he did not acknowledge her, but seemed lost in thought, she offered in a most sympathetic voice, "I can guess the subject of your reverie."

Darcy was somewhat startled, but he replied coolly, "I should imagine not."

"You are considering how insupportable it would be to pass many evenings in this manner -- in such society; and indeed I am quite of your opinion. I have never been more annoyed! The insipidity and yet the noise; the nothingness and yet the self-importance of all these people! What would I give to hear your strictures on them!"

"Your conjecture is totally wrong. While I do agree that there are some here that are noisy and carry about them an air of perceived self-importance, I find that there are pleasures that can be found in country manners if one looks in the right places." In truth, he knew the only true pleasure he could imagine finding here would be Elizabeth.

This did not sit well with Caroline, but she remained steadfast at his side.

The evening passed ever too slowly for Darcy. With Miss Bingley now at his side making every possible hint that she would greatly appreciate being asked to dance, he was becoming more and more agitated. He was uncommunicative, remaining aloof, and solely trying to figure out how to eliminate this family as being Elizabeth's. Although he was not having any luck in that area, he began to hear bits and pieces of talk from those around him of "Bingley's wealth," "a good match for Jane," and "Mrs. Bennet will be so pleased." Even a fool would have been able to discern that the tide of sentiment among the people in this neighbourhood was that Miss Jane Bennet would benefit greatly from a marriage to a man of Bingley's means and they were beginning to expect it. The more he watched Mrs. Bennet, the more he realized she was one of those pushy, marriage-minded mothers who would do anything to secure her daughter in a marriage with a man of fortune.

He finally decided the only course of action he could take to ascertain any relation to Elizabeth would be to ask Miss Bennet to dance. But before he did that, he knew it would be only proper to ask Miss Bingley first. Reluctantly, he asked Miss Bingley, who was ever so appreciative, to join him on the dance floor.

As he struggled to maintain a polite manner as Miss Bingley's dance partner, he remained preoccupied with Bingley's partner. He had to admit he had never seen Bingley so enamoured, so cheerful. She did seem to bring out, even more, his gregarious manner. But the young lady did not seem similarly affected. His concern rose as he considered Bingley did not even notice her cool, unaffected demeanour. There was no harm in being sweet and pretty, but he had to make sure that his good friend married a woman who loved and respected him for who he was and not for what he had.

He thought of Elizabeth and how different, even from this young lady, she was. A vivid recollection of her lively and playful spirit suddenly came upon him and he could not believe how he ached for her. He looked back upon Caroline, who was methodically performing the steps of the dance with an air of distinction. She may have all the external attributes of a well-bred, fashionable woman of society, but Elizabeth was overflowing with internal qualities that put her on a higher pedestal that Caroline Bingley would ever be.

With the agony of the obligatory dance finally over, he excused himself and walked back over to Bingley.

Bingley was readily willing to allow Darcy a dance with his angel. He was eager for his friend's approval, and he had no doubt that he would get it.

As the dance began, and Darcy stood facing the sweet faced Jane Bennet, he wondered whether the two would ever begin a conversation. She was very quiet, and Darcy was at a loss to know how to begin the dialogue that might offer up the information he so desired to hear, or not to hear.

A few rounds into the number, Jane finally spoke up. "Mr. Darcy, how long have you known Mr. Bingley?"

"We have been friends for about eight years now, I think."

Jane smiled. Darcy sighed. It is now or never.

"Miss Bennet, I believe you have three sisters here. Is that correct?"

"Yes, Sir."

The two dancers separated and Darcy's heart lifted. Perhaps that is all she has! Elizabeth is not her sister!

When they came back together again, her voice faltered. "But I have one who is not here."

Darcy was brought abruptly to a halt with her words. He waited for her to continue, as he watched tears form in her eyes.

"She has been gone for several months now."

Darcy leaned his head toward her as he asked, most reluctantly, but he had to know. "Forgive me if this is none of my business, but did something happen to her?

Suddenly Jane smiled, "Oh, no, Sir. Please forgive me." She wiped a tear from her eye. "It is just that we are so close, and I miss her so."

Darcy's heart pounded and he could hear nothing else in the room save what she was saying. "She left for America to visit my aunt and uncle five months ago, although we do expect them to return any day now."

Darcy closed his eyes as he fought a wave of dizziness come over him. He had to make a mental effort to recall the next steps to the dance as he wanted nothing at this moment but solitude so he could rationally ponder this revelation.

"You expect her to return shortly?" he endeavoured to ask.

"Yes, the last we heard they were in Liverpool, about to head for home."

Darcy felt his chest tighten up and he struggled to even breathe. He looked around the room, seeing her mother and three sisters. He could not reconcile that this quiet, demure woman dancing with him, the three vulgar sisters, their mother, and Elizabeth were all from the same family.

A small voice, resonating from his past, his upbringing, and his connections spoke out, *You can still annul the marriage and she need never know you actually considered otherwise!*

They finished the dance in silence, for which Darcy was grateful. He was anxious to leave and settle his nerves and rationally think out all the implications of this!

That night in his room, Darcy tried to decide what to say to Bingley or whether to say anything at all. The fact that his friend had developed an interest in Elizabeth's sister provided a very interesting state of affairs. He pulled out the marriage certificate, which he had secured in a dresser drawer inside a book, and fingered it gently.

He looked at her signature and ran his finger lightly over it. How did she ever end up in that family of hers? Her eldest sister was sweet and kind; he could easily credit her with that. But her other sisters and her mother would be a disgrace to his family! He shook his head, determining he would think of them no longer tonight.

~~*

At breakfast the next morning, Darcy encountered a highly agitated Caroline Bingley. "Mr. Darcy, please come sit down and settle something for us." Somehow he had a feeling this had to do with Miss Bennet. The fact that her brother was not amongst them at the moment prompted him to suspect that Miss Bingley would unleash all her pent-up anger and sisterly concerns.

She waited until Darcy seated himself and helped himself to some food, sitting like a lioness ready to pounce on its unsuspecting prey. Darcy purposely avoided looking at her, as he was not looking forward to hearing what was so upsetting to her.

She cleared her throat before she began. "Mr. Darcy, you know how concerned we are for Charles' welfare, and how he sometimes acts in very foolish ways, making unwise decisions."

"Especially in the area of love," Louisa added.

"Bingley's affairs are his own concern, Miss Bingley."

"Miss Bennet is a sweet girl, Mr. Darcy. But look at her family, her connections; she has nothing to offer him. She is just not the kind of girl and her family is not the kind of family that Charles should marry into. Her mother... certainly you observed last night how ill mannered her mother is!"

Darcy closed his eyes, mentally preparing how he should respond. It was true that Charles had made some unwise decisions before in the area of love. He was not so much concerned now that Miss Bennet was wrong for him, wrong at least in the way Caroline thought she was wrong. He was more concerned that his friend would continue to shower his undivided attention upon this lady and then, as he had frequently done in the past, decide she was not the one for him and leave her. That might eventually put him in an awkward situation with Elizabeth.

"Please do something, Mr. Darcy. Say something to him. He will listen to you, I know!" She leaned in further to him. "You are staying with us for some time, are you not?"

Darcy looked at her. "As it turns out, I will most likely remain here for awhile."

A look spread across Caroline's face that seemed to erase any previous thought or concern she may have had. A wide smile appeared, and she thought, at least she hoped, it was because of *her* that he chose to remain at Netherfield. She was satisfied that the longer he remained here, the better opportunity for him to see for himself the insupportable situation Charles was putting himself into. Caroline was also determined to take full advantage of his presence in her home for her own ambitions.

She was quite astonished, then, with Mr. Darcy's next suggestion.

"Miss Bingley, I think it would be most cordial for you to invite Miss Bennet to lunch or tea with you and Mrs. Hurst."

Caroline looked at him open-mouthed. "You cannot be serious! Why should I encourage this intolerable infatuation of his?"

Darcy looked at her intently. "Because he is your brother and at the moment, Miss Jane Bennet is the object of his regard. If, indeed, he were to decide to marry her, there is nothing that you or I would be able to do about it, and it would be best if you had exhibited friendliness to her at the onset."

Caroline pinched her eyebrows together. "Mr. Darcy, you underestimate your influence over my brother. Just say the word; give him some sort of warning or discouragement, and he shall end it. I tell you he greatly respects your opinion."

Darcy let out a short breath, knowing she was most likely correct. "Still, Miss Bingley, I should extend the invitation if I were you. It will be an indication of your goodwill toward both your brother and this young lady, and it will give you an opportunity to get to know her better."

Caroline knew that if she continued to argue with him, it might spoil her chances with him. She had to let him know she respected his opinion as well.

"Mr. Darcy, now that you mention it, I think it is an exceptionally good idea to invite Miss Bennet over, do you not agree, Sister?" She looked over at Louisa with a sly smile pinned to her face.

Louisa looked at her suspiciously, with every intention of speaking to her candidly about this later when they were alone. "Certainly, Caroline."

"I shall write her directly and invite her to come to tea with us tomorrow!"

Darcy drew the napkin from his lap, dabbed it across his mouth, and then set it down. He pushed the chair back and brought himself up from the table. "If you will excuse me, ladies, I shall be out riding and seeing all that this neighbourhood has to offer."

Caroline only let out a disappointed "hmmm," as she watched him leave the room.

Louisa immediately leaned over. "Upon my word, Caroline! Why would you want to invite Miss Bennet over for tea?"

"Louisa, I am greatly surprised you have to ask. I do believe you have been married too long! I am trying my hardest to get that man to notice me while he is here, and letting him know I think highly of his opinion and totally agree with him is one way to do it!" She looked over at the now empty door. "Besides, Mr. Darcy is most likely aware that while Jane Bennet is here, we might be able to discover all sorts of disreputable information about her family that we shall be able to use against her!"

The two sisters looked at each other and snickered, while Mr. Hurst continued to deplete the plates on the table of their food.

Darcy walked out to the stable, asking the stable hand to ready his horse, Thunder, for riding. With some seemingly innocent questions, he ascertained the whereabouts of Meryton as well as Longbourn. He would do some riding to clear his head and while he was at it, see if he could find the place Elizabeth called home.

Thunder was saddled and eager for an outing around the countryside. Darcy understood Longbourn was three miles southeast of Netherfield, so he set out in that direction. Thunder was more than anxious to expend some of his energy and Darcy allowed him the freedom to gallop through some open fields. As the horse was given free rein, Darcy tried to rein in his thoughts.

He could not get Elizabeth's family out of his mind. Their behaviour was rude, unrefined, and completely inappropriate. So unlike Elizabeth! Her eldest sister seemed to be of the same upbringing as Elizabeth and he wondered how there could be such a disparity between them and their sisters. *Her mother.* He sighed as the uninvited thought challenged him as to how he would ever be able to introduce her family to his own family… to his friends.

Pushing that thought brusquely aside, he came upon a road and slowed down, following it at a brisk canter. Not much farther along he came across a modest two story home that was set back a ways from the road. A wooden sign marker off to the side was inscribed with the name *Longbourn.*

His heart skipped a beat as he looked across at the home, wondering if it indeed was Elizabeth's. *Is this where she grew up? Where she took her walks? Where she formed all her hopes and dreams?*

A noise drew his attention and he saw two young girls come flying out of the house; one carrying a bonnet. He did not want to draw attention to himself, so he gave his horse a slight kick and walked it slowly down the road, occasionally turning to see if he could recognize the girls as the Bennet daughters from the night before.

They were not paying any attention to the road out front, and so were quite careless in their behaviour. One desperately screamed, "Give me back my bonnet!" while the other, who was being chased, waved the bonnet in the air, taunting the other with, "Just try and get it back! It looks much better on me!"

Darcy's stomach churned into a knot as he realized he *was* watching the Bennet girls he had seen last night and that this must be the Bennet household. He hated to admit it, but this little display between the two sisters was another example to reinforce Caroline's partially correct views of the unsuitability of the Bennet family.

Darcy rode on a little further up the road, enjoying the crisp autumn day, but knew he ought to return shortly. He felt a chill in the air and if he suspected correctly, it felt like rain. As he turned back, he imagined Elizabeth taking walks along this very road. He pondered whether her love for walking was drawn from a desire to escape the oddities that were displayed in her house by her family or to merely enjoy the beauty of the hills and dales around her home.

Noticing the skies above and the clouds which began to collect and hover, he decided to head directly back to Netherfield. He could feel a north wind sending its tendrils of shivering cold penetrate him. He brought Thunder to a gallop again, making it back to Netherfield easily.

When he returned, Charles had joined his sisters. Darcy walked in and handed his coat and riding stick off to one of the servants.

"Did you have a nice ride, Mr. Darcy?" asked Caroline.

"Splendid, thank you."

"I was just telling Charles that I will be sending a note to Miss Bennet inviting her to join us for tea tomorrow while you men are out."

Charles perked up. "I think that is a marvellous idea, Caroline. I am glad you thought of it."

Caroline smiled a contented smile, but then quickly added, "Oh, but Charles, I must give the credit to Mr. Darcy. He is the one who came up with that most agreeable suggestion."

"I believe Caroline and Louisa will have a wonderful time with Miss Bennet tomorrow!" Charles exuberantly declared. Charles looked over at his friend. "Do you like her, Darcy? Do you not think that she is an angel?"

"She seems very sweet, Bingley. But why are we to be out? Where are we going?"

"We, good friend, have been invited to dine with the officers."

"We have?"

"Yes. The timing could not be more perfect. Miss Bennet can spend the time getting to know my sisters while we enjoy the company of the officers."

Darcy pursed his lips upon hearing this, feeling disposed to think that what he had intended in his suggestion may now not be feasible. He had hoped to be able to glean a little more information about Elizabeth from her sister. Now he could only hope that the visit with the officers would end early enough for them to return to Netherfield before Miss Bennet left, although he doubted it would. He certainly could not expect to hear any favourable information about her from Charles' sisters.

He resigned himself to the fact that he would be dining with the officers the next day and viewed Miss Bennet's coming to Netherfield whilst he was away in disappointment. He could only hope it would not be too long for another opportunity to present itself to find out more about the woman for whom he impatiently longed.

Chapter 18

The following morning, Bingley boasted of his joyful anticipation of spending a day with the officers, Darcy, and Hurst. He also verbosely delighted in the fact that Miss Bennet would be spending the day getting to know his sisters. He had no doubt that the ladies would get along just splendidly.

After the men had departed, Caroline and Louisa settled in to wait for Jane. As they sat, rather impatiently in the sitting room, they noticed the spattering of rain drops against the window.

"Oh dear," muttered Caroline. "It is beginning to rain." She stood up and walked over to the window and looked out. "How unfortunate that the men are out in it!" She turned to Louisa. "I hope they do not remain long with the officers. I shall have the dullest day if they stay out too long."

With a surprised look on her face, Louisa looked up at her sister. "How can you say that, Caroline? We shall have Miss Bennet here to keep us entertained. Did you forget?"

"Of course not! I simply cannot imagine we shall have very lively or profitable conversation with her. I must admit, I am not looking forward to it in the least bit, but we shall do our duty by her for our brother's sake."

Louisa laughed softly. "And Mr. Darcy's sake?"

Caroline looked at her innocently, with raised eyebrows. "Hmmm?"

"To please Mr. Darcy, as it was *his* suggestion to invite Miss Bennet to dine with us."

"Oh, yes, that." She tilted her head with a sly smile. "All I need is a little time, Louisa. As he does not seem inclined to leave Netherfield any time soon, I am more than confident that things will turn out as I have always believed they would."

As she looked back out the window, she felt more confident that it was solely because of *her* that he had remained on and she let out a reflective sigh. The rain began to pound more fiercely against the window, and Caroline noticed the wind pick up. She tightly wrapped her arms about her as a shiver ran through her. At that moment she saw a lone figure approaching on a horse.

"Now *who* could that be!" asked Caroline in disbelief. "Who would be out on a horse on a day like this?"

Believing it to be someone delivering a post or on some sort of business, she went back and sat next to her sister as they patiently awaited Jane's arrival. It was with a sense of surprise then, that after just a few moments, a servant came to the door followed by a very wet, embarrassed, and uncomfortable Jane Bennet, as she was announced and escorted into the room.

"Why, Miss Bennet! You are all wet! Did you not come in a carriage?"

"Uh, no… Miss Bingley. Unfortunately the horses were engaged elsewhere."

"So you travelled all the way over here on horseback… in the rain?"

Jane meekly nodded. "But it had not begun to rain when I started out."

Her cloak had covered her for the most part, but because of the downpour, it had soaked through and she was quite cold and wet, looking somewhat like a lost puppy caught out in the rain.

Louisa walked over to her. "Dear girl, let us see if we can get you into some dry clothes."

"I would not want to put you through any trouble."

"No trouble at all," Miss Bingley offered, as she looked archly at her sister, wondering if any of the Bennets had any common sense.

They escorted Jane upstairs and secured a change of clothes for her. They left her with a maid who helped her to dry off and change. While she was away doing this, the two ladies returned downstairs and commented to each other on her arrival.

"Can you believe it, Louisa? I have never in my life seen anything so appalling!"

"To be sure. Riding on a horse on a day like today, as if she was a mere simpleton."

"But I cannot say that I am surprised, having seen her family exhibit other thoughtless and foolish displays."

"I must agree with you, Caroline."

"We must convince Charles that she is not suitable at all. We must find out all we can about her family and about her connections while she is with us today. There are some rumours I have heard about her and her family that I should like to confirm."

"That should not be terribly difficult, Caroline. We shall simply show her how interested we are in her whole family." The two women snickered. "Shhhh, here she comes."

Jane returned and joined the ladies, feeling very much more comfortable and grateful for the dry clothes, while at the same time suffering the initial effects of being out in the cold and rain. She felt slightly dizzy and the symptoms of a cold began to course through her.

The three ladies proceeded to the dining room where a delicious hot meal awaited them. As much as Jane enjoyed it and looked forward to getting to know Charles' sisters better, and as much as she applied herself to the two ladies' questions and conversation, she found herself feeling increasingly poor.

"I understand, Miss Bennet," Caroline Bingley addressed Jane in her most polite voice, "that Longbourn has been entailed away from the female line. Did I understand that correctly?"

Jane brought her hand up to her head as she struggled to assuage her dizziness. "That is correct, Miss Bingley."

"And you have no brothers?"

Jane took in a deep breath and brought both her hands up, laying them flat on the table as she felt herself begin to sway. "No, only four sisters."

"So this would mean, most unfortunately, that all of you will at some point be turned out of Longbourn. What a pity. That means that one of you must…" Suddenly Caroline stopped. "Excuse me, Miss Bennet, but you said you have four sisters. I believe we have only met three. Is there *another*?" She turned and looked suspiciously at her sister, pinching her eyebrows heavy upon her eyes.

"Yes, my next eldest sister has been away for the past several months."

"Miss Bennet, you say she has been *away*?" Caroline then raised her eyebrows at Louisa with a look of disdainful interest. "And just *where* has she been and *why* has she been away?

Jane fought off another wave of dizziness as she answered Miss Bingley's questions. "She left to go to America several months ago to visit my aunt and uncle who were there on business."

"Business?"

"Yes. He is in trade in London and was making arrangements to do some exporting to America. As they were to be there for several months, my sister was able to join them."

"He is in trade, is he? And your sister went off to America, just like that?"

Jane nodded, feeling a stronger and stronger sense of light-headedness.

"And your aunt and uncle… just where in London do they live?"

"They live at Gracechurch Street." When this last question was answered, Jane could no longer fight off the overpowering dizziness and she suddenly slumped down in the chair.

The two women called immediately for help, and Jane was carried upstairs to a guestroom and secured in bed. It was determined that she had a cold and fever, and it was best not to move her. When Jane felt able, although still somewhat disconcerted, she scribbled a quick missive home letting them know she had taken ill, was in good hands, and would remain at Netherfield until she felt improved enough to return home.

When she had fallen asleep, Caroline and Louisa returned to the sitting room to await the return of the men. "Now who would have imagined this?" she asked. "I would not put it past her, or her mother, to have designed her coming on horseback with the sole intent of catching cold and having to remain here!"

"Now, Caroline. It may not be such a bad thing that she has to stay on here. Look at it this way. This is a perfect opportunity for you to show Mr. Darcy just how kind and caring you can be. Let him see how well you care for Miss Bennet and tend to her needs. He will not be able to overlook how hospitable you are, and that is just the type of person he needs to be Mistress of Pemberley!"

Caroline turned to her and smiled. "Oh, Louisa, how right you are! I must say that is brilliant! Oh, to think of being Mistress of Pemberley! I can barely breathe just thinking about it!"

The ladies took turns up in Jane's room for the remainder of the afternoon waiting on her and applying themselves to her care. The fever seemed to quickly grip her, and it was soon determined that they should send for Mr. Jones, the doctor.

~~*

The time the men spent visiting with the officers was entirely too short for Bingley, too stuffy for Hurst, and too disconcerting for Darcy. His heart was not in it, and while he normally enjoyed a good discussion with an officer, he could not concentrate. He sat and pretended to listen, all the while anxious to get back to Netherfield with the hope that he could have some opportunity to speak with Miss Bennet.

The afternoon did not end soon enough for him. It began to rain and a cold seemed to take delight in assaulting everything in its path.

When they finally arrived back at Netherfield, they were welcomed at the door by Miss Bingley, as though the woman herself had been keeping an eye open for their return. She excitedly began to tell them how Miss Bennet had unexpectedly taken ill, was going to remain at Netherfield until she was feeling improved, and that she had been doing all she could to make her more comfortable. While her words spoke of her concern for Jane, her focused attention on Darcy reflected solely her true interest in him and her desire for his good opinion of her.

Bingley quickly removed his coat and shook off the water, handing it to a servant, a look of alarm having swept across his features. "Miss Bennet has taken ill? Say it is not true!"

"She certainly is most unwell. I believed her to be too ill to travel back home and have put her up in a guestroom. I have dispatched a note from her to her family at Longbourn."

"Good, good." Bingley rubbed his hands nervously together. "She is being well taken care of, then?"

Caroline sweetly smiled. "We are doing all we can for her. Louisa is up with her now if you would like to see how she is faring. She is upstairs, the second room on the left."

Bingley briskly ran off, taking the stairs two at a time toward the room where his poor, sweet Jane was ailing and now resting.

Hurst's greatcoat was removed and he sauntered into the dining room in search of something to eat.

Caroline looked back at Darcy, congratulating herself on getting them some time by themselves.

Darcy handed off his coat and was removing his gloves as he began to walk toward the stairs himself.

Not wishing him to leave so soon, Miss Bingley asked, "Did you enjoy your time with the officers, Sir?"

"They are an excellent group of men," Darcy replied. Her question did bring him to a halt. He turned and asked her, "Just how seriously ill is Miss Bennet?"

"I believe it to be only a trifling cold and fever. We have called for Mr. Jones and he will be here in the morning. I have done all I can for her to make her comfortable. She has been most grateful for my attentiveness toward her."

"I am glad to hear that."

Caroline smiled triumphantly. But she found it beyond her patience to continue talking to him about Miss Bennet and turned the conversation to her concern for him. "Mr. Darcy, you must take care not to come down with a cold, as well, having been out in the rain as you were."

Darcy looked at her and smiled. "You are so right, Miss Bingley, and I appreciate your concern. If you will excuse me, then, I shall retire to my room to change."

Bowing, he turned and walked away, leaving Caroline appreciating his compliment, but vexed at his leaving her side.

Darcy went upstairs, passing the room where Jane was resting and heard Bingley giving her words of encouragement as well as regret that she had taken ill. His room was a little further down and on the right. As he entered it, another tremor of hope filled him that with Miss Bennet being in their midst for awhile, he might just have the opportunity to talk with her and perhaps something about Elizabeth might come up in the conversation.

How he would love to hear anything about her. What she was like growing up. What are her likes and dislikes? What dreams and aspirations does she have?

He chuckled at himself. He was being ridiculous. He could not, in all propriety, carry on a conversation with Miss Bennet solely about her sister without good reason and without raising suspicion. He smiled as he considered that even one little morsel of information about Elizabeth would satisfy him until he was able to see her again.

~~*

That night, after Jane had been settled into bed for the evening and had fallen asleep, the ladies eagerly made their way to the drawing room to spend their time in a much more agreeable fashion. Darcy walked in a little after them and found them with Mr. Hurst and Bingley at cards.

"Would you care to join us, Sir?" asked Miss Bingley.

"No thank you. I should prefer to read.

Miss Bingley looked impatient, wishing for some bright light of inspiration to engage him. "And what are you reading? Is it something *I* would enjoy?"

"I think not."

"Is it from Charles' library or did you bring it from Pemberley's library?

Darcy closed his eyes to steel his patience. "I brought it from mine."

"Pemberley has such a grand library! Would you not agree, Charles?"

"I believe it does," Bingley concurred with her.

"And did you find Pemberley well taken care of when you returned from America?"

"Yes I did, thank you."

"You have such excellent help. It is so good to be able to entrust the care of something as elegant as Pemberley into such capable hands."

"It practically runs itself."

"I would have to beg to disagree, Sir. Your influence, your decisions, have made it what it is today."

"Hmmm."

At this point Darcy was absorbed into his book and Bingley was calculating how to play out his hand. Caroline was left with no other alternative but to turn her attention back to the card game.

When two games of cards had been completed, Bingley was the first to excuse himself for the night. He stood up from the table and stretched. "As we will be having some sport in the morning, I believe I shall turn in now if you do not mind."

"Good night, Charles." Darcy looked up from his book.

Caroline reached out her hand and said in a voice loud enough for Darcy to hear, "Do not worry about Miss Bennet, Charles. I shall look in on her before I retire and make sure she is comfortable and has everything she needs."

"Thank you, Caroline."

Bingley left the room. The card game had come to an end with his departure, and if Darcy had not been so engrossed in his book, he may have planned a little more shrewdly and taken his leave when Bingley did. But as he did not, he unwittingly found himself again in the midst of a conversation about the unsuitability of Miss Bennet, or at least the unsuitability of the Bennet family.

"Mr. Darcy, you would have been appalled at the state in which Miss Bennet arrived today. She was completely soaked from the rain." She leaned toward Darcy as she said, "She had actually ridden on horseback all the way here! Can you imagine?"

"Perhaps that was her only source of transportation."

"But certainly you see how imprudent it was! And now look what it has resulted in! How long will she have to remain here?" Caroline looked to Mrs. Hurst who gave her an affirming nod. "I find this whole situation with Charles and this Bennet family highly disconcerting!"

"Charles is an adult. I am sure he is perfectly capable of deciding what is best."

She remained quiet but for only a few moments. "Mr. Darcy, you would not believe what else we discovered today about her family!"

Darcy continued to read, inwardly cringed, but politely asked, "And what was that?"

"Well, first of all, their home has been entailed away from the female line and that makes it absolutely imperative that one of the daughters marry well. You must see that her interest in Charles is solely to ensure that her sisters and mother will one day be well taken care of!"

"I do not see that at all."

"Oh, come, Mr. Darcy. Have you ever seen in Miss Bennet any evidence of strong attachment?"

Darcy closed his book. "I have not had the opportunity to see them together enough to make that sort of judgment. There is nothing in her demeanour to suggest she has only mercenary motives for marrying." Although he had been of the same opinion before he knew who she was, he would never admit that to Miss Bingley. He felt until he knew more, he would give her the benefit of the doubt.

"But there is something else we discovered just today."

"And what is that?" Darcy's impatience had just about reached its limit.

"That she has *another* sister who has been in America these past few months."

Darcy's eyes jolted up as his heart lurched. Catching himself, he replied, "Does she?"

Caroline stood up from the table and began to walk around. "Are not *three* Bennet sisters enough? Now we find out she has *four*!" The contempt in her voice did not go unnoticed by Darcy. "Exactly what could this other sister have been doing in America? What reason could there be for *anyone* to go over there?"

"Excuse me?" Darcy asked.

"Oh, except for you, Mr. Darcy, who had to go over there to return with your sister. How kind of you that was!"

"Did she say anything else about her?"

"Anything else?" Caroline mulled over his question. "Only that she expected her home any day now."

Darcy eyed Miss Bingley with suspicion. She did not seem to be finished with her scrutiny of this unknown fourth sister.

"If you ask me," she said in a hushed whisper, "the only reason I can fathom young, single woman to travel to America and back to visit an aunt and uncle, would be to take care of some impropriety on her part."

Louisa again nodded her agreement.

"It would not surprise me if she found herself in a most unseemly way and travelled abroad so no one here would find out she was…"

"Miss Bingley!" Darcy stood up, affronted at her insinuations against Elizabeth.

She looked up at him in surprise, silenced by his anger.

Darcy took in a breath as he attempted to calm himself. "Miss Bingley, you have no reason and no right to assume any such thing and I, for one, will not allow you to spread rumours of that nature."

A wave of regret crossed her face. She regretted that she had caused him such indignation and that it was directed towards her. "I am sorry, Mr. Darcy. It was… it was… thoughtless of me." She had never seen such a look of anger on his face before, and could not, for the life of her, understand why he was so determined to defend Miss Bennet's family.

Darcy stood up abruptly. "If you will excuse me…" Without saying any more, he left the room.

~~*

The next morning the sun eagerly broke through the lingering clouds giving the hope that it would pour forth its desired warmth upon the land. A freshness that only a recent rain can produce filled the air.

Darcy awoke eager to engage his mind and body in a day of hunting. He loved the thrill of the hunt, the challenge and skill that was required, and being in the outdoors. He walked over to the window and looked outside. The rain had certainly left its imprint. The grounds down below were a jumble of mud and puddles. But that should not deter the men. They were ardent hunters and would manage most adequately in it and enjoy their day.

As he prepared to go downstairs, his thoughts went to Miss Bennet. Perhaps if she was feeling improved, she would join them for breakfast. Then he might have a chance to subtly bring up the subject of Elizabeth. He was unsettled with the fact that Caroline seemed so inclined to jump to the most abhorrent conclusions about the Bennets. She was not happy with them and was determined to make her opinion known, at least to him.

He let out a breathy laugh as he considered how appalled she would be if she found out he had formed a strong attachment to this fourth Bennet sister. She would never understand it. As he considered the Bennet family, he was faced with the hard truth that undoubtedly no one in his family would understand it either; at least until they became well acquainted with Elizabeth. Then, some of them might understand, but only some.

Joining the others downstairs in the breakfast parlour, he was disappointed to find Miss Bennet not in their midst. He greeted the others and inquired after her.

"Has anyone seen after Miss Bennet this morning?"

Caroline answered. "Yes, I stopped by her room this morning to see how she was faring. Apparently she did not sleep well at all. She is very feverish and drowsy. All she wants to do is sleep, which is perhaps, the best thing for her."

"I am sorry to hear that she is feeling so poorly." Darcy was served a plate of sliced ham topped with some eggs and poured a cup of coffee. "It is probably wise that she not be moved just yet."

The conversation around the table remained on Miss Bennet, spurred on by Bingley's continued interest and concern for her. Darcy easily noticed the spiteful looks between Caroline and Louisa, which spoke much louder than any of their words, and yet were a truer indication to him that they had heard enough of Miss Bennet and their concern for her comfort was merely an outward show.

When he had finished eating, Darcy stood up and walked over to the window with his coffee, glancing outside as he took the last sips from the cup. Hurst was anxious to get out on the grounds and begin hunting, but Bingley desired to wait for Mr. Jones to come so he could ascertain how Miss Bennet was faring. Mr. Jones was expected at any time and Bingley had to repeat to Hurst several times that he would be the poorest sportsman if he set out before hearing something of her condition.

The door to the parlour opened and a servant stepped in. "A visitor for Miss Bennet." He stepped aside to allow the visitor to step in.

As Darcy was just bringing his cup of coffee up to take a sip, he looked up and suddenly froze in his movement. There, appearing in the doorway with weary ankles, dirty stockings, and a face glowing with the warmth of exercise, stood Elizabeth!

The clanging of Darcy's coffee cup back into his saucer brought all eyes to himself, including the woman at the door. She turned her head and their eyes instantly met; Elizabeth's cheeks being overspread with the deepest blush. Her mouth dropped in shock and surprise, and, without thinking, she cried out, "Will…" The rest of his name was swallowed under her breath as she realized what she was about to say.

Elizabeth was rendered immoveable from surprise and Darcy took a step toward her, propelled, not by perfect composure, but by perfect astonishment and overwhelming pleasure at seeing her. Elizabeth paled, feeling quite close to fainting, wondering if the man she saw before her was a vision or truly him. In a final steeling of her nerves, she turned back to the others in the room and asked in a trembling voice which betrayed her discomfiture, "Will… will someone be so kind as to tell me how my sister is?"

Chapter 19

Silence settled upon the group in the breakfast parlour with death-like stillness as all eyes were upon the lady at the door. Darcy was rendered mute by just the beautiful, long awaited sight of her; Bingley was in awe of this fourth sister of Jane's that he had heard so much about; and his sisters could not believe the appearance of the woman at the door. The state of the lady before them rivalled her sister's appearance the day previous. Mr. Hurst was, of course, completely absorbed with the plates of food before him.

Darcy was grateful the eyes were no longer turned to him, as the blood had all but drained from his face and he took the cup and saucer in both hands to prevent them from shaking and rattling the china.

Bingley, after being momentarily stunned by the unexpected appearance of Jane's beloved sister, jumped up and rushed over to her, introducing himself. "Good morning! I am Charles Bingley!"

"I am Jane's sister, Elizabeth Bennet."

"I have heard so much about you! It is good to finally meet you!"

"Thank you," Elizabeth said softly, her voice still quavering, stealing a nervous, questioning glance at Darcy.

"And this is my sister, Caroline Bingley, and my other sister Louisa Hurst, and her husband Mr. Hurst." Everyone nodded in acknowledgement.

Elizabeth's gaze was directed at the lady dressed in a most abhorrent orange. *Caroline!* The name William had called out the night of the storm. Upon scrutiny of the table she could readily see that the empty place beside hers was where he had been seated. A stiffening chill coursed through her as she wondered just what sort of relationship the two had.

"And this is my good friend, Mr. Darcy."

Elizabeth tentatively turned to him and looked down, closing her eyes briefly as she felt her heart begin pounding. As she opened them, she winced as she noticed the mud that encased her shoes and left trails up her ankles up onto her petticoat. Being so anxious to get out and see Jane, she carelessly skipped across a large field along the way and had landed in some fairly large mud puddles. She closed her eyes again as she imagined how he would consider her in this state. It took all her strength to look upon him calmly when he was the last person she had expected to see, especially in the condition she was in.

"A pleasure, Miss... Bennet." Darcy quickly interjected, a nervous smile settling across his face, and he bowed. Elizabeth sensed his awkwardness as greatly as she felt her own.

Elizabeth discreetly curtseyed, feeling a sense of unsteadiness threaten to overwhelm her. She could not bring her mind to understand why he, of all people, would be here, of all places.

Caroline stood up and walked over to her as her gaze swept up and down her clothing. She obliged herself to take her hand. "Unfortunately, your sister did not sleep well, Miss Elizabeth. She is still very feverish and not able to leave her room. Mr. Jones has been sent for, and he should be here any moment." She urgently turned Elizabeth toward the door. "Come, I will take you to her."

Elizabeth was glad to be ushered out of the room. Her mind and heart swirled in conflicting sensations. As she followed Miss Bingley, she found it difficult to comprehend finding him here so close to her home. She barely returned to Longbourn last night with the Gardiners, had only just caught up with her family, had not even seen Jane, and now she encountered the man who had so frequently occupied her thoughts and settled into her heart these past several months.

Following Miss Bingley up the stairs, Elizabeth tried in vain to fathom his presence in this house. She concentrated on taking each step as Caroline Bingley, guiding her to her sister, seemed to be chatting on about something, but Elizabeth was too unsettled to hear and appreciate her words.

When she walked into Jane's room, her sister's eyes were closed and she appeared asleep. Elizabeth was suddenly overwhelmed with how much she had missed Jane and how grateful she was to see her again.

She looked back to Miss Bingley and offered up a hurried thank you to her and asked to be alone. She sat down on Jane's bed as the ache within gave way to a release of tears.

The slight stirring of the bed awakened Jane, and as she looked upon Elizabeth, she lay still for some time as if she was not sure whether she was dreaming.

"Lizzy?"

"Yes, Jane. I am here. I have come home."

Jane could not have been more delighted. As she noticed Elizabeth's tears of joy, she joined her in a very tearful reunion and fervent embrace.

"Oh, Lizzy! When did you return?"

"Just last night, Jane. Oh, it is so good to see you!" The two seemed reluctant to let each other go, but however weak Jane's embrace was due to her illness, Elizabeth made up for it in fervency because of the unrivalled gravity of her feelings.

"I have felt so downcast, Lizzy, feeling sorry for myself. I wished so much that you were here, and now, here you are!"

"I am so sorry you are unwell, Jane. Are they treating you kindly?" She pulled away, looking closely at her face and noticing how tired and weak she appeared.

"Oh, yes. They have been very kind."

"I am glad." Elizabeth took her hand and held it tightly, gaining a modicum of composure. "Mama told us last night about how you had taken ill, *and* about you and Mr. Bingley." Elizabeth smiled. "She claims that he danced several dances with you at the Meryton Assembly, and spent almost his whole time with you at Lucas Lodge. Is this true, Jane, or just another one of mother's exaggerations?"

As she saw Jane blush, Elizabeth realized her mother was probably correct in her assessment between Jane and this gentleman. "You know how Mama is."

"So, tell me, Jane. What is your Charles Bingley like?" she asked as she drew out a handkerchief and wiped the tears from Jane's eyes and then her own. "I only briefly met him downstairs."

"Oh, Lizzy, he is not *my* Mr. Bingley!"

Elizabeth drew closer to her and whispered, "Is he everything a young man ought to be?"

Jane smiled, "He is, Lizzy. He is."

Elizabeth detected a slight sigh that gave her the deepest conviction that Jane held him in the highest esteem.

"And do you think, dear Jane, that he shall pass my critical scrutiny when I get to know him better?"

Jane turned to her and grasped both her hands in hers. "I do hope so. He is extremely agreeable, is lively and sensible with such pleasing manners."

Elizabeth smiled. "That is all well and good, Jane. But do you think him handsome?"

Jane looked down and a blush tinged her cheeks. "Yes, Lizzy, I think him most handsome!"

Elizabeth leaned over and hugged her. "Good! Then I give you leave to like him!" The two women laughed; Elizabeth grateful for the diversion from her thoughts.

Jane, fighting fatigue and the effects of her illness, inquired of her sister, "I am so anxious to hear about your trip. Will the Gardiners be at Longbourn very long?"

"They had to depart this morning. Mr. Gardiner is needed back at his business in a few days. They asked me to send you their love and were so sorry to have missed you. And as for the trip, it was wonderful, but we have plenty of time to talk about it when you are feeling better."

Jane smiled and closed her eyes.

"I fear I have made you weary, dear Jane, but answer me one more question if you will." Elizabeth took in a deep breath and took one of Jane's hands in her own. "What do you know of Mr. Bingley's friend, Mr. Darcy?"

"Hmmm," Jane sighed. "I am afraid I do not know much. I met him just once at Lucas Lodge the other night. He danced one set with me. He seems very kind, but quiet. He kept pretty much to himself the whole evening, except when in Miss Bingley's company. I did see him dance once with Miss Bingley, but none other."

Elizabeth could not help her eyebrows to pinch together. "That is *Caroline* Bingley?"

Jane nodded. "Why do you ask?"

"He… he seems familiar, that is all."

"Mr. Bingley said the Mr. Darcy just returned from America as you did. Perhaps you saw him over there."

"Perhaps."

Elizabeth set her mind to straightening out the blankets as Jane closed her eyes. Elizabeth thought it best to postpone any further conversation until later.

Jane quickly fell asleep and Elizabeth stood up and walked to the window. Looking out on the furthest horizon, she contemplated with great pain what this would mean, being again in the presence of Mr. Darcy, in this same house with him, along with Caroline Bingley.

~~*

After Caroline returned from taking Elizabeth to Jane, Mr. Jones arrived, and she took him to attend to her. Bingley anxiously awaited downstairs for him to return with news of her condition.

He spent a good half hour with her, and when he returned, he confirmed that she had caught a violent cold and advised that she remain in bed. Her feverish symptoms had increased and Bingley was concerned. It was only through Elizabeth's reassurance that she would stay by her sister's side throughout the day that he decided to go ahead with his plans and spend the day out on the grounds hunting with the other gentlemen.

Returning to the breakfast parlour after the men set out, Caroline could not wait to make her feelings about Miss Elizabeth known to her sister.

"Did you notice, Louisa, how Miss Elizabeth simply *gaped* at Mr. Darcy when she walked in this morning? I found it positively shocking!"

"She did seem quite overt in her admiration."

"I do not know if I like her, Louisa, or like her being here! If she went to America for the reason I suspect, who is to say *what* she will do to try and capture Mr. Darcy's attention!"

Louisa was not quite as sure as her sister that there had ever been any impropriety on Miss Elizabeth's part, but nevertheless she nodded in agreement.

Caroline felt strongly that it would be her sole responsibility, and in Mr. Darcy's best interest, to keep an eye on this fourth sister who was most decidedly deficient in manners, shirking all propriety, and more than likely eager to employ some improper enticements against him.

~~*

The day warmed up nicely for the men to go out hunting, but the woods and fields abounded in mud. This would not usually be enough to discourage men who are ardent hunters, but Bingley was surprised to see that Darcy's heart was not in it. Whereas he normally took down two or three birds quite easily, today he had not hit one. It appeared to Bingley that Darcy's steadiness was not quite what it usually was. Much to Hurst's disappointment, Bingley decided to call it an afternoon with a good three hours still remaining of daylight.

As the men returned to the house, Darcy walked with determined strides, propelled by the anxious hope of seeing Elizabeth again soon. He knew it had been her unexpected appearance this morning that had so disconcerted him both in the breakfast parlour and while out on the grounds. He was anxious to get back, anxious to know what she was thinking about him being there, and anxious to talk to her.

When the men walked in, they discovered Elizabeth speaking with Caroline about arrangements for her to take the carriage home.

Darcy caught Elizabeth's eye as he walked in and, feeling a little more disposed to encounter her, allowed a heartfelt smile to grace his lips as he nodded at Elizabeth. As she attended to Caroline's conversation, she perceived his tender acknowledgement of her and a warmth crept across her face.

Miss Bingley spoke in her most accommodating voice. "I am sure, Miss Elizabeth, that your sister will fare most adequately here for the night. Perhaps by tomorrow she will be ready to return home. There is really no need for you to remain here; you just barely returned home yourself. I am sure you are anxious to spend some time with your family."

"I admit I worry too much," Elizabeth replied. "I am sure she will do quite well without me." Although Elizabeth wished to remain with her sister and her sister desired the same, she wondered whether Darcy would prefer her to not remain here for the night and the sisters unquestionably seemed disinclined to extend the invitation.

"Now there is no need to worry, Miss Elizabeth. She is in very good hands. We will take exceedingly good care of her."

Darcy's voice interrupted their discussion. "Perhaps Miss Elizabeth prefers to remain here at Netherfield for the night with her sister. If that is acceptable with you, Miss Bingley."

Both women looked at Darcy in surprise.

"I would not wish to impose," Elizabeth offered nervously.

Caroline waved her hands in artificial protest. "Why, Miss Elizabeth, it would not be an imposition! I was just about to suggest that myself!"

Elizabeth looked suspiciously back at Miss Bingley. "That is very kind of you. If you do not mind, I shall return to Jane and inform her of my staying. I appreciate this immensely. Thank you. Please advise me when supper is served."

"Yes, well, it is no trouble. I shall dispatch a note to Longbourn; acquaint them with your stay and ask for some clothes to be sent over for you."

"You are too kind, Miss Bingley."

Elizabeth promptly returned to Jane, and Caroline was more than pleased that Darcy witnessed her close attention to this matter; sending the note and asking for a change of clothes.

Darcy took the opportunity while Elizabeth was with Jane to go up to his room and clean up in a hot bath. When his bath was prepared, he slipped in, leaning his head back as he finally had the freedom to dwell on Elizabeth. Not that he had neglected to think of her today. But he had been engaged in other things that required his attention, and although he knew his success out hunting today had been gravely affected by unremitting thoughts of her, he now enjoyed the prospect of giving her his undivided attention.

He could hardly believe that she was here, in this very house, and would be, for at least another day. He knew she would spend her time attending to her sister, but they would certainly have the opportunity to talk. He noticed her demeanour when she saw him this morning. He could tell she felt all the awkwardness of seeing him again unexpectedly. Even he had been completely caught off guard by her sudden appearance and he had the advantage of knowing she might return any day.

He knew they would not be able to talk about what happened between them in the presence of the others, and hoped that it would not be too long before he could take some time to talk with her in private.

He closed his eyes as he contemplated what her reaction had been to seeing him. *What did she think now? Was she angry? Pleased?* He wondered if she had thought at all about him since that last night on the ship. What would be her response to the news that he had not annulled their marriage?

That would be the crucial point to address. He did not feel it would be best to unleash that news first thing to her. Perhaps he should allow her to recognize what his feelings toward her really were so that she might eventually come to return them as well. At that point he might casually mention the fact that he had never annulled the marriage.

Darcy opened his mouth and took in a deep breath, sliding completely under the water. He came up shaking his head as the water flew out from his hair and let out the intake of breath slowly through his nose. Now that he was faced with the certainty of being near her again, his heart began to pound erratically. He futilely tried to calm his nerves. He had hoped a hot bath would help, but until he talked with her, until he knew for certain her feelings for him, he would most likely remain in this disturbed state.

Pulling himself out from the bath and wrapping a towel around him, he walked over to the window and looked out, watching as a rain had begun to pelt the glass again. It ran down in rivulets, blurring the view beyond. He thought of the storm on the ship and how pleasant it had been to have Elizabeth in his arms that night. Would he ever have that opportunity again?

After he dressed, Darcy stood before the mirror, looking at his reflection, wondering if the clothing Durnham laid out for him after the bath would be the best in which to see Elizabeth tonight. Taking his hand and running it through his hair, he realized he had not concerned himself with his appearance since that last day on the ship.

~~*

Elizabeth returned to Jane, surprised, yet pleased that Darcy suggested that she stay. Certainly he must feel the awkwardness of this situation. Jane was asleep when she entered the room, and she sat down quietly in a chair next to the bed. She was grateful that he was not against her remaining at Netherfield. She felt, however, that Caroline Bingley was *not* happy with her staying on.

Caroline! Just the thought of her made Elizabeth recoil. If there was something between them, what did he see in her? She was certainly not the type Elizabeth would have imagined he would find favour with! She closed her eyes as she recalled the looks that Miss Bingley had given her at different times throughout the day. Although her words were very polite and caring, there was little substance behind them. In fact, she felt that although her words said one thing, her feelings were actually the opposite.

She had the impression that Miss Bingley felt intruded upon by her presence and was impatient for her to leave. She closed her eyes. *Please do not let me find out she has secured William's love and admiration! Anyone but her!*

Just before dinner, her clothes arrived with the servant who was sent to Longbourn. She quickly changed and made sure Jane had all she needed before she went downstairs to join the others.

As she came to the dining room, she was joined by Miss Bingley who was also on her way in. The gentlemen were already there and seated, and they stood when the ladies entered. Miss Bingley quickly made her way to Darcy's side, and Elizabeth was left to sit at the far side of Mr. Hurst.

She had barely been seated when Bingley asked about Jane.

"Tell me, Miss Elizabeth. Is Miss Bennet any better?"

"I am afraid not. She seems quite taken down by this cold and fever."

"I am so sorry! What a shame. But I know she is most grateful that you are here with her!"

Elizabeth smiled and could not prevent her eyes from travelling to Mr. Darcy.

The two sisters expressed several times how much they were grieved to hear this, how shocking it was to have a bad cold, and how excessively they disliked being ill themselves. With that, they changed the subject and Miss Bingley continually redirected the conversation to Darcy.

Elizabeth was aware of the difference between Bingley's show of concern for Jane and his sisters' concern. His anxiety for Jane was evident, and his attentions to her most pleasing. His sisters' concern, however, displayed merely a façade and was not indicative of their true feelings.

Elizabeth's dinner partner, Mr. Hurst, seemed not at all inclined to engage in conversation, and as Miss Bingley was so wholly engrossed by Mr. Darcy, Elizabeth sat at the table eating silently, wishing all the while she did not have to witness such a display of enticing conversation and manner that Miss Bingley directed toward him.

Darcy made several unsuccessful attempts to entertain a conversation with Elizabeth and each time Miss Bingley quite determinedly steered it away from her and back to him. Elizabeth was seated too far away to attempt much of anything else. It was all he could do to simply look across the table, past Mr. Hurst and set his eyes upon that face he had longed to behold for so many months. He would have to wait for a more suitable time.

As Elizabeth watched Miss Bingley engage Darcy in conversation, she became aware of the look of longing and admiration the woman exhibited. She swallowed as her eyes returned to him. The nerves inside her swirled violently, and the thought of eating anymore seemed a complete impossibility.

Miss Bingley was now discussing how much she missed London and what, she wondered, was new since her last visit. Elizabeth believed it to be a good time to politely excuse herself to return to her sister. She quickly left the room, prohibiting herself from taking one last look at Darcy before she exited.

Miss Bingley began abusing her as soon as she was gone. Her manners were pronounced very bad indeed, a mixture of pride and impertinence; and she had no conversation, no style, no taste, and no beauty.

Mrs. Hurst added, "She has nothing, in short, to recommend her, but being an excellent walker. I shall never forget her appearance this morning. She really looked almost wild."

"She did indeed, Louisa. I could hardly keep my countenance. She looked as though she had been scampering about the whole country! Her hair so untidy!"

"Yes, and her petticoat; I hope you saw her petticoat, six inches deep in mud, I am absolutely certain; and the gown which had been let down to hide it, not doing its office."

"This was all lost upon me," Bingley cried. "I thought Miss Elizabeth Bennet looked remarkably well when she came into the room this morning. I was simply pleased to finally make her acquaintance."

"You observed it, Mr. Darcy, I am sure," said Miss Bingley; "And I am inclined to think that you would not wish to see your sister make such an exhibition."

"Certainly not."

"What could she mean by walking three miles in dirt? It seems to me to show an abominable sort of conceited independence, a most country town indifference to decorum."

Darcy stood up and walked to the window, looking out as he fought the rising tide of angry words he wished to lash out in Elizabeth's defence. But from years of discipline, he was able to coolly reply, "As much as you find her behaviour offensive, I found her devotion to her sister, whom she had not seen in several months, very engaging, and the result of her exercise to be a most brilliant complexion."

"I agree!" exclaimed Bingley. "I could not have stated it better!"

Mrs. Hurst expressed her views. "I have an excessive regard for Jane Bennet, she is really a very sweet girl. But I am afraid there is very little chance of her marrying well with her mother and father having such low connections."

Caroline continued, "One of their uncles is an attorney in Meryton, and another lives somewhere near Cheapside." Both sisters laughed.

"If they had uncles enough to fill all Cheapside," cried Bingley, "it would not make them one jot less agreeable."

Darcy moved to the door. "I, for one, have had enough of this attack on Miss Jane Bennet, Miss Elizabeth, and the rest of the family. They are both fine ladies and who their family connections are, how they choose to travel around the neighbourhood, and even their decided lack of fashion, is not enough to convince me of any poor manners or lack of anything to recommend them. If you will excuse me…"

Caroline Bingley was left with a most nagging, distressful thought that somehow Mr. Darcy had come under the spell of the Bennets, just as her brother unfortunately had.

~~*

Darcy returned to his room and remained there as long as he felt that propriety allowed him. Just the thought that Elizabeth was down the hall from him was both a great source of joy and temptation to him. How much he wanted to walk down there now, confess his love, take her in his arms, tell her they were still married, and carry her back to Pemberley… to London… or to his room.

At length he determined he ought to join the others downstairs. He had finished his book and decided he would stop by Bingley's library first.

It was true that Bingley's library was only a tenth of what Pemberley's was, but he was confident he would be able to find a book he would enjoy reading. He walked around the room, looking up and down the shelves, picking up a book here and there. He pulled a book from the shelf noticing the title, smiled, and then placed it back where it had been. He walked to the far wall and stood reading the titles when he heard someone walk in.

He turned and saw that it was Elizabeth. She stepped in and walked toward the wall on the opposite side of the room.

Not wanting to startle her, he whispered softly, "Elizabeth."

She turned quickly and in response to seeing him, she cried out, "William! I mean… Mr. Darcy."

Darcy smiled, slowly taking a step toward her, aware only of how beautiful she looked to him. "You do recall how much I wanted you to call me William when we were alone together on the ship, but you refused to do it unless we were in the company of others."

Elizabeth looked down, feeling quite shaken. He took another step, bridging some of the distance between them.

"As much as I enjoy hearing you call me by my given name, I think it would be prudent if you do *not* call me that while you are here. It might cause some scandalous conjecture by one Caroline Bingley."

Elizabeth saw him smile and his gaze was intent upon her face as he took yet another step toward her. She wondered if he was teasing her, warning her, or simply stating the truth. Her mind refused to comprehend any rational thought.

Finding it difficult to look upon him standing so close to her, she turned toward the bookshelf, as if to study the titles. "I must admit I was surprised to see you here. I had no idea you were at Netherfield."

"You had no way of knowing I would be here."

Elizabeth looked down suddenly. She took in a deep breath as her fingers tightly gripped the muslin on her dress once she noticed she had come completely under his shadow, his tall frame blocking the candlelight in the room.

Sensing the distress she was feeling, he calmly and deliberately told her, "I beg you not to feel uneasy. I only recently discovered you lived so close to my friend Bingley and that you were Miss Jane Bennet's sister, so I was a little better prepared to see you." He took another step toward her so that now, if he wanted to, he could easily reach out and take her hand. "Although since I was unaware you had returned home from America, your appearance this morning took me by surprise as well."

They stood in silence for what seemed an eternity.

When Elizabeth did not seem inclined to respond, Darcy said to her, "You left our cabin that last night on the ship and did not return. You got off the ship the next morning without saying goodbye. Why?"

Elizabeth closed her eyes and her heart skipped a beat. Did she just imagine that his soft voice seemed tinged with a bit of sadness? She knew not how to answer him and turned briefly back towards him, needing to take a deep breath and gather her thoughts.

"And you conveniently neglected to tell me that you were the owner of *Pemberley's Promise*."

Elizabeth heard him breathe in deeply. "Yes, that is true."

Darcy's jaw tightened as he saw Elizabeth's turmoil. There was so much he wanted to say, and did not know where to even begin.

"How did you find out…"

He was interrupted by the sound of very determined strides walking in, and Elizabeth, still reeling from the encounter, only vaguely noticed a dash of orange come toward them. A very audible groan escaped from Darcy as he took a quick step away from Elizabeth, but she took no notice.

"Ah, there you are, Mr. Darcy!" Caroline's eyes flashed like daggers at Elizabeth, noticing how close they were standing to each other, and the fact that they were alone together in the library. She was quite of the opinion that she had arrived just in time to rescue Darcy from a most indelicate situation.

Elizabeth watched Caroline sidle up next to him and slip her hand snugly inside his arm. She kept her gaze upon Elizabeth, who was suffering the effects of being either quite pale from alarm or quite red from confusion.

"Come, Mr. Darcy," Caroline adamantly insisted. "We are waiting for you to join us in the drawing room." She turned to Elizabeth. "You may come along as well, if you like, Miss Bennet."

Not wishing to provide Miss Bingley with any further fodder to kindle her speculations and gossip about Elizabeth, Darcy quickly said to her, "Miss Bennet, that book I recommended is on the second shelf there."

Elizabeth looked at him with a perplexed look across her face. He simply pointed to the bookshelf behind her and said, "It is the one with the black cover and gold filigree writing. Second shelf, behind you. I think you will enjoy it."

Elizabeth watched him walk out with Caroline still possessively holding his arm. She closed her eyes as she considered how quickly he had reassured Charles' sister that their conversation in the library had been solely for the purpose of finding a book.

She turned slowly back to the shelf, her heart beginning to feel the slightest tear in the realization he did not wish Caroline to get the wrong impression.

Her eyes drifted to the second shelf as he had mentioned and was surprised when she *did* see a black book with gold filigree writing.

Absently she pulled it off the shelf. *Hmmm. Richard III. I read that a couple of years ago*, she said to herself, as she opened it. Upon looking at the first line of the book, she gasped.

Now is the winter of our discontent; made glorious summer by this sun of York.

She turned back to the now empty door and then looked back down at the book in her hands, the same one she had been reading two years ago in the carriage when she first met him. And now her heart, she was certain, pounded relentlessly. *Certainly he could not remember! Could he?*

Chapter 20

Elizabeth lingered in the library for several minutes after Caroline walked out with Darcy, letting her eyes rest on the book she was now holding in her hand. While her heart felt the painful tug at seeing the two of them together, it was at the same time grasping at any hint, any indication, that he might hold tender regard for her.

She closed her eyes and shook her head. Of *course* he would hold her in his esteem, if ever so slightly! They had a most amiable relationship on board the ship. They lived for almost a month together posing as man and wife. *Well, practically man and wife,* Lizzy reminded herself, willing herself to remember the terms of their marriage. Suddenly the pain in her heart and the rationale of her thoughts began to war with each other whether there was any chance that his feelings for her would outweigh any feelings for or previous arrangement he had with Miss Bingley.

She looked down at the book in her hands and chided herself for even thinking he remembered that day in the carriage two years ago, let alone remember what she had been reading. He most likely just said the first thing that came to his mind when Caroline discovered them in there, and the black book with the gold filigree writing just happened to be this particular one.

She slowly turned and walked out of the library, compelled more by a sense of right than of pleasure, to join the others in the drawing room.

When she walked in, she found the whole party at loo and was immediately invited to join them; but she declined, saying she would amuse herself for a short time with her book. Mr. Hurst looked at her with astonishment.

"Do you prefer reading to cards?" said he. "That is rather singular."

"Miss Eliza Bennet," said Miss Bingley, "despises cards. She is a great reader and has no pleasure in anything else."

"I deserve neither such praise nor such censure, "cried Elizabeth. "I am *not* a great reader and I take pleasure in many things."

"In nursing your sister I am sure you have pleasure," said Bingley; "and I hope it will soon be increased by seeing her quite well."

"And I would not be surprised that she finds pleasure in helping others, as well." Darcy spoke matter-of-factly as he kept his eyes tuned to his cards.

Elizabeth, unable to turn her eyes to Darcy, and feeling all the conviction that she could *not* look upon him for fear of exposing her aching heart, thanked both gentlemen and turned her attention to the book.

"Did you find the book I suggested?"

This time Elizabeth's eyes shot up involuntarily to Darcy, who had now turned to her, and she felt the revealing warmth of a blush pass over her face. "I… uh… yes, I did, thank you." Her eyes tentatively looked away as she detected a warmth and a mirth in his.

"Had you read it before?"

Her pulse quickened and she felt her mouth go dry at his words. She steeled herself to meet his gaze again, and offered a quick reply, "Yes, Sir, but it has been several years, so I do not mind reading it again."

He seemed content with her answer and turned his attention back to the game. As she opened the book to the first chapter, she tried to concentrate on the words before her, but she could not. The conversation around the table then turned to Pemberley's library, and Caroline gushed words of praise of how delightful it is and how Charles should aspire to have a library just as noble.

Elizabeth listened with amusement to the conversation while feigning an interest in her book. She wished that she could say just how much she had enjoyed Pemberley's library and how grand it was, but she could not. When the conversation turned to Miss Darcy, Elizabeth found herself looking up.

Miss Bingley seemed to have a very intimate knowledge of Pemberley and Miss Darcy. Regrettably, Elizabeth experienced pangs of jealousy that shot right through her. She braced herself as Miss Bingley talked about this young girl as though they were the closest of acquaintances, and although Elizabeth had spent not an hour with the young girl herself, she had a very difficult time believing Miss Darcy would feel as close to Miss Bingley as the woman thought.

"Is Miss Darcy much grown since the spring?" asked Miss Bingley. "Will she be as tall as I am?"

"I think she will," Darcy spoke softly as he looked at his cards. "She is now about Miss Elizabeth Bennet's height, or rather taller." When he said her name, he looked up from his cards and she barely detected the slightest lift of his eyebrow, before he turned his attention back to his hand.

As Elizabeth looked down at her book, still held open at the first page of the first chapter, she tried to calm her violently beating heart. If her heart began beating as wildly when he simply mentioned her name, how was she to survive in this household with him?

The conversation now turned to Miss Darcy's accomplishments and Bingley graciously commented about the virtues of women in all their accomplishments. "They all paint tables, cover screens, and net purses. I scarcely know any one who cannot do all this, and I am sure I never heard a young lady spoken of for the first time, without being informed that she was very accomplished."

Darcy commented on Bingley's list of what made up an accomplished woman. "I am very far from agreeing with you in your estimation of what makes up an accomplished woman. I cannot boast of knowing more than half a dozen, in my whole range of acquaintance, that are really accomplished."

"Nor I, I am sure," concurred Miss Bingley. "One cannot be really esteemed accomplished, who does not greatly surpass what is usually met with. A woman must have a thorough knowledge of music, singing, drawing, dancing, and the modern languages. And besides all this, she must possess a certain something in her air and manner of walking, the tone of her voice, her address and expressions, or the word will be but half deserved."

"Yes, all these may be important," added Darcy, "But to all this she must yet add something more substantial; in the improvement of her mind by extensive reading and the desire to learn more about the world by taking every opportunity to travel."

Elizabeth, whose attention had again been captured by this conversation, was rendered motionless by his words, wondering again of his intent, and when she came to her senses, she discovered she had been staring quite opening at Darcy, and his gaze, in return, was focused on her.

It was actually Miss Bingley's reaction to not only his words, but the direction of his gaze, that stirred Elizabeth from her reverie. "Yes, Mr. Darcy, how right you are. But truly, only a woman in the highest circles of society would have the opportunities to avail herself of all those things you speak of." She slyly looked over to Elizabeth. "For example, one would hardly find a woman in *this* neighbourhood that would satisfy your description of an accomplished woman."

Elizabeth's eyes widened as she understood quite clearly the insinuation of the remark.

"Why… I would have to object, Miss Bingley!" Darcy looked to Elizabeth, recognizing quite unmistakably, the look of anger and insult written across her face, coupled with a very determined look of wishing to speak her mind. "We may not have all the advantages one has in town, but we certainly have opportunities that we may take advantage of to improve ourselves."

"Perhaps it would not be the norm," Darcy interjected, "but I do believe one could easily find an unblemished pearl, or two, in a country neighbourhood such as this, if one knew where to look and what exactly they were looking for.

Elizabeth's anger was slightly appeased by Darcy's words, but felt as though she was in the way. Darcy had, at least, stood up for her, and for that she was grateful. If he had remained silent, she could only suppose he agreed with Miss Bingley and she did not think she could bear that.

Finally, not making any progress in her book, she stood up and excused herself, saying she wished to check in on Jane and then retire for the evening.

When Elizabeth walked into Jane's room, she awakened. Elizabeth found her to be even more feverish, and poured her a glass of water from the pitcher in the room. Elizabeth secured a blanket for herself, choosing not to sleep in her room, which was next to Jane's, but to sleep in the chair in Jane's.

When Jane finally settled down again, Elizabeth sat at the mirror and let down her hair, brushing it vigorously in the light of one small candle. She decided to sleep in her dress, and would change into another come morning.

Elizabeth slept little, hoping to keep Jane's body temperature down and encouraging her to drink as much fluid as possible. Jane had fallen asleep again, the house was very still, and Elizabeth was certain everyone had retired for the night. She soon found herself in need of refilling the pitcher with water.

She picked up the pitcher and quietly went to the door, opening it slowly, and closing it behind her. She had taken a few steps towards the staircase when the sound of footsteps coming up the staircase and the flickering of a candle could be seen.

She came to a stop when she found herself face to face with Darcy.

"Good evening, Elizabeth," he whispered softly. "How is your sister tonight?"

"She is quite feverish. I have used up all the water. I was just on my way down to refill the pitcher."

"Let me do that for you." He took the final two steps up to reach her at the top of the stairs.

"No, there is no need for you…" She stopped, as did her heart, when she felt his free hand come around hers on the pitcher.

"Please, Elizabeth. I know exactly where to go to refill it."

Looking at him through the flickering candlelight, and having the warmth of his hand securely around hers, she felt a tremor pass through her.

Darcy could not take his eyes off of her, not having had the pleasure for several months of beholding her beauty in candlelit darkness. She was too close for him not to feel the gentle stirrings of admiration build within him, and thought back to their kiss that last night on the ship, and how much he wanted to take her in his arms again at that very moment.

Her tiny hand felt so right held in his, but he forced himself to let go and reach up above hers and grasp the handle of the pitcher. "Go back to your sister, Elizabeth," he whispered. "I shall fill this up and bring it back to you shortly."

Darcy took it from her hands and turned to head back downstairs, leaving Elizabeth quite immoveable from where she had stood. *If only he would treat me with indifference, it would make it so much easier for me!* She slowly turned and walked back down the darkened hallway to Jane's room. *He is too kind to me.* She let out a soft sigh.

Elizabeth sat patiently in the room, waiting for him to return. At length there was a slight knock on the door. She opened it, and Darcy walked in, carrying the pitcher of water. He carried it over to the small table and set it down.

"If there is anything else you need, just let me know. I am across the hall, three doors down."

"Thank you," Elizabeth said softly, her eyelashes covering her eyes as she looked toward the floor.

Darcy took a sharp intake of breath and brought his fingers up to her chin, lifting it up ever so slightly. "Elizabeth, this is not good. We have to talk."

Looking over at Jane to make sure she was still sleeping, she replied, "But certainly, we cannot here! Not tonight, not in this room!"

"No, not tonight. I ought to leave." His fingers lingered under her chin, holding her face up to his. He thought how easy it would be, how pleasant it would be, to bridge the short distance between their lips and leave her with a kiss of hope, of promise, of purposeful intentions.

But that thought was quickly erased from his mind as he heard a door down the hall open. Glancing back at the door, he whispered to her, "Now I *know* I must leave!"

Darcy quickly walked to the door and as he stepped out into the hall, he was met by a tall figure. "Mr. Darcy! Is there some problem here?"

Elizabeth shuddered to think that Miss Bingley had just discovered him walking out of the room.

"There is not, now. Miss Elizabeth needed to refill the pitcher of water, and I encountered her in the hallway on the way downstairs. I refilled it for her and just now carried it into her sister's room."

In the silence that ensued, Elizabeth felt she must say something to reassure Miss Bingley that nothing of a questionable nature had transpired. "Yes, Miss Bingley. Mr. Darcy was kind enough to refill the pitcher for me." Turning to Darcy, she said. "Thank you, again, Mr. Darcy." She was quite sure Miss Bingley noted the slightest trembling that affected her words.

Darcy proceeded to his room, leaving Caroline with countless speculations about this woman, her character, her intentions, and just how easily Darcy could be ensnared by her.

~~*

Having spent the night in her sister's room, the next morning she had the pleasure of being able to send a tolerable answer to the enquiries which she very early received from Mr. Bingley by a housemaid, and some time afterwards from the two elegant ladies who waited on his sisters. Jane had improved over the course of the night. Her fever had broken and Elizabeth was quite convinced she was on her way to recovery. But it was Mr. Darcy himself who came and inquired after her.

"How is your sister this morning?" he asked when she opened the door to his knock.

"She is much improved, thank you."

"I am glad to hear it." Darcy paused, as if waiting for a response from Elizabeth or deciding to make another himself. He looked over and noticed Jane sitting up in bed and at length he excused himself with, "Shall you come down and join us this morning?"

Elizabeth nodded. "I shall be down shortly."

He smiled and turned to join the others downstairs.

Elizabeth returned to Jane who was enjoying a light breakfast brought earlier by one of the servants. Yes, she was grateful Jane seemed better. But it was her own spirits that had worsened during the night. She thought repeatedly of Darcy's words that they must talk. Each time she conjectured what he would wish to talk to her about, it always came back to their marriage, its annulment, and Miss Bingley.

She wondered whether Darcy viewed their façade of a marriage in a cool, dispassionate light and wanted to ensure that she let nothing slip of its occurrence to anyone in the household. She looked at Jane, and wondered if he was concerned that she would have confided it to her.

She did not think she could bear hearing the words from his own mouth that the leanings of his heart were for Miss Bingley. Elizabeth closed her eyes as she pondered this. Just the thought of it brought her much distress, and she knew not how she would hold up if he spoke to her on this matter.

When Elizabeth had ascertained that Jane was comfortable, she went downstairs and joined the others in the breakfast parlour.

Upon walking in, she found Miss Bingley to be in a very animated discussion with Darcy. She believed the expression on his face betrayed a look of discomfort.

As her presence was noticed, all eyes turned to her, and Bingley expressed with great enthusiasm, "It is so good to hear that Miss Bennet is improved! Should we send a note home to your family? Should we extend an invitation for your mother to come and see for herself how she is faring?"

Elizabeth, with more apprehension at what Darcy would think of her mother than conviction that her mother actually had a real concern for Jane's recovery, simply said, "I think a note informing her of her improvement would be sufficient. I would not want to burden her to come if she has other engagements."

"Nonsense!" cried Bingley. "We shall send a note and extend the offer, and she may reply as she wishes!"

As Elizabeth sat down to join the others in the meal, she sensed tension in the air, and felt it was directed at her. She wondered whether Miss Bingley's address to Darcy as she was walking in had something to do with finding him with her in Jane's room last evening. He obviously was distressed that she imagined there was more to it than really was.

The breakfast continued in relative silence. Elizabeth was content to concentrate on the plate before her, not because she was particularly hungry, but because she was very much aware of the two pair of eyes across the table bearing down on her. The one pair sent out fiery darts in their connection with hers, the other pair was quite disarming, and if Elizabeth did not know any better, would have supposed it was a look more of tender regard than disinterest.

The note was immediately dispatched, and instead of merely accepting the words of her improvement, Mrs. Bennet, accompanied by her two youngest girls, set out for Netherfield soon after the family breakfast. Her prompt arrival seemed less driven by a desire to dispense any words of comfort to Jane or any encouragement to Elizabeth, but instead, to see how things were progressing with Mr. Bingley.

Had she found Jane in any apparent danger, Mrs. Bennet would have been very miserable indeed; but being satisfied that her illness was not alarming, she had no wish of her recovering immediately, as her restoration to health would probably remove her from Netherfield. She would not listen, therefore, to Elizabeth's proposal for the two of them to return home.

After sitting a little while with Jane, on Miss Bingley's appearance and invitation, the mother and three daughters all attended her into the breakfast parlour. Mr. Bingley met them with hopes that Mrs. Bennet had not found Miss Bennet worse than she expected.

"Indeed, I have, Sir," was her answer. "She is a great deal too ill to be moved just yet. We must trespass a little longer on your kindness."

"Removed!" cried Bingley. "It must not be even thought of. My sister, I am sure, will not hear of her removal."

"You may depend upon it, Madam," said Miss Bingley, with cold civility, "that Miss Bennet shall receive every possible attention while she remains with us."

Mrs. Bennet was profuse in her acknowledgements.

"I am sure," she added, "if it was not for such good friends I do not know what would become of her, for she is very ill indeed, and suffers a vast deal, though with the greatest patience in the world, which is always the way with her, for she has, without exception, the sweetest temper I ever met with. I often tell my other girls they are *nothing* to *her*."

"Indeed, she is welcome here as long as need be." Bingley was gracious in his words and conviction.

The conspiratorial look between the two sisters did not go unnoticed by Elizabeth. A look to Darcy, who stood quietly behind Bingley, was all Elizabeth needed to confirm her fears about his estimation of her mother.

Darcy was very agitated, but his agitation rose not only from Mrs. Bennet's shrill outbursts, but from the very fact that she thoughtlessly demeaned her other daughters -- demeaned Elizabeth -- in her excessive praise of Jane!

Mrs. Bennet glanced around the breakfast parlour. "You have a sweet room, here, Mr. Bingley, and a charming prospect over that gravel walk. I do not know a place in the country that is equal to Netherfield."

Mrs. Bennet noticed the gentleman standing behind Bingley. "And you, Sir, I believe I noticed you at Lucas Lodge the other evening."

Bingley looked behind him and apologized. "Oh, I am sorry; this is my good friend, Mr. Darcy. Mr. Darcy, this is Mrs. Bennet, and her two daughters, Miss Lydia Bennet and Miss Catherine Bennet."

Darcy bowed.

"It is a pleasure to meet you, Sir. And do you not think Netherfield is simply grand?"

"Bingley has made a very wise choice in Netherfield."

Bingley laughed and turned back to Mrs. Bennet. "He is being polite. His estate is ten times grander than Netherfield."

Mrs. Bennet clasped her hands in glee. "Is it? Why girls, is that not splendid news?" Turning back to Darcy she asked, "And just where is your estate, Sir?"

"Derbyshire, Mrs. Bennet."

"But that is so far. You are thinking of staying at Netherfield for awhile, are you not?"

"I have not yet determined how long I shall remain here."

Elizabeth stood with her hands in front of her, her right hand holding on to her left at the wrist. To the casual observer, she would appear calm, but her grip tightened around her wrist with each outburst from her mother, and she soon found the fingers on her left hand tingling from lack of blood flow.

She could no longer look at Darcy, for fear of what she would see. She would not be surprised if her mother soon began extolling the virtues of her remaining daughters, and so she interjected before her mother could continue. "Have you seen Charlotte Lucas yet, Mama, to tell her I have returned?"

"Yes, she called yesterday, with her father. She was very happy to hear you were returned."

"Did she dine with you?"

"No, she would go home. I fancy she was wanted about the mince pies. For my part, Mr. Bingley and Mr. Darcy, I always keep servants that can do their own work; my daughters are brought up differently. The Lucases are very good sort of girls, I assure you. It is a pity they are not handsome!"

"Miss Lucas seems a very pleasant young woman," said Bingley.

"Oh, dear yes! But you must own she is very plain. Lady Lucas herself has often said so, and envied me Jane's beauty. I do not like to boast of my own child, but to be sure, Jane -- one does not often see anybody better looking."

When Lydia spiritedly insisted that Mr. Bingley give a ball to own up to a promise, Elizabeth was quite certain that her family's character had been decided by Mr. Darcy and found lacking. When Bingley kindly announced he would be most happy to give a ball when her sister was recovered, an eruption of joy by Mrs. Bennet and Lydia herself added the final touch, grating everyone's nerves.

Mrs. Bennet and her daughters departed, and Elizabeth returned instantly to Jane, leaving her own and her relations' behaviour to the remarks of the two ladies and, she was sure Mr. Darcy; the latter of whom, however unknown to Elizabeth, could not be prevailed upon to join in their censure.

In the silence of the room as Jane slumbered, Elizabeth could not relax and she felt the greatest humiliation at the hands of her mother. *How he must congratulate himself that he has annulled the marriage and will not have to endure being married into a family with a mother such as mine! It would be a wonder if he were not thinking at this very moment that had he known of my family, he would have never even considered such an alignment with me.*

"Ohhh!" Elizabeth cried out and pounded her fists down onto her lap.

Jane opened her eyes. "Lizzy, is something the matter?"

"Oh, Jane." Elizabeth came over and sat down next to her on the bed. "I may tell you someday, but for now, just believe me that I did a foolish thing a while back, and it has come back to haunt me."

Elizabeth spent the rest of the day with Jane, certain of two things: that Darcy did not wish her company and the two sisters desired her gone. Mr. Bingley had proven himself to be most gracious, and Elizabeth saw such goodness and acceptance from him that she felt he could love Jane completely despite all their family oddities. For that she was grateful.

Darcy retired to the solitary confines of his room for the rest of the day. He had struggled; it was to be expected, with the unbridled outbursts of Elizabeth's mother. Several times he had to fight the prevailing will to silently turn away. Again the quiet, persistent voices from his past rose up; needling him to put aside these irrational feelings and do what was required of him in finding a suitable wife. *But Elizabeth is suitable! She is more than suitable for me!* He walked to the window and looked out, slapping his hand against the wall and then leaving it to rest there.

As he looked out, mulling over the disparity in Elizabeth's station and his, the refined Darcy name and her unchecked family, he came to one conclusion. He could not live without her. And until she told him, to his face, that she had no wish -- no desire -- to keep their marriage intact, he would do nothing to dissolve it. He took a deep breath. He told her last night he needed to talk to her. He needed to talk to her *alone,* and it was apparent that was not going to happen on its own. Darcy had to come up with a plan.

Jane continued, though slowly, to mend, but remained in her room, and in the evening Elizabeth joined the rest of the party in the drawing room. The loo table, however, did not appear. Mr. Darcy was writing, and Miss Bingley, seated near him, was watching the progress of his letter and repeatedly calling off his attention to it by messages to his sister. Mr. Hurst and Mr. Bingley were at piquet, and Mrs. Hurst was observing their game.

Elizabeth picked up her book, hoping to attend fully to completing it, although she watched with great interest what passed between Darcy and his companion. As Miss Bingley repeatedly praised either his letter writing, or the evenness of his lines, or the length of his letter, Elizabeth wondered at the woman's behaviour. If she had already secured his affections, she was not behaving as if she had.

Miss Bingley was completely unconcerned with the way in which her praises were received by him.

Elizabeth almost laughed as she regarded his short, stilted answers to Miss Bingley's words of praise. Sometimes he answered not at all. As she looked on curiously, Darcy turned to her.

"Have you finished the book yet, Miss Bennet?"

His address to her startled her. "I have a little bit left."

"Then you think you will finish it tonight?"

"I imagine so."

Elizabeth watched him for a few moments, her heart caught in her throat as she met his gaze. She had avoided turning her eyes upon him ever since her mother left earlier that day, afraid to see his censure.

Darcy's gaze remained on her face several more seconds before Miss Bingley, feeling ever so slightly threatened by something that hung in the air between them, spoke up again, wishing him to send off a missive to Georgiana. When he replied that he could not, she continued in her praise of him in every possible area of writing. Darcy responded as if he cared very little, if not at all.

When he finished his letter, he applied to Miss Bingley and Elizabeth for some music, having a great desire to hear Elizabeth play and sing. Elizabeth watched him fold his letter ever so precisely and slip it into his pocket. Miss Bingley moved with alacrity to the pianoforte, and after a polite request that Elizabeth would lead the way, which she politely and most earnestly declined, she seated herself. Mrs. Hurst joined her and sang while Miss Bingley played.

Elizabeth walked over to look through the music books that were lying on the instrument, and became aware of how frequently Darcy's eyes were fixed on her. She hardly knew how to comprehend it, mindful of the fact that he had been exposed to her mother's foolish oddities that day, and perhaps to an even greater extent the night at Lucas Lodge. To think that she could be the object of his admiration she dared not hope. He lingered at the table where she had been seated, picked up the book she had been reading, and then just as quickly placed it back on the table.

After playing several songs, Darcy drew to Elizabeth's side, quietly saying to her, "I would be very much honoured to hear you play, Miss Bennet. While Miss Bingley is very proficient, her style does not always suit me." He looked through the books himself, so as not to draw suspicion from Charles' sister.

Elizabeth kept her gaze upon the music books, but felt the warmth of his breath as he spoke. "I play very ill, indeed, Mr. Darcy."

"Let me be the judge." He picked up a piece of music and gently nudged Elizabeth toward the piano. When Miss Bingley finished playing, he produced the piece of music and Elizabeth to her, asking her to allow her to play.

With an air of decided displeasure, Miss Bingley conceded the piano playing to Elizabeth. Sitting down at the pianoforte, her nerves were still resounding from his closeness and she was not sure she would be able to play even two measures without her fingers getting all tangled up together. The piece he selected was a fairly easy piece, and she knew the words by heart. But she was not sure she could sing them and do them justice, particularly the way she was feeling at the moment.

As she turned her attention to the piece before her, her fingers began to move across the keys with a mind of their own, and as she began to sing, she was suddenly no longer aware of anything in the room, except a pair of dark, tender eyes that had settled upon her.

Darcy had taken a seat where he could watch her expression as she played and sang. As she lifted her eyes from her fingers moving across the keys up to the music, she could see his dark eyes immobile and resting upon her. Instead of making her nervous or wondering what he thought of her or her family, instead of conjecturing whether Miss Bingley was an object of his admiration or not, she put all her heart and soul into the song, and the room listened in silence.

Darcy could not take his eyes off her. He had endured two days being in her presence and being unable to talk to her without Caroline interfering. At breakfast, before Elizabeth joined them, Caroline voiced again her suspicions of Elizabeth's character and warned Darcy that she might resort to unsavoury means to attract his attention. It was apparent that Miss Bingley was making a concerted effort to remain in one or the other's presence, as he had not found one time conducive to speaking to Elizabeth alone.

He hoped his plan would work. As he watched her, as everyone watched her in polite silence, her playing and singing affected him in an even greater way. Her piano playing was very moving; flowing with an interpretation that he enjoyed immensely. But as she sang, the words and the soft, sweet tone of her voice wrapped around him as if they were as real as two arms in an embrace.

At the conclusion of her piece, everyone graciously applauded her, and a grin came across Darcy's face that neither Elizabeth nor Miss Bingley missed. Each was just as surprised as the other.

Elizabeth, growing tired, and needing some time alone to ponder some of Darcy's behaviour, excused herself.

As she turned to leave the room, Darcy stood up as she walked past. "Do not forget your book!" He picked up the book she had left sitting on the table, and placed it firmly in her hands.

Elizabeth nervously smiled and thanked him.

She walked to Jane's room to check on her and found her sleeping contentedly. Returning to her room, she placed the book next to the bed and readied herself for sleep. As she crawled in, she decided she would finish reading, as there was little left. As she opened the book, a small folded piece of paper fell out. She picked it up curiously and slowly opened it.

Looking down at the scrap of paper and reading what it said, Elizabeth gasped.

It read, *There is no greater delightful diversion than a walk at sunrise. Tomorrow. William.*

Chapter 21

Elizabeth held the small scrap of paper tightly within her fingers. Her heart pounded fiercely and she felt a shiver course through her. Darcy had purposely placed this piece of paper in the book with the full intention of her finding it tonight and arranging to meet her while walking on the grounds of Netherfield at dawn.

She sat in her room, bringing the small missive up to her heart, wanting with every fibre of her being to believe that it was written purely out of a desire to begin the day with her out on a walk as they had done so often on the ship. She was very well aware he wanted to talk; they had a great need to talk. She prayed he was not planning to tell her something that would be difficult to bear.

Elizabeth sat in her bed, knowing now that she would find it difficult to concentrate on the book and finish it. All she cared to do was to stare at the missive; written, as Miss Bingley had so eloquently stated, in such an even hand, and yet there was more: an elegance and a style that most men would not possess in their handwriting. She absently ran her fingers across the simple message and across his name.

She could hear, very slightly, a discussion from downstairs and recognized Miss Bingley's shrill voice and Darcy's calm, soothing voice. She could not discern their words, but began to feel a bit more confident that he was not blinded by that woman's character and would not choose to align himself with someone such as her. At least that was her conviction if she had really come to know and understand the man as well as she thought she had.

She let out a hopeful sigh and crawled into her bed, pulling the covers up tightly under her chin. Her heart was not going to let her easily forget that tomorrow morning she would start the day just as she had those days on *Pemberley's Promise;* walking with her husband. She let her head fall to her chest, remembering with a sudden ache in her heart that she could no longer claim him as such.

Elizabeth's mind would not let go of the clear memory of the two of them walking together aboard the ship, and she was not even sure when her wilful meditation gave way to dreams that were of the very same nature.

Later, as Darcy returned to his room, he paused ever so slightly as he walked passed Elizabeth's door. Had she read his note? Would she understand his meaning? Would she oblige him by meeting him tomorrow morning?

He put two fingers to his lips and then reached out, letting them slide silently down the length of her door; his heart stirring at the thought of her just inside. He wondered just how much he should say to her tomorrow if she came. He was still unsure of her feelings for him as her manner in his presence since arriving at Netherfield had been very dissimilar to her manner on board *Pemberley's Promise* with him.

He knew she felt awkward around him and he even believed at times that she intentionally avoided him. He could not believe, however, that she felt nothing for him. *Or am I being foolishly arrogant in that consideration? I have been known to be arrogant before.* Darcy slowly walked down the hall to his room.

If he knew for a certainty that she would remain at Netherfield a few more days, it would be easier. He decided that first he should get some basic issues out in the open with her. Curiosity and the pain that it caused him drove his determination to find out why she left the room that night and why she did not return to at least say goodbye. That would give him a good indication of her true sentiments toward him. If he were to discover any encouragement in her words, then his next step would be to subtly, without Miss Bingley's observing, give Elizabeth some very definite hints that his feelings leaned toward a very strong regard. Dare he say love? His heart pounded at the thought.

Would she embrace his words warmly? Would he be even able to express the depth of his feeling to her in a way she would understand? Would she look favourably upon him as still being her husband when he told her he had never annulled the marriage?

He would take one step at a time, and then he could only hope.

~~*

As the sun slowly made its appearance above the horizon, sending its first ray of light into Elizabeth's room, she stirred. Stretching her arms out high above her, she opened her eyes and it took her a few moments to begin thinking lucidly. As her mind cleared, she suddenly sat upright in her bed. *The walk!* Her heart began thunderously pounding as she looked toward the window and saw the dawn of a new day. She contemplated, with a thread of hope outweighing her doubt, and anticipation instead of apprehension, that soon she would be out walking again with Fitzwilliam Darcy.   The chill of the late autumn night had inhabited her room, but the warmth of that anticipation flooded her. She slowly swung her legs off the bed and stretched them out before her. She sat for a few moments, allowing her body time to awaken, as well as allowing time for her heart to calm its incessant throbbing.

As she sat there, however, her heart was given little chance to recover. She heard a door open down the hall and footsteps walk past her room, pausing, she noticed, just outside her door. She kept her eyes upon the door, half expecting a knock, but soon the steps continued on down the hall.

Elizabeth quickly arose, slipped on her dress, and sat at the dressing table, scooping her hair into her hands and easily bringing it up. She looked at herself, at her dress, and began to think those same thoughts she had on the ship; her dress so simple, especially now compared with the fashionable attire of Bingley's sisters and to what William himself was most likely used to.

Taking in a deep breath and opening her eyes wide, she let out a speculative sigh. *Well, it is now or never!*

She picked up her coat, knowing that the air outside would be brisk, slipped it on, and quietly opened the door. She could hear the sounds of people at work coming from the kitchen, but knew everyone else was most likely still asleep. She chose to allow Jane to sleep in as long as she could, and reasoned that she would not be gone too long.

She was able to slip out without encountering anyone, and chided herself for feeling as though she was doing something improper. She rolled her eyes as she considered Miss Bingley would have ways to construe it as being such!

She walked out and deeply breathed in the cool morning air. Little patches of mud still remained and as she looked around, not seeing Darcy, she tried to determine which way to go. Off to the right was a gravel path, and she settled on that direction, reasoning that there would be less of a chance of getting caught in the mud as she had the other day.

The path took her to a grove of trees, down below which was a small body of water. As she entered the grove, the path wound its way down, and in turning, she saw Darcy standing with his back resting against a tree. She saw him look up at her, pull himself away from the tree, nervously straighten his coat, and take the few long strides needed to bring him to her.

She stopped as he did. "Elizabeth, you came."

"Yes."

"I was uncertain whether you would see the note, and then, whether you would choose to come at all."

How could I pass up an invitation for such a delightful diversion as an early morning walk with you? she said to herself. "Yes, the note fell out of my book when I began reading it." She avoided addressing his other thought.

Darcy noticed a faint glimmer in her eyes before she answered him, and it took him a moment to turn and point in the direction of the pond. "Shall we?"

The two began to walk, awkwardly at first, thoughts of their walks on the ship flooding their minds.

At length, Darcy spoke. "I knew it was imperative we find an occasion to talk without interruption. I was not sure how else to propose it, as we have, *both of us,* been under the most diligent, watchful, and speculative eye of Miss Bingley."

"Oh, yes. Miss Bingley. We would not want to give her the wrong impression."

"She gets the wrong impression too easily and too wilfully, I fear." Darcy looked down and smiled at her, although she missed seeing it as she was staring straight ahead at the path before her. "But I do not believe her to be too early a riser, and thought this would be the best way to have a little time together without her interference."

Elizabeth walked with her hands clasped together in front of her, as Darcy mirrored her, walking with his clasped behind him. Each could not help rubbing their hands nervously together.

"I…"

"You…"

They looked at each other and nervously laughed, as they had both begun to speak at the same time.

"You first, Elizabeth."

"No, please you may go first."

Darcy stopped and turned toward her. "You left our room that last night on the ship, and then left the ship the next day without saying goodbye. I just wondered why."

Elizabeth's brows furrowed and she bit her lower lip as she contemplated what she would say. Being unable to meet his gaze she lowered her head and answered, "I... I just felt I should not stay in our... in the room that night."

He gingerly brought a few of his fingers under her chin and lifted it up, forcing her to look at him, and he looked intently into her eyes. "Was it... because I kissed you? Please accept my apology if it offended you."

Elizabeth quickly closed her eyes, her ragged breath betraying her feelings. "No, it was not the kiss itself." His fingers still pressed lightly under her chin and the mention of the kiss flooded her with a warmth that prompted her to turn away.

"Did you not like it?"

Elizabeth nervously laughed. "No, I mean yes. I mean..." Elizabeth paused.

"I do not wish you to be uncomfortable, Elizabeth."

"It was... it was because of Caroline."

Darcy's eyes widened. "Caroline? Caroline Bingley?"

Elizabeth nodded.

"You did not even *know* Caroline Bingley then, did you?"

Elizabeth turned back to him. "No, but you called me her name the night... the night of the storm."

"I called you Caroline?"

Elizabeth nodded.

"And you assumed that by my calling you Caroline, there was someone back home that I held in favourable regard."

"Yes, something like that, and therefore I should not have kissed you."

Suddenly Darcy began to gently laugh and Elizabeth wondered what he thought was so funny.

"I am sorry you find my conjecture so humorous, Sir."

"I do not find your conjecture humorous at all, Elizabeth. What I find humorous is the reason I called you Caroline."

Narrowing her eyes, Elizabeth asked, "And what, may I ask, *was* the reason?"

"I am not sure I should divulge it."

"Well you certainly must now, as you have piqued my curiosity."

"Let us walk." Darcy reached over and took her hand, tucking it inside his other arm and they turned. As they both faced forward and began slowly walking, Darcy told her, "I awoke that night and found you had turned and were sleeping in my arms. It was quite... disconcerting... in a good way. I found myself fighting a terribly difficult temptation, having you so close to me."

As he spoke, Elizabeth blushed, remembering the mortification she felt when she had awakened and found herself entangled with him.

"So, I steeled myself to think of you as Caroline Bingley, which apparently worked all too well."

"Think of me as Caroline Bingley?"

Darcy shook his head. "You have seen Miss Bingley. Do you really think someone like that could be a temptation to me?"

Elizabeth looked down, overwhelmed by his words.

Darcy stopped and turned back to her. "Elizabeth, you did not think… certainly you could not think Miss Bingley means anything to me."

"I confess I found it difficult to comprehend, but yes, I have wondered."

They stood staring at each other; Darcy's eyes travelling down to her lips and back up to her eyes.

"I am sorry, Elizabeth, that you have suffered under such a misapprehension. I had no idea…" The words no longer came as he found himself entranced by the glow in her eyes.

Elizabeth, feeling drawn in by his fervent gaze, finally shook herself free from his magnetizing spell and turned to walk again. Darcy quickly joined her.

The ardour that had come over him was quickly dispelled by Elizabeth's disparaging words. "And why was it that *you* purposefully neglected to tell me you owned *Pemberley's Promise*? Was it your belief that you could not entrust me with that information?"

"How did you come to learn of that?"

"That is not important right now."

Darcy brought up his hand to rub his chin. It was not a simple answer. He considered it was not even a sufficient answer. "When I came on board, I did not want anyone to know I owned the ship. I did not want to be burdened with complaints and problems and requests for special treatment. In essence, I wanted to be left alone in regards to the dealings with the ship."

This time, Elizabeth stopped and waited while he explained.

"I knew that in my asking you… in making the arrangement we did… I would be able to persuade the captain to agree to it because of my position. I feared afterwards, that if you found out, you would be angry, or no longer trust me."

Elizabeth looked away harshly. "Did you truly believe that of me?"

"Remember, Elizabeth, you were the one who claimed, most emphatically, that the captain would not agree to marry us. I felt that if you found out I was his superior, you would believe he had little or no choice because of who I was; you would come to regret it and resent me."

After a few moments of silence, he asked, "How *did* you find out, Elizabeth?"

Elizabeth knew this would be more difficult to tell him. Not that she was ashamed or felt she had done anything wrong, but because the whole experience at Pemberley evoked such strong feelings within her.

"We took a ship back to Liverpool from America, where my uncle finished up some business details. Upon leaving Liverpool, we stopped at Lambton, where my aunt had lived as a young girl."

"Lambton?" Darcy stopped. "Why, that is not five miles from my home!"

"Yes," answered Elizabeth. "Pemberley. One day my aunt and uncle and I took in the sights around Derbyshire, and my aunt mentioned visiting Pemberley. I was a little surprised by the name, mentioning that Pemberley was the name of the ship I had come over on, and she began to tell us of Pemberley and that it was owned by the Darcys. You can imagine my surprise."

"I am sorry that I did not tell you. But Elizabeth, tell me, did you go see Pemberley?"

Elizabeth nodded. "Yes, we did."

"And, may I ask, what you thought of it?"

"I thought it was quite grand, as most anyone would."

Darcy felt a great sense of contentment that Elizabeth had walked the very halls of his home.

"And I had the pleasure of meeting your sister. She is very sweet and kind and a very accomplished pianist."

"You met Georgiana?"

"Yes."

"You heard her play?"

Elizabeth nodded.

"I am amazed. Georgiana usually hides herself in her room when strangers are touring the home. She is extremely shy."

"Yes, but she can be encouraged out of her shyness. And the only reason we heard her play was because she did not realize we were there. She came out to meet us after Mrs. Reynolds informed her that I had been on the same ship as you on the crossing to America."

"This is remarkable news to me! Georgiana actually came out to meet you?"

"She was concerned about you and asked me questions about the trip."

Suddenly Darcy's face turned serious. "What did you tell her?"

"She wanted to know what may have happened because you had been so despondent when you arrived in America. I told her I had no way of knowing." She looked up at Darcy's face and searched the depths of his eyes. "She seemed very concerned. She cares for you greatly."

"She is very kind and caring. I am glad you met her. I only wish I had been there when you arrived."

They walked down to the pond and Darcy stooped down to pick up some small stones and casually began to throw them in. Elizabeth stood with her arms tucked together in front, marvelling at all they had said to each other.

Elizabeth laughed, "I am afraid, William, that we would not have visited if you had been home. I had my uncle inquire whether you were there. If you had been home, I would have felt too awkward to take the tour of it."

Darcy held one last stone in his hand, throwing it lightly in the air and catching it. "First of all," he said, "there would be no reason for you to have felt awkward if I had been there. And secondly," he tossed the rock into the pond, "you just called me William, we are alone, and you did not correct yourself."

"Yes, William, I did."

He stood looking at Elizabeth, taking in a very satisfied breath and wearing a slight smile that looked on the verge of bursting into a full-fledged grin. The smallest encouragement was all he needed to lean the short distance over and experience the joy and pleasure of kissing her lips again.

But before he had an opportunity to satisfy that thought, he looked up towards the top of the path, noticing a flash of orange coming down. "I fear, Elizabeth, that we are about to be intruded upon." He nodded up in the direction of the house and Elizabeth followed his gaze. "Shall we give Miss Bingley something to speculate about, do you think?"

Elizabeth, unsure of his meaning, but not inclined to further Miss Bingley's suspicious mind replied, "If you do not mind, I should prefer to continue walking on. I would not wish for her to give a shocking report to Mr. Bingley of Jane's sister." Her smile disarmed him and he reached out for her arm to briefly detain her.

"We could easily climb this tree, could we not, and escape her notice? I heard once that climbing trees can be a good way to avoid someone you do not wish to encounter."

Elizabeth gasped and stood transfixed, unable to move as she considered his words. The only way he would know of her climbing a tree was if he remembered the carriage ride, the conversation in the carriage, and her!

"I… uh… I must go!" Elizabeth turned and quickly continued down the path, away from the all-knowing, smiling gaze of William and the all suspicious gaze of Miss Bingley.

~~*

Elizabeth walked quickly around the path that eventually brought her back up to the house. She slipped in and went directly to Jane's room, grateful to see that Jane was up and sitting in a chair.

"Good morning, Jane. Are you feeling better today?"

"Yes, Lizzy. Have you been out for a walk this morning?"

"Yes. It was a grand morning for a walk!"

"You look… you look very vibrant! Walking certainly agrees with you."

"That it does, on certain occasions. Come, Jane, let me help you get ready to go downstairs."

"I believe I am ready to go home, as well. Can you see about securing the carriage from home?"

Elizabeth paused in attending to Jane, realizing with a start that now she had no desire to leave. If she had spoken the very same words yesterday, Elizabeth would have been inclined to leave at a moment's notice. Now she was hoping for every possible opportunity to remain on longer.

"We shall see, Jane. Let us see how you do once you are up.

~~*

When they both came to the breakfast parlour, Bingley was there with the Hursts. Darcy and Miss Bingley were nowhere to be seen. Bingley was pleased to see Jane even more improved and able to come downstairs to join them for breakfast.

They sat down at the table and answered the polite inquiries from everyone. It was some time later that Darcy and Caroline walked in. Darcy appeared invigorated by the walk, his eyes emanating a gleeful warmth as he looked at Elizabeth. Miss Bingley seemed exhausted by the walk and not at all satisfied with life in general.

The atmosphere around the table focused on the improvement of Jane, her being well enough to come down to the table, and from Bingley, how regrettable it was that she would be leaving. Miss Bingley was unusually quiet, forcing a smile and every now and then, making a trite comment. Darcy seemed very satisfied with things, and he openly, and quite warmly, looked up and glanced at Elizabeth. He had accomplished the first thing he had set out to do, and he was very pleased with the outcome.

Later, he would tell her the extent of his feelings and that they were still married. His throat suddenly dried as he merely *contemplated* doing this. He wondered how he would fare when faced when *actually* telling her!

Elizabeth sat next to Jane at the table and down from Darcy, and found herself actually smile as she witnessed Miss Bingley's occasional attempts to garner his attention again. It was sad, actually, but Elizabeth did not feel sorry enough for her to take away from her enjoyment in watching her make a spectacle of herself in front of him.

When the subject of Jane feeling better and the possibility of her returning home were brought up by Caroline, Jane suggested that they send a note home and ask for the carriage to be sent. Bingley agreed, but the prospect of her having to leave dampened his spirits ever so slightly.

Darcy's eyes narrowed as he contemplated Elizabeth leaving and not having another chance to speak with her. There was so much more he wanted to say!

A note was dispatched to Longbourn, asking for the use of the carriage to bring them home, and a reply from Mrs. Bennet emphatically stated that it was out of the question, and would not be available until Tuesday. Bingley graciously offered his own carriage, but informed them it would be best to leave the following day as it would be in use most of the day. Both sisters agreed and the two men's countenances shone of their satisfaction of keeping the ladies one more day.

Bingley harnessed Darcy in his study for most of the afternoon while Jane rested. While she was much improved, she had spent a great deal of energy that morning down with the others, and wished to spend their last evening in the drawing room in the company of everyone. Elizabeth sat in the room with her, feeling for the first time, a great sense of contentment.

Later that evening after supper, Elizabeth and Jane came down to the drawing room. Jane sat off to the side with Bingley, the two engaged in very private and concentrated conversation. Elizabeth brought her book to read, Darcy sat in a chair reading his own book, and Miss Bingley appeared as though her nerves would not settle down. She paced the floor, picking up a book at one point and then putting it down. She walked to where Darcy was seated and peered over his shoulder, looking down at what he was reading, but as he paid her no heed, she returned to her pacing.

At length she called upon Elizabeth to join her. "Miss Eliza Bennet, let me persuade you to follow my example, and take a turn about the room. I assure you it is very refreshing after sitting so long in one attitude."

Elizabeth viewed her with curious suspicion, but agreed. Miss Bingley took her arm as they walked and succeeded no less in the real object of her civility; Mr. Darcy closed his book and looked up. He was as much awake to the novelty of Miss Bingley's attention to Elizabeth as she herself was, and as the two women passed him, he lifted an eyebrow in question to Elizabeth's shrug of her shoulders in wonderment. He was directly invited to join their party by Miss Bingley, but he declined it, observing, that he could imagine but two motives for their walking the room together, with either of which motives his joining them would interfere.

Miss Bingley insisted on knowing his meaning.

Darcy twisted his mouth in a smug smile. "I have not the smallest objection to explaining my meaning," he said. "You either choose this method of passing the evening because you are in each other's confidence and have secret affairs to discuss, or because you are conscious that your figures appear to the greatest advantage in walking. If the first, I should be completely in your way, and if the second, I can admire you much better as I sit by the fire."

"Oh, shocking!" cried Miss Bingley, who was, at least, rather gratified that he included her in his statement of admiring their figures. Elizabeth merely blushed, not quite sure how she was to respond to such a bold statement by him.

Miss Bingley continued walking with Elizabeth, and as they came to pass by Jane and Bingley, she spoke again.

"Tell me, Miss Eliza. You have been here at Netherfield practically ever since your return from America. Is there not some favourite of yours that you left all those months ago whom you are anxious to see? Some gentleman who must have been pining for your return?"

"There is none that I call a favourite, no."

"Upon my word, Miss Eliza. Certainly there is someone!" She turned to Jane. "Tell us, Miss Bennet, does your sister speak the truth? With her great beauty, she is keeping a great secret from us! Tell us who Miss Eliza favours!"

Elizabeth shook her head, as she considered the desperate measures of this woman.

"There is no one," Jane answered softly.

Elizabeth was confident that Jane's answer would suffice in bringing Miss Bingley's assertions to a halt. But Jane unexpectedly continued, "Unless you would consider Mr. Wright." Jane gave Elizabeth a smile, which was met by Elizabeth's startled gaze.

Behind her, Darcy reacted with a start, remembering this as the name Elizabeth cried out when she had a fever. He had only briefly considered him to have been someone she held in her regard, and now began to wonder if indeed he was. He unknowingly held his breath as he waited for Elizabeth or her sister to continue.

"Oh? And just who is this Mr. Wright?" Miss Bingley seemed most interested.

"Jane, I really do not think *anyone* is interested in Mr. Wright!" Elizabeth said firmly as she directed an imposing stare at Jane.

Jane, being encouraged along solely by Bingley's smile, did not notice Elizabeth's threatening words or piercing stare. Yet in truth, Elizabeth had very rarely ever given Jane either, and therefore she was not inclined to notice them as such.

As Jane looked to Bingley, she said, "He is someone she met a couple of years ago in a carriage."

"Jane, *please!* I do not think anyone is inclined to hear this!"

"I would be very interested in hearing who Mr. Wright is." Elizabeth closed her eyes as she heard Darcy's appeal to Jane.

"Please, Jane, *no!*" This time she shook her head for emphasis, but Bingley was now applying to Jane to continue.

Jane could only smile at Bingley and oblige him. "Mr. Wright was someone Elizabeth met in a carriage ride from a few years back." She looked up at Elizabeth and could not understand why her eyes were closed. "Actually, she never got his name, but she felt that he was so right for her, that whenever she talked about him, and she did quite often, she referred to him as Mr. Wright."

Elizabeth dropped her head, speechless, as Caroline eagerly jumped in. "You are saying that Miss Elizabeth has been pining all these years for a nameless man she only met in a carriage? Is that not sweet?" Caroline patted the arm she held in hers. "You are really quite the romantic, Miss Eliza. I do hope that someday you shall meet this man and that he shall be everything you have imagined him to be all these years."

Darcy sat motionless, finally able to take in a greatly needed deep breath that filled his lungs with air as he considered the words Miss Bennet spoke. A wave of joy swept over him as he realized that all along, Elizabeth had remembered him from that day two years ago and not only that, remembered him with a fervent partiality.

Bingley was most engaged by this thought and asked Jane, "And what was there about this man that your sister found so appealing?"

Jane continued. "Even though they only spent a short time in the carriage, Elizabeth had decided he was the most handsome, most intelligent, most gracious man she had ever made the acquaintance of. She really did not think any other man would even come close to comparing favourably to him."

Elizabeth's face was flushed. She could not move, and if she had been able to, she would have seen a look on Darcy's face buoyantly displaying that every doubt he had entertained about Elizabeth's feelings toward him were now wiped away. It was a few moments before he was able to speak.

"And, Miss Elizabeth, if you were to meet this man again, do you think you would know him?"

Elizabeth took a deep breath, pursed her lips together and slowly turned. "I believe I may not recognize him immediately, but in time, I would come to know it was him."

Darcy smiled. "And I am quite certain that he, in turn, would remember you from that carriage ride. Indeed, he would have to consider himself a most fortunate man."

The two stared at each other, completely oblivious to the others in the room.

"Do let us have a little music," cried Miss Bingley, more than aware that something just happened in this conversation but unfortunately found it to be completely baffling to her. "Louisa, you will not mind my waking Mr. Hurst."

Her sister made not the smallest objection, and the pianoforte was opened. With Miss Bingley's command at the pianoforte, all conversation seemed suspended. After a few songs, as much as Jane and Bingley would have preferred to linger together for the duration of the evening, Jane had grown more tired and Elizabeth thought she should take her back upstairs.

As they excused themselves, Elizabeth readily noticed the smile frozen on Darcy's face that did not seem inclined to leave. In fact, if she had been able to watch him once she left, she would have seen a man reading a very serious historical novel with a sly grin that had taken hold of his features.

Chapter 22

As Elizabeth helped her sister get ready for bed, Jane turned to her. "Lizzy, you seemed upset when I spoke of Mr. Wright tonight."

Elizabeth waved her hand as if to dismiss the thought.

"I was speaking about him even before I realized that perhaps I should not," she smiled. "Mr. Bingley seemed so interested."

And Miss Bingley, Elizabeth said to herself. She took in a deep breath, wondering how much to tell Jane. "I will not say that I was upset, Jane, but perhaps I was more unsettled about how certain people in the room would react to such a sentiment."

"But why? It has been so many years; I thought everyone would enjoy hearing the story. I am so sorry if I embarrassed you."

Elizabeth sat on the bed next to her after she was settled in and took her hands in hers. "Jane, remember the other night when I said I had done something that I regretted?"

Jane nodded.

Elizabeth pondered how much she should tell her sister. As long as they were at Netherfield, she did not want to disclose that Darcy had been on the ship with her. "Well, I shall not go into all the details, but…" Elizabeth closed her eyes and breathed in deeply. When she let out the breath, she continued. "Mr. Darcy is… he is… you see… he is Mr. Wright."

Jane's eyes widened. "You mean… the real one? The one from two years ago? Or just a new one?"

Elizabeth let out a soft chuckle and nodded. "He is the one who was in the carriage two years ago. And he knows it."

"Oh, you should have told me! I mean, I had no idea."

"Of course not. And I had no idea the subject of Mr. Wright, the man in the carriage, would come up."

"Oh, Lizzy! Mr. Darcy? I can scarce believe it! But what was it you did that you regret?"

Elizabeth shook her head. "Not tonight. Some other time. You need to get some sleep. But please, dear Jane, keep this to yourself for now. I do not want Miss Bingley finding out that Mr. Wright is Mr. Darcy."

"I promise I will, Lizzy."

Elizabeth smiled. "Good night, dear sister."

"Good night."

Elizabeth tucked in the blankets on Jane's bed, and then walked into her room. Her heart had not slowed down one bit since the subject of Mr. Wright came up, but now it was not beating thunderously out of distress, but out of reassurance. The look William gave her had given her pause to consider that he *did* care for her; he cared for her a great deal. She flung herself onto her bed and smiled.

~~*

The next morning Elizabeth awoke to the sun gently nudging her to rise. She had slept much more soundly, but now felt the all too familiar lurching of her heartbeat as her thoughts went to William. She lay in bed watching the light slowly creep up the far bedroom wall and wondered whether she should get up and take another early morning walk.

Elizabeth smiled and threw off the comforter. *Whether she should* was not the issue. She *wanted* to, and promptly rose to get herself ready. As she was finishing her hair, she heard the telltale sound of a door opening down the hall and footsteps walking past. Since coming to Netherfield she had come to recognize the distinct sound of his walking past her door. Her heart fluttered even more.

She grasped the brush to her chest, and willed herself to sit for but a few minutes longer. She knew it would not do for her to walk out with Darcy, knowing Caroline was still doing all she could to keep her from spending any time alone with him.

Elizabeth waited a little longer, and then quietly opened the door and walked downstairs. She breathed in the aromas coming from the kitchen of coffee being made and breads baking. Her stomach gave her a little reminder that she had yet to eat, but at the moment there were more important things to tend to. She stepped outdoors and the early morning air beckoned her to breathe in deeply. It was a little cooler than it was yesterday and she pulled her coat around her tightly and hugged her arms around her as she began walking in the same direction she set out the day before.

As if experiencing a sense of déjà vu, she came upon the turn in the gravel path, and saw Darcy leaning against the same tree, in almost the same position as he had been the day before. But instead of feeling the apprehension that she felt yesterday, this morning she approached him with a sense of confident elation.

"Good morning, Elizabeth."

"Good morning, William."

Elizabeth was amazed how the simple gesture of calling him 'William' brought a smile to his face, accentuating the dimples that remained obstinately hidden save for the times he exhibited a full grin.

"I was hoping you would see the benefit of another early morning walk."

"You should know that I am quite fond of them."

Darcy smiled and extended his arm to her and Elizabeth responded in what seemed to her to be a most natural way, slipping her hand around it. They had walked together this way on the ship several times, but then it was more of an attempt to convey a picture of a married couple. This morning, for her, it was truly out of a desire to feel the warmth and strength of his arm in her small hand.

As they walked, their conversation began very fundamentally. "Did you sleep well, Elizabeth?"

"Yes, thank you; much better than the two previous nights."

"I am glad to hear that." Darcy took in a deep lungful of fresh morning air. "I must admit I slept quite soundly myself."

"Perhaps it was the evening meal we had," Elizabeth offered. "I understand some foods are more conducive to allowing one to have a good night's sleep."

Darcy laughed. "Or perhaps it was the evening conversation. I, personally, have found certain topics of conversation to put one in a rather content mood."

Elizabeth stopped and detected a mischievous twinkle in his eyes. "Perhaps, instead of being content, you were merely bored. Boredom does tend to leave one in a somnolent state."

"I think not, Elizabeth. Last evening, I was definitely not bored by the conversation."

Darcy prompted her to begin walking again.

"I think it would be best if we do not stop every time we have something to say. I have been made aware that Miss Bingley has the most attentive lady who waits on her and thus keeps her apprised of my every move. I would not be surprised if she is up and readying herself to come outdoors as we speak."

"I would not have considered Miss Bingley an avid walker."

"Oh, she is not. So I propose that we take a brisk, longer walk this morning, thereby curtailing the chances of encountering her."

Elizabeth smiled. "I highly concur with your suggestion, William."

"Good." The two began walking at a moderate pace and then Darcy added, "Although, as much as I wish to avoid Miss Bingley, I do owe her a debt of gratitude for her inquisitiveness last night."

Elizabeth happened to look up to him and watched as a very roguish air settled across his features.

"Mr. Darcy, you appear to be on the verge of imparting some remark that I would imagine might be at my expense."

"Do you really think I would do such a thing?" He brought his other hand over and placed it on hers. "Have you reverted back to calling me Mr. Darcy?"

Elizabeth pursed her lips. "There are times when your behaviour necessitates it, Mr. Darcy. Now is one of those times, as I must put you in your place before you attempt to tease me unmercifully." She looked up and his smirk had not dissipated. "Mr. Darcy, just say what you must. I shall bear up under it, I am sure."

He paused, knowing his penchant for unsuccessful teasing, but had felt too much elation at what he had heard last night to let it pass.

"Your Mr. Wright, that your sister mentioned last night..."

Elizabeth closed her eyes, but allowed a smile to touch her mouth. "Yes?"

"When you were feverish that first night in our room, you called out his name."

Elizabeth looked sharply to him and stopped, not expecting this. "I did?"

He nodded. "You said something like, 'Mr. Wright, I did not know.' Now what do you suppose you meant by that?" His smile became more pronounced.

Elizabeth rolled her eyes as she knew what he wanted her to say. "Mr. Darcy, what would you have me to say in answer to that? I have become aware these past few days that you remember that carriage ride, that you remember certain aspects of that carriage ride, and that last night, you became aware that I… that I…"

"Yes?" he leaned his head in, anxious for her to finish.

"Sometimes you can be impossible!" She stamped her foot, folded her arms together in front of her, and turned off to the side, more to hide the smile that had graced her lips than to make a firm point.

"I am only encouraging you to finish your sentence."

"Very smugly, I might add." She turned and took a few steps. "I believe we should begin walking again, Sir."

As the two began walking, Darcy took her arm. "You were going to say?"

She took a breath and coolly replied, "Yes, Mr. Darcy, you *are* Mr. Wright."

She actually felt relieved that it was out in the open, felt a sense of relief that at least he knew how she felt. In a softer voice she continued, "But I actually did not realize it until that last night during the storm." After a pause, she added with a laugh, "It seems as though something deep inside was a little quicker to recognize you than I was, though."

They walked along in silence and finally Elizabeth asked, "I never imagined that you would have remembered the carriage ride, let alone that I was the one in it. When did you remember?"

"That day you fell on the stairs. I had been enjoying our lively discussions during our morning walks and vaguely remembered thinking the same about the woman in the carriage those years back. When you told me how you had sprained your ankle two years earlier in a fall, I was fairly certain it was you."

Elizabeth thought back to that day. "That was the very day you made your… your offer."

"Yes, it was."

Elizabeth, having a lively and spirited nature, which, in the past few months had been quite subdued, felt an overwhelming tug within her heart to respond in kind.

"Mr. Darcy, you appear to me to have a very self-satisfied, smug look emblazoned across your face. What you heard last night and what you confirmed just now seems to sit well with you."

"That it does, Elizabeth. It does sit *very* well with me. And is it still to be Mr. Darcy?"

"At the moment, yes, Mr. Darcy." She stopped again and looked at him. "But there is something that *I* can view just as smugly."

Darcy narrowed his eyes and looked at her curiously. "And what would that be?"

She turned and briskly began walking, and Darcy, taking two long strides easily caught up with her.

"When my aunt and uncle and I visited Pemberley, Mrs. Reynolds was kind enough to include your study in the tour."

"Your aunt and uncle. These are the two people you spoke so highly of while on the ship."

"Yes. To me, they are dearest family. They are also the ones from Cheapside." Elizabeth cast a furtive glance up at Darcy to watch his reaction.

Darcy's only response was to smile. "But they are the ones you hold in highest…" He stopped abruptly. "The study has never been part of the public tour. Now why would she have done that? Mrs. Reynolds showed you my *study*?"

Elizabeth nodded, pursing her lips together and tilting her head only slightly to look at him up out of the corner of her eyes. She remained silent for a moment, as she watched his face.

He looked down at her, his eyebrows creased together, his head tilted, but the remnants of a smile still touching his lips. Elizabeth knew the moment he realized what she was talking about. His head lifted up and his eyes opened wide. He let out a small chuckle.

"Your sampler."

"Yes, you can imagine my surprise when, upon coming into your study, I saw my sampler on the mantel. Mrs. Reynolds was so generous to explain how that mantel carried all of your favourite treasures. There was my sampler, framed no less, among miniature portraits of your family and other favourite tokens."

They reached the pond and Darcy stopped this time, his heart about to burst, and believing he could not feel any greater depth of feeling, he reached out for Elizabeth's arm, not taking it as he would if he were escorting her, but in a way that brought her to a halt. She turned back surprised, and was met by his dark eyes searching hers. It was not a time for words, as Darcy brought his other hand around her, drawing her close, finally joining his two hands together behind her at her waist. She stood motionless, mesmerized by his closeness, his strong arms embracing her and pulling her against his firm chest. She tilted her head up just as his came down and claimed her lips.

His kiss was gentle at first, their lips lightly touching. Darcy tightened his arms around her as the kiss grew more ardent in its intensity. His arms had pinned hers against her side, but she managed, in a concerted effort to steady herself as well as return the embrace, to bend her arms at her elbows and bring her hands to grasp him lightly around his waist.

The rising sun's reflection on the pond seemed to give life to everything around it, and celebrate a love that was just mutually realized. They were framed by an arch of trees that seemed to swoop down in the gentle breeze and embrace them as they held and kissed each other.

Darcy was the one who finally, and most reluctantly, drew himself away. As he looked at Elizabeth's face in that first moment apart, he stopped in the midst of a breath as he beheld her eyes closed, her dark lashes splayed down across her eyes. He watched as she slowly opened them, and the green flecks in her hazel eyes shone in the sunlight.

Seeing his gaze upon her and at a loss to know what one says after such a formidable kiss, she merely fixed her eyes back upon him. He brought up a hand and reached for a loose strand of her hair, rubbing it between his fingers. How long had he been dreaming of this day, when he knew, in all assurance, that Elizabeth returned his love!

"William," Elizabeth finally whispered, finding it difficult to catch her breath, "is there nothing you have to say to me about the presence of my sampler there?"

"Your sampler, and its presence there, Elizabeth, speak for themselves, I believe."

Bringing both hands around her neck, and gently rubbing her jaw with his thumbs, he lowered his forehead to touch hers. "Elizabeth," he said gently, "I will be leaving for London soon after you leave for home today. I have some business that requires my attention there." He pulled his forehead away and replaced it with a kiss. "I shall, hopefully, be away no longer than a week."

Her eyes closed again when she felt his lips touch her forehead lightly. Still holding him at his waist, her hold grew firmer as she grew more unsteady. The only thing she could do, the only thing she wanted to do, was to lean her head forward and rest it against his chest.

His arms went around her again and they remained transfixed in each other's arms, seemingly content to remain that way. At length Darcy stiffened and pulled away again, thoroughly convinced that he must convey the news to Elizabeth that they were still married, but just as unsure what her reception of that news would be.

"Come, Elizabeth, let us walk on a little further." With the beating of their hearts urging them on, they walked in silence for some time until Darcy was sure they were far enough to be beyond Caroline's reach should she venture out.

He stopped again and turned to her. Elizabeth looked up to him, seeing a mixture of love and respect in his eyes that was, however, tempered by some disquieting thought. "William?"

He took in a quick, sharp breath, with every expectation of letting it out as he told her, but suddenly the words eluded him. He looked to the side and closed his eyes, as if offering a prayer for his words to be bathed in a spirit of wisdom and to be received in a spirit of acceptance.

Feeling a little more disconcerted herself, Elizabeth asked again, "William, what is it?"

He brought his hands up to her shoulders, as if to hold her up as well as give him strength. "Elizabeth, there is something I need to tell you. I am just not sure how to say it."

"A forthright manner is always a viable option."

He gently squeezed her shoulders as he began. "Elizabeth, our marriage…"

Elizabeth's eyes narrowed as she heard him mention that one thing that had been avoided in all their discussions since meeting at Netherfield.

"Yes?"

No words seemed to come forth from Darcy's mouth. He looked everywhere but at her as she waited very impatiently.

Elizabeth reacted by reaching out and grabbing his arm. "Tell me, William! What is it?"

"We are… Elizabeth, I… I never annulled the marriage. We are still married!"

Elizabeth paled, her eyes widened as her heart faltered, and her body quivered. She swallowed hard, her mouth went dry and words refused to come. She felt the briefest moment when she thought she would lose her ability to remain upright, and Darcy, sensing it, steadied her with his hands.

She reached up and grabbed both of his arms that were still on her shoulders. "We are still married?"

Darcy nodded. Holding on to her tighter, he said, "I know this must come as a shock to you. I am sorry if I have distressed you with this news."

"No, no, I am well," she whispered, feeling a bit more steady. Then she looked directly into his eyes. "I am faring *quite* well, actually." She gave him a smile.

"Once I got off that ship, I knew that I did not want to annul the marriage. My only objective was to find you again."

"And now?"

He cupped her face in his hands. "I still have no wish to end it. If it is acceptable to you, we must now decide when and how we will tell everyone. As soon as I return from London, I want to work towards that end. Elizabeth." He looked intently into her eyes. "Will you do me the honour of remaining my wife?"

Elizabeth's heart beat incessantly at his words and her eyes filled with tears. To think that they were still married was a wish she had not allowed herself to even consider. To think that he wished to remain wed to her was unfathomable.

"I would consider it an honour and a privilege."

A smile crossed Darcy's face that seemed to reach into the depths of him. Taking a deep breath he pulled her close, content to just hold her. Elizabeth wrapped her arms around him, pressing her hands against his back and nestling her head against his chest.

"Telling our families will be difficult," Darcy whispered.

She sighed.

"What is it, Elizabeth?"

"Oh, if only I could talk to my Aunt and Uncle Gardiner. They would know the best way to go about it."

He pulled away and bestowed another brief kiss on her willing lips. "It will work out, Elizabeth. Come, we ought to get back."

They turned and began walking silently back towards the house.

They reached the pond again and at the same time both noticed Miss Bingley making difficult progress down the path towards them. Darcy casually walked over to the edge of the pond and picked up a few stones as he had done the day before while Elizabeth remained back.

"I really should leave," she said again as Miss Bingley was almost upon them.

"You stay right where you are. She can find no fault in our both happening to be here at the same time! And I will not have Miss Bingley dictate when and where I can speak with you!"

Elizabeth watched as Darcy began to throw the stones he was holding, one by one, into the pond. Her heart pounded fiercely as she considered all of the implications of his words. They were still married and he had never been inclined to annul it! As her heart pounded out of great joy, she watched him throw one stone at a time into the pond, and stood back admiring his tall, lean form. His movement in simply throwing a stone was very striking and graceful. With joyful elation, she sighed quietly as Miss Bingley approached him.

"Mr. Darcy! What a surprise to see you again this morning!"

"Good morning, Miss Bingley."

"Is it not a lovely…" Caroline's eyes caught a movement off to the side and she turned to find Elizabeth standing there. Her eyes darkened and narrowed, going back to Darcy.

Feeling quite flustered, she turned back to Elizabeth and spoke in a most disagreeable way, "Oh, Miss Elizabeth. I see you are here as well. I forgot that you enjoy walks, too."

Elizabeth nodded and gave Caroline a genuine smile. "It *is* a lovely morning for a walk."

Turning back to Darcy, she saw that neither was inclined to move. Her suspicious mind suddenly began churning, and she surmised that Mr. Darcy must be trying to ignore this country nobody who had come out with the sole intention of entrapping him! She could only assume that her coming upon them when she did was providential.

She walked over to Darcy, struggling to keep her balance as she walked down the slope to the edge of the pond. As her foot, shod in a most elegant shoe, suddenly turned in the soft dirt, her arms went flailing as she tried to keep from falling. She managed to keep herself upright, but her composure was a little less steady. Elizabeth could not keep herself from chuckling.

As she came up to Darcy, he was throwing the last stone in the pond.

"Mr. Darcy," she said under her breath, "Just say the word and I shall send Miss Elizabeth, along with her sister, packing for Longbourn the moment we get back! If she has provoked you or imposed on you in any way, I shall…"

"Miss Bingley, what makes you think a charming woman such a Miss Bennet would impose herself on me? Does it appear that she is imposing?"

Her eyes narrowed as she looked over at Elizabeth. "Mr. Darcy, you do not know her as I do. I see things that you may not see."

Elizabeth watched from the side, unable to hear their words, but ever confident that Darcy was putting her in her place, as reflected on her face.

"Miss Bingley, I am afraid you will *never* know Miss Bennet as well as *I* do."

The look that crossed Caroline's face was worth every agonizing speculation Elizabeth had endured. A pained expression imprinted itself and she sharply flinched back, appearing to Elizabeth as if she had actually been slapped, rather than merely spoken to.

Caroline was too stubborn to let Elizabeth remain alone with Darcy, and too ignorant to realize hers was a lost cause. The three of them quietly returned to the house, with two out of the three very content to walk in blissful silence, and the third very inclined to consider Mr. Darcy not quite in his right mind.

When they arrived at the house, Jane was up, and some very able ladies had been sent up to pack hers and Elizabeth's things. As they all gathered in the breakfast room for their last meal, Bingley sombrely commented on how greatly he would suffer the impending loss of Jane, but expressed a wish to see her completely recovered soon and come again to Netherfield when he gave the ball.

Miss Bingley was all too cordial in her address to Jane, but seemed not inclined to address Elizabeth or Darcy at all. Her finding them together and his words to her had completely disconcerted her and she was counting down the minutes for Elizabeth and her sister to be out of her house.

For the first time since coming to Netherfield, Darcy was able to secure the place next to Elizabeth at the table. As he and Elizabeth listened to Bingley overindulging in his feelings for Jane, doting on her every need, and painfully wondering how he would endure without her captivating presence any longer, Darcy and Elizabeth were content to sit at the table with their fingers intertwined beneath the concealing layers of linen and lace that graced the fine table.

When they were ready to leave, the two Bennet ladies expressed their gratitude to Charles' sisters for their hospitality, although Elizabeth was far more aware of Miss Bingley's true feelings than Jane ever was. Elizabeth felt that Miss Bingley and her sister considered Jane a sweet girl, but that they would never view her as an acceptable choice for their brother to marry. And now, Elizabeth was sure, Miss Bingley's contemptuous estimation of her was quite irreversible.

Later, as the two men escorted the ladies out to the waiting carriage, Darcy walked alongside Elizabeth. "I shall see you in a week's time," he whispered, as Bingley occupied himself with talking to Jane. "There is much we need to discuss." When they reached the carriage, Darcy helped Elizabeth up, letting his hand linger around hers as she climbed in. He stepped back and smiled, taking a very contented deep breath. As the carriage pulled away, Elizabeth turned back and watched him until they were out of sight.

"Oh, Darce," Bingley said when the carriage could no longer be seen. "You just have no idea what it is to love someone as much as I love Jane. We must see to finding you someone just as wonderful." He sighed and Darcy could only smile at his lovesick friend who had been so infatuated with the presence of one Bennet sister that he never noticed his best friend was just as deeply in love with the other.

Chapter 23

Elizabeth's return to Longbourn was quite an adjustment for her. She had only been home one evening since returning from America before setting off to Netherfield to assist her ailing sister. The unrestrained behaviour of her youngest sisters and uncontrolled outbursts by her mother reminded her just how agreeable her life had been these past six months in the refined presence of her aunt and uncle and in the delightful, close presence of her husband. She smiled as she considered with great delight how wonderful it felt to think of him as her husband and be assured that he still was!

Elizabeth's moments of contentment and pleasant dreams of one gentleman, however, were increasingly intruded upon by Lydia and Kitty openly and boisterously admiring the officers that had come to Meryton. Her mother did nothing to discourage their behaviour and actually made matters worse by relentlessly declaring how good it was for their girls that there should be so many officers encamped in the neighbourhood.

Mrs. Bennet was also quite convinced that Mr. Bingley would soon make an offer to Jane and reminded everyone she met what a good choice he was for her. A match between Jane and Bingley was not disagreeable to Elizabeth at all, but things were not as settled between him and her sister as her mother would have everyone believe. The way she spoke of this match to all their neighbours, one would have thought it was a decided thing. If things did not turn out as Jane desired and her mother expected, Elizabeth feared it would be especially difficult for Jane to face everyone, let alone deal with her own broken heart.

After being home only a few days, Elizabeth finally found herself somewhat adjusted to, or at least beginning to tolerate, living in the Bennet household again. One evening, she found herself, along with her mother and sisters, surprised by the news Mr. Bennet gave at dinner. He announced to the family the imminent arrival of one cousin, from whom he had received a letter a few weeks earlier. The cousin was a Mr. William Collins, who was the clergyman of Hunsford Parish, whom the family had never before met, and who, upon the death of Mr. Bennet, was next in line to inherit Longbourn. The very thought of this cruel act caused Mrs. Bennet an undue amount of vexations and rattled nerves and everyone in the household was made to be aware of it. Everyone also came to know her opinion of this man and that she did not look with favour upon his coming to Longbourn for a visit.

His arrival caused much consternation and speculation. From the contents of his letter, both Elizabeth and her father were inclined to view him as being a rather foolish man. It was with great curiosity that the family gathered to meet him the day he was to arrive.

Mr. Collins turned out to be an odd combination of melodramatic discourses and flattering nothings. The whole Bennet family listened to him in disbelieving awe as he spoke of his regret at the rift that had existed between his father and Mr. Bennet for so many years. He apologized profusely for the fact that entails were a common occurrence, although Mrs. Bennet was of the opinion that he did not feel one bit of remorse and one day he would, most unmercifully, drive them all out of Longbourn.

Collins also spoke most liberally about his exceptional patroness, Lady Catherine de Bourgh, and with great zeal gave explicit details about the home she lived in with all its chimneys, fireplaces, and windows; adding that he was separated from it only by a small lane.

Elizabeth spent most of the week trying to avoid her cousin's presence while counting down the days for Darcy's return. Jane was greatly improved with each passing day, and as the weather accommodated them, they were able to spend a great deal of time out of doors.

Their times together were usually accompanied by Mr. Collins, as well, and Elizabeth felt certain that he had come to Longbourn to secure a wife for himself from among one of her sisters. At first, his inclination seemed to lean toward Jane, but Elizabeth believed that her mother gave him direct advice, declaring Jane was very close to becoming engaged, and that he should turn his attentions elsewhere. Unfortunately, this meant his attentions soon turned towards her.

Elizabeth did all she could to discourage him, but to no avail. She often wondered what he would think of her if he knew she was already married. She wondered what *all* of her family would think, but worried particularly how her father and Jane would view it. She believed that neither would understand, although she felt quite secure that Jane would be more merciful toward her than her father. Her concern with telling Jane too soon about her marriage was that everyone had always expected her to marry first. Everyone anticipated that she would receive an offer of marriage from Mr. Bingley, but it had not yet come. Elizabeth decided she would only tell Jane when she felt it was an absolute necessity.

The days passed slowly, and soon it had been a week since Jane and Elizabeth had left Netherfield. Elizabeth's desire to see Darcy grew stronger with each passing day, as did her determination to avoid Collins.

It was on a mildly pleasant afternoon that the Bennet sisters decided to walk into Meryton to run some errands. Mr. Collins, taking a continued, determined, and most persistent liking to Elizabeth, decided to join them, much to everyone's consternation.

The walk was long, but the girls were young and did it frequently, so it was an easy distance for them. But by the time they reached the little village, Mr. Collins was quite fatigued, and his little round face was splotched with areas of red and enveloped in perspiration. It was all he could do to summons the energy to pull out his handkerchief and dab it across his face.

The first thing Kitty and Lydia did when they arrived was to run ahead of the others to the window of the milliner's shop to see if there was anything new in it.

As they looked at a newly displayed bonnet, they argued who it would look best on and what they could do to make it prettier.

When Kitty had enough of Lydia's boasting about how *she* would look much better in the bonnet, she turned away and caught sight of an officer across the road.

"Look, Lydia, there is Denny!"

The attention of every young lady was soon caught by a young man, whom they had never seen before, of most gentlemanlike appearance, walking with Denny on the other side of the way. All were struck with the stranger's air and wondered who he could be. Kitty and Lydia, determined to find out, led the way across the street.

Mr. Denny addressed them directly, and entreated permission to introduce his friend, Mr. Wickham, who had returned with him the day before from town, and, he was happy to say, had accepted a commission in their corps. This was exactly as it should be; for the young man wanted only regimentals to make him completely charming. His appearance was greatly in his favour; he had all the best part of beauty, a fine countenance, a good figure, and very pleasing address.

Denny and Wickham seemed quite content to talk with Lydia, who knew how to draw the men in with her teasing and laughter. Wickham walked around the group to stand by her, getting out of the bright sun by placing himself in the shadow the eave of the small building they were standing by.

Everyone waited impatiently as Lydia seemed to garner both men's undivided interest. Elizabeth watched with concern as her youngest sister certainly knew how to captivate a man's attention and that worried her. She only wished her parents showed more care to check her flirtatious ways, lest she bring scandal to her family. Unfortunately, her mother would only encourage her behaviour.

As they talked, two men on horseback slowly made their way down the road. They both noticed the group of women talking with the men. Darcy's eyes immediately picked out Elizabeth and he felt that increasingly familiar lurch of his heart. He could not take his eyes from her.

Bingley let out an audible gasp as he noticed Jane, and the two men, without speaking, led their horses in their direction.

Darcy noticed the five Bennet sisters, but did not notice any of the others in their party distinctly; his eyes were content to rest solely on Elizabeth. When one of the sisters pointed out the two men coming down the road, all eyes went to them and Darcy was only barely aware that one of the men, the one standing in the shadows, had briskly turned and began walking away down the street.

Bingley jumped off his horse and cheerfully greeted Jane and the others. Jane, at first, seemed embarrassed by this surprise meeting, but Bingley's endearing personality soon had her engaged in conversation and she quickly lost all coherent thought.

Darcy slid off his horse, taking off his hat, and slowly walked over as well, greeting Elizabeth with a smile in his eyes. He was introduced to Jane's and Elizabeth's sisters and the men were then both introduced to a cousin of the Bennet sisters, a Mr. Collins, and the remaining officer. Denny excused himself after the introduction and left to rejoin his friend.

Mr. Collins bowed repeatedly, a hint of nervousness and excitement consuming his features as he slowly moved closer to the place where Darcy and Elizabeth were standing together.

Bingley spoke animatedly to Jane while Darcy and Elizabeth exchanged a quieter conversation.

"How was London, Mr. Darcy?"

"It was most profitable for me. I took care of some business that required meeting with some business associates and then attended to a matter that required making new, rather pleasant personal acquaintances."

Elizabeth could not read the look on his face except to be sure he was not going to explain any further. At least not now.

"I am glad."

Collins hovered close to the pair, seemingly intent to listen to their conversation. Darcy knew he could not overtly express his joy at seeing Elizabeth, with Collins in such close proximity, as much as he would have liked to. He looked at Collins and then back at Elizabeth. "As much as London has to offer, I found myself greatly longing for the pleasant company that I have found in this neighbourhood."

Elizabeth noticed the twinkle in his eyes and the slight tilt of his lips in a smile. She returned a smile, accompanied by a slight blush, knowing his words were meant for her.

Collins could not contain himself any longer, and when he noticed the pause in the conversation between Darcy and his fairest cousin, he broke in. "Mr. Darcy," he excitedly addressed the tall, fashionable man, "Would you be, by some small chance," and here he brought his finger and thumb close to one another and continued to make repeated small gestures that resembled a bow, "of the same Darcy family that is so inexorably linked to my generous, most noble patroness, Lady Catherine de Bourgh?"

Darcy looked at him as surprise and concern spread over his features. "Indeed, she is my aunt."

Collins clasped his hands together in jubilant satisfaction. "Is this not grand news? To actually make your acquaintance! She speaks so highly of you!" His nervousness seemed to propel his wordiness. "I am most pleased to tell you that she was, when I left her a few days ago, in exceedingly good health!"

"I am glad to hear that."

Elizabeth noticed the look of discomfiture that seemed to come over Darcy. She could not imagine why he would not feel inclined to receive the news that Collins was his aunt's clergyman with any pleasure.

Bingley then told everyone that they were just on their way to Longbourn to deliver the invitation to a ball he was having a Netherfield.

"Oh, Mr. Bingley!" exclaimed Lydia. "How wonderful! A ball at Netherfield, just as you promised!"

Lydia and Kitty were soon beside themselves in anticipation of the ball. Mr. Bingley was now looked upon with great admiration by the two girls, although it was only because he was giving the ball as promised and assured them the officers would also receive an invitation.

Darcy was grateful for the distraction as it took everyone's attention off himself and he took the opportunity to lean in to Elizabeth. "Elizabeth, how long is your cousin to remain at Longbourn?"

"I believe he is leaving Saturday next."

Darcy pursed his lips as Collins cast a glance toward the two and then turned back to the others.

In a soft whisper, he said, "It will not be good for me to talk with your father while Collins is still in your home. I would not want word getting back to my aunt before I am able to talk to her. Unfortunately, that means it will not be until after the ball that I am able to come. Does that disappoint you too much, my beloved?"

Elizabeth's disappointment was soothed by his endearing address. "If that is best, I understand."

Using the hat he was holding in one hand, he brought it over his other as he gently reached over and took her hand in his. Letting his fingers intersect with hers, he gave her hand, which felt so soft and tiny in his, a tender squeeze.

Darcy smiled at Elizabeth's blush and pulled away his hand as Collins turned back. Collins had noticed the particular attention the esteemed Mr. Darcy had been extending to Miss Elizabeth. He sighed as he contemplated with great pleasure that if this man, the nephew of his patroness, condescended graciously to associate with her, certainly Lady Catherine would find it within her to accept his choice for a wife with the same condescension.

Denny caught up with Wickham who had stopped and turned back toward the group at the far end of the street.

"You left very suddenly there, Wickham."

"Yes," he said slowly, his eyes on the group gathered. "I deemed it to be to my best advantage to remain unseen by a certain gentleman."

As Wickham watched Darcy, his old childhood chum, something unusual caught his eye. Normally, Darcy shunned country neighbourhoods and distanced himself from those of that class. And yet, here he was approaching this group, so far beneath his station, as if they were his equals. He noticed that the two elder Bennet daughters were quite pretty, and from the looks of things, the other gentleman with Darcy seemed to have an attachment to the eldest. Could that mean that Darcy had taken a fancy to Miss Elizabeth?

He shook his head and laughed, thinking to himself, *Ol' Darcy, has this country lady somehow touched your heart? How sweet. But knowing you are in the neighbourhood should prove quite profitable for me if I keep out of your sight and play my cards right!*

Wickham turned and slapped his friend on the back. "Come, Denny, I suddenly find myself with quite an appetite!"

Chapter 24

The Bennet ladies remained in Meryton to visit their Aunt and Uncle Phillips, while Darcy and Bingley went on their way, expressing the hope to pay a visit to Longbourn later in the week. For the remainder of the afternoon, the subject of the ball was first and foremost on Lydia's mind as well as Kitty's. That was all that would satisfy the two girls as the topic of conversation. Elizabeth was content to silently reflect on her husband, knowing he had returned safely and she looked forward, with a quieter, but just as joyful anticipation, to the fact that soon she would not have to conceal her affections and regard for her husband.

While visiting their aunt and uncle, Lydia wasted no time in securing an invitation to return the next night with the promise that her uncle would extend the invitation to Wickham himself, along with several other officers. With all the excitement and anticipation of the upcoming ball and the prospect of seeing Mr. Wickham the following night, Lydia was quite sure life could not be more perfect!

Later, as they walked home, Mr. Collins brought up the subject of his patroness and Mr. Darcy. "I would have you know, Miss Elizabeth, that Lady Catherine speaks ever so highly of her nephew. I cannot wait to inform her that I made his acquaintance this very day! She is very mindful of these things and it will please her to no end." His outburst of enthusiasm was almost too much for Elizabeth to bear, even if it did concern William. She turned to Jane, raising her eyebrows and concealing a smirk.

Because Collins' words had a way of grating on her nerves, she had come to form a rather negative opinion of Lady Catherine and she deemed it wise to begin viewing the great lady in a more favourable light. She thought with amusement that she was now *her* aunt, as well. But at length, as Collins continued with his excessive verbosity about her, Elizabeth found herself no longer listening.

His endless effusions about the woman, her home, and her excessive attentions continued with nary an audience but himself. It was some moments later that she heard him say, "…one day hers and Mr. Darcy's great estates shall be united."

Elizabeth heard Mr. Darcy's name mentioned and looked at him curiously. "Excuse me? What did you just say?"

Collins looked at her, pleased that Elizabeth was taking an interest.

"Whenever I am invited to dine with her, I hear wonderful stories of how she is Mr. Darcy's closest family, and how one day their two great estates shall be united."

Elizabeth gave him a puzzled glance. "Their two estates united? What does she mean by this?"

With a contented grin, he answered, "Ah, my dearest Cousin Elizabeth, do you not see? Lady Catherine's daughter, Anne, a princess is what I would call her, although it is very unfortunate that she has a weakly constitution, but still, she is a gem, as I often tell Lady Catherine…"

Elizabeth shook her head in exasperation. "Yes, you have often spoken of her. But what of uniting the two estates?

"Why, that she is engaged to be married to Mr. Darcy! And by this, their two great estates, Pemberley and Rosings, will be united." Collins clasped his hands as he most eagerly relayed this information to Elizabeth, thinking again that his patroness would be quite pleased when he wrote and informed her that his second eldest cousin was the choice for his wife.

Elizabeth paled. "They are engaged?" she asked meekly as she reached over to Jane and took her arm to give her some support.

"Oh, most certainly! And what joy that will give my patroness when they are finally united in matrimony! Lady Catherine has told me how she and her sister, Mr. Darcy's mother, promised them to each other as infants. I believe Mr. Darcy has only been waiting until his cousin improves in health before he marries her, but her mother is eagerly anticipating their marriage exceedingly soon."

Elizabeth looked down to conceal the feelings that suddenly began to overwhelm her as Mr. Collins continued. *Certainly William's aunt would understand that he did not necessarily hold to the hopes that two women made years ago,* Elizabeth thought to herself. *Or would she?* She wondered how much Lady Catherine would feel he was bound, either by moral or familial obligation, to this engagement and what would the neglect of it mean to him and his relationship with his family? If indeed it was expected that he was engaged to his cousin, where would that ultimately place Elizabeth in his family's regard? Elizabeth no longer heard her cousin as all these questions flooded her thoughts and she walked the rest of the way home in silent contemplation.

~~*

The following evening, the coach conveyed Mr. Collins and his five cousins at a suitable hour to Meryton; and the girls had the pleasure of hearing, as they entered the drawing-room, that Mr. Wickham had accepted their uncle's invitation, and was then in the house.

As Mr. Collins was drawn into a game of whist, the two youngest girls were occupied with some of the officers in a game of cards; Mary was exhibiting on the pianoforte; Jane was politely listening; and Elizabeth found herself alone. At length, Mr. Wickham approached. He was definitely far above the rest of the officers in person, countenance, air, and walk. She watched Lydia's look of disappointment as he came over to Elizabeth and asked if he could join her.

"Do you not care to play, Mr. Wickham?"

"No, I know little of the game they are playing."

Elizabeth smiled and there was a slight pause in the conversation. Elizabeth finally commented, "You left quite suddenly yesterday afternoon. We were not even able to pay our respects."

"Yes, and I do apologize. I had a pressing engagement."

The two were distracted by an outburst by Lydia.

"Your youngest sister, Lydia, is a very lively sixteen year-old."

Elizabeth raised her eyes at him, wondering if he was attracted or indifferent to her. "She is only fifteen, and yes, sometimes she behaves in a most unreserved manner."

Wickham suddenly lowered his voice and looked intently at Elizabeth. "When I left the other day, two gentlemen were approaching. Could you tell me who they are?"

Elizabeth turned her head and met his intense gaze. "One was Mr. Bingley, who recently let Netherfield, and the other was his friend, Mr. Darcy."

"Hmm, do you know them both well?"

"I... um..." Elizabeth took in a deep breath and felt her face involuntarily blush. "I recently spent a few days at Netherfield, when Jane had taken ill there, and I did come to know them both fairly well. Why do you ask?"

"Oh, nothing in particular. One merely seemed familiar, that is all."

The subject of the two men was dropped, and soon Wickham left her side to spend most of the remaining time in Lydia's presence. Elizabeth watched as Lydia continued to engage her flirtatious way with him and he seemed disinclined to dismiss them. Elizabeth shook her head, wondering just how far Lydia was willing to go to attract a man's attention. She only hoped Wickham was wise enough to know when to walk away and gentleman enough to do it.

~~*

The prospect of the ball at Netherfield had sent the home at Longbourn into such a disarray of feminine emotions that Mr. Bennet quite believed he would not be able to endure it.

Mrs. Bennet chose to credit Bingley for giving it in compliment of her eldest daughter and was particularly flattered by receiving the invitation from Mr. Bingley himself, instead of a ceremonious card. She was frequently overcome by such a variety of nerves causing her both rapture and distress that she knew not how to coherently articulate her feelings save for a frequent eruption of wails accompanied by a very animated set of gestures and flailing of her hands.

Jane's thoughts on the subject of the ball were more subdued, but her emotions were actually beginning to spill over in anticipation of being able to see and dance with Mr. Bingley again. More than once she was found to be daydreaming when her father addressed her, and although she denied that she was distracted by thoughts of one Charles Bingley, her blushing countenance suggested otherwise.

The happiness anticipated by Catherine and Lydia depended on the hope that Mr. Wickham would be in attendance and that they could dance half the evening with him.

Mary assured her family that she had no disinclination for a ball, although she could not speak as highly in favour of it or as frequently as everyone else did. She often sided with Mr. Bennet as he commented on the tone of the Bennet household that the ball seemed to be the only topic of conversation and everyone was dwelling to a far greater extent upon it than they should. But Mr. Bennet would not allow that he and Mary were of the same opinion and continually contradicted her just for his own caprice.

Elizabeth's thoughts on the ball were mixed with all the anticipation that the pleasure of being with William would bring, but it was tempered with the gnawing realization that they had several storms to pass through before all would be smooth sailing for them. Mr. Collins' revelation about this expected engagement between Darcy and his cousin prompted her to wonder of his family's acceptance of their marriage.

Elizabeth also found herself battling another most discomfiting realization. Mr. Collins, despite Elizabeth's fervent discouragement, was singling her out and displaying quite overt signs of amiable behaviour toward her, which she had to assume, was for reasons of matrimonial deliberation.

Politely discouraging Mr. Collins without offending him became increasingly difficult. To add to her dilemma, a few days before the anticipated ball, he unfortunately solicited her hand for the first two dances. She accepted with as much good grace as she could, mostly at the insistence of her mother, and could barely endure his company as she became the object of his increasing civilities and frequent attempts at complimenting her on her wit and vivacity. Although she was more astonished than gratified by this effect of her charms, it was not long before her mother gave her to understand that the probability of a marriage between her and Collins was exceedingly agreeable to her.

As long as he continued at Longbourn, she would be painfully miserable having to endure his presence and her husband would be prevented from coming to speak to her father because of the association between Collins and his aunt.

To avoid the misery of Mr. Collins' attentions, coupled by a wish to encounter Darcy out on a walk, Elizabeth wakened every morning with the hope to venture outside. But unfortunately, from the day they received the invitation to the ball to the day of the event itself, there was such a succession of rain as to prevent anyone from walking or visiting anywhere. This left not only Elizabeth in a pitiable state, but Lydia and Kitty, as well, as that meant there was no visit to their aunt in Meryton, no officers, and no news that could be sought after.

Jane seemed to take the lack of a visit from Bingley with expected serenity and was more concerned with how quiet and withdrawn Elizabeth had become. She knew her sister had taken a liking to Darcy; the fact that he was her *Mr. Wright* made that very apparent. But she wondered if there was something more than just an infatuation with the man from two years ago. If the attachment on her part had grown stronger by his presence at Netherfield, the announcement by Collins must have disconcerted her. She decided they must talk.

A few days before the ball, she came into Elizabeth's room when everyone had gone to bed and sat on the edge of her bed.

Elizabeth had been reading, or at least trying to read, when Jane came in and she recognized at once that look of sisterly concern written across her face. She closed the book and set it aside.

"What brings you in here tonight, Jane?"

"I thought we might talk."

"Hmm," muttered Elizabeth. "About anything in particular?"

"Is there not something *you* would like to talk about?"

"You must have something in mind, dear sister. What is it?"

Jane nervously rubbed her hands together. "Ever since the day we walked to Meryton," she watched her sister's face, "when Mr. Collins mentioned that Mr. Darcy was engaged to his cousin, you seem distracted, faraway."

Elizabeth smiled and patted Jane's hand. "I appreciate your concern, Jane, but…"

"Lizzy, I know how fond you were of *Mr. Wright* after you met him, and now, having been in his presence, that is, Mr. Darcy's presence, it cannot be easy to dismiss those feelings you had for him. But you must know that people of their class often marry for reasons of obligation, to improve their status and expand their wealth or, as Mr. Collins said, unite two estates." She then put her hand on top of Elizabeth's, which still rested on her other hand. "He is of a completely different class, Lizzy. Even if there was not an arranged engagement with his cousin, you could not rationally cling to any hope that he would view you as anything more than an acquaintance of his friend. He may have been your *Mr. Wright*, but you cannot expect him to necessarily view you in the same light." Jane gave her sister a smile. "However, in my opinion, he would be a fool to overlook you solely for those reasons."

Elizabeth took a deep breath and looked away for a moment. When she turned back, she bit her lips in a determination of what to say. She had not wanted to tell Jane this soon, but felt there would be no better opportunity. Finally, she took both her hands and grasped each of Jane's.

"Jane, there is something that I must tell you. But you must promise me not to tell a soul!"

Jane withdrew a little at the intensity in Elizabeth's face. "What is it, Lizzy?"

"I told you that Mr. Darcy was on the ship going over to America."

Jane nodded.

"Well there is one small, minor thing that happened that I did not tell you."

Jane's eyes were now wide with anticipation.

Elizabeth gulped and gripped her hands more tightly. There were a few moments of silence before she went on. "Jane… while we were on the ship… Mr. Darcy and I… we…"

Jane gasped. "You did something you regret?"

"Yes and no."

"Yes and no? What does that mean?"

"It means when I told you I had done something I regretted, I did, indeed regret it. But now I do not."

"Oh, Lizzy, whatever do you mean?" Elizabeth had never seen such alarm written across her sister's face.

Elizabeth closed her eyes as she said in a soft, muffled voice, "…we got married."

Jane's eyes were now wide with astonishment. "Married? You mean you and Mr. Darcy married… each other?"

"Shhhh," Elizabeth laughed lightly and nodded. "Oh, Jane, it is a very long story. But the short of it is that he had the only available bed on the ship in his room and I needed one. We married solely so that I could sleep in that bed without any appearance of impropriety. The whole marriage was a pretence and he was going to annul it once he returned to England."

Jane's mouth dropped open, but she could not produce one audible sound.

"But something happened on the ship that neither of us expected."

Jane was not sure she dared ask, but found herself compelled to. "What was that?"

"We fell in love," Elizabeth sighed. "But both of us were afraid to tell the other. We travelled all the way to America *pretending* to be a couple who fell in love on the ship and married, while, in all truth, we really *were*. Each of us thought the other was holding to the expectation that the marriage was only a temporary solution to a problem and would be later annulled, so neither of us confessed our love to the other."

Jane found it difficult to breathe, but finally took in a deep breath of relief. "Oh, Lizzy, my head is spinning with all this news. But tell me, has he annulled the marriage?"

Elizabeth shook her head and patted Jane's hand. "No, and he does not intend to. He told me the last morning we were at Netherfield. In fact, I really was not aware of his feelings for me until that morning."

"Oh, Elizabeth, I must admit I am quite astonished! And to find out that he and Charles are best friends!"

Elizabeth smiled at her use of his Christian name. "Yes. When I first saw him at Netherfield, I was quite surprised. Surprised and shaken. I knew how strong my feelings were for him, but I believed him to be indifferent to me, having a fondness, at best. In fact, I was under the false assumption that he and Miss Bingley shared a mutual regard."

"Charles has told me that his sister has long desired his good opinion."

"That is very apparent."

"But Lizzy, what of this engagement Mr. Collins spoke of?"

"Knowing Lady Catherine has lived with this expectation that William is to marry her daughter, my main concern is how she will feel about me once she knows the truth. I cannot imagine I will sit well in her graces now."

"When are you going to tell everyone? I mean… Lizzy! You are married!" Suddenly a serious look swept across Jane's face. "What about Papa? He will not be happy either!"

Elizabeth nodded. "I have thought about that. That is something William and I… Mr. Darcy and I need to discuss now that he is returned from London. Unfortunately with the weather as bad as it has been, neither of our suitors seems inclined to visit us."

"Oh, but Lizzy, Mr. Darcy is not your suitor, he is your *husband!* I can scarce believe it! Married to Mr. Darcy!"

"Jane, it is still hard for me to believe, but it is true."

Jane pulled her sister close and gave her a fervent embrace. Tears pooled in her eyes as she shared in the joy of her sister's marriage and hoped that the same would be true of her shortly.

Elizabeth could not have been more pleased with Jane's reception of the news and could only hope and pray that Mr. Bingley would soon make the offer that her sister so greatly desired. She also offered up a prayer that she and William would find the most suitable time and appropriate way to tell everyone else of their marriage before word of it was somehow found out.

Chapter 25

On the day of the ball, the Bennet household displayed a total disregard for Mr. Bennet's sanity as they readied themselves for the event of the season, at least so considered by all in their neighbourhood. They were of the firm opinion that it was to be a ball unlike any other. To be held at such an illustrious place as Netherfield, to have all the fine officers in attendance, and to conjecture that Bingley might, before long, make an offer to Jane was enough to cause an abundance of folly, particularly from Mrs. Bennet's quarter. That, in turn, prompted Mr. Bennet to wonder how he would ever endure the remainder of the afternoon and evening.

"Oh, Mr. Bennet!" exclaimed Mrs. Bennet, unable to contain herself. "Just think of it! A ball at Netherfield, our Jane with Mr. Bingley, and I am quite sure he intends to ask for her hand soon, and all the officers looking so handsome for all our other daughters! It shall be the most delightful affair!"

Mr. Bennet, having been one too many times on the receiving end of an emotional outburst, stood up to retreat to his study and was heard to cry out, "Oh, that the ball had been a week ago and all your hopes and dreams for it had been dashed!"

Elizabeth preferred the solitary confines of her room, which allowed her to deliberate on her situation, away from the trying goings on of the other members of her family.

She often thought of Miss Anne de Bourgh. Was her heart as inescapably entwined with William's as Elizabeth's was? Did she harbour feelings of love for him that would be crushed when she learned of his marriage to her? Was his esteem for his aunt so great that he would find it difficult to announce it to her? His own declaration that he could not speak to her father while Mr. Collins remained at Longbourn gave her pause to consider he was concerned how his aunt would receive the news.

As much as Elizabeth looked forward to this evening, she knew she needed to talk to him about some very critical issues.

Elizabeth finished readying herself and when her hair had been drawn up and embellished with flowers and ribbon, she looked at herself in the mirror. Her dress was one of her nicer ones, although she was certain Darcy would have seen many that were much more elegant in the circles he frequented.

As she stood before her mirror and turned from side to side, her first inclination at seeing her reflection was to tell herself she would not be dressed as fashionably as he was accustomed to seeing. But she took in a deep breath resolving that she would not let herself dwell on that thought. She then walked out of her room with a smile, anxious to join the others, travel to Netherfield, and see the man she loved and whom she had not seen in almost a week's time.

When she came downstairs, Mr. Collins was waiting. He reminded her that she had promised to dance the first two with him tonight and subtly suggested she save another one later in the evening for him. Elizabeth sighed as she contemplated what a thorn this man was to her happiness and peace of mind. She could not view him with indifference, finding herself continually annoyed by his hovering presence.

Mr. Bennet kept to himself in his study, having readied himself before anyone else, but chose to wait in comfort until they were all ready to depart. He was not fond of these types of affairs; he would prefer to remain home and read. But he knew this was an event of some import, and so resigned himself to oblige his family and attend. He only hoped that there would be some intelligent conversation to be had and that the evening would pass quickly.

When the last of the Bennet daughters came downstairs (and it was Lydia, who spent a great deal of time doing and redoing her hair until she was satisfied), Mr. Bennet joined them and they set out for the ball.

Upon arriving at Netherfield, Elizabeth entered the ballroom and cast a glance around her at the array of people from her neighbourhood, dressed in their finest. Almost everyone gaped quite openly at the opulence of the house that had been opened for them and they seemed in the highest spirits, as they anticipated a most pleasant evening. Unfortunately, the man she most wanted to see was not to be seen.

Elizabeth looked around for Darcy, while Lydia and Kitty, in turn, anxiously looked around for Wickham. They were greatly disappointed, therefore, to hear from Denny that he had been obliged to go to town on business the day before, and was not yet returned. This dismayed them to no end, particularly Lydia, as she felt he had singled her out with his attentions earlier in the week at the Phillips' home. At length, however, the two girls became enamoured by any officer that took notice of them and soon Wickham was forgotten.

Elizabeth noticed that Bingley had come along Jane's side and he was escorting her around the room visiting with his guests. Elizabeth smiled. The serene happiness that shone in Jane's face seemed to spur on the pure bliss that radiated from Mr. Bingley's. Their contentment seemed to infect everyone with whom they spoke.

Elizabeth looked around the room for Darcy, and not seeing him, noticed Charlotte standing off by herself. They had only seen each other once since Elizabeth's return, and she walked over to her, giving her a warm embrace.

"Charlotte, it is so good to see you."

"Elizabeth, I cannot tell you how happy I am to see you, as well. I had planned to visit several times this week, but the poor weather prevented me."

The two ladies talked joyfully until Elizabeth received a distressing reminder from Mr. Collins that he was intent on claiming those first two dances. Elizabeth casually introduced her friend to her cousin, and then, rather reluctantly, walked with him over to the set.

Elizabeth's attention during the dance was not quite what it should be, as she kept a resolute eye open for Darcy, and it was not until they were halfway through the first set that she saw his tall, lean frame walk in. Being momentarily distracted by his elegance and stature, his meticulous look of fashion, and the smile that formed on his lips when their eyes met, she stepped to the side instead of moving toward her partner, as was her next required movement.

"This way, Miss Elizabeth," prompted Collins. Elizabeth looked back and quickly altered her movement to bring her back to her correct place in the dance set. She felt quite flushed at suddenly seeing him thus and was all too aware that Darcy noticed her blunder. Elizabeth's nervousness was enhanced when he came and stood behind the dancers in the set, directly opposite her. He watched her dance bearing an amused smile on his face as Mr. Collins then compounded her distress by making several mistakes of his own.

When the dance ended, Collins hovered by her side, quite content that this was only the first of many dances they would share together and looked forward to the second she had promised him.

The look of impatience etched across Darcy's face did not go unnoticed by Elizabeth. She knew not how to rid herself of Mr. Collins' presence until after her obligatory second dance. She watched as Darcy turned and walked out of the room.

Elizabeth endured the second, and she hoped final, dance with him. As they walked away from the set, she eagerly pointed Mary out to him and encouraged him to ask her to dance the next, as she had been without a partner for the first two. Elizabeth was relieved to get rid of, at least temporarily, her exceedingly attentive cousin. Looking around for Darcy and not seeing him, she found Charlotte and eagerly joined her friend again. As a new set began, they watched as Bingley and Jane danced their third together. They admired how well they seemed to get along; Charlotte commenting on how she ought to show a little more outward display of her affections.

As they were talking, a tall figure came up and stood before them. Charlotte looked curiously to him and then to Elizabeth. Elizabeth warmly smiled.

"Good evening, Mr. Darcy."

"Good evening, Miss Bennet."

"Mr. Darcy, have you met my friend, Miss Charlotte Lucas?"

"I believe I made your acquaintance at Lucas' Lodge. It is a pleasure to see you again."

"Thank you, Sir."

Darcy looked awkwardly at the two ladies, and finally asked in a most anxious way, "May I have the honour of the next dance, Miss Bennet?"

"I would be happy to, Mr. Darcy."

He bowed and walked away, content to wait until the dance began to speak with her.

Charlotte looked curiously at Elizabeth. "That is quite a compliment to you, Lizzy. Everyone around here knows that at the dance at my father's lodge, Mr. Darcy only danced with Miss Bingley and just once with Jane."

Elizabeth looked over at Mr. Darcy, who had gone to stand off to the side. She thought back to her first impression of him on the ship and his tendency to withdraw in situations where he knew very few people. "You must remember, Charlotte, that he knew no one at that dance. Perhaps he is reserved in unfamiliar situations."

"Well if that is so, he certainly makes up for it in looks and fashion, let alone wealth." She looked at Elizabeth slyly. "You know I am not a romantic, Elizabeth, and that I only look to be married to someone who will give me happiness and security."

Elizabeth smiled. "Yes, I am all too aware of your feelings about matrimony, Charlotte."

"Yes I know you are," she said with a faraway look in her eyes, "but, I think I should be in a fair way most content if my husband happened to be as nice looking as him."

Elizabeth shook her head with a smile and a slight laugh as the music began playing and Darcy approached to claim her hand. Before he arrived at her side, Charlotte could not help cautioning her in a whisper to please try and suppress her playful disposition and make an attempt to display a refined set of manners so as not to make her appear unpleasant in the eyes of a man of his consequence. Elizabeth made no answer, but only smiled to herself as Darcy took her hand and they walked over to the set.

"I had no idea I would have to wait so long for a dance with you, Elizabeth." Squeezing her hand, he said, "It appears as though I am not your only ardent admirer here."

"William, please," she said in exasperation. "He has asked to dance with *each* of his cousins."

"I see," Darcy replied, instead believing that Collins was unduly charmed by Elizabeth. "And does he look upon each of his cousins with that blatant look of silly admiration across his face?"

Elizabeth raised her eyebrows and then narrowed her eyes at him. "Do you think him silly for having admiration for me, then, Mr. Darcy? Is that what you are implying?"

Darcy leaned in. "No, that is not what I am implying. I meant that he is a silly man if he thinks he can win your heart."

"Yes, how easily you can say that, knowing what you do know about me… about us. You can say that quite confidently because you know something he does not know."

Darcy stopped her before they reached the set and turned to look at her. "Elizabeth, I believe I can conjecture with complete confidence that, if I had not already secured your hand, you would *still* have never welcomed his attentions."

She smiled up at him and then replied, playfully, "We shall never know, shall we? And I think from now on, we ought to use our formal address, Mr. Darcy."

"As you wish, *Miss* Elizabeth," Darcy replied with a smile, with a most definite emphasis on the Miss.

As they took their place in the set, Elizabeth standing opposite Darcy, she read in the faces of her neighbours around her their amazement in beholding their pairing, and she realized that she and Darcy were now to become the object of much speculation and gossip.

They stood for some time without speaking a word; both were content to stare at each other from their position in line waiting for the music to begin. Darcy was quite under the impression that as Mr. Collins bore that silly look of admiration on his face as he danced with Elizabeth, his own was radiating with love and the highest esteem.

As they stepped together, grasping hands, Elizabeth felt all the warmth from that simple contact that she had from his kiss. His hand was warm, unlike Collins, whose had been cool and moist. His arm went around her waist and he applied a little more subtle pressure than one who might be a casual acquaintance. Darcy seemed content to dance in silence, his hands bestowing expressions of his love and regard instead of words.

Walking down the centre of the set, Darcy finally broke the silence. "How have you been this past week, *Miss* Elizabeth?" A quick raise of his eyebrow acknowledged her use of her formal name, and Elizabeth responded in kind by nodding her head.

"I have been well. And yourself, Mr. Darcy?"

"I have been most intolerably bored," he answered. "There is very little liveliness at Netherfield now for some reason."

"I am sorry to hear that." Elizabeth looked at him sympathetically.

"I would have hoped you would *not* be sorry to hear that!"

They were silent as the movement of the dance separated them. When they came back together, Darcy said, "I have missed seeing you. If it had not been for the excessive rain, I believe Bingley and I would have tried at least once to call on Longbourn."

Elizabeth gave him a reserved smile. "I would have liked that. I was hoping you could meet my father."

"I *have* met your father," Darcy said. When Elizabeth looked at him with a questioning glance, he answered, "During your second dance with Mr. Collins, I sought him out and secured an introduction. I could not bear to watch that Collins look so smug as he danced with you. Besides, I felt it was imperative that I meet the father of the woman I am married to."

Elizabeth's heart skipped a beat at his words and the look of open admiration on his face. She easily returned his smile, but curious of his opinion of her father, she asked, "And how do you find him?"

"I can certainly see where you get your intelligence and lively disposition. He has an interesting sense of humour, yet does not use it unnecessarily often." He smiled at Elizabeth. "I enjoyed the short time I spent with him."

Elizabeth felt a warmth permeate within her as he spoke those words. She had wanted so much for him to appreciate her father and see the good in him. "I am glad." She also wondered what her father's opinion of *him* had been.

Elizabeth was quite impressed with how well Darcy danced, believing he was one of the better partners with whom she had ever had the privilege of dancing. His movements flowed perfectly with hers, and he seemed to move gracefully across the floor with very little effort. Elizabeth felt as though she was dancing on a cloud!

They settled into an easy silence as they danced. Each time they turned away from each other, Darcy anxiously waited for the movement that would bring him back to face her. Then he would look forward to stepping forward and taking her hand and bringing his arm around her.

As they met in the centre of the set and walked around the couple next to them, Darcy spoke. "I was rather surprised to discover that my aunt is Mr. Collins' patroness." A sudden pale came across Elizabeth's face and her eyes suddenly flinched in pain. Darcy searched her face, noticing her discomfiture. At length, he finally said, "Elizabeth, tell me what is wrong."

Elizabeth's eyes turned serious as she contemplated his question. She knew what was troubling her, but was unsure how to state it. When the steps brought him to her side again, Elizabeth looked up at Darcy. "My cousin mentioned the other day that Lady Catherine considers you to be engaged to her daughter."

They parted on the dance floor just as she finished the sentence. Darcy returned to his side of the set and briskly turned to face her, looking at the concern on her face. He took a deep breath as she appealed to him with questioning eyes. They had to wait several moments before they were close enough to speak again, and Darcy took her hand and held it tightly.

"Trust me, Elizabeth, it is not as it might seem, but I cannot talk of it while we dance."

They danced in silence until the set ended, and Darcy quickly stepped toward her, taking her hand and drawing her close to himself. As they stepped away from the other couples, Darcy continued in a firm, but whispered voice, "Elizabeth, my aunt has held this absurd notion in her heart and mind all my life, and she refuses to listen to reason and my insistence that it will never happen!" His voice raised in irritation. "Neither my cousin nor I have ever been inclined to be married to one another!" He closed his eyes as he noticed the concern in Elizabeth's. "Do you believe me? Even before I met you, I never had any intention of marrying her."

"And go against your family's wishes?" she asked softly.

"She is the only member of my family who holds to such nonsense. And yes, I am more than willing to go against any family wishes in this," he answered her emphatically, sensing that Elizabeth was still disconcerted.

"Will your aunt not be angry at you? At *us*? And what of your cousin?"

"Do not worry about my aunt, because *nothing* ever pleases her. If by some miracle she is pleased, she will refuse to admit it. And as for my cousin, I am quite confident that she will hold you in the highest regard."

His eyes beseeched her with the plea to trust him and be assured of his words. "I was afraid you might hear something to that effect when I found out your cousin knew my aunt. She does tend to speak as though a marriage between us is a settled thing."

He looked down at her, securing her hand in both of his. "Trust me, Elizabeth. I will stand between you and her if she voices any objection."

Elizabeth looked up at him and finally allowed an effusive smile to take hold of her features.

"Now *that* is what I have been longing to see all evening. May I be so bold as to claim a second dance with you, Elizabeth."

"Perhaps later. I believe there is already an excess of speculation going around, and I would not want my father to question your character or your intentions and think poorly of you even before this evening comes to an end."

Darcy gave her hand a squeeze before letting it go and spoke softly to her. "Elizabeth, I need to talk to you about my going to him. I need to talk to you *alone*. Perhaps we can meet out in the side alcove later. Would that be agreeable to you?"

Elizabeth's head nodded while her heart fluttered at the thought of meeting him outside alone.

"Good. I shall let you know when it seems like a good time." He bowed. "Thank you, *Miss* Elizabeth, for an enjoyable dance, and I look forward to one more later in the evening if I may be so fortunate."

Elizabeth watched him walk away and felt an irrepressible joy in her heart as she considered that it could not be soon enough for him to speak with her father about their marriage and announce to all that they were married.

They had not long separated when Miss Bingley came towards her and, with an expression of civil disdain, thus accosted her, "Miss Eliza, I noticed you dancing with Mr. Darcy. I wish to advise you that he has obligations in consideration of the relative situation of any woman he aligns himself with, and although he may have found himself to be enamoured by you, I would not read anything into his securing you as a dance partner and would advise against dancing another with him."

"Upon my word, Miss Bingley! I will dance with whom I choose, and I believe Mr. Darcy will do likewise."

Caroline attempted a compassionate smile. "I would not wish for you to be hurt."

Elizabeth met her challenging gaze. "Let me be the one who decides that."

"I beg your pardon," replied Miss Bingley, her smile becoming insolent. "Excuse my interference. It was kindly meant." She hastened away, leaving Elizabeth to ponder her words.

Elizabeth fumed quietly to herself. *If only you knew how little effect such a paltry attack as this has on me. I see nothing in it but your own wilful ignorance and infatuation with William!*

~~*

A little later, when the meal was served, Elizabeth found herself seated behind the table at which her mother and father were sitting. Darcy had been placed next to Elizabeth and Charles and Jane were seated across from them. She wondered whether Jane had any influence over the seating arrangements. She noticed the twinkle in Jane's eyes as she looked upon Mr. Darcy now in a new light, but it was apparent that Mr. Bingley was either completely oblivious to their attachment or he was too captivated by Jane to pay them any heed. Whereas Jane and Mr. Bingley openly admired one another, with eyes all around them, there was little Darcy and Elizabeth could do but act as mere acquaintances.

She was deeply disconcerted to find Lady Lucas seated nearby her mother, and could easily overhear her mother talking freely, openly, and of nothing else but of her expectation that Jane would soon be married to Mr. Bingley. Mrs. Bennet seemed incapable of fatigue while enumerating the advantages of such a match. It was, moreover, such a promising thing for her younger daughters, as Jane's marrying so greatly must throw them in the way of other rich men.

There was nothing that Elizabeth could do to check the rapidity of her mother's words or to caution her to speak in a less audible whisper. To her inexpressible vexation, she could well perceive that the chief of it was overheard by Darcy.

Elizabeth blushed and felt shame as her mother continued on a variety of subjects and let her views be known in the same loud tone. As she glanced at Darcy, he gallantly feigned being unaware of her words, but Elizabeth was quite confident he heard her every outburst as the expression on his face became more and more disengaged. She had seen that look before. It appeared when he was in the company of people he felt exceedingly uncomfortable around or who were taxing his patience. She was sure that in her mother's case, it was both.

He and Elizabeth remained, for the most part, quiet, as Bingley seemed quite content to keep the conversation going around their table. Elizabeth wondered whether her husband was quietly listening with increasing indignation at her mother's words or whether he was truly applying himself to his friend's conversation. She hoped it was the latter, but feared it was the former.

When her mother finally had no more to say, Elizabeth breathed a sigh of relief, only to have but a single moment's respite from humiliation. When singing and playing was talked of, Mary obliged, eager for the chance to exhibit, and it was a most painful song. Mary's powers were by no means fitted for such a display; her voice was weak, and her manner affected. Elizabeth was in agonies. When Mary finished, with very little encouragement she seemed inclined to begin again. Elizabeth winced as her father stood up and loudly asked her to let someone else play.

Her cousin, Mr. Collins, for whatever absurd prompting, decided to give a lengthy discourse on the merit of music, and how, if he were so fortunate to be able to sing, he would oblige the company with an air. His voice was loud, heard by half the room. Many stared, many smiled, but no one looked more amused than Mr. Bennet. While Elizabeth and Mr. Bennet had often shared a laugh at the man's expense, this time she had no inclination to do so.

To Elizabeth it appeared, that had her family made an agreement to expose themselves as much as they could during the evening, it would have been impossible for them to play their parts with more spirit, or finer success; and happy did she think it for Bingley and her sister that some of the exhibition had escaped *his* notice, and that *his* feelings were not of a sort to be much distressed by the folly which he must have witnessed. His two sisters, however, who were seated next to Bingley and across the table from Elizabeth, were a different matter. Elizabeth could see by their spiteful looks to each other that they were quite openly offended. And then there was Darcy. What was *he* to think of the family of the woman to whom he was married?

She could no longer bear the mortification and with a pained expression, excused herself from the table as soon as she finished eating. She walked over to a table to get a refill of liquid refreshment. As she sipped the cup, she struggled to steady her hand, afraid to look back over at Darcy and see the effect of her family's behaviour on his countenance.

As she stood with her back to her husband and her family, she heard her sister Lydia let out a playful wail, and Elizabeth closed her eyes as she felt her whole body tense at yet another display of reckless behaviour. Her eyes were closed in shame when she suddenly heard a voice behind her whisper, "I think now would be a good time, Elizabeth. Will you meet me out in the side alcove?"

She turned slightly to see Darcy standing there. People had begun to depart the room, and, as she knew many of the ladies would be attending to personal obligations and refreshing themselves, she silently nodded. No one would particularly miss her.

Darcy continued. "I do not deem it wise that we go out together. I shall go first, and you follow in a few minutes."

Elizabeth nodded and watched him leave. She waited a few moments, and watching to make sure no one took notice, she stealthily left, walking down a long hallway and through a utility room that was at the far end of the house. She was grateful for the days she spent at Netherfield, as she knew the house well, and did not need any direction to get to the alcove. She also knew that those who wanted to step outside for some fresh air would go out to either the front or the back courtyard.

She came to the door that led outside, and carefully looking around, opened it, feeling a cool blast of air hit her from the late autumn evening. While attempting to accustom her eyes to the darkness, she was suddenly aware of Darcy's presence. He took her by the hand, pulling her into the shadows of the alcove, drawing her close to him.

Darcy breathed in the floral scent that seemed to emanate from her. He knew they could not remain out here too long as there was always the chance that someone would come out, but he knew, in addition to talking to her, there was one more thing he greatly desired to do. As the two looked at each other in the darkness, he caressed her face softly with his fingers, touching her lips lightly. As he moved his fingers slowly away, he simply paused, looking into her eyes.

Elizabeth looked up to see his silhouette, her thoughts just barely coherent, and before she was able to entertain any kind of verbal reflection, Darcy enveloped her with his arms and placed his lips over hers. Elizabeth's answer was to close her eyes and she returned his fervent embrace. A sense of reassurance swept over her, convinced that he still loved her despite her family's behaviour and loved her enough to be willing to go against Lady Catherine's wishes and defend her to his aunt, if need be.

Slowly he pulled away. "I hope you do not find my behaviour inexcusable, Elizabeth, and although I did miss you terribly this past week, I did not ask you out here solely to steal a kiss, however pleasant it may have been." He gently stroked her cheek.

Elizabeth looked up into his face, shadowed by the darkness of the moonless night. The light of some distant torches cast a very pale light upon their faces.

Darcy's arms went around her again, holding her tightly. "Elizabeth, as soon as Collins leaves, I should like to come and speak with your father."

"About our marriage?"

"Not quite yet."

Elizabeth lifted her head and gave him a curious glance.

"I have it on good advice, from someone who knows your father well; that I ought to first go to him and tell him I wish to court you. Then, once I am secured of his approval, which hopefully, will not be too great a length of time, I shall tell him the truth that we are already married."

"Someone who knows my father well?"

Darcy drew away and smiled. "Yes. While I was in London last week I paid a visit to Cheapside. I met your aunt and uncle."

"You met my Aunt and Uncle Gardiner?" Her great joy in hearing this was suddenly tempered by the realization that he most likely told them. "And you told them about us?" she asked softly.

"Yes. Everything."

Elizabeth tried to catch her breath. "What did they say?"

"Obviously they were surprised and of course, concerned. They knew something had happened to you because you were so altered when you arrived in America. Of course they had no idea you had married some strange man on the ship with the agreement that the marriage would be annulled later."

Elizabeth tried to fathom this information. "And what did they say?"

Darcy laughed. "Your uncle gave me quite the interrogation and your aunt gave me the strictest lecture I have ever received about how you deserve only the best. I did assure them that I have no intention of annulling the marriage and that I am deeply in love with you. I believe we all left fairly satisfied in the end."

Elizabeth shook her head in great incredulity. "I cannot believe you visited my aunt and uncle!"

"Neither can I," Darcy laughed. "But I did! And I found them very pleasant, indeed! You should expect a letter from your aunt shortly."

The love and admiration Elizabeth felt for her husband in taking the initiative to visit her aunt and uncle suddenly gave way to a lucid realization of the words he had just spoken.

"What did you just say?"

"You should expect a letter from your aunt shortly."

"No, before that. You told them that you have no intention of annulling the marriage and..."

He reached out and took each of Elizabeth's hands in his. "I am deeply in love with you, Elizabeth."

Tears unexpectedly came to her eyes as he tenderly spoke these words. Searching his face in the darkness that surrounded them, she was able to detect a glimmer in his eyes, as well. "William, I love you, too."

He pulled her close, wrapping her with his arms. Lowering his head, he placed a few kisses along her cheek, drawing closer to her ear. Upon reaching it with his lips, he whispered, "I should like to come specifically to talk with your father on the Saturday that Collins leaves, if that is acceptable to you."

His attentions caused shivers of delight to course through her and prevented her from being able to attend to his words without making a concerted effort. "That… should be fine."

"Good," he said, bringing his hands up to her shoulders and gently stroking her neck with his thumbs. "In the meantime, I believe I should like to join Bingley when he visits your family. Would tomorrow or the following day be satisfactory?"

Elizabeth took in a deep breath to counter the pleasant assault his simple touch was waging within her. "I believe tomorrow would be the better of the two. My two youngest sisters have invited the officers over the following day, and my father is likely to be in a most disagreeable mood that whole day because of it."

Darcy laughed. "Then if it suits Bingley, we shall come the following day."

Elizabeth shook her head. "No, that is the day the officers are coming and my father…"

Darcy nodded and laughed. "And that is why *I* plan to be there!"

The music began and Darcy extended his hand. "Shall we return inside?"

Instead of answering him, she unexpectedly reached up on her toes and placed a quick, tender kiss on his cheek.

"What was that for?"

Elizabeth tilted her head as she answered. "Does there have to be a reason?"

Darcy laughed. "No, I would never demand a reason for you to kiss me, my love."

Elizabeth looked up, wishing she could see her husband's expression. "There is a reason. It is for loving me despite my family."

She heard him take in a deep breath and he could discern the pain in her voice.

Darcy pulled her close as he said to her, "I was well aware of the distress you were suffering in there."

"And what of yourself, William? I cannot help but wonder what influence my family's ill-mannered behaviour would have had if we had been mere acquaintances and not already married when you met them."

Darcy paused as he considered her thought.

At length, when he did not answer, Elizabeth responded. "I believe they would have driven you away. You would have been conflicted in your heart and mind, struggling to know whether to follow your feelings or listen to all you have been taught about the woman whom you should marry and the type of family she must have."

Darcy breathed in deeply, gathering his thoughts. "Elizabeth, it is of no use conjecturing what would have happened if this or that had or had not occurred. I am married to you, I love you, and I would not wish it to be any different. Do you believe me?"

Elizabeth's heart gave a small leap as he spoke those words. Her eyes filled with tears of joy as she whispered back, "Yes, I believe you."

He held her close to him, leaning over and placing a kiss on the top of her head just as he had the night she slept in his arms on the ship. Only this time, she was aware of it, digging her head more deeply into his chest.

They remained still, content to keep themselves in the solitude of this alcove, but Darcy, hearing a rustling in the shrubbery nearby, quickly said, "We must get back. You go on inside, and I shall be in within a few minutes."

Elizabeth reluctantly pulled away and returned inside the house. Darcy glanced out over to the row of trees and bushes that bordered the alcove. It was too dark to see anything, and not hearing anything more, he quickly opened the door and took himself in.

When they met back inside, they were finally able to dance their second dance, which they did in almost complete silence, quite confident of their love for each other and content to simply enjoy each other's presence.

As the dance ended, people began to leave and Mrs. Bennet was perfectly satisfied with the events of the evening. She quitted the house under the delightful persuasion that, allowing for the necessary preparation of settlements, new carriages and wedding clothes, she should undoubtedly see her eldest daughter settled at Netherfield in the course of three or four months.

Of having another daughter married to Mr. Collins, she thought with equal certainty, and with considerable, though not equal pleasure. Elizabeth was the least dear to her of all her children; and though the man and the match were quite good enough for her, the worth of each was eclipsed by Mr. Bingley and Netherfield.

If she had not been so set in her second eldest daughter marrying Mr. Collins, she might have paid more heed to the talk that was beginning to circulate about Elizabeth and Mr. Darcy, but she did not consider Elizabeth good enough to tempt a man of his means and therefore paid it no notice.

Darcy watched as the Bennets walked out the door. As far as he was concerned the ball was over, but he knew he must remain until the final guests took their leave. He walked over to a window that overlooked the front, and in the subdued light of the torches, watched as Elizabeth was brought up into the carriage.

With a small smile of satisfaction touching his face, he thought to himself, *It went superbly!* He reproached himself for those days on the ship when he had been reluctant to express his feelings to her. If he had, neither of them would have had these months of wondering, misery, and resignation. How good it felt to tell her he loved her, and even greater to hear her voice the same.

The sound of footsteps behind him and the shrill voice of Caroline Bingley shook him out of his reverie. "Mr. Darcy, there you are!" He closed his eyes.

Caroline came up to him and joined him looking out the window into the darkness. "I cannot tell you how grateful I am that this ball is almost over! Has it not been simply the most wearisome gathering of people you have ever seen?"

When he did not answer, she proceeded. "Those Bennets! You must agree with me, Mr. Darcy, that their incessantly ill behaviour tonight far exceeded anything one would deem acceptable in the finer societies."

Darcy pursed his lips to prevent him from lashing out in anger.

"And that Miss Elizabeth Bennet! I am still quite unsure as to her reasons for travelling to America. What do we really know of her character? I am still firmly of the opinion that she found herself disgraced and…"

Darcy did not answer her immediately, making a futile attempt to calm himself. He finally broke the silence in a definite, but controlled, anger. "Miss Bingley, I have it on the highest authority that she did not travel there to take care of any *disgrace*, as you call it!"

Caroline's eyes widened at his anger, but held her ground. "Certainly Sir, anything you hear from her friends and family around this uncivilized neighbourhood would be biased, I am sure, to keep it…"

"It is on my *own* authority, Miss Bingley!" Darcy's eyes glared at her. "Elizabeth Bennet was on the same ship as myself travelling to America! And I can guarantee that she was *not in any way disgraced!*"

Caroline's jaw dropped and she felt herself grow suddenly cold. As she gasped at his words, her throat constricted and more of a squawk came out. She quickly swallowed and muttered a conciliatory, "Oh."

"Now, Miss Bingley, if you will excuse me!"

As Darcy left, he was approached by one of the Netherfield's servants. "Sir, if you would please come up to your room. You are needed there."

Darcy quickly left for his room, and was met by Durnham, who informed him that a man had been seen leaving his room by one of the maids.

"I have made a thorough going over of the room, and there are a few pieces of expensive jewellery missing. Your set of diamond cufflinks and neckcloth pin. I believe it was most likely some ruffian wanting some easy money."

"Thank you, Durnham."

The servant looked at Darcy. "Is there anything we can do for you, Sir? We deeply apologize for this inconvenience."

Darcy turned and told him, "There was nothing of consequence taken that cannot be replaced. Let Bingley know so he can have the rest of the house looked over in case he went through other rooms."

"Yes, Sir."

Darcy was quite surprised by how little this upset him. He was feeling too intoxicated by the lingering warmth of Elizabeth's embrace and their confession of love to one another to allow a petty theft to annoy him or to dwell on it too fully.

Chapter 26

George Wickham made his way through the darkness to the horse he had tethered in the midst of the dense grove of trees that formed a convenient cover for him as he stole away from Netherfield. He mounted his horse and rode back at a daunting pace in the darkness of night to his quarters in Meryton. When he returned to the solitude of his room, he looked through the various items that he had liberated from his old chum's room. But it was the simple piece of paper that proved to be most interesting.

A malevolent wave of elation swept over him as he thought back to the events of the evening. He could not determine whether he was more greatly satisfied at what he had been able to secure, what he had seen, what he had heard, or that he was able to accomplish it all without being caught.

He tossed aside the few pieces of jewellery that would garner him a more than adequate amount of gambling money. But in light of the other things he came away with, these small items were inconsequential. His eyes narrowed as he perused what was apparently a marriage certificate. He shook his head as he tried to fathom the circumstances of a marriage between Fitzwilliam Darcy and Elizabeth Bennet. A sly smile crept across his face as he realized that no one in this trifling neighbourhood seemed to be aware of it!

Wickham chuckled as he considered how easily he had been able to charm one of Netherfield's young servant girls, who had come to Meryton the other day, into telling him which room Darcy occupied at Netherfield. He leaned back into his chair, giving this piece of paper his undivided attention. The brief thought crossed his mind to attempt to blackmail his old friend but chances are Darcy would choose to do something noble, such as divulge the truth to everyone rather than pay.

He thought about the bits and pieces of conversation that he overheard as Darcy and this young lady, who bore the esteemed honour of being his secret wife, stood in the shadows. *Something about getting married only to have it annulled later. Must have changed their minds, although they obviously are not living together as man and wife.*

Wickham shook his head, unsure how all this fit together. He was quite confident, however, that there was some scheme he could come up with using this little piece of paper and this most enlightening morsel of news to his best advantage; something that would pad his pockets at least for a while.

He put the certificate down and began to take off the dark clothing that he had worn to sneak in. As he pulled off his shirt, a rather novel idea came to him. *Ahhh, yes. I do believe there is someone who would be most interested in what ol' Darce has been doing these past few months. She ought to pay very handsomely to keep me quiet while she pursues her options to take care of this... problem.*

He ran his fingers over the paper and smiled. When he planned to sneak into Darcy's room, he had been quite confident he would be able to garner a few items of value from his room, perhaps shake him up a bit. But he had no idea he would find something like this. *And to think I was also able to witness their little clandestine meeting where they thought no one would see or hear them!*

It had been dark in the alcove, but Wickham was able to get a good look at Darcy as he came out the door. He had just approached the house, waiting for the right opportunity to sneak in. He had no idea he would witness quite the romantic display to entertain him while he waited in the shadows.

As he thought about this piece of information that no one else seemed to be aware of, a new idea came to him. A sinister grin spread across his face as he dwelt more on this very promising thought. *This could prove to be even more lucrative than I first imagined! This can set me up for life!*

He balled his fist and tapped at his chin several times as he considered this. *But first, I must get Darcy out of the way for a few days. I cannot let him find out I am here until my plan is complete.*

He pondered the best way to ensure that Darcy would immediately leave. *What would make Darcy return to Pemberley?* Another smile, even more sinister than the first, touched his lips. *Of course! I shall use myself!*

Picking up a pen and a piece of stationery, Wickham began writing. *Darcy ~ I think it would be wise for you to return to Pemberley at once. Wickham has been seen for several days now around Lambton and even once on Pemberley's property. Am concerned for Georgiana, as you might imagine.*

He wondered how to sign it and finally decided to simply scrawl an illegible signature.

"There! That should get Darcy hightailing it to Pemberley!"

He folded up the deceptive missive and made plans to have it delivered to Netherfield first thing in the morning.

~~*

The next morning, the topic of conversation around the Netherfield breakfast table dwelt mainly on the theft. There was much conjecturing from the men about who would have done such a thing and some disparaging remarks from the sisters about the type of people that must live in this neighbourhood. But in all her remarks, for some reason, Caroline seemed unusually subdued.

When they were almost finished eating, a note that had just been delivered was brought in for Darcy. He looked at the writing, and not recognizing it, curiously ripped it open. As he read it, his jaw tightened and he slammed his fist down. "Heaven forbid!"

"What is it, Darcy?"

Darcy looked at his friend, in whom he had never confided about his sister and childhood friend, George Wickham. "Some problems at Pemberley. Unfortunately I must return at once!"

Darcy stood up and summoned Durnham. He sent him up to pack a small bag and a change of clothes and then asked to meet with Bingley alone.

When the two men walked in his study, Bingley closed the door and turned to Darcy. "What it is, Darce?"

"Bingley, I must ask you to relay a message for me. I can only trust you to do it and I would ask that you do not say anything to anyone, particularly your sister. Do you understand?"

"Yes, friend. Anything. What is it?"

"Miss Elizabeth Bennet must be told that I had to return to Pemberley because of an emergency that has arisen, and I will not be back for at least four days. Because of that, I will not be able to pay her a visit as I had hoped. I will put it all in a note. Will you be so kind and see that she discreetly receives it?"

"Of course." Bingley looked at him oddly. "Darce, may I ask a question?"

"Certainly."

"Did something happen here at Netherfield between you and Miss Elizabeth that I was not aware of? Have you taken a liking to her?"

Darcy looked up into Bingley's jovial face. "I have taken more than a liking to her, Bingley, but it did not happen at Netherfield." Turning his head and looking out the window, he said, "It happened two years ago."

~~*

Mr. Bingley came by Longbourn in the late morning. He brought along with him the note from Darcy, and was able to give it to Elizabeth undetected.

She stole away to the privacy of her room to read his words to her.

My dearest Elizabeth,

I hope this finds you well. Unfortunately, this morning I received some news that has disturbed me greatly. I find it necessary to leave immediately for Pemberley for the sake of my sister and my own peace of mind.

Please accept my regret at having to leave again. Trust that my thoughts will dwell on you for the duration of my journey. Once I have secured the safety of Georgiana, I shall return to Netherfield with her and hope that we can begin on that course that we determined. I look forward, as well, to you renewing your acquaintance with my beloved sister.

I leave the greater piece of my heart with you here as I depart for Pemberley.

Until my return,
FD

Elizabeth was quite disappointed to learn that he had been forced to return to Pemberley and she would have to wait again for his return. But her heart was touched by his words and she treasured them deep within her.

She returned downstairs and was able to visit with Jane and Bingley for a short time before they left to spend the day at Netherfield with his sisters.

Her distress increased, however, when Mr. Collins decided this would be the day he would make his declaration in form. On finding Mrs. Bennet, Elizabeth, and one of the younger girls together, he addressed the mother in these words,

"May I hope, Madam, for your interest with your fair daughter, Elizabeth, when I solicit for the honour of a private audience with her in the course of the day?"

With a wave of mortification passing over Elizabeth and a forceful acquiescence from her mother, Elizabeth found herself alone with Mr. Collins.

The few minutes she hoped it would take to politely refuse his proposal turned into several minutes as he would not believe that her 'no' truly meant no. With every reason he put forward as to his reasons for wishing to marry her, Elizabeth had to repeatedly decline, yet it seemed to no avail, believing her to be acting out of delicate modesty.

Collins continued to prattle on and began speaking about Lady Catherine de Bourgh. As he spoke, Elizabeth's thoughts took her a different direction as she suddenly realized what a precarious situation she was now in, in regard to this woman. How would she now be viewed by her? Elizabeth was now not only the one who married her nephew instead of her own daughter, but she would also be the one who refused her clergyman's offer of marriage.

She came to dread that the only response that might satisfy him was if she declared she was already married. Knowing not what else to do, she turned to depart the room.

As Elizabeth quickly left, eager to seek the solitude of her own room, she encountered her mother who possessed a rather congratulatory look about her. As Elizabeth passed toward the staircase, her mother joined Collins, offering up such warm terms on the happy prospect of their nearer connection. Mr. Collins, however, related to her what happened, still believing her refusal to be part of her bashful modesty and the genuine delicacy of her character.

Mrs. Bennet saw it otherwise and soon Collins realized that he had, indeed, been refused. He then changed his opinion of this daughter and began speaking as though he would not reconsider her.

Mrs. Bennet knew she must appeal to her husband and quickly left Collins before he was able to say another word. As she entered the library, she called out, "Oh! Mr. Bennet, you are wanted immediately; we are all in an uproar. You must come and make Lizzy marry Mr. Collins, for she vows she will not have him, and if you do not make haste he will change his mind and not have her."

Mr. Bennet raised his eyes from his book as she entered, and fixed them on her face with a calm unconcern which was not in the least altered by her communication.

"I have not the pleasure of understanding you," said he, when she had finished her speech. "Of what are you talking?"

"Of Mr. Collins and Lizzy. Lizzy declares she will not have Mr. Collins, and Mr. Collins begins to say that he will not have Lizzy."

"And what am I to do on the occasion? It seems a hopeless business."

"Speak to Lizzy about it yourself. Tell her that you insist upon her marrying him."

"Let her be called down. She shall definitely hear my opinion."

Mrs. Bennet rang the bell, and Miss Elizabeth was summoned to the library.

"Come here, child," cried her father as she appeared. "I have sent for you on an affair of importance. I understand that Mr. Collins has made you an offer of marriage. Is that true?"

Elizabeth replied that it was.

"Very well, and this offer of marriage you have refused?"

"I have, Sir."

"Very well. We now come to the point. Your mother insists upon your accepting it. Is it not so, Mrs. Bennet?"

"Yes, or I will never see her again."

"An unhappy alternative is before you, Elizabeth. From this day you must be a stranger to one of your parents. Your mother will never see you again if you do not marry Mr. Collins, and I will never see you again if you do."

Elizabeth smiled and felt a great deal of relief at the conclusion of such a beginning; but Mrs. Bennet was excessively disappointed. When she left the room enumerating the agonies she suffered, Elizabeth gave her father a hug.

"Now, now, Lizzy, enough of that. You should know me well enough by now to know that I am not inclined to give my consent to just any man who is silly enough to imagine he has regard for you and thinks he can simply ask for your hand. Presently I do not feel as though *any* man is worthy of you, let alone Collins. So, my dear, even if *you* had said yes to the man, *I* would have absolutely refused it!"

Elizabeth smiled, grateful for her father's scrupulous opinion in this matter, but wondering how William would fare under it.

The household was in turmoil the rest of the day as Collins refused to be mollified and Mrs. Bennet blamed Elizabeth for ruining everything.

Elizabeth consoled herself with the fact that this would soon be all forgotten once her mother was informed of her marriage to a man of £10,000 a year!

~~*

While Elizabeth was suffering from this most unsettling day, Darcy endured, most impatiently and fretfully, the long carriage ride back to Pemberley. His heart was tossed about thinking with joy on Elizabeth, but with trepidation on Georgiana. He did not trust Wickham one bit and would not put it past him to still harbour a grudge and resort to some revenge upon him, his home, or, as much as he did not want to think upon it, his sister.

He knew how enraged Wickham had been earlier in the year when he separated him from Georgiana. Wickham obviously thought he had succeeded in a plan that would give him the fortune he always desired but was never willing to work for. Darcy's intervention foiled that plan.

His chest tightened just thinking back to those painful days. He considered himself a failure as Georgiana's guardian. He wondered of his own ability to raise her. Where had he been when she had made that errant decision to elope? Had he been negligent in discussing with her the things of the world? Had he been too inattentive to her that he missed signs of her vulnerability?

Darcy rested his arm against the window of the carriage and let his head fall into his hand. Georgiana seemed so young then, and he wondered if her willingness to go with that charlatan had to do with the fact that Wickham had treated her like a grown lady, whereas *he* did not. She was his younger sister, and he zealously wanted keep her young and innocent. Darcy took in a long, deep breath.

If he arrived too late and Wickham did anything to Georgiana, he would never forgive himself.

Darcy watched the passing scenery, anxiously anticipating the familiar landscape of Derbyshire to show itself. He knew it would be an all-day journey and he would be subject to every thought of apprehension for his sister battling for prominence in his mind with all his admiration and regard for Elizabeth. He allowed himself to smile as he thought of Elizabeth, his wife. His anticipation of bringing her back to Pemberley with him instilled in him great joy.

Needing a respite from his anxiety, he thought upon Elizabeth having walked the grounds of Pemberley and it gave him a great sense of contentment. To know she had graced some of the rooms with her presence and even talked to his sister pleased him immensely. How he looked forward to returning with her in his arms. He knew Georgiana would think well of her.

His eyes narrowed as he considered what the rest of his family would say about her. His aunt… Darcy closed his eyes. She still clung tenaciously to that foolish notion that he would marry her daughter. He knew she would be the most difficult, but he was determined to defend Elizabeth to her at all costs.

He allowed himself to ponder Elizabeth's family. On the three occasions that he had been in their presence, there had been some markedly objectionable behaviour displayed. The night he went to Lucas Lodge and did not know they were her family he was appalled at them. He regretted that he had agreed with Miss Bingley in her criticism of them. How he wished he had learned somewhere in his life to control his tongue in regards to people he deemed beneath him! But it was when her mother and two sisters came to Netherfield and he heard her disparaging remarks directed at Elizabeth! That still angered him.

And then there was the ball. He thought about how he tried to block her mother's loud, obtrusive discourse from his mind, but found it to be increasingly difficult. He remembered looking over at Bingley and wishing he could have that same easygoing countenance and ignore the follies and faults of people around him. That was a trait he had never acquired. He closed his eyes as he thought of Elizabeth's father and how even he behaved in a most ill-mannered way that night, followed by foolish displays by her cousin and her sisters.

Would he, in all honesty, be able to accept them as he would wish to accept the family of his wife? He had not allowed himself to even dwell on this, and unfortunately, on the long day of travel, he found himself without a strong inclination that he would.

When Elizabeth asked him last night whether he would have accepted her family if they had not already been married, he had already asked himself the same. He was only thankful that they *were* married, and he did not have to conjecture how things would have turned out if events in their lives occurred in a completely different manner.

In all truth, as he dwelt upon her family, he was grateful for the vast distance between Longbourn and Pemberley, and knew that would figure in the frequency of visits. But London was immeasurably closer, and he had to admit that when he and Elizabeth were in residence there, it would be a much easier distance for either to travel for a visit. If the Bennets came to London, their behaviour would be noticed and scrutinized. If the Bennets wanted to visit, he would more greatly prefer that they visit Pemberley, in all its seclusion, than London, in all its display. At Pemberley they would only have themselves and the Pemberley staff as spectators to the oddity of their behaviour.

Oddity. He smiled as he thought of the conversation he and Elizabeth had on the ship. Elizabeth claimed to have some odd relatives. Perhaps in a way she had been warning him, but then he certainly had to admit his own aunt was an oddity. She was worse than that. If anyone dared to cross her, she showed little restraint in lashing out at them most vehemently. If she sensed any threat to her neatly ordered and planned out life, she would show very little forbearance.

Darcy sighed. Perhaps all Elizabeth's family needed was a little exposure to genteel living. He absently shook his head. Her mother was probably too set in her ways to change, and the two youngest sisters, particularly the youngest, would need some sharp discipline! Her father had hope, though. His only fault would be negligence of teaching his family proper manners and then reacting too harshly when they behaved outside acceptable bounds.

He consoled himself with the fact that her Aunt and Uncle Gardiner were very a decent, respectable couple. He regarded them highly from his visit with them in London. They were a couple that he deemed he could befriend easily; in fact, he greatly desired to deepen his friendship with them. He believed them to have been one very positive influence in Elizabeth's life.

Darcy's thoughts went to his aunt who was fiercely protective of her name and her circle of society, and that sense of protection extended to Darcy and Pemberley. He could only imagine what might happen the first time he introduced Elizabeth to her as his wife. He was quite sure there would be enough sparks between them to start a fire in all of her fireplaces without any kindling.

Darcy determined that it would be best to inform his aunt when Elizabeth was not in their presence. He had no idea if he would ever be able to sway her opinion of his wife, but he would make a gallant effort. He would also have to make a gallant effort to view Elizabeth's family with a little more clemency.

Darcy arrived at Pemberley at dusk and immediately sought out Georgiana. He greeted his surprised sister warmly. It was too late to do any investigation into Wickham's presence, although he did check discreetly with the household staff to see if anyone knew who wrote the note or if any had seen Wickham. He was not afforded any knowing response.

He spent the rest of the evening visiting with Georgiana, each informing the other what they had been doing the past few weeks.

~~*

The following day at Longbourn, Elizabeth was sitting with Jane and enjoying the cool, crisp day that afforded them the pleasure of spending it outdoors. They were watching as the officers visiting Longbourn enjoyed the company of her two youngest sisters.

The two sisters talked as they watched Kitty and Lydia entertain the group of four officers to whom they had extended the invitation. Jane had felt the extent of her mother's disapprobation toward Elizabeth yesterday that had continued even into this new day. They were both grateful that Collins had excused himself and was spending the day with the Lucases.

As they heard the squeals and laughter coming from their sisters, they glanced over. But neither Elizabeth nor Jane were inclined to join in the activities that Lydia and Kitty were engaged in with the men.

"Did you enjoy your visit with Mr. Bingley yesterday, Jane?"

"We did enjoy ourselves. I had a most enjoyable time at Netherfield."

Elizabeth smiled, knowing that Miss Bingley would have to have been on her best behaviour in front of her brother. "Yes, and it is good you were *there* when Mr. Collins was *here* humiliating me as well as himself as he made his offer of marriage to me!" Elizabeth looked at Jane and rolled her eyes. "I have never been so uncomfortable in my whole life!"

"I am so sorry that happened!"

"Well, Jane, I believe there are just some things in life that are meant to happen that you cannot avoid."

Jane took her hand. "You miss Mr. Darcy. I can tell."

Elizabeth sighed. "Sometimes I feel that just knowing he loves me gives me strength to endure anything. But, yes, Jane, I do miss him."

"I enjoyed watching the two of you at the ball. It was also interesting hearing the thread of gossip that began to circulate after your first dance, and then quite exploded after your second."

"And just what were they saying?"

"That the esteemed Mr. Darcy certainly has good taste, and wherever he goes, he can have the best pick of dance partners."

Elizabeth raised her eyebrows. "And?"

Jane looked down. "And... that you better not hold to any expectations about his having danced two with you."

"I shall remember that, as Miss Bingley gave me the same warning."

Both sisters laughed.

Elizabeth reached over and put her hand on Jane's. "Have you told Mr. Bingley... about William and me?"

Jane shook her head. "I do not feel as though I should; at least, not until he makes an offer of marriage to me. I do not feel it right to mention that his best friend is secretly married to my sister."

"That is probably very wise, Jane."

"I know that he shall be greatly pleased, Elizabeth; do not fret about that. I merely would not want him thinking that I am telling him solely to prompt him into making me an offer of marriage."

As the two began talking of other things, they saw the object of their conversation approach them on horseback, surprising Jane with a visit. He joined the two sisters as they visited, and at length, Charles and Jane departed to go for a walk.

Elizabeth turned her attention back to her sisters and the officers and continued to watch in concern as one of the officers, George Wickham, seemed to concentrate his attentions on Lydia. Her youngest sister seemed to respond more and more to him in what seemed, to Elizabeth, to be an overly flirtatious and even provocative way. He had a charming personality, but Elizabeth wondered of his intentions. Certainly a man in his position would not bother with someone with as little fortune as Lydia. And although Lydia had a very gregarious personality, unless he had some unsavoury objectives in her regard, she could not understand his attention. She determined to keep an eye on them.

She realized she knew him only slightly. She had come to know him but a little at her Aunt and Uncle Phillips' home after their initial meeting in Meryton. He had been cordial and attentive, charming and outgoing, but seemed very modest in sharing anything personal about himself.

She was a little surprised, then, to see him leave Lydia and come over towards her.

"Do you mind if I sit with you on the bench?"

"No, Mr. Wickham. I could use a little company."

"Good," he said, seating himself next to her.

"You have a very pleasant family, Miss Elizabeth."

"Thank you, Mr. Wickham." For some unknown reason, Elizabeth felt his words were a little too coated in sweetness.

"And your sister and Mr. Bingley seem very happy."

"Yes, they are."

Wickham smiled and paused, as if searching for a way to say something.

"And his friend, what is his name?"

Elizabeth quickly turned to him with a blush sweeping over her face, startled at his reference to her husband. "He... his name is Mr. Darcy."

Wickham smiled at her obvious nervousness.

"And is he from around here?"

Elizabeth inwardly chided herself for her sudden nervousness. "He lives in Derbyshire." Elizabeth unknowingly began rubbing her hands together.

"And you said you had only come to know him spending those few days at Netherfield?" He flashed her a charming smile, meant to disarm and assure her of his trustworthiness.

Elizabeth turned her face from him, feeling as if she was being interrogated.

"I... he..." Elizabeth had the gnawing suspicion that his questions were not as casual as they seemed. "I have not known him long, no."

Wickham narrowed his eyes, noticing her obvious discomfort.

"I notice that he did not join his friend today. Is he no longer in the neighbourhood, then?"

Elizabeth looked at him, searching the face behind the charming smile, suave voice, and penetrating eyes. "No, I believe he had some business that took him back to his home in Derbyshire."

Wickham's charming smile was quickly replaced by a satisfied grin.

Further conversation was prevented by Lydia briskly walking towards them.

"Mr. Wickham, I wondered where you had gone off to!"

"Well, Miss Elizabeth, it appears as though your sister desires my company.

If you will excuse me, it has been a pleasure conversing with you." Wickham gave her a polite bow, and then eagerly went off with Lydia.

As he walked away, Elizabeth was annoyed at herself for reacting as she did. *Why did I feel so uneasy when he spoke of William?* She gripped her hands together and shook her head. *There was no reason to react that way.* She could not help in turning her gaze back on him, nevertheless, wondering what it was about him that so disconcerted her.

Chapter 27

Darcy arose at dawn the next day to get an early start making inquiries. With the help of Durnham, they sought out all the staff that worked at Pemberley to whom they had not already spoken. When no one seemed to recall seeing Wickham in quite a long time, they set out for the surrounding villages and made inquiries. Wickham had not been seen by anyone.

That night Darcy retreated to his study. It had been a long day and he was too restless to sit and relax, wondering what Wickham could be doing and who it was that saw him. *What is it that I am not seeing?* he asked himself. He relentlessly paced back and forth before walking over to the mantel and picking up Elizabeth's sampler. As he looked at it, Georgiana walked in.

"Am I disturbing you?"

Darcy quickly put the sampler down and returned to his chair. "No, please, come in and sit."

Instead of sitting, Georgiana walked up to her brother's desk, facing him. She had just come to learn from one of the servants that his preoccupation since arriving had something to do with Wickham.

She decided to ask him outright. "William, what brought you home so suddenly?"

Her eyes searched his and noticed the pain that flooded them.

"I... I received a note that there was a matter of urgency here that needed my attention."

Georgiana waited, but he seemed reluctant to go on. He tapped his fingers lightly on the desk. Over the years, Georgiana had come to recognize that as a sign he was nervous and concealing something.

"Does it have to do with George Wickham?"

Darcy started at this, looking up into the wise, maturing face of his sister. Her look of tenacity surprised him at first, and then softened his guard.

"Have you seen him recently?"

Georgiana shook her head. "No, and I do not wish to, but I would have liked to have been informed of this."

"You have grown up, Georgiana, and sometimes it is difficult for me to remember that." He stood up and beckoned her to come to him. She walked around the desk and he drew her into his arms.

"I received a note that Wickham had been seen around Lambton and Pemberley. I was worried about you."

"Did you not trust me, William?"

"I trust you, Georgiana. I do not trust him."

He drew her away and looked at her. "I will make some final inquiries into this matter tomorrow, and then on the following day I want you to join me when I return to Netherfield."

She gave him a sly smile, and walked over to the mantel. "You have been spending a great deal of time with your good friend, Charles Bingley. You must be enjoying his company."

"Yes, I am."

"And Miss Bingley?"

"Miss Bingley is, and always will be, an unfortunate accessory to my friendship with Bingley."

Darcy watched as Georgiana casually picked up the sampler.

"And what of Miss Bennet?"

A lump in Darcy's throat forced him to swallow and he watched her turn slowly and give him a piercing gaze.

"Miss Bennet?"

"Yes." She turned and bore her eyes into him. "You claim that you trust me, William. Would you please trust me enough to tell me exactly who Miss Elizabeth Bennet is?"

Darcy stared at her for some length, unable to speak. Finally, Darcy nervously laughed.

"Oh, I had forgotten. She mentioned that she met you when she and her aunt and uncle toured Pemberley."

"So you *have* seen her at Hertfordshire!"

"Yes, I have. But how did you know?"

Georgiana walked back around to the chair opposite his desk and sat, still holding on to the sampler. "Too many things were all too conveniently linked together. You called out the name *Elizabeth* from the carriage in America and reacted in a way I had never seen you act. And then there was the strange note from Willoughby, with only the word *Longbourn* written on it. When Miss Bennet visited Pemberley, she mentioned that she lived at Longbourn, which is in Hertfordshire, which just happened to be where you set off to so suddenly."

"You are quite the detective, I see."

"Oh, I have all the clues, but I do not know what they mean! The final clue, however, I have just recently discovered while you have been gone."

"And what is that?"

She held up the sampler. "I had not noticed this before, but a few days ago I was looking at this sampler and I saw the initials of the one who stitched it. *EB*. They are cleverly concealed among the tendrils of the vine, but definitely an *EB*. Now please do not tell me it is all a coincidence!" Georgiana crossed her arms in front of her, as if she was not going to leave until he explained this all for her.

Darcy looked up, taking a deep breath as he did. "I met Miss Bennet on the ship going to America."

"I thought as much."

Darcy tightened his jaw as he contemplated how much to tell her. "I grew quite attached to her, but did not come to learn any particulars about where she lived or where she was staying upon arriving in America. That morning when we docked, I went in search for her, but she had already disembarked and was on a carriage to I know not where."

"And that is why you seemed so despondent when you arrived in America?"

Darcy nodded. "All I knew was that she was staying with her aunt and uncle in New York for a few months and then would return to England. I knew she lived in Hertfordshire. Willoughby said he would do some checking for me to see if he could find out exactly where she lived. That was what his note was for, which, by the way, was addressed to *me,* and younger sisters should *not* be sneaking a peek at!"

Georgiana smiled and looked down, then slowly lifted her eyes to look innocently at him.

"So you found her at Longbourn in Hertfordshire?"

Darcy nodded, a wide grin spreading across his face.

Georgiana clasped her hands. "I am glad!"

"You are glad?"

"Yes. William, I liked her so much, and I prayed and prayed that she was someone of whom you were fond and that she cared for you in return." She nervously looked down at her hands. "I have very often thought about the fact that you would someday marry, and that it might be someone whom I would not like or who would not understand me."

Darcy reached across the desk with his hand and Georgiana met his with one of hers. He gave it a gentle squeeze. "And what did you think of Elizabeth? I mean, Miss Bennet?"

"I liked her, William. Just in that small amount of time I spent with her, I came to like her very much." She looked at him and smiled. "She is so very unlike any other woman I have seen you with."

Darcy looked down, feeling somewhat embarrassed. "Now you know very well, Georgiana, that I have never really taken a strong liking to any of the women I have been forced to accompany to some event, or that I have been forced to have accompany me! Usually it was out of duty or obligation or some familial association. There may have been a few whose company I enjoyed, but none that I would have sought out as my wife."

"Oh, but there were certainly many who wanted you to take a liking to them and who would have, without the slightest hesitation, consented to being your wife!"

"Yes, and I can remember all your comments you made to me after I would introduce one of those women to you."

Georgiana looked down, displaying a childlike pout for her brother. "I was not *that* bad, was I, William?"

William laughed. "I quickly discovered, Georgiana, that the quieter you were around the lady, the more vocal you would be to me after she left!"

Georgiana smiled at her brother's complete understanding of her.

"Your shyness certainly did not hold you in its grip around *me* on those occasions!"

Georgiana tilted her head and looked at him oddly. "I never realized the connection between my shyness and how well I liked or disliked someone. I imagine it was the degree of discomfort I felt in their presence that led to the degree of shyness I exhibited. And the greater degree of discomfort, the greater I disliked them and was determined to tell you I did not approve."

Darcy smiled at his sister. He had often wondered over the years if she would have approved of *any* lady. He often speculated that his sister would be more reticent to give her approval of a woman than his mother would have been. "And how did you find Elizabeth?"

She smiled. "I enjoyed her company. I felt as though I could talk to her easily. As a matter of fact, William, I felt perfectly comfortable around her."

Darcy stood up, guiding Georgiana's hand around the desk until she was by his side and pulled her close in a hug. "I could not be any happier, knowing my two favourite ladies enjoy one another's company."

"Did she say anything about *me?*"

Darcy nodded. "As a matter of fact she did. She likes you very much."

Georgiana sighed, and Darcy knew it was a sigh of contentment.

Darcy was grateful for Georgiana's regard for Elizabeth and knew it was only a matter of time before he told her that she was already his wife.

The following day, Darcy made some final inquiries and concluded that Wickham was nowhere in the vicinity, becoming quite suspicious as to the origins of the note. He fixed on departing the following morning to return to Netherfield and Darcy determined he would spend the rest of this afternoon with Georgiana.

He returned just after midday and after eating a light meal, he suggested that they take a walk together around the grounds. He had enjoyed their talk the previous day and wanted to hear more about what she had been doing while he was gone.

It was a cool day and the days were succumbing to the approaching chill of December. They bundled up and walked down to the lake.

"So what have you been doing with yourself these past few weeks since I have been gone?"

"Studies, of course. The Metcalfs stopped by one day to pay a visit with their son."

Darcy eyed her suspiciously. "Their son? The one you always hated?"

"Yes. But he is not the scrawny little boy who always wanted to pull my hair any more. He is quite amiable now… and rather nice looking."

Darcy gave her a warning glance that told her he thought she was too young to be thinking along those lines.

"Well, you *do* approve of the Metcalfs do you not?"

"Yes, but…"

"Good!" She tucked her hand into her brother's arm. "Pray, do not make any protective brother remarks. I am a grown up young lady!"

She heard her brother breathe in deeply and let it out in a huff.

"Well I am! I have learned my lesson about men! I will never fall for anyone like Wickham again!"

"I know, Georgiana. Sometimes it is just hard for me to realize you are grown up. Or perhaps I do not want to admit it to myself. When I received the letter that

Wickham may be near, it frightened me greatly, knowing that I might be too far away to prevent him from doing anything rash."

"Whom do you believe wrote the letter, William?"

"I really do not know. I could not decipher the signature."

"Perhaps I can. If you still have it, I might look at it when we return."

"I have it here," Darcy said, as he reached into a pocket and pulled it out. Georgiana took it, and Darcy watched as her eyes narrowed.

"What is it, Georgiana?"

"Well, overall, the handwriting does not look familiar, but...."

"Yes?"

"But the way the 'W' is made in Wickham's name. There is only one person I know who makes a 'W' like that."

"Who is that?"

Georgiana looked up with a serious look on her face. "Mr. Wickham."

Darcy's heart suddenly began to race and a cold chill swept through him as he began to ask himself all of kinds of questions. "Wickham! But why would he...?"

Darcy turned and grabbed Georgiana by the shoulders. "Are you sure of this?"

Georgiana nodded, frightened by the look in his eyes.

"We must get back to Hertfordshire right away!"

"What is it, William? Why would Wickham want you to come here?"

"The bigger question is why did he want me to *leave* Netherfield? And how did he even *know* I was there?"

The two began walking briskly toward the house, Darcy bringing his hand up to his head, raking his fingers through his hair. "The theft!"

"What theft?"

"Someone broke into my room the night of the ball. I just assumed it was someone who wanted some small items that he could easily grab and sell for some easy money."

"Do you think it was Wickham?"

"I have no doubt it was him."

Darcy was taking brisk, long strides and Georgiana was having a difficult time keeping up with him.

They rushed into the house and Darcy ordered his bag packed as well as a trunk packed for Georgiana as quickly as possible. He was not sure how long they would be gone.

Durnham returned with Darcy's bag. "It is a full day's journey, Sir. We will not make it there before dark."

"I know. We will travel as far as we can today and then make the rest of the distance in the morning."

Darcy paced the floor waiting for Georgiana's things to be packed. He was confident that the man who broke into his room was Wickham. He shook his head. *Is he that desperate for money?* There seemed to be something else that he was not seeing. *What was it?*

Darcy thought back to that night, how Durnham had searched the room after the theft for any missing valuables. Darcy had sensed that he was missing something. He thought back to his room. He kept most of his valuables in the armoire and they had searched all the drawers in it. Just a few things gone. There was the closet, but apart from his hanging clothes, nothing really of value that would be easy to lift.

His mind's eye travelled to the bed and the small table next to it. Normally, he just kept his reading book…

Suddenly Darcy stopped in his tracks. His eyes widened as he considered what he had neglected to check for that night. *The marriage certificate!* His heart lurched as he realized with great anguish that he had not looked in that drawer. And if Durnham checked it, he would not have been aware of its presence there, let alone its absence. If Wickham discovered his and Elizabeth's marriage certificate, what damage has he been doing with it these past few days?

What a fool I am! How did I not think of it?

When Darcy had been apart from Elizabeth, not knowing where she was, that marriage certificate had become a sort of lifeline to her. But now that she was back in his life, she was the only thing he thought of. He had not even thought to check to see if it was still hidden in the drawer.

Darcy restlessly waited for everything to be readied for their departure and then he rushed through a farewell to the Pemberley staff.

When Darcy and Georgiana were settled in the carriage, the two travelled in silence for quite a distance. At length, after observing her brother's demeanour for some time, she stated, "I suspect, dear brother, that you have determined what Wickham's reasons were for insuring you leave Netherfield."

Darcy turned sharply and looked at his sister, seeing something in her for the very first time. "How do you know me so well, Georgiana?"

Georgiana smiled. "You wear your great depth of feeling on your face, William. Over the years, I learned to read your face when you refused to tell me what you were feeling."

"I never wanted to burden you."

"I am old enough now, William. Tell me, what do you think Wickham is up to?"

Darcy balled his hand into a fist, brought it up to his jaw, and repeatedly pounded it.

"Before I tell you what I think Wickham is doing, Georgiana, I must tell you something first, that ultimately I believe will please you, but initially it will confound you. I fear at first you will not understand."

"I am listening."

Darcy began rubbing his hands nervously together, while Georgiana waited patiently.

"It is a long story."

"We have a long ride ahead of us."

"Yes." She watched as he turned to look out the window and then turned back and faced her directly. "I told you that Elizabeth and I had been on the ship together that took us to America."

Georgiana nodded."

"Yes... well..." Darcy took a deep breath. "What I did not tell you... was that she and I..." He reached over and took his sister's hands. "Georgiana, Elizabeth and I are married. We got married on the ship."

As Georgiana comprehended his words, her jaw dropped and her eyes opened wide. She nervously looked to her right and then her left, finally coming back to look upon her brother. Darcy held on to her hands tightly as she began to pull them away.

She looked down to hide the tears that were beginning to pool in her eyes and said softly, "You are right, Fitzwilliam. I do not understand. How you could be married without telling me?"

Darcy calmly and deliberately explained to Georgiana how everything came about. She shed a few more tears in her struggle to comprehend, however grateful she was that his wife was, indeed, Elizabeth. Darcy moved himself so that he was seated next to her and pulled her close. She buried her head against him as he wrapped his arms about her and she let her tears fall.

At length, she did recover; her tears ceased, and she was able to view this announcement with joy. She was able to understand a little more, as they discussed it and she asked questions of how this all came about.

It was then that he told her what he believed Wickham may have found.

"Whoever broke in stole some items of minimal value. Nothing that cannot be replaced. But there was something in the room that I had not thought to look for. I am not sure if he found it, but if he did, I cannot even grasp what he is doing with it."

"What is it?" asked Georgiana.

"Elizabeth's and my wedding certificate."

~~*

At Longbourn the following day, two events of great import took place.

The first occurred when Bingley came for a visit for the third day in a row. Elizabeth secretly smiled as she noticed the nervousness with which Jane greeted him this day and wondered if she was anticipating that this would be day he might make her an offer.

As they sat and visited in the sitting room, a nervous expectation seemed to quell everyone's ability to converse in a rational manner. Most were rendered mute by it, except for Mrs. Bennet, who seemed to be propelled into mindless chatter by the quiet that overtook the others.

Elizabeth finally made a suggestion that they venture out for a walk, and Mrs. Bennet heartily agreed. Elizabeth agreed to accompany them, but in her wish to give them some privacy, let her amblings slow down and soon they were far ahead of her. She tarried as she pretended to take notice of the variety of plants that lined the path, woodland animals that scurried away, and the views from different lookouts as they walked up Oakham Mount.

They were soon out of her sight and Elizabeth paused just a little longer. Her heart pounded mercilessly and she thought Mr. Bingley better be making good use of this time alone or she might do something impulsive to propel him along.

She began walking again, and at length, she caught up with the couple, who had stopped. Jane greeted Elizabeth with such an abundance of joy that Elizabeth could only assume he had asked for her hand and she had accepted. She hugged her sister warmly.

"Oh, I am so happy, Lizzy! Charles and I are to be married!"

Elizabeth pulled away from Jane and looked at Bingley. "I am so happy for you both!"

"Thank you, Miss Elizabeth. I believe we are quite happy as well."

As they walked back down together, they talked of their wedding. Jane had such a look of contentment on her face that Elizabeth was quite confident they would be happy all their lives. She was also grateful that this announcement would finally draw her mother's negative attention from herself and transfer it to Jane in a most positive way.

As to be expected, Mrs. Bennet wailed with glee. The sisters were all in support of this, and Mr. Bennet, although not visibly exhibiting much emotion, dwelt on this occasion with great pleasure, knowing that his family should now be well taken care of.

While this one marital announcement was taking place, another offer was being made. Mr. Collins made an offer to Charlotte, who readily accepted. When it was announced to the Bennets, the reception of it was quite dissimilar from what Charles' and Jane's had produced.

Mrs. Bennet reminded Elizabeth that this announcement might have been hers and that now the Lucases must be already viewing Longbourn as belonging to them. However, her distress was diffused greatly in light of the joy and elation she experienced in Jane's engagement. The Bennet daughters were all completely in shock at Charlotte's acceptance, particularly Elizabeth, who felt that her friend was making a very foolish mistake. And with a sarcastic chuckle, Mr. Bennet was convinced that Mr. Lucas would, without a doubt, proudly boast of his fine, new son-in-law.

~~*

After the excitement of the previous day, Elizabeth found herself alone late in the morning. Everyone had errands to run or visits to pay. Mr. Collins was making final arrangements with the Lucases for his and Charlotte's wedding before he left for Hunsford. Jane was paying a visit to Bingley and his sisters at Netherfield to talk of their wedding plans. Her parents, along with Mary and Kitty, had set out to Meryton on some errands and to visit the Phillips, and Lydia had been invited to spend the day with Colonel Forster's wife. She was grateful for the solitude, as a letter from her aunt arrived after everyone had left.

She eagerly retreated to her room, closing the door behind her and carefully opened the sealed missive. Flinging herself onto her bed, she began reading.

My Dear Niece,

I know you have been expecting this letter and I hope it finds you well. I must say that I began writing three other times and resorted to tearing up each of them, as I was not satisfied with any. So I shall devote this whole morning to formulating a letter that, hopefully, expresses your uncle's and my sentiments.

You know that Edmund and I hold you in the highest esteem and I treasure our familial relationship as well as our close friendship.

You might suspect, dearest Elizabeth, that Mr. Darcy's appearance at our doorstep when he was in London was quite unexpected and astounding. But what he went on to tell us, dear one, could not have taken us more by surprise. That you and he are married! Oh, how confused we were to hear that!

As he went on to explain how this came to be, I thought back to our visit to Derbyshire and Pemberley, and suddenly, I understood your extreme nervousness in viewing Pemberley and wishing to visit only with the certainty that Mr. Darcy, who we thought had merely been a fellow passenger on the ship, was not at home. I thought back to the little sampler he had on his mantel, remembering the verse that you so often quote. Did you, indeed, do the stitchery yourself? And then there was, of course, your melancholy countenance upon arriving in America.

Oh, Elizabeth, suddenly everything made sense and how I wished that you had felt secure enough in our love to tell us! But do not be mistaken, I do understand. Mr. Darcy acquainted us with all the circumstances surrounding your decision to marry, how it was to be annulled, and how, upon your meeting back in Hertfordshire, you both very strongly desired to keep your marriage intact.

Elizabeth, may I say that Mr. Darcy loves you a great deal? I know that this secret marriage will be difficult for your father to understand. His love for you is most protective and we have advised Mr. Darcy to take some time getting to know him before he tells him of your marriage.

I know this means that the two of you will have to continue in the secrecy of your marriage, but we think it will be best. We do hope that when you do inform your family and friends, (and we are quite sure your mother will be thrilled and can only hope that she learns to appreciate the man and not just his wealth) that everyone will understand.

Edmund and I will make every effort to come to Longbourn should you feel the need for some additional support! I would take this opportunity to say how much we like and approve of him. His behaviour was, in every respect, very pleasing and honourable. Edmund and I can certainly put in some very good words for Mr. Darcy to your father, if need be.

Have peace, Elizabeth, in all this.

Yours, very sincerely,
Madlyn Gardiner

Elizabeth, may I discreetly tell you how greatly I look forward to visiting Pemberley again when you are settled in as its Mistress?

Elizabeth read and reread the letter several times and was stirred from her reverie as she heard the sound of a carriage come up the drive to the front of the house. She pulled herself up out of her bed and walked over to the window and gasped at the sight of the opulent carriage that stopped. She watched as an older woman was helped out of the carriage and brought to the door. She had never seen the woman before in her life.

Assuming it was someone paying a visit to her mother, Elizabeth stayed in her room. She was quite surprised, then, when there was a knock on her door. Elizabeth quickly folded up the letter and called out, "Come in."

Hill walked in very nervously. "There is a Lady Catherine de Bourgh here to see you, Miss."

Chapter 28

"Lady Catherine de Bourgh? To see me?"

"Yes, Miss."

Elizabeth raised her eyebrows in surprise and then immediately lowered them in contemplation that Lady Catherine was soliciting her. She imagined the only grounds for her requesting her company would be due to her hearing of Mr. Collins' proposal... or Elizabeth's refusal of it. Her chest tightened as she considered that any misapprehension would surely make it more difficult to receive Lady Catherine's approbation when Darcy informed her of their marriage.

Elizabeth looked in the mirror and straightened her dress, tucking a few wayward strands of hair back in place before walking downstairs. She desired to be presentable in appearance as well as in manners to her husband's esteemed aunt.

As she reached the bottom of the stairs, she observed a very well-dressed lady, standing erect and bearing a most decidedly stern look across her face, which was aged well beyond her years. Her clothes, which were quite opulent in design and fabric, reinforced the decidedly haughty expression on her face. Elizabeth walked up and waited for the woman to address her.

Instead, the woman eyed her up and down, with a most dissatisfied look upon her face.

Elizabeth took it upon herself to introduce herself. "Good morning, Lady Catherine. I am Miss Elizabeth Bennet..."

"I am well aware who you are." The sarcastic tone in Lady Catherine's voice was unmistakable. "I noticed a prettyish kind of a little wilderness on one side of your lawn. I request your presence in joining me there."

"Yes, come this way, please," offered Elizabeth, already discomfited by this lady's insolent manners.

Before they had even entered the copse to which Elizabeth brought her, Lady Catherine turned and began to release a diatribe against her.

"You can be at no loss, Miss Bennet, to understand the reason of my journey hither. Your own heart, your own conscience, must tell you why I have come."

Elizabeth looked at her with complete astonishment at her brash greeting, but steeled herself to remain calm and polite. "Indeed, Madam. I am not at all able to account for the honour of your visit and to finally make your acquaintance. I have heard much about you from..."

"Miss Bennet," she replied in an angry tone, "I will have you know that I am not to be trifled with. But however insincere you may choose to be, you shall not find *me* so. A report of a most alarming and grievous nature reached me two days ago." Lady Catherine's face became quite red with anger as she narrowed her eyes upon Elizabeth.

"Lady Catherine, I believe there is no need for you to be upset. You see, although I did turn down…"

"I will not be interrupted!" She pounded her cane into the ground. "Have you no respect for your elders?"

Elizabeth's ire began to rise as she struggled to maintain a measure of composure, believing this woman had no right to treat her thusly for refusing her clergyman's proposal. She took several deep breaths in an attempt to calm herself. "I do, Madam, when I am, in turn, treated with respect."

"You expect *me* to treat *you* with respect?"

"I would certainly ask for and expect nothing less."

"How dare you, when I have been told that you, Miss Elizabeth Bennet, have covertly formed an alliance with my nephew, Fitzwilliam Darcy; that you have, much to my shock and dismay, secretly married him!"

She stopped and watched the expression on Elizabeth's face betray the truth. Elizabeth paled and felt as though the world was spinning around her.

She continued, "I had every hope that it was a scandalous falsehood when I was informed of this grave situation. I instantly resolved on ascertaining for myself its fabrication."

"If you believe it to be a falsehood," said Elizabeth, colouring with astonishment and rising disdain, "I am sorry you took the time to come so far to verify it. I will say nothing to your allegation."

"Impertinent girl! As much as I wished it to be untrue, what I was given proves otherwise!" Lady Catherine pulled out a piece of paper and waved it in front of her. When Elizabeth was able to look at it more closely, she could see that it was a marriage certificate. *Their* marriage certificate!

"How did you come by that?" she asked, her voice cracking and her whole body beginning to tense up.

"It is not important who placed it in my hands. I need only say that a concerned, long-time friend of the family came upon it and knew that it would be in my family's best interest to be aware of the infamous scheme in which you have placed him.

Elizabeth was rendered mute by the sight of the marriage certificate in Lady Catherine's possession and the accusation against her.

Lady Catherine continued. "And just what do you have to say to this, Miss Bennet - or should I say, Mrs. Darcy - however disinclined I am to do so. Do you pretend to be ignorant of it?"

"Lady Catherine, do you not think you should take this up with your nephew instead of me?"

"This is not to be borne! Miss Bennet, I insist on being gratified. Has he, has my nephew entered into a matrimonial union with you?"

"Your ladyship has a piece of paper claiming to be proof of it. How can I answer against such strong evidence?"

"I want to hear it from your own mouth. I demand to know what arts and allurements you used to cause him, in a moment of infatuation or obsession, to forget what he owes to himself and to all his family. I want to know how you have drawn him in!"

"If I had been the one to draw him in, I would be the last one to confess it."

"Miss Bennet, do you know who I am? I have not been accustomed to such language as this. I am almost the nearest relation he has in the world, and am entitled to know all his dearest concerns."

"Then to him you must apply!"

Lady Catherine hesitated for a moment, and then replied. "Unfortunately, he has left for Pemberley."

Her voice became more deliberate and harsh. "Let me be rightly understood. This match to which you had the presumption to aspire is impossible! I want you to assure me that this is a falsehood! That this certificate is some sort of fabrication!"

Elizabeth looked at her oddly; anger and confusion hindering her ability to comprehend all she was hearing. "I am sorry you took the trouble to come here and accuse me, your ladyship. It is not a falsehood. I did marry your nephew. I humbly suggest and fervently hope that you will accept it."

Lady Catherine drew in some haggard breaths, closing her eyes as if wishing to close out the truth of what she just heard. She opened her eyes and glared at Elizabeth, pointing to the certificate. "Accept it? You ask me to accept a marriage between my nephew and someone like you? Never! And who is this Captain Willoughby?" she asked as he pointed to the certificate.

"He was the captain of the ship on which we were sailing, Madam. He performed the marriage."

The angry woman lifted one eyebrow in disdain at the young lady standing in front of her. She pounded her cane into the ground again for emphasis. "This is not to be borne! You stand there and tell me that my nephew has not only entered into a marital relationship with someone so decidedly beneath his notice, with little or no connections, but he did not even have the decency to marry in a church? Heaven forbid! What have you done to him? Have you no scruples, girl? How is it that you came to be married to him?"

Elizabeth fought the strongest impulse to retort back harshly to the woman, remembering she was now family. She closed her eyes, vainly wishing her husband was here.

"Answer my question! How is it that you came to be married to him on this ship?"

Elizabeth paled at Lady Catherine's relentless verbal assault of her. She took in a few breaths to calm herself before she answered. "He made an offer and I accepted it. It is as simple as that."

Lady Catherine's eyes darkened, then questioned. "I understand it was a marriage of a peculiar nature."

Elizabeth started. "I am sorry, I do not know to what you are referring."

"Do you not?" Taking in a deep breath she began, "I understand that you were married with the intention that it would later be annulled."

Elizabeth felt a tremor course through her. "Where did you hear that?"

"That does not matter. What matters is that I insist on knowing whether it is true!"

Elizabeth could not look upon her, wondering how she came to have this information.

"With all due respect, Lady Catherine, this is not something I wish to discuss."

Lady Catherine persisted, ignoring her response. "On what basis was it to be annulled?"

Elizabeth straightened her shoulders. "Lady Catherine, I have answered all the questions I wish to answer. If you will excuse me!"

"I will have you know," she countered, as she stepped in Elizabeth's path, "that my nephew has been promised to my daughter since their birth. It was his mother's design as well as mine! And now you expect me to simply ignore the fact that you and he were married, that you degraded him? Do you really believe that I can overlook your marriage to him when he marries my Anne, knowing he has been in an annulled marriage? You have no idea what this will do to my daughter! And what about Mr. Collins? Does he know that the woman he plans to marry has had a marriage annulled?"

"Mr. Collins?" Elizabeth could not believe she was bringing him into their conversation and realized that Lady Catherine assumed their marriage would be annulled if it had not already been.

"The disgrace of it all! First I receive a letter from my clergyman informing me that he is planning to ask for your hand in marriage. Naturally I was pleased that he had found someone to marry. Then, to my horror, this is placed in my hand, and I find that not only is the object of his intention already married, but she is married to my nephew!"

"Please, Lady Catherine, you must understand. I never intended to marry Mr. Collins. In fact, I refused his proposal."

"You refused his proposal? Who do you think you are, you unpolished country girl, to aspire to keep my nephew yoked to you? Heaven and earth - of what are you thinking? Are the shades of Pemberley to be thus polluted? Insolent girl! Tell me, has my nephew annulled this marriage?" Lady Catherine asked in a commanding voice.

"I would beseech you to apply to Mr. Darcy for that answer!" Elizabeth replied, her voice edged with the turmoil building up inside her.

"Do you know to whom you are talking? I insist on you telling me! Tell me, once and for all, has my nephew annulled the marriage?"

Though Elizabeth would not, for the mere purpose of obliging Lady Catherine, have answered this question, she could not but say, after a moment's deliberation refusing to be intimidated this woman, "No, he has not, nor does he intend to. I love him and he loves me!"

Elizabeth watched as Lady Catherine's face grew red with rage. "Not annulled! Obstinate, headstrong girl! You cannot even know what marriage to my nephew requires!"

"I beg to differ, Madam."

Suddenly, a gleam appeared in Lady Catherine's eyes and a cruel smile etched her face. She leaned in closely to Elizabeth. "Ah yes. Now I fully understand." Her bulging eyes narrowed and she looked upon Elizabeth as though she was eyeing the most distasteful object one could lay their eyes on. "He had planned all along to annul the marriage. For whatever reason, you married with the intent that it would be annulled." She nodded to herself as she let her mind speculate. "It must have been platonic. He must have determined to keep things chaste so he could easily annul it."

Elizabeth watched a harshness sweep over the woman's face as she raised her voice. "But you tricked him! In a moment of weakness, you tricked him into succumbing to your enticing wiles… and now he feels he must honour the marriage."

"I did not trick him, your ladyship. Your assumption is the furthest thing from the truth!" Elizabeth interjected, greatly affronted by the accusations and assumptions of this woman. She held on to the fabric of her dress with tight fists as she struggled to maintain her composure. "That is *not* the reason our marriage has not been annulled."

"Do you expect me to believe that? How can you even live with yourself?"

She turned away from Elizabeth in anger, but just as suddenly, her body posture softened, and she turned back. She looked squarely at Elizabeth. "I understand that you are still not living together and that no one seems to be aware of this union."

Elizabeth stiffened, noting the change in Lady Catherine's manner. "We… we have yet to tell our families."

"Tell me, girl, has this marriage ever been consummated?"

Elizabeth gasped at her question. First she questioned her very morality and now she demanded to know the most intimate details of their marriage. She grasped her hands together tightly and softly answered, as a blush crept across her face, "I beg your pardon, Lady Catherine, but that is something that I refuse to answer."

Lady Catherine's eyes narrowed. "By the looks of you, I will assume it has not!" Suddenly, a rather pleased, sardonic smile came across her lips.

Elizabeth watched her as a great pain began building up inside of her.

Lady Catherine stood erect, straightening her bonnet and looking Elizabeth directly in the eye. "It is most apparent that you have no regard, then, for the honour and credit of my nephew! Unfeeling, selfish girl! Do you not consider that a connection with you must disgrace him in the eyes of his family and society?"

"Lady Catherine, it will not disgrace him in the eyes of anyone who is truly a friend. I have nothing more to add. I have said all that I wish to say to you on the matter."

"It is well. You refuse, then, to oblige me. You refuse to obey the claims of duty, honour, and gratitude. You are determined to ruin him in the opinion of all his friends and make him the contempt of the world!"

"No principle has been violated by my marriage to Mr. Darcy!"

"And this is your final opinion! This is your final resolve! Very well. I shall now know how to act. You need not worry whether my nephew annuls this marriage. I shall do it for him. I will make certain that it is annulled and that there will never be a trace of it having ever existed!" She raised a finger at Elizabeth. "And do not think… or hope… young lady, that you shall ever have any connection with my nephew again! I have influence and power that you could not even dream existed."

Lady Catherine turned and stormed off, taking no leave of the distraught Elizabeth. She stood motionless; trying to grasp what had just happened, what she had just been told, and wondering what, if anything, she could do. With a wave of distress and unsteadiness threatening to consume her, she walked over to the bench that was nearby and collapsed onto it.

~~*

After spending the night in a small town, Darcy and Georgiana awoke early and began the half day journey that would return them to Netherfield. He was eager to see Elizabeth again and for Georgiana to renew their short acquaintance. He only hoped Wickham had not done anything that could not be undone.

When they arrived, Darcy escorted Georgiana in and they were greeted by one of Netherfield's servants. "It is good to have you back, Mr. Darcy. But I am sorry to say that you missed seeing your aunt, who stopped by earlier."

"My aunt?" he exclaimed? "My aunt was here? Which aunt?"

"A Lady Catherine de Bourgh, Sir."

"Heavens! What was she doing here?"

"I am afraid I do not know. She inquired as to your whereabouts, and when we informed her you had left for Pemberley for a few days, she then inquired about Miss Elizabeth Bennet's household and directions to it."

Darcy's heart stood still in shock as he heard these words. Very slowly, he asked, "How long ago was that, please?"

"No more than a few hours ago, Sir."

"Have one of Bingley's horses, a fresh one, readied for me! I shall be down in a moment!" he said to the servant and then turned to Georgiana.

"Georgiana, I must go to Elizabeth. Do you mind if I leave you here?"

"William, I shall find my way around and I am sure Miss Bingley is somewhere and more than willing to assist me. You must go."

Darcy leaned over and kissed her. "Thank you!"

"Go, Brother," she reassured him. "She may need your help more than I."

Darcy gasped in a quick breath. "Thank you, Georgiana, but first, I must check my room!"

He turned toward the stairs and she followed him, along with Durnham. Darcy walked into the room he had occupied since coming to Netherfield and went immediately to the small table next to the bed. He slowly opened the drawer. His eyes lit upon the book that was lying in its place. He lifted up the book and closed his eyes when he saw that nothing else was in the drawer. He opened the book, leafing through the pages and found nothing.

"What is it, Sir? Did you discover something else missing?"

He dropped his head and then slowly nodded.

"What is it, Mr. Darcy? What is it that you find missing?" He waited patiently until Darcy finally answered.

"Merely a piece of paper that, if placed in the wrong hands, could be to me merely a minor nuisance, but for a young lady, it could cause more serious distress."

Durnham looked at him with a look of confusion in his eyes. "Sir, if it is not any of my business, I understand, but I am not sure I know what you mean."

Darcy put up his hand to stay the conversation as he heard Bingley come upstairs.

"Darce, I heard you and Georgiana had returned. Miss Bennet and I are visiting with my sisters in the sitting room if you wish to join us."

"Thank you, no, Bingley. Georgiana will join you shortly, but I have an urgent errand I must attend to!"

"Certainly. But you can at least offer me your congratulations. Jane and I are to be married!"

Darcy reached out and grasped his friend's hand. "Congratulations, Bingley, I know the two of you will be most happy."

A grin spread across Bingley's face as the two men shook hands.

"Must you be off so soon, Darce? You have only just arrived!"

"Yes. I shall return as soon as possible. Please see to Georgiana for me."

"I will, friend. And let me know if there is anything I can do."

"Thank you, Bingley."

Once Bingley left, Darcy looked back to Durnham. "I believe it is about time you know."

"Yes, Mr. Darcy?"

"Help me change into a clean shirt as quickly as you can and I will tell you."

Durnham quickly drew out one of Darcy's shirts that he had left behind when he set out for Pemberley. As the valet began attending to Darcy, he explained, "What I just confirmed that was missing from the drawer was a marriage certificate."

Durnham eyed him with a look of sheer astonishment. "Whose marriage certificate, Sir?" he asked his master, warily.

Darcy remained silent for a few moments. "Mine."

His reply rendered Durnham dumbfounded. "Excuse me, Sir, but when did you get married and just whom did you marry?"

"It was on *Pemberley's Promise* on the crossing to America." Darcy looked up at Durnham. "I took your advice, Durnham, and secured myself a wife. I married Miss Elizabeth Bennet."

Durnham's eyes closed as he tried to take in all this information. "Go on, Sir."

Darcy enlightened Durnham as to the events that led up to their marriage as he was helped into his clothes.

Durnham watched his master, completely astounded. "But Sir, in all these months, I have never seen a marriage certificate."

Darcy looked over to him, very much aware that Durnham's first response was not surprise that Darcy had secretly married a woman, but that he had not discovered it himself. Durnham was loyal, to be sure, and had always prided himself on knowing all about his master. This was one time Darcy's actions had eluded him.

"That is partly because I kept it in the dresser next to my bed either under a book or hidden in the book. I knew that you never check that drawer and felt it was safe to keep it there."

Durnham stood up. "Could it have been misplaced, do you think? I beg your pardon, but why would anyone take a marriage certificate?"

"To possibly extort some money… possibly exact some revenge on me."

Suddenly Durnham caught on. "Wickham?"

"Without a doubt!" Darcy stated, emphatically as Durnham finished dressing him.

As he rushed downstairs, he told Durnham. "I am not sure when I will return. Please take note of any talk that is being circulated among the staff. Oh, and please apprise Winston of the situation. I do not want him to be caught off guard if indeed rumours are circulating."

"Yes, Sir!" Durnham watched Darcy leave, and then went to the kitchen to see if there was anything to be found out from the servants there.

The horse was ready when Darcy stepped outside. He easily mounted it and rode as fast as he could to Longbourn, hoping he was not too late; hoping his fears were not confirmed.

When the horse pulled up to Longbourn, he slid off of it even before it came to a stop. He slid the reins over a post and hurried to the front door.

He knocked impatiently and it was answered by a middle-aged woman.

"My name is Fitzwilliam Darcy. My aunt is Lady Catherine de Bourgh. I understand she may have been here." He unknowingly held his breath as he waited for her response, hoping she would tell him his aunt had not come by.

The woman nodded. "She was here, Sir, but left quite a while ago."

He let out his breath as his heart quickened. "Did she talk to anyone?"

"Yes, Sir. She asked for Miss Elizabeth. They stepped outside to talk. I believe Miss Elizabeth is still out there, off to the side of the house. At least, she has not returned."

Darcy nodded gratefully and ran off toward in the direction she pointed. He heard Elizabeth before he saw her; she was sobbing, curled up on the bench, her head buried in her hands.

Darcy's worst fears were realized.

"Elizabeth…"

Elizabeth slowly lifted her head, and upon seeing Darcy, another wave of grief swept over her.

"Elizabeth, please, tell me what happened."

It was a while before she was able to say anything. She did not wish him to see her this way and attempted to regain her composure before she began speaking.

"Your aunt came by. Lady Catherine. She… she has our certificate of marriage."

Darcy closed his eyes in anger.

"Did she say how she came to have it in her possession?" Darcy asked.

Elizabeth answered, shaking from distress, "Only that a close family friend brought it to her."

Darcy angrily raked his hand through his hair and softly cursed. "I should have known!"

"But who was it?"

Darcy reached out and took her hand. "I believe it was an old family acquaintance, the son of my father's steward, thinking he could extort some money for it. Considering that my aunt now has it, I believe he must have been successful. He most likely asked for some sort of payment before he turned it over and then possibly even more to keep him quiet about it."

Elizabeth looked up at him, wondering what he was trying to say. "I do not understand."

He squeezed her hand more tightly. "Elizabeth, I am not sure about all the details. I feel terrible that I did not discover it gone the night of the ball. If I had, all this most likely would not have happened."

"She was so very angry!"

Darcy sat down next to Elizabeth, putting his arm around shoulder and brushing his lips up to her hair. "I am greatly sorrowed that you had to endure her wrath, my dearest Elizabeth. Tell me what happened? What did she say to you?"

"She said that if you did not annul the marriage, she would!" Elizabeth nestled her head against his chest, allowing herself to feel the strength and assurance that his mere presence gave her, yet with tears welling up in her eyes. "Can she really do that?"

Darcy's eyes closed. "She has no say over my life, over my affairs." He grasped one of Elizabeth's hands. "She may have intended it to be an idle threat meant to cause you undue distress. I am more concerned that she brought this upon you than belief that she can actually annul our marriage."

Elizabeth turned her head and it fell against Darcy's chest. "I would do anything to ensure she does not succeed. I never wanted the marriage annulled, William. Never! I wish I had not left the room that night on the ship. I…"

Darcy wrapped his arms around her. "Elizabeth, we both made mistakes. It is futile to speculate what may have happened if we had done things differently." Elizabeth could feel her husband's heartbeat against her cheek. She felt very safe in his arms, yet was not completely confident that their marriage would not be annulled by this woman who was very resolute to ensure that there would never be any evidence left of their having been married.

"William, how can we know for sure of what she is capable? I have heard of annulments being sold. Do you suppose, if one has enough money, one could be bought?"

"Elizabeth, I want nothing more than to assuage your fears. I shall travel to Town and confront her."

Elizabeth grasped his arm with both her hands. "Must you leave again?"

Darcy took in a deep breath. "Yes, Elizabeth, I must."

He placed both hands on her shoulders. "Elizabeth, this time, I do not wish to leave before…" Darcy stopped.

Elizabeth pulled away and looked at him. "Before what?"

"Elizabeth, this time, before I leave, I must speak with your father."

For a moment Elizabeth did not think she could breathe. "You are going to tell him?"

Darcy was silent for a moment. "I am well aware this is not what your uncle advised, but disguise of any sort is my abhorrence. The threat no longer exists that my aunt might discover our marriage, as she already has. I believe that the most prudent course now is to inform your father."

Elizabeth understood his words and was actually grateful for his decision. Her deepest concern was that her father would most likely be quite upset by it.

"And then?"

"I will leave immediately for London. My aunt will travel slowly in her carriage and I might reach Town in a reasonable amount of time if I ride. I doubt that I will be able to overtake her, depending on when I am able to leave, but she should not have the opportunity to do anything tonight. It will be very late when she arrives."

Tears again pooled in Elizabeth's eyes.

"Elizabeth?"

She closed her eyes and a tear trailed down each side of her face. "I am sorry." She felt absolutely helpless to do anything about her tears.

Darcy pulled out a handkerchief and gently dabbed at her tears, then handed it to Elizabeth. "My heart is breaking that you are in such distress."

"When I was in America, I realized that being married to you was all I wanted. I wanted to honour those vows I spoke to you; even though at the time, it was not our intent to keep them. I determined that, in my heart, I would always keep those vows to you, even though I believed you would annul our marriage."

Darcy's heart swelled at her words. Darcy stroked her cheek, his heart feeling quite unworthy to receive such love and devotion. "You were willing to keep those vows even believing that I would not?"

With tears streaming down her face, Elizabeth silently nodded. "William, we cannot allow her to annul our marriage!"

Darcy took both of her hands in his, feeling all the urgency of her words. Grateful for the shielding of the trees and shrubbery around them, he then drew her against his chest and wrapped his arms around her. "I will not let her do anything, Elizabeth. I promise. You have my love for eternity."

Elizabeth looked up at him and he came down and kissed her, taking her lips passionately and purposefully. Pulling her tightly against him, he was overwhelmed by the depth of love he had for his wife. He did not think he could love anyone more.

As they remained in their passionate embrace, shielded from anyone's eyes, the sound of an approaching carriage drew them apart.

"That must be my family returning."

Darcy knew what this meant. He could only hope that he would be able to put into words the strength of his admiration and regard for Elizabeth. He would help her father to understand that despite the unusual beginning of their marriage, he had the deepest love for her and that he would put all his heart and soul into pleasing this woman so worthy of being pleased.

"So it would seem." Darcy inhaled deeply and let it out slowly. "Shall we go in?"

Chapter 29

Darcy and Elizabeth both turned and began walking in the direction of the house, becoming barely aware of the commotion coming from Mrs. Bennet as she stepped down from the carriage.

Elizabeth instinctively turned and grasped Darcy's coat, effectually bringing him to a stop before they stepped out into a clearing. "Are you certain you wish to do this now?"

"I have never been more certain. There is no longer any need to delay and I cannot take the chance of encountering some other impediment before it is announced. I am resolute, Elizabeth."

Elizabeth sighed and turned to walk again. "I only hope we will find my father in good spirits."

This time Darcy stopped her. Taking a quick glance toward the house to ensure no one could see them, he took both of her hands in his, cupping them together, and brought them up to his lips. "Elizabeth, my love, there is nothing to fear. I shall make your father understand."

Elizabeth looked into his eyes and she felt her whole body quiver as his lower lip remained pressed against her hands as he spoke. She felt his warm breath gently encircle her cool fingers.

Darcy wished he could remain here with Elizabeth indefinitely. How he wanted to hold her close and kiss her endlessly! Before turning to walk into the house, he was determined to enjoy one last kiss. He released her hands and brought his arms around her waist, pulling her the short distance to him. She was firm, yet so soft, against him. He lowered his mouth and met hers, enjoying the feel of her feminine softness pressing against his unyielding body. His arms tightened as he felt intoxicated by her presence and her response.

Elizabeth closed her eyes. She felt herself spinning, as if in a swirling current, as his kiss deepened. She returned his embrace by bringing her arms up around his neck, as much to steady herself as to show her affection. His kiss and touch had the most pleasant effect of leaving her quite light-headed, positively breathless, and in a most pleasantly disconcerted state.

At length, Darcy pulled slightly away, looking down at Elizabeth's flushed face. He took in a deep breath before he was able to say anything. "I think it would be prudent for us to join your family directly, Elizabeth." He fingered a loose curl that framed her face and smiled. "However, I would have you know it is a good thing we are about to announce our marriage to your father, as all I wish to do is steal away with you to Pemberley directly!"

The set of his eyes as he looked upon Elizabeth immobilized her. Even if she wanted to, she could not remove her arms from around his neck. He brought up both hands and gently took hers in his, bringing them down.

"Come, Elizabeth, it is time for us to go in."

They walked toward the house, united together in purpose, yet separated a respectable distance from each other by the conventions of their day. Elizabeth wanted nothing more but to draw the strength she needed by entwining her arm within her husband's, but as no one yet knew of their mutual attachment, they walked divided by, what seemed to Elizabeth, an ocean of distance.

As they approached the house, they were greeted by a multitude of wails and loud exclamations from the other room, mostly from Elizabeth's mother.

"Oh, Mr. Bennet, my nerves! Please do not say such things!"

"Mrs. Bennet! I am saying only what I believe is the reality of the situation. Your wailings will do nothing to remedy our troubles!"

Elizabeth glanced at Darcy with a look of alarm. "Perhaps now is not a good time, William."

"Let us find out, first."

He gave her a reassuring smile which was immediately followed by a pained expression as he overheard Mrs. Bennet exclaim in an enraged voice, "But of course he will marry her!"

"I find that quite improbable, my dear wife! She has no fortune and nothing to recommend her!"

Elizabeth paled and looked with great fear at Darcy, wondering with mortification if her parents had somehow come to hear some misconstrued report about them. Elizabeth's heart thundered within her chest as she contemplated this.

Darcy returned her look as he began to suspect that Wickham may have furthered his evil scheme and spread some venomous lies about him and Elizabeth that the Bennets had come to hear.

Darcy followed Elizabeth into the room and all eyes turned to the couple.

"Mama? Papa?" Her voice was weak as she looked at the alarm and anger engraved upon their faces.

"It is about time you came home, Lizzy!" Mr. Bennet directed his anger at Elizabeth in a harsh and bitter voice.

She looked with great alarm from her mother to her father. "What has happened?"

"Oh, Lizzy! Lydia has run off. She has eloped, but your father insists they are not to be married!"

Both Elizabeth and Darcy breathed a momentary sigh of relief that the news which was wreaking havoc in the Bennet household was not due to them.

Mr. Bennet continued. "He has no need for a woman with no fortune! I fear your hopes for a marriage between them, my dear, are unfounded!"

"Lydia? Elope? How did this happen?" cried Elizabeth.

"We thought she was visiting the Forsters today," her mother explained, "but Hill just recently discovered this letter left by her." She frantically pointed to a note held by Mr. Bennet. "She had never gone to the Forsters!"

Elizabeth felt herself grow unsteady. "I cannot believe this!"

Her father came and looked at her gravely. "Hill sent someone for us immediately when the note was discovered. We stopped by the Forsters' upon leaving the Phillips' and when we applied for Lydia, they said they had not seen her all day." It was all he could do to explain the situation to Elizabeth in a calm, rational manner.

"But with whom did she elope?" Elizabeth asked, her voice and countenance distressed.

"According to this," Mr. Bennet shook the note angrily, "she and that Wickham have run off together; proving to me that she has not an ounce of sense in her!"

Darcy started at the mention of Wickham's name, growing incensed at what he heard, attempting to calm every fibre in his body before he spoke. "With whom did you say she ran off with?" His voice was low and raspy.

Mr. Bennet looked at Darcy curiously, suddenly wondering why he was here, but in no mood to try and establish the reason. "Mr. Wickham. And it makes absolutely no sense that he would run off with the intention of marrying our Lydia! She has nothing to offer him!"

"Oh, Mr. Bennet, please," cried Mrs. Bennet. "Perhaps they love each other! He had certainly been singling her out with his attentions."

"Nonsense! He has absolutely no use for her... at least as a wife!"

"Oh, do you have to say such things?" Mrs. Bennet pointed to her smelling salts, indicating her wish that someone bring them to her.

Darcy looked down at Elizabeth, tightening his hands into a fist, and finally recovering a semblance of control, whispered to Elizabeth, "Is that George Wickham?"

"Yes," Elizabeth said, feeling quite distraught that Lydia was putting her family through this, but also that her husband was witness to the scene. "Are you acquainted with him?"

Darcy closed his eyes and brusquely rubbed his chin with his hand. "Unfortunately, I am."

Suddenly, Mr. Bennet looked again at Darcy, noticing his most severe countenance. "And might I inquire as to your presence here, Mr. Darcy? Are you enjoying the trials and tribulations of our family?"

Darcy stiffened, unable to calm himself enough to make a rational response.

"And where have you been, Lizzy? No one seemed to know where you were off to."

"I was out... walking, Papa."

"At least you have not run off, eh?" He looked at his wife, who flailed a handkerchief in the air to circulate some air around her.

Elizabeth looked at Darcy; her eyes wide as she shook her head, giving him a look that said, now would definitely *not* be the time to say anything!

Crying relentlessly, Mrs. Bennet said, "I am sure he intends to marry her, Mr. Bennet! Lydia would not do this do us!" She dramatically dabbed at her tears with her handkerchief. "Oh, my poor, dear girl!"

"Madam," Mr. Bennet answered gravely, "I can guarantee that he will not! Lydia may be under the foolish impression they are to be married, but I am most certain this Wickham will leave her disgraced when he is through with her! Colonel Forster himself told me that he had just come to learn of his disreputable behaviour! He has unpaid gambling debts throughout Meryton! He certainly cannot expect our family's fortune sufficient to pay them off!"

A loud wail was heard from Mrs. Bennet as Kitty and Mary looked at each other with wide eyes, astonished that several people, including their youngest sister, were deceived by this man's character.

"Excuse me, Sir," Darcy said. "But I must agree with Mrs. Bennet. I believe Wickham *is* going to marry your daughter."

Darcy's words halted all thought and movement on Mr. Bennet's part. "Mr. Darcy," he said slowly. "I appreciate your trying to console us in our time of distress, but you can hardly know the circumstances."

"Sir, I beg to disagree. I have known George Wickham from childhood and there is some information of which you are not aware that will shed some light on his willingness... indeed, his purposeful resolve... to marry your daughter."

Suddenly, Elizabeth's eyes shot open wide as she realized Mr. Wickham must have been the long-time family friend who took their marriage certificate to Lady Catherine. That meant he knew about their marriage. And that meant her husband was about to tell her father the truth about them!

"Pray, Mr. Darcy, what is this information?"

"Yes! Yes!" cried Mrs. Bennet. "What do you know? I knew he would marry her! I just knew it!"

"I would speak with you alone, Sir."

"You have some information that will explain his singling out Lydia?" Darcy nodded.

Elizabeth pleaded with him with her eyes. "Perhaps now is not the best time, Mr. Darcy."

"No, I believe there is no better time."

A sense of dread began to rise up within Elizabeth, knowing her father's propensity to be overcome with anger and see very little else objectively. She said, "Please, then, I beg leave to join you."

"No, I believe I need to discuss this with your father alone." He turned to the middle-aged gentleman. "Shall we?"

Elizabeth's hand came up and her fingers covered her mouth in distress as she watched them turn to leave.

"What is Mr. Darcy about, Lizzy? Tell me what he knows!"

"Something about Mr. Wickham, I presume." Elizabeth's response was deceptively calm, however her heart raced as she watched them walk toward her father's study.

"Oh, Lizzy! If he does not marry Lydia, what shall we do? What shall become of us? This would destroy my meagre hopes for you girls to marry well! Oh, but he will marry her! I just know it! He must!"

Elizabeth sighed at her mother's clashing emotions. She did not know it for a certainty, but felt very strongly that it would not be in Lydia's best interest to marry this man. The alternative, however, was just as dreadful.

She wondered how her husband would fare breaking the news to her father.

As a tremor unexpectedly passed through her, she excused herself and quickly caught up with the men.

She knew her mother would only persist in attempting to garner information from her and at the moment she felt she would rather endure her father's interrogation than her mother's.

Her father looked at her oddly as he reached the door to his study and began to walk in.

"Lizzy, was there something you wanted before we go in?"

Elizabeth straightened her carriage and took in a deep breath. "I wish to come in with you and Mr. Darcy, Papa."

"Elizabeth, no!" Darcy ordered, and then closed his eyes contritely as he felt the wrathful gaze of Mr. Bennet upon him. Softly, he muttered, "Please no, *Miss* Elizabeth."

Looking at the stubborn determination of Elizabeth and the awkward, countenance of this man of great wealth and position, Mr. Bennet was more than a little curious. To Darcy's disbelief, he shrugged his shoulders and said, "Come, Lizzy. I recognize that determined look on your face. If you feel as though you should be here, then who am I to stop you?"

They walked into the room. Elizabeth quickly sat down in one of the chairs while Darcy remained standing. "Come, Mr. Darcy, sit," offered Mr. Bennet.

"Thank you, no, Sir." Instead of taking the proffered seat, Darcy walked over to the window and looked out. He then turned back to Elizabeth and in a firm, yet gentle, voice said, "Please allow me to do all the talking."

Elizabeth folded her hands tightly and silently nodded her agreement.

Eyeing them both suspiciously, Mr. Bennet said, "You have some information for me… something about this Wickham."

"Yes, but it is not all about Wickham. Part of it concerns me… and your daughter."

"Lydia?"

Darcy shook his head. "No, Sir. Miss Elizabeth."

Mr. Bennet's eyes narrowed at his words and he looked at the blushing countenance of his daughter. "Lizzy? What does this have to do with her?"

Elizabeth took a breath as if to answer, and Darcy slowly reached out with a hand to stop her. He then returned it to join his other hand, rubbing them together as he pondered how to go about telling this gentleman that he was married to his daughter. "What I have to tell you will most likely be… difficult to understand."

"Mr. Darcy, nothing that has happened today has been easy to understand."

"I am not quite sure how to tell you this."

"Telling me directly is a viable option."

Darcy looked over, glancing furtively at Elizabeth, and nervously said, "Someone else once said something to that effect to me."

Mr. Bennet narrowed his eyes at the man pacing the floor in front of him. "Pray, Mr. Darcy, what is the relationship between you and my daughter?"

Darcy made an attempt at a smile, however difficult it was for him to produce one. "I…" Darcy's heart raced as he searched for the right words. "I seem to have found myself in possession of a strong love and admiration for her, Sir. Very strong."

Elizabeth could not meet the eyes of her father and stared intently at her hands which were nervously fidgeting in her lap. His words, admitting his love for her to her father, made her heart swell and she stole a glance at her father to behold his response.

Mr. Bennet stood up and alternated glances between the two. "You have piqued my curiosity, Mr. Darcy. I do not know whether I have a greater desire for you to pursue this line of conversation about my second eldest daughter or ask what you know of Wickham and my youngest daughter. But I shall leave it to you to continue."

"Thank you, Sir. If I may, I should prefer to begin with Wickham. We grew up together as boys as his father was my father's steward. As he grew into adulthood, I saw him embrace some excessively improper behaviour and disagreeable habits."

Darcy paused, wondering whether to mention Wickham's deceitful scheme involving his sister, but when Mr. Bennet seemed to accept his words without question, he determined that revealing those painful circumstances were presently unnecessary.

"He had indicated an interest in being a clergyman, and before his early death my father secured a living for him. Wickham then refused the living, settling instead for a large sum of money. The greater part of that money was gambled away or wasted on reckless living."

"Go on."

"Unfortunately he is not a man to be trusted. He has lived his life trying to secure a fortune for himself doing as little as possible. He gambles, cheats, steals, extorts... does everything with purely selfish motives."

"Your words do not instil in me any confidence that he is either suitable for my daughter or intent on marrying her. As I said before, I do not believe he is going to marry her! And from what you have said, I cannot see why you believe he will!"

"Because, Mr. Bennet, Wickham knows that by marrying Lydia, he is marrying into a family connection that has a substantial amount of wealth."

Mr. Bennet looked at him oddly. "You refer to Jane's marriage to Mr. Bingley? Come, Mr. Darcy. Mr. Bingley may have a slight fortune, but certainly not enough to induce this type of man into marriage!"

"You are quite right in your assessment of what will induce Wickham, and no, it is not Bingley's fortune."

"Then whose fortune do you mean? Certainly you are not blind! Our family's fortune could not elicit that type of inducement!"

Elizabeth closed her eyes tightly as she gripped her hands together, her heart about to burst from its incessant pounding as she awaited his revelation.

Darcy came over to the desk, in front of Mr. Bennet, and stretched both hands out, planting them firmly on the desk.

"My fortune, Mr. Bennet."

"Yours?" Mr. Bennet looked at him with bewilderment and promptly sat down.

"I told you that I have a strong... *very* strong admiration for your daughter."

"Yes, Mr. Darcy? Just exactly what are you trying to tell me?" Mr. Bennet found himself struggling to maintain a steady demeanour. Glancing at Elizabeth and then back to Darcy, he asked, "Or is there something you would prefer to ask me?"

"With all due respect, Sir, I wish I could have the honour of asking you what ought to be your due. But unfortunately, I cannot."

Mr. Bennet eyed him suspiciously. "I do not take your meaning, Mr. Darcy. I repeat, Sir, just what, exactly, are you trying to tell me?"

Darcy took a deep breath before answering. "Elizabeth and I are married, Sir."

Mr. Bennet narrowed his eyes at the man in front of him. He tried to grasp the words he just heard, determining if he could have somehow misunderstood the words. Slowly, and most deliberately, he spoke. "Excuse me, Mr. Darcy, but I believe you just said that you and my daughter are married."

"Yes, Sir, I did."

Mr. Bennet slowly stood up from his chair, bringing himself eye level with Darcy. Elizabeth bolted from her chair, reaching out to her father in an attempt to calm him. "Lizzy? You married my Lizzy?" The indignation in his voice could not be mistaken.

"Papa, please..."

Darcy nodded, bracing himself for the anger he heard in Mr. Bennet's voice and saw rising in his face.

Mr. Bennet pounded a fist down upon the desk. "How dare you come here and tell me that you and Lizzy are married! How can this be?"

"Mr. Bennet, if you will only allow me to explain!"

"Explain? Explain? What sort of explanation can there be?" He turned away, pulling a handkerchief out and wiping his brow. "My Lizzy!" Turning to his daughter, he cried, "All I ever wanted was your happiness and now I discover you have married this man, whom I hardly know, without even informing me! Without ever asking for my consent?"

He turned back abruptly at Darcy, pointing his finger at him. "All right, young man, but it had better be an explanation that is to my satisfaction!"

"Sir," beads of perspiration began to form on Darcy's brow as he struggled to maintain his composure. "We were on the ship together going to America. Down in steerage, where Eliza... Miss Elizabeth was staying, they had doubled up the children in beds. When sickness broke out, Elizabeth charitably gave up her bed to a child and subsequently was left to sleep on the floor. She then took ill, herself. I had the only available bed on the ship so we had the captain marry us so she could sleep in that bed without any semblance of impropriety. We agreed that I would annul the marriage when I returned to England."

"You agreed to enter the holy state of matrimony... on a ship... only to have it later annulled?" He slammed his fist on the desk. "I find it easier to understand Lydia running off as she did than what you just told me Elizabeth agreed to!"

"I was ill, Papa ..."

His eyes glared at Darcy. "So you took advantage of my Lizzy when she was ill?"

"Sir, I never…" Darcy paused and turned to his wife. "Perhaps you best leave while your father and I continue this conversation."

"But…"

"Please," Darcy's eyes implored her.

"I shall be just outside the door." Elizabeth gave pleading looks to both her husband and father before turning toward the door.

The two men watched as she exited and closed the door behind her. Darcy turned back to Mr. Bennet. The look in the older gentleman's eyes and expression on his face were certainly not lost to Darcy's understanding. He was angry and Darcy regretted that his anger was compounded against him due to Lydia's indiscretion. The possibility that Elizabeth had acted imprudently was overwhelming him. "Sir, I hope you will believe me when I say that I have only behaved in an honourable manner towards your daughter."

Mr. Bennet was taken aback by this. "You expect me to believe that you spent all that time together in the same room and she remains as virtuous as when I escorted her onto the ship?"

Darcy felt all the approbation of her father weighed upon his answer.   "Yes, Sir." Darcy closed his eyes as he fought off the imposing awkwardness that this discussion was creating within him. "I give you my word, Sir." Darcy managed to take in a few breaths to bolster his resolve. He continued, "Mr. Bennet, our marriage initially was one of convenience. However, while on the ship, I grew to love and admire your daughter but, regrettably, did not openly confess it due to my belief that she wished the marriage to be annulled. When we met again at Netherfield, I was delighted to discover that she returned my regard and, like myself, desired to keep our marriage intact. I want to assure you that our love for each other is strong and we desire nothing less than being able to openly acknowledge our marriage. I appeal to you, Sir. We will do whatever you wish for us. Unfortunately, although I cannot ask for your permission to marry your daughter, I respect her beyond measure and would not wish to compromise her reputation without securing your blessing upon our marriage." He held his breath, waiting for Mr. Bennet's response.

Mr. Bennet was quite moved by Darcy's admission, but was still too stunned to respond favourably. "At the moment, I am not inclined to give my blessing; however, I am willing to give it some thought."

Darcy slowly let out his breath. "I would appreciate that, Sir."

Mr. Bennet had almost forgotten about the reason for their conversation in the first place. When at last he did, he said to Darcy, "But back to my other daughter. This Wickham somehow learned of your marriage to my Lizzy and figured he could entice our Lydia into marrying him so he could, through some means, tap into your fortune?"

"That is what I assume, Sir. His sole motive for everything he does is to secure riches for himself with as little effort as possible. It would not benefit him to run off with Lydia and then cast her off. No, I believe he does intend to marry her and eventually use his connection to me through your family to support his habits and lifestyle."

"And knowing this, you still wish to remain married to my daughter?"

"More than anything, Sir.

Mr. Bennet knew Mr. Darcy was not a man one should ever refuse. He was rightly angered by his daughter's secret marriage, but deeply gratified by the measure of this man before him, not just his wealth -- that would make Mrs. Bennet undeniably happy -- but the strength of his principles and conviction. However he was not inclined to let the man off so easily.

"Well, Mr. Darcy, I must say that today has been the most taxing day of my whole existence. To go from hearing of the unfortunate elopement of one daughter to the reprehensible secret marriage of another... I truly cannot think too clearly on any of this at the moment."

"Sir, I offer my deepest apologies for any suffering this may have caused you; however, I do not apologize for marrying your daughter. While my original intent may not have been what it ought to have been, I wish for nothing else but to keep our marriage from being annulled."

"And are you fearful that I will insist on having it annulled, then?"

"I would hope you would not, Sir. But the truth is, at this very moment my aunt is making her way to London to see if she can dissolve it. George Wickham was more than expedient in informing her of our marriage as soon as he learned of it. But his disclosure was most likely not out of any sort of kind-hearted gesture. I imagine he was able to extort some money from her before producing our marriage certificate to her as proof. My aunt called on Elizabeth earlier today and left her with the threat that she would do all she could to have it annulled. I would beseech you to calmly think about all I have said."

Mr. Bennet looked at the man before him. To say that he looked desperate was not an exaggeration. He quite enjoyed it and wondered just how much this man was willing to take for his favourite daughter.

"Mr. Darcy, on what basis should I accept you as my daughter's husband? How do I know that you are not as deceitful as this Wickham, or perhaps more so? How can I give my blessing when I hardly know, you save from one conversation at a ball?"

"Sir, do you trust your daughter's judgment?"

Thoughts of his favourite daughter filled his mind. She was indeed the wisest discerner of a person's character of anyone he knew. He nodded, knowing that of all his daughters, he trusted Elizabeth's judgment the greatest. "I will give it some thought, Mr. Darcy."

Darcy looked down, not knowing whether he was in Mr. Bennet's good graces or not. "Thank for you that, Sir." Darcy then looked back up at his father-in-law. "Mr. Bennet, there is one more thing that I might be able to accomplish in Town if I leave immediately."

"And what is that?"

"Find Wickham and remove your daughter from his presence."

"Do you think you can actually find them?"

"I know of several acquaintances that he has there that he may have contacted. My only concern for your daughter is that I might not arrive in time, if you take my meaning, Sir."

"I do and would be most grateful, Mr. Darcy, if you did remove Lydia from that rake. But now you must decide what matter of business you see to first when you arrive; preventing the annulment of your marriage with my one daughter or securing the innocence of my other daughter. You have a difficult choice before you, young man."

"I will do what I can."

"I am quite confident you will." Mr. Bennet looked closely at the man before him. "Colonel Forster and I talked about leaving in the morning for London to see what we can do to find them. We shall go to the Gardiners' home and meet you there. Will that suffice?"

"Yes, Sir. And hopefully, Mr. Gardiner will have your daughter in his possession."

"We shall hope, shall we not?" Mr. Bennet looked to the door. "Should we ask Lizzy to join us again?"

"Yes, I should like that very much."

Mr. Bennet opened the door, finding Elizabeth lingering suspiciously close. "Come, Elizabeth. I would like some words with you."

Elizabeth walked in and cast a worried glance at her husband, whose face gave her no inclination as to the outcome of their meeting.

"Well, Lizzy, I would offer you a seat, but if you are inclined to follow your husband's lead, you will remain standing."

Elizabeth nervously looked at her father.

"Papa, I do hope you will find it in your heart to forgive me… to forgive us. We never meant to hurt anyone."

"Hmmm. I must say that finding out twice in one week that you had an offer of marriage is certainly something I never suspected."

Darcy looked at him oddly. "Twice?"

Elizabeth shook her head and said softly, "I will enlighten you later."

"But now, we must decide what we are going to do about this little bit of news. I must confess that I am not at all pleased with this disclosure; however, what is done is done. Until I decide what we are to do about it, neither of you are to speak a word of it to anyone unless absolutely necessary and, of course, you are not to live together as man and wife."

"Yes, Sir, anything you say."

Mr. Bennet came around from behind his desk and walked toward the door. "You go do what you must in Town, Mr. Darcy. I suggest you find the fastest horse with the greatest endurance that will get you to London in time. Do what you can about Lydia. But I warn you, if you return to Longbourn only to inform me that my Lizzy's marriage has been annulled, I will be seriously displeased!"

"Thank you, Sir. I will do all I can."

Mr. Bennet left the room with a "Hmmph."

Darcy turned to Elizabeth. "I am fairly uncertain whether he is completely angry at me still or has accepted our marriage."

Elizabeth looked toward the door through which her father just disappeared. She turned back and smiled. "I believe he is considering how insupportable it would be for me to be in a marriage that has been annulled. Presently, he finds the alternative, being married to you, the lesser of the two offences."

Darcy raised his eyebrows in contemplation of Mr. Bennet's words. "I suppose I shall have to be content with that at present and only hope that his opinion of me will improve in the future. I will do all that I can, Elizabeth."

With Mr. Bennet leaving them alone, he took a bold initiative and grasped her hand, bringing it to his lips, lifting his eyes to meet hers just as his lips touched the back of her hand.

As he continued to hold her hand, he asked her, "What did your father mean by a second proposal?"

Elizabeth looked away sharply and took in a deep breath. "Mr. Collins," she said softly.

"Mr. Collins?" Darcy looked at her incredulously. "He actually asked for your hand?"

She nodded as she looked back at him. "Do you find it surprising that he would ask for my hand?"

"On the contrary. It was quite apparent to me that he wanted nothing more than to garner your favour." Darcy smiled. "What did you say?"

"I told him no, of course!"

Darcy smiled. "Good! I only wanted to be assured of your answer." He squeezed her hand and looked down at it. "I brought Georgiana back to Netherfield with me. If it is acceptable to you, may I ask her to send for you while I am away?"

"I should like that very much."

"It would give me great pleasure for you both to become better acquainted. She only had the kindest words about you and your meeting at Pemberley."

"I am glad."

"I have told her about our marriage, Elizabeth."

"Then I believe that we shall not only be the closest of friends, but the closest of sisters when you return!"

A smile readily came upon Darcy's face. "You do not know how much that means to me." Darcy's breath caught as he beheld the gleam in Elizabeth's eyes. "I regret leaving again, but I promise I shall return promptly." He closed his eyes for a moment, and as if in a prayer he added, "With our marriage intact, my beloved wife."

He kissed her hand again before quickly leaving the room, grateful that he was able to leave the house without encountering the questioning glances or remarks by Mrs. Bennet.

Elizabeth remained in the room and her father soon returned to join her.

"Well, Lizzy. What have you to say for yourself?" Mr. Bennet inquired.

"Papa, he is a good man. You must see that he has the finest character."

"Oh, I have it on good authority that he is a solid gentleman; a decent, principled man; one that I should never lament having as a son-in-law." His eyes twinkled as he looked at Elizabeth. "Or being your husband."

"Papa, I do not understand."

Mr. Bennet reached into his desk drawer and drew out a letter. "From your

Uncle Gardiner." He absently scratched at his jaw as he held the missive out towards Elizabeth. "He thought it best to warn me that Mr. Darcy would be coming to talk with me about something of a most astonishing nature and that I should try to be open and give him my full attention. He and Mrs. Gardiner had only words of praise for him and gave him their ultimate approval. Not that I knew why they were bestowing such elaborate praises on the man."

"And now you do."

He looked down at her. "Yes, Lizzy, now I do. Although, even having received somewhat of a warning in the letter, I am still shocked. And I could not allow him to think I approved of what the two of you did. No, as much as I have respect for the man, I thought I needed to unsettle him just a bit."

"But you do forgive us?"

"Yes, Elizabeth, I do. But I am going to be adamant that for the moment we tell no one about this marriage and we wait until Mr… your… your husband returns before we do or say anything. If his aunt does somehow annul your marriage, however unlikely it is, it would be best not to have told anyone of it. Do you understand?"

Elizabeth wrapped her arms tightly around her father's neck. "Yes, Papa. I do, and thank you!"

Chapter 30

Darcy pounded his horse toward London. He was barely aware of the scenery passing by and those things on either side of him that were soon covered with a fine dusting of dirt, kicked up by the animal's hooves. He was intent on arriving in London before darkness settled. His only uncertainty was in regards to what he would see to first.

As the horse maintained a constant gallop, Darcy grasped the reins tightly, his mind in turmoil as he considered the plight of Miss Lydia Bennet. Finding Wickham and this youngest Bennet daughter was of the utmost urgency. Before leaving Hertfordshire, he inquired at the post station and determined that Wickham had indeed left with Lydia in the direction of London. He was grateful they had not gone in the direction of Gretna Green.

He could only hope that he would find them before nightfall. Once evening came, Lydia would likely be lost; taken, but not yet as his wife. He knew Wickham could not have planned this elopement far enough in advance to have already secured a license to be married in London today. Darcy shuddered as he considered that Wickham would not likely wait to have his way with her, if only to ensure that they marry. Darcy knew for a certainty that if he did not find them tonight, then it would be a matter of choosing disgrace over an imprudent, ill-fated marriage.

He shook his head in anger as he considered the lengths Wickham would go to secure his own welfare. Darcy wondered, though, how much of Wickham's actions were solely to spite him for interfering in his plans to marry Georgiana. Not that he ever loved her, but her fortune would have suited him very nicely. What could Wickham ever hope to gain by marrying Lydia? Darcy could only imagine that Wickham thought he would use Lydia as an intermediary between the two of them, most likely through Elizabeth. In anger, he dug his heels into the horse's flanks to spur him on even faster.

These concerns for Lydia battled with the issue of his aunt's threats to Elizabeth in regards to their marriage. What plans she had, once she arrived in London, he could only conjecture.

Darcy shuddered as he recollected times when some flagrant indiscretion was completely hushed up through ruthless manipulation by his aunt or, conversely, a minor offence was made public and the offender brutally scandalized by her own dispersal of exaggerated particulars. He had many more questions than he had answers.

His only consolation was that his aunt, conveyed in her carriage and requiring frequent stops, most likely arrived too late in the day to begin her implacable course of action. He expected her late arrival would necessitate waiting till the morrow. He fought against all selfishness in wanting to seek out his aunt immediately, but knew Lydia's situation would be settled most unfavourably once her virtue was lost. Being a man with a great sense of honour, he deemed it more prudent to seek out Lydia and Wickham first.

Darcy wiped his face with the back of his hand. The dirt and grit stung his face as he rode. He had given instructions to Durnham and Winston to convey the carriage to London the following day. He was not sure he would need their assistance, but he knew he would greatly appreciate the comfort of a carriage for the ride back.

About halfway to London, Darcy stopped at a livery post to change horses and freshen up. He did not take the time he normally did, securing only something to drink and a light fare to get him by until evening. He left a substantial sum with the livery hand to cool the horse down and keep him until he returned. He mounted the fresh horse and was quickly on his way again.

Darcy was tired; physically tired from travelling all morning to Netherfield and now to London and emotionally drained from the events of the day. He felt as though the past several days collided into one blur as he travelled from place to place attempting to quell one mishap after another. Perhaps this was his due penance for marrying Elizabeth with such a light regard for the vows he took. Not that he took them lightly now; in fact, the very thought of any action on his aunt's part against his wife or against their marriage produced a rage that consumed the depths of him. It prompted him to take whatever actions he deemed necessary to protect the one he loved beyond measure.

He was grateful for the change in horses, as this one was eager to take to the road in full stride. He should make it to London before darkness settled on the outlying roads.

At length, he began to see the familiar sights of the outskirts of London. He began to ponder where he should go. Wickham's acquaintance, Mrs. Younge, a co-conspirator in his scheme to elope with Georgiana, managed a boarding house. Although it was located in a rather squalid part of town, he was quite confident Wickham would seek her out for accommodations.

He would need a place for Lydia to go once she was removed from Wickham. He was confident he could enlist the aid of Mr. Gardiner.

When he finally came upon the streets of London, the sun had just dipped over the horizon. The lamps were being lit along the streets and he allowed the horse to slow its pace. It let out a few grunts, letting Darcy know it was most grateful.

As he came into the city, he directed his horse toward Cheapside. He would stop by the Gardiners first, acquaint them with the situation, and then set out to find Wickham.

He manoeuvred the horse down busy streets, walking around horse-drawn carts laden with items for sale or implements which a tradesman would use. The Gardiners' modest home was in the heart of Cheapside on Gracechurch Street. It was well kept and clean and located in a small area of similarly respectable homes. He alit from the horse, slapped the reins around a post, and walked up to the front door and knocked.

When the door was answered, the maid recognized him from his earlier visit. "Good evening, Mr. Darcy. What can I do for you?"

Darcy took off his hat. "Are either Mr. or Mrs. Gardiner at home?" he asked.

"Yes, they are just sitting down to dine. If you will wait here, I shall inform them that you are calling."

"Thank you."

The maid walked into the dining room and Darcy heard Mr. Gardiner's voice boom in a loud, surprised fashion. "Mr. Darcy? Well, invite him in, by all means!"

The maid returned. "This way, please."

As Darcy entered the small dining room, Mr. Gardiner was up on his feet and walking toward him. "What a surprise this is, Mr. Darcy! To what do we owe the honour of this visit?"

His grin was soon displaced by a more sombre look as he met Darcy's gaze. "What is it, my friend?"

"I am afraid I do not bring good tidings." He looked over at Mrs. Gardiner and the children. "Good evening, Mrs. Gardiner." He nodded at the children. "May we speak alone?"

"Certainly! This way."

Mr. Gardiner led the way to his study as Darcy followed. Both men vividly recalled this was where the two had sat just a few weeks earlier when he came to tell him of his marriage to Elizabeth. At that visit, Darcy had appeared nervous and on edge. This evening, he appeared far more distressed.

"Pray, what has happened, Mr. Darcy?"

Darcy's eyes looked up from staring disconsolately upon the hat he held in one hand and brushed his other hand through his hair. "Mr. Gardiner, I regret to inform you that your youngest niece, Miss Lydia Bennet, has run off with one of the officers stationed in Meryton with the intention to elope with him."

Mr. Gardiner shook his head. "This is very disturbing, indeed! I always feared she would be one who would do something reckless!" He turned back and looked upon the gentleman standing across from him. "But how is it that *you* have come to inform me of this?"

"I am well acquainted with the… the… officer in question. He grew up with me; his father being my father's steward. Unfortunately, he is not a man of honourable character. He discovered Elizabeth and I were married and I believe he is choosing to marry Lydia with some nefarious intent to tap into my wealth. I believe they have come to London."

"When did all this happen?"

"They departed Meryton sometime today. It was only discovered this afternoon."

"And what can be done about it?"

"I know some of his acquaintances that reside in Town. There is one in particular with whom he will likely make contact. I am sure you agree that it is of the utmost urgency to recover her tonight. I do not trust the man."

Mr. Gardiner took in a deep, solemn breath. "We must make every attempt to remove her tonight!"

"May I depend upon you to take her into your home?"

"Mr. Darcy, you may be assured we will and not only that, I shall accompany you. Let us leave directly. I only hope that my presence might do a little more to bring her to her senses."

"Thank you, Mr. Gardiner. However, I do not have a carriage. As you may have guessed from my attire, I rode all the way from Hertfordshire."

"We shall take mine. Allow me to inform my wife, and we shall be off without delay!"

After quietly informing Mrs. Gardiner what happened, Mr. Gardiner joined Darcy for the ride to Mrs. Young's boarding house. Darcy had the strongest inclination they would have secured a room for the night from her and he gave the driver the directions. Along the way, he relayed to the gentleman the particulars of Wickham's acquaintance with her.

Darcy also acquainted Mr. Gardiner with Wickham's corrupt habits, including how he informed his aunt of their marriage in return for, Darcy believed, some sort of payment. However, he chose not to breach Georgiana's confidence and therefore, did not tell him of Wickham's attempt to elope with her. "Knowing Wickham as I do," Darcy concluded, "if he was able to separate my aunt from some of her money in exchange for the marriage certificate, chances are he will be intent to find himself a high stakes card game and hope to win even more!"

Darcy went on to tell Mr. Gardiner of his aunt's subsequent threats to Elizabeth that she was going to annul the marriage and then, of Mr. Bennet's reaction to being informed of their marriage.

"You have had quite a trying day, have you not, Mr. Darcy?"

"That would be one way to describe it."

"And your aunt, what do you suppose she intends to do?"

Darcy shook his head. "I do believe she will attempt to discredit our marriage or perhaps even Elizabeth. I know my aunt too well. She does not make idle threats." Darcy shook his head. "She may not be able to use her wealth and power to annul our marriage, but she will do what she can to make a definitive display of her disapproval of it."

Mr. Gardiner raised his eyebrows as he pictured this woman who was now also Elizabeth's aunt. He smiled reassuringly to the man seated next to him. "Surely your aunt is not as vindictive as you think. My niece is a fine, young woman. I am certain you will help her to see reason, Mr. Darcy."

"Elizabeth is a wonderful woman, but you do not know my aunt. I may be required to resort to some threats of my own to ensure she behaves in a way that respects my wife as well as my decisions."

The men rode the remainder of the way in silence. As the carriage slowed down, Darcy looked out and saw that they were approaching the boarding house that Mrs. Younge owned.

The carriage stopped and Mr. Gardiner exited the carriage first, turning to Darcy. "Is this Mrs. Younge acquainted with you, Mr. Darcy?"

"I doubt she will ever forget my face in view of my behaviour toward her the last time I was in her company."

"Hmmm." Mr. Gardiner stood at the door to the carriage, effectually blocking it so Darcy could not get out himself. "I do not believe she will willingly give you the information you seek about this Wickham, given your history. Perhaps I should go in and inquire of his whereabouts."

Darcy looked at Mr. Gardiner with much respect. "I had planned to offer her a rather large monetary enticement to ensure her cooperation."

Mr. Gardiner put up his hand and waved it through the air. "No need to bribe her, Darcy. Why reward her when her character is just as despicable as Wickham's?"

"I doubt that she will give us the information without it!"

"Just leave it to me," Mr. Gardiner assured Darcy. "If you will allow me to see to the lady, alone, Sir, I hope to return promptly with his whereabouts."

Darcy watched the middle-aged gentleman turn and walk up to the boarding house. Mr. Gardiner tilted his hat askew, loosened his neckcloth, and began to stagger his walk. Darcy let out a soft chuckle as he realized Mr. Gardiner was going to portray himself as a man quite inebriated.

Mr. Gardiner approached the front door of the boarding house and knocked. The door opened and a young woman peered out.

"May I help you, Sir?" she asked nervously.

He removed his hat and gave an exaggerated bow. "I certainly hope… so." He slurred his speech in long, drawn out syllables. "I am lookin' for a Mrs. Younge."

"Just a minute, Sir."

The girl stepped away from the door and Mr. Gardiner placed a foot strategically against the open door, thereby preventing it from being closed on him.

Another woman approached him. "I am Mrs. Younge. Do you wish for a room?"

"No, not tonight. I unner… unner… stand…my good ol' friend… George Wickham… came into… Town… to… today." He swayed a little to reinforce his character.

"I am sorry, Sir, I do not know a Mr. Wickham."

"Ohhh." He said, looking down at his hands. "Are you… are you… Mrs. Younge?"

"Yes, but…"

"Good!" Mr. Gardiner clapped his hands loudly and leaned toward her. "He told me to come see you… he told me to let him know if I could get him in some decent card games with some high… some high stakes… I found just the game he is looking for! Yep! Should make Wickham quite happy, knowing his cir… circum… stance." Placing his hands against the doorframe as if to steady himself, he looked up at her and winked. "Some… easy, well-to do-targets… in this one."

Mrs. Younge narrowed her eyes at the man before her. His dress was only moderately fashionable, he was obviously intoxicated, but certainly not a man of the finer circles of society. "And you said the stakes are high in this game?"

As Mr. Gardiner watched this woman's face, he saw her suspicion and scepticism fade away, replaced by a look of outright greed.

"Most assuredly. Mr. Wickham will be most... will be most pleased... to know we have some aff... aff... affluent players who are little concerned about parting with their... parting with their money. You know how su... superior Wickham's card playing is... and with the bundle I un... understand he has, he will stand up nicely with these men. If you know wha... what I mean, Madam."

Mrs. Younge smiled. She knew Wickham had come into a respectably large sum and wished to increase it to get him by until everything was arranged for his and Lydia's marriage. At that point, he had reassured her, he would have no difficulty securing a nice amount of spending money from his brother-in-law, Fitzwilliam Darcy! She sneered to herself as she thought of the man who previously ruined their similar plans with Georgiana.

"Very well," said Mrs. Younge. "But he is not in this boarding house. It was full. He is staying across the road in one of the cottages in the back. It is number seven. Just cross the road and it is off to the right. You cannot miss it."

"I thank you very much!" smiled Mr. Gardiner and tipped his hat. He turned to leave, and just as he was about to walk out the door he looked back at her. "And Mr. Fitzwilliam Darcy thanks you, as well!" He straightened up and spoke as clearly and as soberly as a judge.

As Mr. Gardiner stepped out, Darcy briskly walked up the steps behind him. Mrs. Younge flung the door open, demanding to know what Gardiner meant by that and found herself face to face with the man himself.

"Mrs. Younge, I cannot say that it is a pleasure to see you again, but I certainly hope that you have given my good friend here the information he requested."

Her eyes glared at him. "You deceived me! How dare you!"

"You are perfectly right, Madam. Disguise of any sort is my abhorrence and I am excessively sorry to have to resort to your method of choice. If I were you, I would remain here. It might not be a very pleasant sight."

The two men departed and hurriedly crossed the road; darkness and a bitter cold seemed to sweep over them. Upon reaching the cottages, they easily found number seven. The two men gave a determined glance at each other as if to say, "Let us go to it!"

Darcy's hands were already clenched in a fist when he hurried up the steps and pounded on the door.

An irritated voice called out, "Who is it?"

Darcy recoiled at the familiar sound of Wickham's voice. Mr. Gardiner put up a hand to Darcy to indicate he would take care of this.

"Sir, Mrs. Younge sent me over with some things for your stay."

"Just a minute," came the answer.

Darcy stepped up to the door and as it swung wide open, he took a step forward, filling the frame. Darcy's and Wickham's eyes met at equal stature of height but not equal stature as men. Wickham quickly assessed the situation and realized the most likely reason for his presence. He attempted to close the door, but Darcy's body blocked it. Mr. Gardiner did not miss the venomous look in

Darcy's eyes and wondered what all had been the cause of such a strong hatred for this man. Knowing his character was one thing, but it seemed to be spurred on by something intensely personal.

"Turn over the girl, Wickham," Darcy spoke through a taut jaw.

Wickham sneered at his long time rival. "She will not come with you. She and I are to be married."

Mr. Gardiner stepped into Wickham's sight. "She may not go with Mr. Darcy, but she certainly is going to come with me!"

"Who is it?" a young girl's voice could be heard from the other side of the room, followed by footsteps which brought her to the door. Her eyes widened and her head wrenched back in surprise. "Uncle Gardiner! Mr. Darcy! What are you both doing here?"

Mr. Gardiner spoke. "I am here to remove you from this man, Lydia. Your family is most concerned and there is much we need to talk about. Did it not even cross your mind that what you were doing was wrong?"

Giving him a look of derision as she rolled her eyes she clipped back, "I am old enough to know what I am doing! I love Mr. Wickham and he loves me and we are to be married!"

Wickham gave Darcy a rather smug look as he wrapped his arm around the girl. "You see, Darcy? She will tell you! We are to be married!"

Mr. Gardiner easily saw the failings and wickedness of this man; certainly not the type of husband one would wish for one's niece. Glaring at Wickham for the overly familiar embrace in which he held Lydia, he retorted, "You are not married yet and she should not be here with you! I demand that you unhand her immediately and release her to me!"

Lydia did not think she had ever seen her uncle look so stern and pulled in closer to Wickham. A brief look of apprehension crossed her face, but she quickly steeled herself and answered back, "You cannot make me go!"

Instead of arguing with his niece, Mr. Gardiner unexpectedly pushed past them, catching the two of them off guard. Without saying a word to either one, he determinedly walked toward the back room.

"Where is he going?" asked Wickham, taken by surprise. "You cannot walk in here without my permission! I demand that both of you leave immediately!"

Mr. Gardiner ignored him and when he walked in the room, he breathed a sigh of relief. The bed was perfectly made. They had arrived in time.

As he came back out he looked only at Darcy, saying with an air of relief, "We are not too late."

"Wickham, release the girl to her uncle immediately." Darcy spoke in a firm, controlled voice that Wickham had long come to recognize.

Wickham narrowed his eyes at Darcy. "It will not work this time, Darcy. Lydia knows exactly what she is doing!"

"Does she?"

"Of course I do!" exclaimed Lydia. "Uncle Gardiner, Mama cannot be but pleased that I am marrying an officer. She has the deepest respect for officers. And I love George!"

"Lydia, you will come with me now!" Her uncle's voice was unyielding.

"Once we have talked about this, I trust you will see it was a mistake!"

Lydia let out a frustrated groan and Wickham held on more tightly.

Darcy pointedly addressed Wickham. "Wickham, holding on to Miss Bennet more tightly will not work once she knows the truth. Do you want me to tell her how you attempted the same thing with my sister? How you schemed to elope with her only because you wanted her fortune?"

Lydia's eyes, as well as Mr. Gardiner's, widened at this revelation.

"I was foolish back then, I admit it! But Lydia does not have any fortune so you cannot say my motive is the same!"

"Yes, but you know differently, Wickham. Do you not?"

Mr. Gardiner looked down at Lydia. "Lydia, Wickham knows that by marrying you he will have a connection to a rather large fortune."

"What?" asked Lydia. "Me? Have a fortune? Surely you are joking!"

Darcy turned and looked at her. "No, not you directly. But your sister, Elizabeth, has one and Wickham hopes some of that fortune will come to him by marrying you."

"Oh, Lord! Elizabeth has a fortune?" Lydia tilted her head. "How?"

Darcy looked directly at the young girl. "Because *I* married her."

Lydia gasped. "*You* married Elizabeth?"

"This is absurd!" Wickham stated coolly. "How would I know something like that when even her sister was not aware of it? Come, Mr. Darcy, this is all a futile attempt on your part to try to interfere with my life; to prevent me from finding happiness! All because you resented your father's love for me!"

Darcy's eyes darkened. "Do not bring my father into this, Wickham!"

Lydia cried out again, "*You* married Elizabeth?"

"You have always interfered with my getting what I want!" Wickham accused, pointing his finger at Darcy.

"The only thing you seek is an easy fortune! Well I can guarantee, Wickham, that marrying Miss Bennet will not procure one ounce of anything from me! Your plans for her would be just cause for the Bennets to cast her off, cutting you off completely from them and, consequently, myself." Darcy leaned in to Wickham, clearly making his point. "Mr. Bennet would never give his permission for you to marry and you would not even be able to collect the 50 pounds a year that the Bennet daughters are to inherit."

Wickham's face was enflamed with anger. "You are still as tight-fisted as you always have been! You have fooled the people around Pemberley into thinking you are generous. Well *I* know otherwise!"

"Wickham, I have been generous toward you to a fault! It is because you chose to mishandle all that was given to you that you are in the dire straits you are today. Does Miss Lydia know of all your gambling debts you left behind in Meryton, let alone all the other places you have fled? Does she know how you have gone from one line of work to another because you must leave in order to escape being forced to pay those debts?"

"That is all a lie!" He paled, though, as Darcy's words struck like arrows, piercing him with the truth. More importantly, they were beginning to awaken Lydia to the truth of who he really was.

"Come, Lydia," urged Mr. Gardiner, as the two men stood quietly now, staring at one another. "Certainly you can see for yourself that this man before you is not the gentleman he led you to believe he was. His intentions have been strictly dishonourable."

Lydia turned to Wickham. "Is this all true? Did you know that my sister was married to Mr. Darcy? Is this the only reason you wanted to marry me?"

Wickham pushed her away toward her uncle. "Oh, go with him! I would be weary of your incessant chattering in but a few days. No amount of money would make it worth marrying you!"

Lydia's eyes widened as she turned back to him. "You lied to me! All those things you said to me were lies!"

"I only said what you wanted to hear!"

"Lydia," Mr. Gardiner gently urged her away, "the carriage is waiting."

He took Lydia's arm to take her to the carriage, glancing at Darcy and urging him to follow suit.

Wickham eyed him with contempt. "Take your tedious sister and return her to her pathetic family. You have done well for yourself, old friend, marrying into the Bennet family. Your pretty little wife must make up for her decidedly inferior station and questionable connections in other ways for you, eh, Darcy?"

Darcy's fist tightened as Wickham made his malicious declaration against his wife and her family.

Wickham looked at him spitefully. "I found her quite dull, myself. Although her figure was certainly something I would not mind getting my hands on."

Wickham gave a low laugh and then abruptly decided he was finished.

"What are you remaining here for? You have Lydia. Now go!"

"There is one more thing I wish to take care of here, Wickham," Darcy said softly, masking his anger.

"And that is?"

Before Wickham could even brace himself, Darcy pulled back his hand that had remained fisted for the duration of their visit and promptly gave him a blow to the stomach. Wickham doubled up, making a futile attempt to catch his breath.

"I leave you with that, Wickham, as well as with a warning. Do not ever speak of my wife in that manner again! And never attempt anything like this with a young girl again or I shall make sure you will suffer more than just the consequences of a blow to the abdomen!"

Darcy wiped off his hands and turned, leaving Wickham crouched and unable to get up for some time.

The carriage returned to the Gardiners' home in relative silence. Lydia was most obstinate in not wanting to listen to any scolding. She was humiliated by Wickham's harsh words against her but felt more strongly the interference by these two men. That she now was required to go to the Gardiners' and bear their lectures on the virtues of women was far too disheartening.

When they arrived at their destination, Darcy did not follow them in, but bid them farewell. Darcy's body ached, prodding him that he needed rest. He knew, however, that he had one more situation which required his immediate attention and he knew this might be even more difficult than what he just endured.

Chapter 31

When Darcy rode up to his townhouse, it greeted him with all the easy familiarity of a close friend. Just setting his eyes upon it helped calm him. But he knew very well that just inside might be something of a different matter.

He walked up to the door and opened it, greeting a very surprised butler, Mr. Andrews. "Mr. Darcy, this is a surprise! We were not expecting you!"

"I am sorry to arrive without notice, Andrews. Tell me, is my aunt here?"

"Yes, Sir. Your aunt arrived but an hour ago and your cousin, Colonel Fitzwilliam is here as well."

"Fitzwilliam?"

"Yes, Sir. He has been here a couple of days. He is in with your aunt now, in the sitting room."

Darcy looked at him. "I beseech you, Andrews; do not let anyone know I am here. I shall be in my study. Please make an attempt to draw Colonel Fitzwilliam away from my aunt and ask him to come into the study without raising her suspicions. Presently, I do not wish for her to know that I am here."

"Yes, Sir."

Darcy slipped into his study and closed the door. He waited. If he could garner the help of his cousin, this might turn out to be easier than he thought.

It was some minutes before Colonel Fitzwilliam came into the study. He opened the door curiously and when he saw Darcy, his eyes travelled up and down the usually immaculate man. Darcy was encrusted with a layer of dirt; his clothes completely soiled. He began to let out a "Cous…"

Darcy put his fingers up to his lips to silence him. "Shhhh, Fitzwilliam. I do not want Lady Catherine to know I am here just yet! I desperately need your help in a matter."

Darcy saw the look of exasperation on his cousin's face. "And I need your help in a matter, Darce! She is extremely upset and irrational! Something has her so enraged, yet she refuses to tell me what it is!"

"I believe I know what has her so enraged. I will tell you and I ask that you return to her and attempt to get her to discuss it with you."

Colonel Fitzwilliam looked askance at him and nodded his head. "Pray, continue."

"First, sit down and promise me you will not utter a word until I have finished."

Fitzwilliam furrowed his eyebrows and smiled. "You are behaving quite oddly, Cousin, but if you insist, not a word!"

"Good. Some news came to her attention about me and she is most definitely not pleased about it."

"What news was that?"

Darcy paused, thinking to himself that disclosing his marriage ought to get easier with all the people he had already told. "She found out I am married."

"Mar…"

"Shhh!" Darcy looked at his cousin's face shocked face. "I married a wonderful, young lady I met on the ship to America. She is exceptional… more than I could have expected to find in a lady… but she does not meet our aunt's expectations of whom she believes I should marry. Although I strongly believe *no* woman would have satisfied her notion, other than Anne."

"Ahhhh, *now* I understand her temper tonight!"

"Well, there is more. We have been secretly married."

At Colonel Fitzwilliam's look of astonishment, Darcy explained briefly how it came to be.

"Very few people know about it, but Wickham found out… in truth, he stole the marriage certificate and took it to her, no doubt seeking some sort of recompense for bringing it to her attention. She, in turn, went directly to Elizabeth, my wife, with the certificate in hand, berating her to her face and threatened that she would annul our marriage!"

"Darcy! In the past we have witnessed some highly inexcusable things she has done, but this surpasses them all! Certainly she has no real ability to annul your marriage, does she?"

"Is there anything our aunt would not attempt, if she was so determined?" He looked at his cousin guardedly. "Think back, Fitzwilliam, on how often she has used her wealth and position for fraudulent means; silencing and influencing authorities; discrediting the honour of someone simply because they stood up to her or were not to her liking."

"I take your meaning."

"You must engage her to talk. Somehow you must get her to show you the marriage certificate and remove it from her possession and return to me! I will rest a little easier having it in my own hands."

"How am I to do that?"

"Give her some reason to enlighten you as to what she comprehends of my situation. Relate to her how badly I have mismanaged Pemberley; how you are concerned about my behaviour of late… anything to get her to confide in you about what she discovered concerning me!"

"You really want me to disparage you in front of her?"

"Only until you are able to secure the certificate. I do not believe she can do anything without it. And once I have it, I will confront her. With your help, of course!"

"Thanks, good cousin! I cannot tell you how I have always wanted to do this!" Fitzwilliam cast Darcy a sarcastic look. "Enumerate your faults, that is, not confront our aunt!"

Darcy shook his head slightly at his cousin's teasing. "But you will do this?"

"Yes, I will see what I can do!" As Fitzwilliam walked out, he turned and gave Darcy a curious glance, unable to believe the man had actually found a woman he deemed worthy to marry. That he had married in such a fashion was even more astounding.

Fitzwilliam left, and Darcy sank down in his chair. He leaned back and closed his eyes, believing he would just rest his weary body while Fitzwilliam was charming his aunt into surrendering the certificate. But resting his body soon gave way and Darcy fell into a deep, much needed sleep.

Fitzwilliam walked through the door, awakening Darcy with a start. "That was certainly prompt!" he said as Fitzwilliam looked at him, holding a piece of paper in his hands.

"Prompt? How can you say that was prompt? It took me more than an hour to get this from her!"

Darcy blinked his eyes a few times. "That long?" He shook his head to clear his thoughts. "I must have fallen asleep."

"You must have fallen into a *deep* sleep!"

"So where is she now?"

"She is still in the drawing room. Mad as a hornet about all the things I said about you. But you were correct, it worked! After all I told her of all your recent troubling behaviour, she was more than willing to tell me all about your *little* indiscretion. However, in her eyes, one would think you had committed treason or some similar offence. When I feigned complete disbelief, I asked her what proof she had and she promptly produced this!"

"Excellent work, Fitzwilliam." He met the look of mirth in his cousin's eyes. "Now I only hope we can undo the damage of the stories you told!"

"Undo them? Why, I only told her what was true!" Fitzwilliam took great delight in teasing his younger cousin.

Darcy shook his head. "Come, Fitzwilliam. I need you beside me now, more than ever!"

The two walked into the drawing room, where Lady Catherine had leaned her head back and had drifted off to sleep.

"It appears as though all that anger has taken its toll on her, Darce. Perhaps we should leave her and wait until morning."

"No, Fitz! We are doing this now!"

Fitzwilliam looked at his cousin and could see the exhaustion that permeated his body. "Darce, there is no need to pursue this tonight. You are exhausted! Let it… and you… rest until morning. You always think better after a good night's sleep. And you know how our aunt hates being disturbed from her sleep. You will not stand a chance with her tonight if we awaken her now."

"Perhaps you are right. I shall retire to my room and will be up at first light. I shall see you in the morning."

"Aye, Cousin. Anything you say!"

As Darcy turned to leave, he admonished his cousin. "If I am not here in the morning, do what you must to keep our aunt from leaving! I have an urgent errand to run and you must keep her here until I return!"

At Fitzwilliam's nod, Darcy walked slowly to his room, anxious for his bed. Passing Andrews, he informed him that he would be turning in and again asked that his aunt not be informed of his presence in his home.

"Shall I have a bath drawn for you, Sir?"

For the first time since arriving, Darcy looked down at his clothes. "Yes, Andrews, that would be splendid. He came into his room and quickly rid himself of his grimy attire. He waited quietly and patiently for the bath to be drawn, and at long last it was ready. He stepped into the bath and leaned back, allowing Andrews to take Durnham's role in scrubbing him clean.

When he finally slipped into bed, he fell into a deep sleep consoling himself with dreams of a beautiful woman he longed so much to have at his side.

~~*

Darcy opened his eyes and he sat up with a start. He looked around him, adjusting his eyes to the semi-darkness of the room, quickly realizing that he was in his room at his townhouse in London. He swung his legs off the bed, knowing that he must ready himself without delay if he was to get the early start he required.

It was some time later that Colonel Fitzwilliam cautiously came downstairs and was grateful when he saw that the dining room was empty. His aunt had not yet come down. He would be able to savour at least a few minutes of undisturbed silence as he enjoyed his morning meal. He was brought a variety of breads and fruit to choose from as well as a steaming cup of coffee. He selected a dark rye and smeared it with a thick layer of butter, taking a large bite from it and enjoying its hearty flavour.

The house was silent save for the murmurs coming from the kitchen and the occasional sound of cookware set upon a counter or utensils drawn from a drawer. He sighed deeply as he recollected the events of the night before.

His aunt's anger was such that he had never seen the whole of his life. He could most assuredly have called it a furious rage. On many occasions he had witnessed her demanding tirades, her stridently voiced dissatisfaction with a trifling annoyance, and even her irritation at his own acts of impudence, but never what he had witnessed last night.

As he drained the last sip of coffee from his cup, he set it down. He wondered to what extent his aunt had berated the woman who was now the object of her contempt -- Darcy's wife. To think that she paid her a visit to express her disapproval, to vehemently denounce their marriage, and to threaten to annul it! The very thought made Fitzwilliam shudder. He only hoped that this woman whom his cousin married had a strong enough constitution to bear this first meeting of their aunt and was kind-hearted enough to forgive her.

Fitzwilliam questioned, however, whether his cousin would ever be able to forgive their aunt. Throughout their life they had, for the sake of family, endured her emotional outbursts and verbal assaults, learning at an early age to simply be silent when she burst into a fit of rage. Was it only his imagination or was she truly becoming more and more malicious of late? Fitzwilliam did not honestly believe that he would be able to forgive her if she came to someone he held in high regard and behaved as abominably as she had toward Darcy's wife.

His eyes drifted toward the door and up toward the second floor as he heard his aunt's voice snapping out orders to her maid. She had arisen! He knew it was only a matter of time before she would come upon him in the dining room and continue with the tirade she began last evening. He looked back down to the empty coffee cup and shook his head. He hoped his cousin would return shortly. He was not sure how long he would be able to detain her from setting out, as Darcy had requested, let alone endure her wrath.

At length, her commanding presence filled the room. Fitzwilliam needed only to take a quick glance at her and notice her erect stance, firmly set jaw, and impatience in slapping the fan she held in one hand against the other to see that she was still quite annoyed. He steeled himself for that with which she was about to engulf him.

She entered the room with a fiery countenance that clearly reflected her dissatisfaction with everything and everyone. At her overly dramatic frustrated sigh, Fitzwilliam looked up. "Good morning, Aunt."

"Until I get a few things settled, I hardly would call it good. Fitzwilliam, do you still have the marriage certificate? You do, do you not?"

"Ah, yes, it is somewhere around here."

"Nephew, you must retrieve it directly and attend me!"

Fitzwilliam gave her an innocent questioning glance. "Pardon? Attend you where?"

"Oh, Fitzwilliam! Have you no recollection of last night? With all that you told me of your cousin's behaviour of late, you must accompany me. Surely with the information we both submit to our attorney, he shall clearly see that Darcy is not in his right mind and that his marriage must therefore be annulled!"

Fitzwilliam forced himself to disguise his horror as he looked at his aunt. "Not in his right mind?" Fitzwilliam smiled at the thought. "Certainly that can wait, Aunt, until after breakfast. Sit down and enjoy something to eat."

"I must attend to this as soon as possible, Fitzwilliam, and you must join me!" She pulled out a piece of paper. "I have written it all down this morning; everything you informed me of last night and all that I have come to be acquainted with in regards to his behaviour of late. He certainly cannot continue to handle all of his responsibilities, particularly managing Pemberley, if he is so mentally incapacitated. And this marriage…"

Fitzwilliam could barely swallow without choking as he heard his aunt's scathing words. He looked up to her with disbelief as she was essentially threatening to take over all of Darcy's affairs. He forced himself to remain calm. "I am sorry, Aunt. I am fear that I cannot. If you wish me to accompany you, it must be later. Something has arisen and I cannot leave at present." He hoped his expressed inability to leave directly would delay his aunt's departure.

"Something has arisen?" Lady Catherine looked at him angrily. "When I arrived yesterday and discovered you here, you informed me that you were here to spend a week free of responsibilities and engagements. Now you say something has arisen? Pray, what?"

"Me!"

The voice behind Lady Catherine startled her. She turned to see Darcy standing in the doorway, his eyes darkened and his hands tightly gripping his riding stick.

Darcy noticed only the slightest thread of dismay cross her face followed by an adjustment of her shoulders and a fortification of her resolve. "Nephew!"

"Lady Catherine," Darcy acknowledged her with a restrained anger.

The two studied each other. Lady Catherine anxiously tried to determine if her nephew knew her reason for being in Town or was aware of the meeting with his… his… She could not bring herself to consider that woman as his wife!

Darcy, on the other hand, braced himself to confront this woman who so insolently berated his Elizabeth.

"I was not aware that you would be in Town," Lady Catherine commented warily.

"I would imagine you rather *hoped* I would not." His jaw tightened and he refused to break his look of cold fury as she nervously sought out Colonel Fitzwilliam.

"Well, Darcy, your cousin and I… we have business we must attend to." The glance she gave to Fitzwilliam demanded that he heed her appeal.

As she turned to walk around Darcy, he sidestepped in front of her to prevent her from getting beyond him. "I would advise you to sit down, first, Aunt. There is a matter I must discuss with you."

"As soon as I return!" She turned to Fitzwilliam. "Fitzwilliam, be so kind as to get that item we were discussing a few moments earlier. It is imperative that I have it in my possession."

Fitzwilliam merely looked at his aunt. "I am sorry, I seem to have misplaced it." Fitzwilliam padded his hands around his pockets and into his coat jacket as if to search for it. Then he settled back with a sly grin, as he was most anxious to watch events unfold. Over the years, he and his cousin had passively endured their aunt's tirades on so many occasions that he was actually looking forward to Darcy putting her in her place.

"Misplaced it?" she exclaimed.

Darcy reached into his pocket and pulled out a piece of paper. "Is this what you were looking for, Aunt?"

Lady Catherine gasped as she saw the marriage certificate in his hands. "And exactly how did you come into possession of that?"

Darcy leaned into her and, in a voice that barely restrained his rage, pointedly stated, "I might ask you the same question!"

Desperately, Lady Catherine reached out to grab it, but Darcy quickly pulled it away. Her voice raised a couple of octaves as she pointed her finger repeatedly at Darcy. "It was in the best interest of the family that it was put into my hands. You have not been in your right mind lately. Your cousin will attest to that! And this marriage that you had the audacity to enter into! Why… why…" Lady Catherine's face grew red and she took a few breaths to calm herself. "It is positively insupportable!"

"And your behaviour to my wife was unspeakable and completely unforgivable!"

"Nephew, I am not used to being treated this way by family! Now hand me the marriage certificate! I shall deal with it so that the family will not go through the disgrace that this travesty of a marriage will bring upon it!"

"Indeed, I will not!" The resonance of his voice reflected the anger he was barely able to control. "My marriage to Elizabeth will bring no disgrace, no dishonour, and no shame to our family! It is you who brings our family disgrace by your insolent actions!"

"How dare you, Nephew!"

"And how dare you approach my wife without my permission and threaten her and berate her as you did."

Lady Catherine met his challenging glance and answered, "You are the one who has chosen to dishonour the family name! Your behaviour of late… your cousin has told me…"

Darcy looked at his cousin. "Just what do you have to say against me, Cousin?"

"Me?" asked Fitzwilliam, feigning innocence by shrugging his shoulders. "I can think of nothing you have done that is not of the highest integrity."

"What?" asked their aunt in horror. "Tell him what you told me last night!" She turned to Darcy. "He knows, Nephew! He knows how you have been mismanaging Pemberley, but fears telling you to your face!"

"On the contrary, Aunt," Fitzwilliam began. "None of those things I told you last night had any bearing of truth to them."

"Certainly, they must!"

Fitzwilliam shook his head. "No, I only said those things so that you would tell me about his marriage and I could obtain his marriage certificate and return it to the rightful owner."

The two cousins watched their aunt as her face contorted in anger. "How dare you treat your aunt with such disrespect! Do you know to whom you are speaking?"

Darcy turned to his cousin. "Fitzwilliam, if you will excuse Lady Catherine and me, I believe we ought to complete this conversation in the privacy of my study."

"This is not to be borne! I refuse to go anywhere with you!" She turned to Fitzwilliam. "Certainly you see that his marriage must be annulled, no matter what you say different today!" She then turned to Darcy. "Keep your marriage certificate, then. I shall not need it. When I inform our attorney what you have done, he will see that you are not in your right mind and turn over all your affairs to my authority!"

She turned to leave, but Darcy's words stopped her.

"I have already paid a visit to Greeley this morning."

She turned back and blinked her eyes, not believing what she heard.

"I have informed him of the circumstances of my marriage and he is under the direct order to take no action against it from anyone, particularly from you! He dutifully agreed, seeing no reason to do otherwise."

Lady Catherine's breathing became ragged and she pounded her foot upon the floor. "Insolent Nephew! You know not what disgrace this marriage will be to our family. And what of Anne? You have been promised to each other since birth! Your mother and I…"

Darcy clenched his teeth. "Aunt, I have told you repeatedly, and your daughter has reaffirmed it, we have no wish to marry. We never have! I have already married another and there is nothing that you or anyone else can do about it!"

"But our two estates… the obligation to your family name… the meagre station of this woman!"

"This woman is my wife. None of those things are of any import to me! She is the only thing that matters! If you cared in the least for my welfare, if you loved me as the son of your sister, you would rejoice with me that this woman has become my wife! You would treat her with kindness and respect. But what you have done, what you have said, your behaviour…" Darcy felt his ire rising and his patience running thin. "I confess I know not how I shall ever be able to forgive you." Darcy's face was iron-clad with anger and resentment.

His aunt was rendered speechless as she looked from one nephew to the other, hoping for some sort of weakening that she could have her way. But both remained resolute.

"Aunt, if you do not wish to discuss this further with me in my study, I think it best for you to remove yourself from my premises without delay." Darcy turned to depart the room but stopped at the door and turned. "One more thing, Aunt. I did advise Greeley that your behaviour of late has been quite unstable and if you come to him with any request that he deems highly unusual, he is to notify me at once and we shall proceed in declaring you unfit to manage Rosings. He is in complete agreement with me that Anne is perfectly capable of handling your affairs if you prove to be incompetent."

Lady Catherine's mouth dropped wide open, her whole body began to tremble, and she was rendered mute by Darcy's threats.

Darcy used her silence to make one final point. "And do not think that you have an open invitation to call here or at Pemberley until you have improved your conduct and made a full apology to my wife."

She looked up at her nephew through narrowed eyes. She had only seen the unyielding look etched across his face on a few occasions. And while she prided herself on never cowering to anyone, the threats he was issuing were enough to make her reconsider. The thought of having Rosings forcefully taken from her set her mind in turmoil

Darcy turned and walked away, leaving Fitzwilliam alone to see the look of anger upon his aunt's face turn to anguish. Looking helplessly at her nephew, she said, "Surely you see… you agree with me, do you not? His marriage… it is unacceptable!"

Fitzwilliam actually felt pity for this woman who held so tightly to what she perceived was family honour and obligation. "No, Aunt. Although I have not met this lady, I am quite confident that Darcy would have chosen well. She must be someone well suited to the intelligent gentleman he is."

"But…" Lady Catherine tried to interrupt, but Fitzwilliam put up his hand to stop her.

"And to him, that is more important than any expectations you may have for his wife." He gave a slight smirk as he looked toward the door Darcy just walked through. "As a matter of fact, I am quite anxious to meet this young lady who was finally able to break through the barriers he has always put up. Already, I find myself holding her in the highest regard!"

Fitzwilliam, with a quick farewell, excused himself and left Lady Catherine quite disturbed and fretful that her invitation to residences in both London and Pemberley had been withdrawn. She felt quite unsteady as she realized the grave results of her actions.

Whatever slight regrets she may have harboured about the consequences of her actions, she was not yet inclined to yield. Lady Catherine was extremely indignant when she left London later that morning. Darcy remained secluded in his study and did not bring himself out to bid her farewell. Neither did she take the opportunity to stop by and advise him she was leaving. Her only companions on her way home to Kent were her very diverse thoughts and feelings about all that had transpired.

She could not imagine being turned away from Pemberley or the London townhouse. It was enough to grieve her indefinitely. But at present, her resentment and anger were in such an excessive state that she could not bear the thought of going to the girl and offering an apology. *My nephew will soon overlook my actions and his familial bonds will bring him around to apologizing to me for such a severe course of action.* But the little voice in her head did not seem to quell the displeasure she felt at her nephew's rebuke and disapprobation.

Darcy retreated to his study and after collapsing in his chair, he dropped his head into his hands. Even though he had no qualms about defending his wife to his aunt and possibly causing a major rift between this stubborn older woman and himself, everything that he had ever learned about loyalty and respect for family assaulted him. He had become proficient at keeping his anger and his words at bay when a member of his family, particularly his aunt, grated against everything he believed.

There were times when his aunt's outbursts exceeded the limits of his patience and he was forced to withdraw from her presence to keep from issuing an angry retort to her. But this time, she had gone too far and he could never have allowed her to remain unchallenged.

Chapter 32

Elizabeth awoke early the next morning. She tossed and turned throughout the night with a heaviness in her heart as she anxiously pondered the state of their marriage.

At one point, she pulled herself from her bed and walked over to the window. It was an overcast night and the moon sneaked peeks at her as clouds passed in front of it. She recollected watching the moon from *Pemberley's Promise* and her father's admonition to say a prayer each time she saw it. Without giving it much thought, she folded her hands together and looked out into the darkened sky.

Entwining her finger tightly together, she closed her eyes and prayed, "Oh, God, certainly You can see that the vows I took that day on the ship are vows that I now cherish and fervently uphold. Let nothing befall our marriage."

She slowly opened her eyes to see the moon shining bright from a break in the clouds. She sat quietly, listening to the clock on the hearth beating rhythmically along with her heart. She suddenly felt an assurance that, no matter what happened, all would be well.

The heaviness that had lingered in her heart for most of the night finally dissipated. Although she wondered of her husband's success the previous day, as it pertained both to confronting his aunt about their marriage and Wickham about Lydia, she knew there was nothing that she could do about it here and there was nothing to be gained by worry.

She saw her father off that morning when Colonel Forster arrived in his carriage to depart for London. She wished him Godspeed as they walked arm in arm toward the carriage. He was grateful that Elizabeth was the only one who had risen to see him off.

"Father, I do hope all goes well."

"Have no fear, Elizabeth. If this husband of yours is as excellent as you think he is, he will have done everything required of him."

Elizabeth closed her eyes as she wondered whether her father did not consider William excellent enough for her.

"Father, you will treat him kindly, even if he was not able to accomplish all you expected him to, will you not?"

He looked at his daughter and smiled. "Fear not, Lizzy. By the time we return to Longbourn, I am quite sure he and I shall be the best of friends."

With that, he climbed into the carriage and it pulled away. Elizabeth enjoyed her father's wit and was usually quite capable of discerning whether he was being serious, mocking, or sarcastic, but now, when his words spoke of someone she loved, she found it difficult to know his true feelings.

Later that morning, Elizabeth was delighted to receive an invitation from Miss Darcy to join her at Netherfield in the afternoon. Elizabeth looked forward to removing herself from the house and her mother's continued emotional outbursts, first snivelling about Lydia and how grievous it would be if Wickham did not marry her, then exclaiming in glee how fortunate it would be if Wickham did marry her, and finally, how much she missed her favourite daughter already.

Later that day, a carriage arrived from Netherfield and Elizabeth and Jane enjoyed the ride over together. They both were grateful for the quiet and solitude of the short journey.

"Oh, Jane! Will Mother ever see reason? Can she not see the folly in her wishes that Lydia marry Wickham?"

"She has been taken in by him as much as Lydia was, Elizabeth. A man in a redcoat, unfortunately, holds more credibility to her than a respectable man such as Mr. Darcy."

"That ought to change soon enough when he and I inform her we are married. Only then, I believe, will his wealth sway her opinion of him for the better."

"When will you tell her, Lizzy?"

Elizabeth shrugged her shoulders and clasped her hands tightly together. "Most likely when William and Papa have both returned from London." She looked down, but lifted one eyebrow as she looked up at Jane. "But, most assuredly, *not* when William is around. I can only imagine how she will behave once she finds out, and I do not wish to be mortified in his presence by her actions." Elizabeth tilted her head and smiled at her sister, reaching out and taking her hand. "Remember when she found out about you and Mr. Bingley?"

The two sisters laughed, and the carriage pulled up at Netherfield.

As they stepped out of the carriage, Elizabeth's heart beat a little nervously. The first time she met Miss Darcy, it was quite unexpected and she was enamoured by the sweet, young girl. Now, they would be meeting as sisters and she only desired to make it a very rewarding occasion for each of them.

They were ushered into the sitting room where Mr. Bingley, Miss Bingley, and Miss Darcy were having afternoon tea.

Miss Bingley did not notice Elizabeth at first, as she was diligently leaning in to Miss Darcy, engaging her in what appeared to Elizabeth, to be a one-sided conversation. All eyes turned to the two sisters as they were announced, followed by a most exasperated glare by Miss Bingley.

Miss Darcy stood up. "Miss Bennet… I am so pleased you could come. It is good to see you again."

Miss Bingley looked from Elizabeth to Miss Darcy and back again to Elizabeth. The expression on her face was, without question, one of great astonishment. Elizabeth could only imagine her desperation in attempting to determine why Mr. Darcy's young sister had sent for her and how they came to be acquainted.

Miss Bingley, in an attempt to recover from her surprise, quickly stood and offered -- as hostess of Netherfield -- a greeting. "Good day, Miss Bennet, Miss

Eliza." She promptly informed them, "Miss Darcy and I were having such a pleasant conversation. She and I have had a long, close acquaintance."

"I hope I did not disturb you," Elizabeth said apologetically and walked up to the young girl.

"No... no," stammered Georgiana and tentatively reached out for one of Elizabeth's hands. "We were merely having afternoon tea."

As Miss Bingley witnessed the interchange between Elizabeth and Miss Darcy, she felt another long held hope within her fade. The first had been when she suspected that Mr. Darcy held a strong regard for Elizabeth Bennet which was confirmed when he told her that he and Miss Bennet had become acquainted on the ship crossing over to America. The second was when her brother made the offer of marriage to Jane Bennet instead of Miss Darcy, as she had hoped for so long. And now, the friendship that she was trying to nurture between herself and the young Miss Darcy was being snatched out of her hands by none other than Miss Elizabeth Bennet. It did not escape her notice how the girl's face lit up when she saw Elizabeth walk in.

She no longer felt hospitable, no longer wished to entertain Jane and her brother, and only wished to leave this insufferable room, these insupportable people, and this intolerably unpleasant neighbourhood!

Miss Bingley was grateful to be relieved of her duties as hostess and any further hospitable pretence when Georgiana asked Elizabeth if she would accompany her for a walk of the grounds.

Elizabeth cheerfully agreed.

As Elizabeth walked out with Georgiana, she felt the young girl's arm tighten around hers. Elizabeth looked at her and noticed the tense look upon her face. "I hope I did not arrive at an inopportune time."

"Oh, no. In fact, your arrival was most timely. I do not think I could bear another minute of Miss Bingley's gruelling conversations."

Elizabeth smiled and patted her hand. "I understand completely, Miss Darcy."

Georgiana turned to Elizabeth. "Please call me Georgiana." She paused and a slight blush passed over her face.

"And you must call me Elizabeth."

As the two walked, Elizabeth noticed Georgiana glance toward her several times, as if about to speak, but saying nothing. Elizabeth remained silent, giving her an occasional encouraging smile, hoping to hearten the young, shy girl to speak.

Finally, Georgiana spoke the words she had been longing to say. "May I say, Elizabeth... that I have always longed to have a sister. I am especially delighted that you and William are married. I could not ask for a finer sister."

Elizabeth smiled warmly at her. "I am most pleased to have you as my sister, as well."

Georgiana looked down nervously. "But then you already have four sisters." Georgiana said this almost apologetically.

"Oh, Georgiana. But none are like you. You shall be a special sister to me, indeed!" Elizabeth wrapped one arm around Georgiana's shoulder and gave it a tender squeeze.

Georgiana smiled. She had so much she wanted to say to Elizabeth and wondered if she could put into words her thoughts and feelings.

They walked in silence for a while and Elizabeth recognized that their steps were taking the two of them down the same path she had walked with William when she was at Netherfield. When they came to the pond, they both stopped and looked out over it. Elizabeth sensed something was weighing heavily on Georgiana and let time and silence be her ally.

At length, Georgiana spoke. "My brother informed me of the reason for his leaving so abruptly for London."

This time it was Elizabeth's turn to look down as she recoiled at the thought of Lydia's unspeakable behaviour. "He told you, then, of my youngest sister's actions?"

Georgiana nodded, "Yes."

Elizabeth pursed her lips together. "Unfortunately, Lydia seems to have made a very reckless decision."

When she glanced at Georgiana, she noticed her draw back and look down. Elizabeth could not miss the scarlet that spread over her features.

"Georgiana?" Elizabeth leaned in to her. "What is it?"

Georgiana's eyebrows pinched together and Elizabeth, still holding her arm, felt her shiver. The younger girl looked away and then emboldened herself to look back at the lady who was now her sister.

"Elizabeth, there is something my brother did not tell you. He thought it would be best if I tell you rather than himself."

"What is it, dearest sister?"

Georgiana looked up and feebly smiled at the endearing words. "I am guilty, as Lydia is, of running off with the intention to elope earlier this year."

Elizabeth reproached herself for making the comment about Lydia's actions. "Georgiana, I am sure the particulars were not similar at all."

Georgiana closed her eyes as she struggled with the painful memories of being deceived and disappointing her brother. "No, Elizabeth, they are quite the same." She paused in an effort to summons the strength to continue. "I also ran off with George Wickham."

Elizabeth's breath was caught in her throat when she heard her words and saw the pain etched across Georgiana's face. Elizabeth drew her arms around the young girl and pulled her close into a hug as tears began to well up in Georgiana's eyes.

"Oh, my dear, sweet Georgiana." Elizabeth closed her eyes in contrition at her thoughtless comment about Lydia's behaviour and thought frantically for something to say to lessen Georgiana's regret. "Georgiana, I understand Mr. Wickham was a long-time friend of your family, is that correct?"

Georgiana sniffled and nodded an affirmative.

"Was he particularly attentive to you?"

"Yes, Elizabeth. He was always kind towards me."

"I thought as much." Elizabeth drew away and clasped each one of Georgiana's hands. "Georgiana, you are still young and have so much to learn.

Mr. Wickham is the sort of man who knows how to charm a young girl by saying the things she wants to hear; by giving her the attention she longs for."

Georgiana looked at Elizabeth and took in a few tremulous breaths. "If I had known someone like you that I could have talked to… and who would have talked with me, I often have thought I would not have made such a dreadful decision."

Elizabeth smiled, aware that this young girl had lived most of her life without a mother or close female friend. She'd had governesses, but she wondered whether they were women with whom she could confide her deepest thoughts and ask her hardest questions. Elizabeth took the girl's hand firmly in hers. She pondered how difficult it must have been for her to have lost both her parents while still young. Did William even know how to talk to this young lady about the things she most needed to hear?

"Georgiana, if there is anything you wish to talk with me about, I would be happy to oblige you. If you have any questions, I would be honoured if you would feel free to come to me." Elizabeth laughed softly. "I may not have all the answers, but I will do my best."

Georgiana took Elizabeth's arm and they both turned and began walking again. "I do want you to know, Elizabeth, that I am terribly sorry for my Aunt Catherine's behaviour towards you and wish to apologize for her. I fervently hope that William is able to make my aunt see just how excellent you are for him… and for me… before she is able to do any harm!"

Elizabeth sighed as she took in the disquiet on Georgiana's face and in her words. "I appreciate your concern, Georgiana, and I do hope your brother can smooth things over with your aunt; I would not wish to be the cause of a rift between them. But there is one thing of which I am certain." She turned her face off toward the southern horizon, looking toward London. "William and I will be married at the end of all this; even if we must marry again!"

Chapter 33

One Month Later

Darcy stood up at the front of the church at Longbourn alongside his best friend, Charles Bingley. The small chapel was filled to overflowing with guests waiting for the ceremony to begin.

Bingley looked out at the people who had become his neighbours since first coming to Netherfield. He made eye contact with several, giving them a wide grin, all the while anxious for his bride-to-be to make her way down the aisle.

In stark contrast to his ebullient friend, Darcy avoided the eyes that were upon him. He kept his eyes set on the back of the church, waiting for Elizabeth to come down. As he patiently waited for her beautiful, reassuring face to appear, he began to suffer that all too familiar sense of being scrutinized by those seated before him in the church and wished that he could disappear into the crowd unnoticed. But he could not. Not today.

Bingley and Darcy. Best friends. Soon to be brothers-in-law. A wedding.

When Darcy left Elizabeth and her father for London that day a month ago, he had been propelled by an unequalled passion to fiercely protect Elizabeth and their marriage. His short stay in Town was successful in that endeavour as he put enough fear into his aunt by threatening to remove Rosings from her control and to forbid her from ever visiting his London townhome or Pemberley again. Upon hearing his vehement declaration, she dared not attempt any of her calculated manipulations that would discredit his wife or their marriage, however little she was inclined to accept either.

When he returned to Hertfordshire, he was welcomed into the Bennet household, particularly by Mrs. Bennet. Elizabeth had the sole responsibility, while her father and husband were still in town, of informing her mother that she and Mr. Darcy had married. Her father had written from London to say that Lydia was acquainted with the situation and that it would be futile to try and keep their marriage a secret any longer.

Mrs. Bennet, however, first received the news that Lydia was not to be married and bore it with great disappointment. It was all Elizabeth could do to soothe her spirits. Her mother had held such strong hopes that Mr. Wickham would marry her sweet Lydia! In her vexation and disappointment, she blamed her husband and Mr. Darcy for their interference. Elizabeth waited until she had calmed down before she told her what she knew she must.

When Elizabeth felt her mother was in a condition to attend her words, she gently told her of her marriage to Mr. Darcy. Mrs. Bennet could not think poorly of Elizabeth's situation, but she hardly understood why a man of Mr. Darcy's stature and wealth would even look twice at her second eldest daughter. But that he did, she considered with great pleasure, although the truth be owned, her attention dwelt a great deal more on Lydia's disappointment than on Elizabeth's happiness. When the reality of Elizabeth's good fortune became clear, suddenly everything paled in comparison. Word of Elizabeth's happy alliance spread quickly about the countryside, propelled mainly by Mrs. Bennet herself.

It was very apparent to Elizabeth that her mother had no qualms about their marrying on a ship, by a captain instead of a clergyman, and she was not even disturbed that they had kept it a secret for all these months. Instead, Mrs. Bennet noted all the advantages to such an alliance; particularly that it would throw her other daughters in the path of rich gentlemen.

This day, Darcy stood alongside his best friend for the wedding. But he was not just standing up with Bingley; he and Elizabeth were going to recite their vows again. Bingley and Jane had already set this day for their wedding and it was decided that Darcy and Elizabeth would participate as well, in that ceremony, renewing their vows to one another again for all to see.

Most guests in attendance eventually knew the truth of this couple's situation. But it was also common knowledge that the couple had not lived together as man and wife, per the fervent admonition of Mr. Bennet. As much as he graciously welcomed Darcy into the family, he did insist that their marriage be solemnized by the church first. And as the guests at the wedding looked upon the striking, but quite nervous Mr. Darcy standing at the front of the church, most had forgotten that he and Miss Elizabeth Bennet had been married for several months already.

Darcy had agreed to abide by Mr. Bennet's constraint for another month's separation to ensure that there would be no scandal to besmirch the union given its unusual start. Fortunately for Darcy, the month passed quickly, as plans for the ceremony took precedence over all other things. He satisfied himself, however, with stolen kisses along solitary walks with Elizabeth and whispered endearments during dinner engagements.

Among those looking up at the two men in the front of the church was Miss Caroline Bingley. It had been her brother who had the daunting task of informing her that the man for whom she had harboured long-time hopes to return her favour was, and had been, married to Elizabeth for some time. She took the news as one would expect she would, making some inane comments about how London society would appreciate the new Mrs. Darcy's attempt to bring country dances to the ton and how she had never understood what women saw in Mr. Darcy anyway.

Noticeably missing from the guests was Lady Catherine de Bourgh. She still stung from her nephew's rebuke and had not reconciled in her mind the need to apologize to his wife. The unfortunate consequence of her decision was that Darcy's cousin, Anne, could not be in attendance. Truly glad for her cousin to have found a wife he so greatly loved, she sent along her best wishes and apologies for her mother's cruel and unrepentant attitude. She hoped in time Lady Catherine would see the error of her ways and accept the woman he had married, and expressed a wish to meet Elizabeth as soon as could be arranged.

The lingering disturbance Darcy felt over his aunt's actions and her adamant refusal to attend today's ceremony was reasonably assuaged by the support and attendance of Colonel Richard Fitzwilliam and his family. Darcy's uncle could offer no excuse for his sister's behaviour and had no reason to question Darcy's good judgment in matters of the heart.

Just when Darcy felt he could no longer abide the scrutinizing eyes of the people in the church, Elizabeth began to walk down the aisle, escorted on her father's arm, with Jane on the other. Suddenly, everyone's attention turned from him to the beautiful women slowly walking towards the two gentlemen. Elizabeth walked intently towards the man waiting up front for her; the man who had waited patiently for almost six months for this day to come to pass when she would, in the eyes of God and society, truly become his wife.

She was delighting in this day - her wedding day. It was a day that she believed she would never be able to experience. As she walked down the aisle with her arm tightly tucked in her father's, she reflected on her earlier decision, that she could not marry another, as her heart irretrievably belonged to Fitzwilliam Darcy. She could never have turned her back on those vows she had spoken to him, even if he had. That she was sharing with her sister in this beautiful wedding ceremony gave her the greatest delight.

Darcy's heart made a leap as the trio came toward him. For those who previously had witnessed only Darcy's controlled demeanour, it came as quite a surprise to see him with a full-fledged, albeit nervous, smile, returning the warm and reassuring one Elizabeth gave him as she approached closer.

Seeing her so close yet still out of his reach, nothing could prevent Darcy from stepping forward to bridge the final distance and taking Elizabeth from her father's side, bringing her alongside himself. Bingley remained firmly planted, eyes wide and a resolute grin etched firmly on his face, as he waited for Jane to take those final steps to reach him. That he displayed a more open admiration was apparent. But at that moment, Meryton society got a small glimpse of the regard that the stoic and proper Mr. Darcy obviously held for his bride.

Darcy and Elizabeth recited their vows again to one another, promising to love one another and remain faithful through all the seasons of their life. Darcy spoke with determination, not taking his eyes off the woman to whom he was making these vows, consumed by the depth of his love and admiration for Elizabeth. This time, Elizabeth spoke each vow with warm conviction, treasuring in her heart all she was saying. When the vows had been recited, he placed a simple elegant ring on her wedding finger and a tender kiss on her lips. Then they were pronounced man and wife… again.

Netherfield hosted the wedding breakfast and to Elizabeth's amusement, Darcy displayed a constant impatience to leave for London. Bingley and Jane's plans were to remain at Netherfield and to take a short journey up north after a few days. Elizabeth did not envy her sister having to remain in a household spilling over with visiting friends and family, although she was quite aware that going to Darcy's townhome in London, which she had never visited before, was going to be awkward enough. Having never met the staff there, she was certain she would be under the strictest scrutiny.

One of the first people eager to meet Mrs. Darcy at the wedding breakfast was Colonel Richard Fitzwilliam. After Lady Catherine departed London that day a month ago, the two cousins did a great deal of talking; mostly pertaining to Elizabeth. Fitzwilliam had never seen his cousin so happy and content and looked forward with great anticipation for the opportunity to finally meet her.

When Darcy left London to return to Hertfordshire, Fitzwilliam was required to report back to duty the following day. He only arrived for the wedding late the previous night, so this was the first occasion he had to meet Elizabeth.

Colonel Fitzwilliam watched the couple intently as they stood side by side during the wedding. He was amused that Darcy was unable to keep his eyes off Elizabeth. He was understandably sympathetic to his cousin's attachment to this fine lady. She met her husband's gaze with a lively one of her own and Colonel Fitzwilliam felt a sudden tug of jealousy that he had yet to find a woman so worthy.

At length, Darcy brought Elizabeth over to meet his cousin, who took her gloved hand and kissed it, all the while keeping his eyes lifted to hers.

"Mrs. Darcy, I have long desired to make your acquaintance."

Elizabeth smiled as this reasonably handsome man, noting several similarities in his features as that of her husband. "I am pleased to finally meet the man my husband holds in the highest regard."

Colonel Fitzwilliam gave a slight bow and smiled. "And I am steadfastly able to say the same about his regard for you, Mrs. Darcy. My cousin spoke admiringly of you while in London. Indeed, I can see the truth of his words."

"Thank you, Colonel Fitzwilliam. You are too kind."

Fitzwilliam put up his hand. "No formalities, please. Please be so kind as to call me Richard."

"And I shall be Elizabeth to you."

Darcy enjoyed listening to the repartee between his cousin and his wife and then watched curiously as his cousin leaned over to whisper something in her ear. His eyes narrowed as he overheard the words Fitzwilliam deliberately spoke loudly enough for him to hear.

"Elizabeth, may I prevail upon you, the next occasion that we meet, to visit with you on some of my cousin's peculiarities. While he may convey a most disciplined and upright comportment to most, I do have many stories I could share with you of his most unconventional behaviour at times."

Elizabeth laughed merrily at Fitzwilliam's words and her husband's grimace. "I should very much enjoy comparing notes with you, Richard."

There were many more introductions that morning between family members and acquaintances. It was with great relief, then, that they were finally able to sit down to enjoy the breakfast. Darcy relished these few moments of reprieve from having to endure the social strictures of meeting so many new people. He was simply able enjoy his wife's company and those few more intimate friends and family that were seated around him. He found himself finally able to relax for the first time that morning.

Following the wedding breakfast, when Elizabeth felt that they had remained long enough to be deemed proper and acceptable, she gave her husband the nod he had been waiting for.

Fitzwilliam and Elizabeth Darcy bade farewell to all the well-wishers. Although Mrs. Bennet was put out that they seemed inclined to leave the gathering so hastily, she felt great satisfaction in her heart knowing that this daughter, her husband's favourite -- whom she had always slighted because of her jealousy for Mr. Bennet's affection -- had secured their future by marrying a man of more than abundant means.

Before leaving, Elizabeth sought out Jane and when she found her, the two brides, who were also the closest of sisters and friends, embraced. They promised they would write to one another often. They were fully aware that they would now be separated again, as they had been when Elizabeth had travelled to America. Both Jane and Elizabeth secretly hoped that some day Charles would see fit to find a home an easy distance from Pemberley so the two families could reside near each other.

Elizabeth then sought out Georgiana, who felt deeply the imminent separation from her brother and his wife. She knew it would be temporary, but she had grown extremely close to Elizabeth during that month. As Elizabeth came towards her to bid her farewell, Georgiana fell into her arms in tears.

"Please forgive me, Elizabeth," Georgiana said through her sobs. "I am truly happy for you, both. But I shall miss you; miss our talks."

"Truly, Georgiana, I am of the same mind," Elizabeth replied. Elizabeth noticed a young man standing nearby, who had been introduced to her earlier, along with his family, as long-time friends of the Darcys. In one of their many talks, Georgiana had confided in Elizabeth that she was experiencing feelings for this young man that she had never felt before.

"I am quite certain," Elizabeth whispered slyly in Georgiana's ear, "that you shall not be lonely for too long after we leave."

Georgiana looked at her curiously.

Elizabeth smiled. "I do believe there is one gentleman here who is just waiting for the opportunity to further his acquaintance with you. Perhaps you might choose to oblige him?"

Georgiana looked in the direction Elizabeth was indicating and saw Adam Metcalf watching them. Instantly, she felt flushed and her heart began to beat mercilessly. "Oh, Elizabeth, it is almost too much for me to bear to think of talking to him." She stole another glance at him. "When his family came to visit at Pemberley, it was all I could do to be the proper hostess, let alone carry on a conversation with him."

"You shall do excellently, Georgiana. Remember, he is but a young man."

The two were laughing as Darcy walked up. "And what do my two favourite ladies find so amusing?"

Elizabeth and Georgiana exchanged conspiratorial looks. "Nothing that would be of interest to you, at present," Elizabeth replied. She turned back to Georgiana and gave her an ardent hug. "I shall look forward to our return to Pemberley and seeing you there, Georgiana. Remember, we both love you."

Tears came again to Georgiana's eyes. "And I love you both, too."

When Elizabeth stepped away from Georgiana, Darcy took the opportunity to embrace her. "We shall not be away too long, Georgiana. You be a good girl now for Lord and Lady Matlock, do you understand?" He pulled away and lifted her chin up with his fingers.

Georgiana smiled and nodded at her brother for his most fatherly display.

Darcy turned before she could see the tears coming to his eyes.

Darcy and Elizabeth walked out to the waiting carriage as the hands of all the well-wishers gleefully waved goodbye. They turned and gave final hugs to those dearest to them and then climbed into awaiting carriage.

As it slowly pulled away, they turned toward the window and waved one final farewell to everyone.

When they were at last out of sight, Darcy turned back to Elizabeth. She looked up at his tightly pressed lips curving slightly upward and noticed his contented sigh.

"May I ask just what you are thinking, my dearest husband?"

He took her hand in his and brought it to his lips, placing several kisses on it. He held it there as he spoke, and she could feel the warmth of his breath and the occasional light touch of his lips brush against it. "My dearest, loveliest, Elizabeth. I am thinking that this day, which I have so long awaited, is finally here. I fear to even turn my head from you, lest I look back and find you gone and that this blessed day has only been a dream."

"It is not a dream, William."

The sight of her seated next to him, her eyes sparkling with love, her lips so inviting, parted in a smile that seemed to call out to him; her fragrance, permeating his senses... He slowly turned and kissed the open palm of her hand and then took her face in both of his.

"I love you, Elizabeth. You are my love, my life." He drew closer to her and kissed her; warmly at first and then allowed it to deepen passionately. At length, he reluctantly pulled away, knowing they had a long ride ahead of them.

Elizabeth took in a deep breath in an attempt to recover from the feelings her husband's kiss had evoked. She nestled against her husband and he encased her with his arms as they settled in for a leisurely -- but occasionally passionate -- ride to London.

As the carriage reached London and ambled through town, Elizabeth curiously looked out the window and then back to her husband. "Did you not tell me your townhouse is near St. James Park?"

Darcy nodded, "Indeed, I did."

She kept her eyes on the buildings passing by. "Is it not, then, on the other side of town? Are we not travelling in the opposite direction?"

"Yes, it is on the other side of town, and yes, we are travelling in the opposite direction."

"But why?" She asked this question as Darcy made an attempt to smother the smile that was forming on his lips.

"There is something I would like us to see one last time."

Elizabeth eyed at him suspiciously. He seemed intent to be silent, although he finally lost in his effort to keep a broad smile from gracing his face.

At length, she realized they were nearing the harbour and the carriage slowed as they passed ship after ship. Elizabeth looked out; her heart pounding as she kept her eyes open for the one ship that would be all too familiar. The carriage soon pulled to a stop and Elizabeth looked out toward the front and saw at once the grand sailing ship with its name engraved on the front, *Pemberley's Promise.*

She looked at Darcy with child-like eyes. Barely even able to form the words, she said to him, "You did not tell me we would be coming to the ship."

"I wanted to keep it a surprise. Come, Elizabeth. I believe we are expected."

As they walked toward the ship, Darcy took her hand and told her that he was in the process of selling the great vessel and wanted to take one last look at it with her.

"Selling it? But why?"

Darcy brought her hand to his lips. "It was a profitable investment when I purchased it and it did well. But my trust in the seaworthiness of this vessel rode heavily on Captain Willoughby's excellent reputation as its captain. As he is getting on in years, he has decided he would like to captain something that perhaps only makes the crossing of the Channel to the continent and back or up and down the coast of England." He looked over at Elizabeth, whose eyes were misting over. "You are not sad it is for sale, are you?"

"I admit I am. After all, this is where we were married."

"That is why I brought you down here. Look, there is Captain Willoughby now."

They walked onto the ship and Elizabeth felt a great sense of awe as she looked around her. Her thoughts assailed her of their time together on board this vessel; their walks, their misunderstandings, and her walking off that last day, believing she would never see him again.

"Mr. and Mrs. Darcy! I am exceedingly pleased to have you back on board! And may I offer my sincere congratulations and deepest satisfaction that you not only found each other, but found one another to be of the same mind in regards to your marriage."

"Thank you, Willoughby," Darcy answered.

"Thank you, Captain," replied Elizabeth.

The captain looked at Darcy. "If you will follow me, Sir, everything is prepared for you."

Willoughby turned and Darcy took Elizabeth's arm, smiling at her inquisitive glance. "Come, dearest Elizabeth."

They walked slowly behind the captain and Elizabeth quickly realized he was leading them to the room that had been theirs the month they had been on the ship. He opened the door and stepped back.

"If you have need of anything, I shall be in my quarters. You meal will be brought to you in approximately an hour."

"Thank you, Captain," Darcy nodded at the gentleman and watched him turn and walk away.

Elizabeth began to take a step into the small room, but Darcy stopped her. "There is one thing I must attend to first, before we walk in," he told her. Without pausing, he reached down and easily lifted her up into his arms. She wrapped her arms around his neck and leaned her head on his shoulder.

"Do you remember this is how I first brought you into this room? By carrying you?"

A wide smile passed Elizabeth's face as she recollected his having to carry her because she had sprained her ankle. "I may have been ill at the time and suffering from a painfully sore ankle, but yes, I do remember." She looked at his face and gently caressed it with her hand. "Even back then, I enjoyed the feel of being held in your arms."

Darcy smiled. "Is that a fact?" He stepped into the room and continued to hold her as their eyes were locked together, one to another. "If I had known that," he said softly, "I would have done it more often!"

They both laughed and suddenly looked around at the room, feeling at once as though they stepped back in time. As they glanced around them, vivid memories flooded their minds from that month they spent together.

As their eyes travelled over to the little table, they both had to catch their breath. It was covered with a crisp linen tablecloth and scattered rose petals. A shallow crystal dish also held rose petals floating in water. Candles were lit just above the table in wall sconces, and there was a bottle of wine and two goblets set out for them.

"William! How beautiful! Was this your idea?"

"I cannot take credit for all of it. I asked Willoughby to make the room look nice as I wanted to bring you back to it. I asked him to have the chef prepare something special and to make the table presentable for our wedding day meal."

Elizabeth giggled. "I do believe if you had brought me to your room that afternoon and it was in this state, I should never have wanted to leave!"

Darcy, still holding her, walked over to the bed that Elizabeth had slept in, sitting down so she was now seated in his lap. Leaning in to her, he gently kissed her. "You have no idea how much I wanted to kiss you that morning I comforted you and held you like this when Mrs. Trimble passed on. You were so beautiful, even in your distress."

Elizabeth sighed. She had to admit that her feelings toward Darcy had truly altered after that day. She felt that he sincerely cared for her as she grieved for Mrs. Trimble. He had held her, consoled her, and let her cry against him. Then later that day, they sat at the table and talked about themselves.

The two found themselves gently swaying along with the rhythm of the boat's rocking. Darcy looked over at the other bed, which had been his on their voyage and suddenly recalled waking each morning and looking directly over to the sheet that had given Elizabeth her privacy. It was hard for him to believe that this night they would sleep in the same bed and there would be no need for ever hanging another sheet. An involuntary sigh escaped him.

"What are you thinking, William?"

Elizabeth's voice startled him from his reverie.

"Hmm." Darcy nestled his head against Elizabeth's neck. "Truth be told, my dearest, I was contemplating the sheet."

Elizabeth pulled slightly out from him and asked, "The sheet?"

"Yes. You remember…"

"Of course, but that is what you were just thinking of?"

Darcy nodded his head. "More along the lines of *not* needing the sheet. Nor a door, nor a room, nor a house ever separating us again."

Elizabeth smiled and looked around her at the small cabin. "Are we to stay here for the night, then?"

Darcy's eyes widened. "Here? I should say not! I have something arranged that I trust you will find more pleasantly accommodating. A little more spacious in regards to certain amenities." He glanced at the bed as he said this and Elizabeth, blushing, turned away.

But a sense of disappointment swept over her and she looked back at Darcy. "I think I would prefer to spend our first night here."

Darcy looked at her incredulously. "But Elizabeth, certainly you cannot expect us…" He looked at the beds and back to her in exasperation. "I have no intention of sleeping in separate beds after all the time I have waited! These beds are barely wide enough for one person, let alone the both of us!"

"Please, my love?" Her drawn out plea and her twinkling eyes gave him a moment's pause to reconsider.

But then, quickly, he answered, "No, Elizabeth. I promise you that you will greatly prefer the plans I have made."

"You were hoping to spend the night at your townhome, were you not?"

Darcy shook his head, *"Our* townhome and, as a matter of fact, *no*, I had something else in mind."

"And what would that be?"

Darcy shook his head. "I wish it to be a surprise."

Elizabeth suddenly pulled herself out of Darcy's lap and stood up, folding her arms in front of her. "Is there any reason, other than your judgment that the beds are too small, that we cannot stay here for the night?"

"That is reason enough for me!"

Darcy stood up and walked over to Elizabeth. A very mischievous look crossed her face and she pulled herself up against her him. "If I recall correctly," Elizabeth began, "when I awoke that night we had to sleep on the floor, we were not taking up much space together at all!"

Darcy smiled as he recollected waking up to Elizabeth snuggled tightly against him and forcing himself to think of her as Caroline Bingley to ensure his behaviour was kept in check. "Are you saying you wish to sleep on the floor?"

Elizabeth smiled. "If we end up there, so be it. I would merely like to spend our wedding night where we were first married."

A wide grin spread across Darcy's face as he battled with Elizabeth's romantic notions and insistence. He finally relented.

Drawing close to Elizabeth again, he said, "I shall inform the captain that we will be spending the night here and have Durnham bring in our overnight bags." He leaned down and gave her a tender kiss.

After Darcy returned and they waited for the meal to be brought in, he poured the wine and the two sat at the table, reflecting on their journey to America and their journey back to each other.

The winter sun descended quickly toward the horizon, and soon the room was illuminated solely from the candles. They ate their perfectly prepared meal in the ambiance of a candlelit room, rocking softly to the rhythm of the gentle swells of the Thames River.

Although Darcy hated to leave Elizabeth, he knew it would be only proper for him to give her some privacy to allow her to ready herself for bed. He stepped out of the cabin and walked toward the dining room where he found Durnham and Winston visiting with some of the crew. He stopped and talked with them and then walked out on the deck.

As he walked, he thought back to those times out here when he had struggled about his feelings for Elizabeth. How could he have waited so long to tell her he loved her? He felt a tremor pass through him as he considered that after they departed the ship, he may never have found her again. He closed his eyes at just the thought of that possibility.

His thoughts took him back to Elizabeth, who was now back in their cabin, readying herself for him to come to her and it was all he could do to not return to the room directly. He walked the deck a couple of times and finally decided he had allowed her sufficient time.

He came to their door and lightly knocked. "Elizabeth…."

"Come in," Elizabeth answered softly.

Just hearing those simple words from Elizabeth's mouth made Darcy's heart race and his mouth go dry. He slowly reached down and took the door handle in his hands, giving it a turn. As the door swung open, he looked in; his eyes needed a few moments to adjust to the soft dimness of it. Elizabeth had extinguished most of the candles save a few.

She was still sitting in front of the mirror when he first walked in and saw her. He was rendered speechless as he watched as she unhurriedly stood up and turned around. His heart pounded in his throat when he saw her. The gown she wore shimmered and clung to her curves. His eyes took in every inch of her standing before him as well as the back of her from the reflection in the mirror.

He was so captivated by the sight of her, he was torn whether to take those few steps and take her in his arms or stand and watch her from afar.

He was finally able to muster the words, "Elizabeth, you are beautiful."

She looked down and smiled. As he still seemed incapable of movement, she began walking towards him. She came up to him and wrapped her arms about his waist, looking up at him. He needed no further prompting to take her in his arms and revelled over her softness.

As his lips came down upon hers, she suddenly felt all apprehensions about the night disappear. She felt right in his arms and he felt so right in hers. Their kiss grew in intensity and soon their passions were ignited beyond abandoning.

At length, Elizabeth noticed that her husband had never closed the door to the room. "Dearest husband, it will not do to have me standing here in this attire and in such a passionate embrace for all the ship's crew to see. Would you please mind closing the door?"

Darcy kept his arms tightly wrapped around Elizabeth as he used his foot to manoeuvre the door closed behind him. It shut with a resounding bang that announced to all that from now until dawn, that they were to be left alone, no visitors would be accepted, and no interruptions would be tolerated.

~~*

The door to the cabin finally opened close to 9:30 the next morning. For two people who enjoyed rising in the early hours, it was tantamount evidence that neither had slept adequately.

They took a leisurely walk arm in arm up on deck and then proceeded to the dining room. The chef in the ship's galley had prepared a simple morning repast and they enjoyed it while sitting alone at the table Elizabeth had been sitting at when Darcy made his unusual offer of marriage. They both looked around them, knowing it might be the last time they would ever see the ship.

"Must you truly sell the ship, William?" Elizabeth asked in a melancholy manner.

"No, but I believe it to be the best thing to do."

His hand gently went to the back of Elizabeth's neck and kneaded it gently.

Elizabeth took in a sigh of contentment laced with a touch of resignation. "I shall truly miss it."

Darcy only nodded and smiled.

When they finished their meal and their bags had been taken out by Durnham and Winston, they stood up to leave the dining room. Elizabeth took Darcy's arm as they walked toward the door that brought them back out on deck. Before they reached it, though, they came to a hanging sign that boasted the name of the ship.

"A moment, please," Darcy said. He called out to one of the crewmen that was working in the dining room and asked if he could assist.

Elizabeth watched curiously as the man helped Darcy remove the sign.

Darcy thanked the man and he turned to Elizabeth, holding out the sign. "A remembrance for you."

Elizabeth smiled. "Oh! Where should we hang it?"

"I am sure we will find the most suitable place for it!"

They walked out and as Elizabeth began walking toward the carriage, Darcy nudged her away from it. "Come, let us walk a ways along the harbour."

Always eager for a walk, Elizabeth obliged. They engaged in small talk as they passed several ships. It was but a few moments later that Darcy stopped suddenly. Elizabeth looked at him curiously.

"Shall we go back, then?"

A furtive smile crept across Darcy's face as he answered, "No."

At Elizabeth's questioning glance, he pointed to the ship moored directly in front of them.

Elizabeth turned and gasped when she found herself facing a smaller replica of *Pemberley's Promise*. Darcy watched her face as her eyes travelled the length of the ship and fell upon the name engraved upon the front, *Pemberley's Promise II.*

She looked at her husband, at the ship, and then back to her husband. "William, what is this?"

"This, my dear, is where I had planned to spend our wedding night." He wrapped his arms around her. "Elizabeth, your wedding gift from me. Our own ship, with our own private cabin, to be captained by Willoughby wherever we wish to go."

"Our own ship?" Elizabeth's eyes were wide and sparkled in delight.

Darcy nodded. "Would you like to see it?"

"Oh, yes!"

The two walked aboard the ship as Darcy explained to her how he had come to London after she left Netherfield to make the arrangements to purchase this ship and sell the larger one. With Willoughby desiring to sail more locally, he did not want the burden of finding another captain for *Pemberley's Promise* on whom he could rely as greatly as he did him. So he decided to sell and found this smaller ship, built by the same builder, and knew he had to have it.

As they boarded the ship, Elizabeth was surprised to see Willoughby already on board.

"Good morning, Mr. and Mrs. Darcy. Welcome aboard your new ship, *Pemberley's Promise II*."

Epilogue

After a short voyage on board *Pemberley's Promise II* sailing up and down the coast of England, they went on to the London townhome. Elizabeth was well pleased with it in all its aspects and could not suggest one change she would wish to make in it. She quickly became acquainted with all the staff and they all gave their hearty approval of the woman their master had chosen to marry.

Charles and Jane lived several years at Netherfield until finally a suitable manor was found for them to purchase but a mere half hour's carriage ride from Pemberley. In the years to come, the three Bingley children and four Darcy children grew up to be the closest of cousins.

Georgiana grew in her admiration and esteem for Mr. Metcalf, but after she was brought out into society, several men drew her attention and eventually she married the son of an Earl who had the sweetest disposition and a respectable fortune that greatly complimented hers.

Kitty married next, a young gentleman from Hertfordshire who owned a small estate. Mary then wed a clergyman and moved south of London.

Lydia found it difficult to settle down with any man. Her wild, impetuous ways were so ingrained within her that, after the episode with Wickham, she pretty much decided she did not want to do the conventional thing and marry. As long as there were soldiers nearby, Lydia was content. She lived with her mother and father at Longbourn for 10 years until Mr. Bennet finally died. Mrs. Bennet and Lydia were then put out of Longbourn by the Collinses.

With the unbearable prospect of Mrs. Bennet and Lydia coming to live with either the Bingleys or the Darcys, a joint decision was made to purchase a respectable home for them in the village of Meryton. There, living close to the Phillips' and having the best source of noteworthy gossip right at hand, Mrs. Bennet was quite content. Lydia often left for unexplained periods of time and when she would return, Mrs. Bennet never questioned her of her whereabouts. But she was always glad to have her back and the two were always in agreement how handsome a man in a redcoat was.

Lady Catherine de Bourgh finally did come to accept Elizabeth and apologized to her about a year after the marriage. But it was mainly the machinations of her daughter, Anne, that prompted this and it was not until Lady Catherine was quite ill and presumed close to death. Anne could not allow her mother to pass on without making amends, so she pleaded with her cousin to come with his wife to Rosings.

Darcy and Elizabeth agreed to make the visit and when they arrived, they could not believe how gravely ill their aunt was. Despite her condition, she continued to make demands and let her strong opinions be known. She did, however, struggle through an apology, which Darcy later reflected must have been the most difficult thing she had ever been required to do.

It was a great surprise that Lady Catherine seemed to recover from her close call with death. Apparently, she had not been as ill as everyone surmised and she lived another five years. Whilst her behaviour did not improve completely, she was very attentive to the things of which she spoke in the presence of her nephew, not wishing to give him any cause to her to contact their attorney.

Darcy and Elizabeth sailed frequently on *Pemberley's Promise II*, making stops in ports around England, Scotland, and Ireland, and then sailing across the Channel to visit different ports in Europe. Sometimes they traveled alone and at other times they brought Charles and Jane, Georgiana and her husband, or some other family members or friends.

Neither forgot the greater ship, *Pemberley's Promise*, and on a rare occasion, when they were at the harbor or out at sea, they would see her moored at the dock or elegantly sailing by. She was a beautiful ship and never ceased to cause both Darcy's and Elizabeth's heart to flutter just at the sight of her.

The sign they removed from the grand ship's dining room was hung on the wall above their bed in *Pemberley's Promise II*. It was a constant reminder to them of the vows and promises they made to each other that day while crossing the Atlantic on *Pemberley's Promise*.

~The End~

Kara Louise lives in Kansas with her husband.
They share their 10 acres with
an ever changing menagerie of animals.
They have one married son who also likes to write.

Other published books by Kara Louise
"Drive and Determination"

Visit her website,
www.ahhhs.net
where you will find the novels
"Assumed Engagement"
"Assumed Obligation"
and
"Master Under Good Regulation"
and a variety of other stories
written by her and Australian author, Sharni.

1181246